romyanna.thomas@talk21.com

@RomyWoodThomas

Word on the Street

Romy

_____

Romy Wood

G000147481

Cillian Press |

First published in Great Britain in 2013
by Cillian Press Limited. 83 Ducie Street, Manchester M1 2JQ
www.cillianpress.co.uk

British Library Cataloguing in Publication Data.
A catalogue record for this book is available from the British Library.

Paperback ISBN: 978-0-9573155-2-5
eBook ISBN: 978-0-9573155-3-2

Cover Design: Roshana Rubin-Mayhew

Published by
Cillian Press – Manchester - 2013
www.cillianpress.co.uk

For Barbara, in the present tense.

Acknowledgements

I would like to thank: the writers at the Fitz; all at Cillian Press; Dee who was my first reader; Charlie, who can spot scabies a mile off (though where I've favoured poetic licence over science, it's my doing); and Megan, Harry and Bobby, who manage to live with a unique blend of Dermatology and Creative Writing, and who light up our world.

For each man kills the thing he loves

Oscar Wilde, 'The Ballad of Reading Gaol'

1

Carol encourages me to tell my story, and I write:

The first person to die rotted for a week. He'd broken into someone's shed, tucked himself up under a blanket, and coughed himself through the pearly gates. When the owner of the shed returned from her all-inclusive golfing break, she was met with a sight and a stench that made the national news.

Carol says this is a powerful hook; now give her the up-close, the dirty realism, the boredom and the itching. I think of Colin telling me his dog had died.

'My dog died.' Colin shrugged his shoulders and stared at my left earlobe. I took his hand.

'I'm sorry,' I said.

We were in the kitchen at the Shelter, which was on one side of a knocked-through room taking up most of the ground floor. On the other side we had a telly with a three piece suite to die for (or possibly on). We had a leaflet rack attached to the wall which we updated from time to time and which people never looked at.

'Shona, you hate dogs.'

'I can still be sorry.' It was true. I am not so heartless as to begrudge a bereavement. Colin twitched and coughed and I let his hand go. He rummaged in a drawer for the tin opener and set to work, humming, on the first of six tins of soup. The floor was sticky from spills that we'd wiped up but never got round to mopping. Ants were dotted around, glued fast where they'd been since the early summer invasion.

'How old was it?' I filled the tea urn.

'Six.'

I didn't know what to say then. Was it good or bad that the dog had been six? I prefer email to conversation, for the thinking time.

'What have you done with it? You don't have to tell me. Sorry.' Sometimes I think my social skills are worse than Colin's. I sighed. It's a shame people correlate niceness with animal-loving, because I really can't stand dogs or cats, I hate horses and I actually have nightmares about being chased by cows. I think it might be the smell that clinches it. When I walk past a dog crapping in the street, and some stroppy-wellied woman is waiting with a plastic bag, I hold my breath and try not to look at either of them.

Colin has always been a great believer in the curative properties of takeaway pizza. So, when everyone was down for the night and the television was on, he sat sideways in the armchair and rang for an extra large spicy pepperoni. Pizza dissolved and vanished inside Colin, like the five chocolate bars I'd seen him guzzle in one night. His stomach was concave and shiny white, with tufts of black hair in a line from his naval down into the top of his jeans. This wasn't something I knew from close inspection; when he stretched to pull off his fleece, his t-shirt would ride up and I'd get a flash if I didn't look away.

'And a –' he waved the phone at me. I shook my head. 'Large Hawaiian,' he said, and gave next door's address. He stretched out his arms and legs and laughed silently, looking at his filthy size zillion trainers and batting away a crane fly.

It was crane fly season. They pitter-pattered their pin-prick feet over the posters and the lampshades in the night, driving you mad until you had to get up and thwack them. The Shelter was the last house in the terrace, and crazy vegetation grew unchecked front, side and back. The crane flies had their headquarters amongst this jungle and sent attack parties out from there. There were nights I thwacked so many that the vision of them stayed under my skin; dislocated heads and torn wings, legs on their own where they'd come off in the tissue.

I picked off the squares of ham and pineapple to eat first, with the vague intention of leaving at least some of the crust. By then I had grease round my mouth and on my hands, and I began to tear at the pizza with my teeth, chewing too much at once. When it was finished, the boxes were soggy on the table between us and there were crumbs on the floor. I couldn't sit like Colin, all floppy and yawny, staring at the television and wiping my hands on my clothes. I wanted the sticky patch cleaned up quickly, as soon as it was over. I thought about saying this as I stood up; a little self-deprecatory joke. But it was the sort of thing Colin could only have coped with in a group; a remark like that with just the two of us to bounce between would leave a crater where it fell. I took the boxes across to the kitchen area and tried to cram them into the recycling bin, but it was overflowing so I pulled out the bag and shoved everything down until I could tie the handles. The top of my jeans was sharp on the bulge of my stomach.

'Am I safe to take the rubbish out?'

Colin looked at the top of my head. 'Safe as houses,' he said. 'Apparently most people now believe the nonsense about sleeping in the fresh air.'

The previous week, we'd had a minor riot outside the front door. The Shadow Minister for Homelessness had said in a television interview that hostels should be shut until the source of the disease was pinpointed, and a rumour went around that people with beds would be able to keep them, like a sort of legalised squat. I stood at the gate, trying to explain that nothing had changed, that people would still be moving through, and Colin twitched his nose a lot and repeated everything I said. Then the very next day, the Minister for Health went on television and said it was definitely much safer to sleep in the open than to go to a hostel, where the disease was at its most virulent. So then we had beds free and couldn't fill them.

I heaved the recycling bag into the hall, and Colin changed the channel on the television.

'Chivalry not dead, then,' I called, sliding the bolts on the front door and catching the skin on my knuckle. 'Ow. Shit.'

Outside, the air was still and smelt of bonfire. It was quiet except for next door's music. (There were six students living there, and they all had iPod speakers on their windowsills.) The lamppost opposite flickered, lethargic, and beyond the rooftops the copper dome of the Whitchurch hospital water tower burnt a hole in the darkness. Wherever you go in Cardiff, the water tower is there; it doesn't seem to matter which way you're facing – and you can be up on a hill looking down or walking along the road looking up – there it is. Leering, dominating the skyline, *you can't touch me, I'm listed.* I used to collect pretentious phrases from the television and radio, and I remember some cheesy-grinned gardening presenter talking about 'borrowed landscapes', which really just meant looking at something that isn't yours. Your neighbour might have a nice tree, for example, which you can see from your decking. The cheesy gardener went so far as to suggest you made an interestingly-shaped hole in your fence in order to borrow a view. But you don't need to go to any such lengths to include the water tower. You could blow it up and, when the dust settled, it would have rearranged itself and be standing gormless and all the more indestructible for its ordeal. I don't know where I got the idea from, that the water tower was where they burnt the suicides. Maybe it was an early playground myth. I imagined a trolley going round the wards, collecting the bodies of people who hadn't been able to face another day, and using them to stoke an everlasting furnace in the tower. At the bottom there was (I imagined) a pile of bones and ashes, and at the top the fumes produced by the boiling blood of people fed on mind-altering substances. Apparently, the purpose of a water tower is to create pressure in the taps.

The Shelter's front garden had six paving slabs, shunted out of place by the roots of a tree that had long since been cut down. I stepped round the stump to wedge the sack between the bin and the fence, and realised that, underneath the massed iPods, I could hear someone breathing. The front door was still open, the stark light from the hall leaking out into the street. I stepped backwards, catching my ankle on the tree stump and falling onto my bum.

A young woman stepped out from behind the bin, clutching a cushiony white handbag and looking apologetic.

'I'm so sorry,' she whispered. 'I don't know why I'm hiding really.' She took the rubbish from me and propped it against the fence while I staggered to my feet.

'Thank you,' I said. She was wearing a neat little skirt and shoes with bows on. 'What are you doing here?'

'My housemates have changed the locks.'

'That's horrible. It's unforgivable, actually, at the moment.'

Her eyes began to swim. 'I quite literally have nowhere else to go. And my bank account is frozen. And I heard you were still letting people in here. But then I couldn't bring myself to knock.' In the light from the hall, I saw that my knuckle was bleeding where I'd caught it on the door.

'Do you want to come in?' I said.

'Could I? Just for tonight, then I can sort myself out tomorrow. Thank you so much. I'm Fflur. Double F-l-u-r.' She offered me her hand to shake and then thought better of it.

'I'm Shona,' I said. 'Pleased to meet you.' I'm sure it was the first time in my life I'd ever said that.

Inside, I saw how crinkled her clothes were. Her cardigan was an elegant little crochet number in pale green. I wouldn't have got an arm through a sleeve let alone stretched it across my back.

'This is Colin,' I said, sucking my knuckle. 'Colin, this is Fflur.'

Colin stood. He did a little jiggle from side to side by way of a greeting and looked at the curtains.

'It's so lovely of you to have me,' said Fflur. 'I'm so grateful. Oh God, I've been so scared.'

'I can believe it,' I said. 'Do you want some soup?'

'Yes,' she said. 'Do you mind if I sit down?' She sat on our antique corduroy sofa and put her handbag at her feet. 'I think I'm in shock. Probably hungry. I had this meeting, you see. I make jewellery. And whilst I was out, they got one of their boyfriends to change the locks.' Colin came across to the kitchen and got in my way. I left him to the soup and went to sit with Fflur. 'I'm babbling a bit. Being homeless is new to me. Do you need my details or anything?' She started crying. Colin drummed a little rhythm on the kitchen work surface. The pizza was heavy and oily inside me. After a bit, Fflur tucked her hair behind her ears and said, 'I'll be able to pay you, when I get things organised. I've got two shops lined up to stock my jewellery, and I'm getting a catalogue printed.'

'That sounds great,' I said. 'Maybe you'll be able to give us a donation or something.' She had a 'please like me' face and a pretty smile.

After she'd eaten the soup, I led her up the stairs, embarrassed suddenly by the state of the runner which was thicker with Suzy's hair than it was with actual carpet.

'Bathroom,' I said, opening the door, hoping Paul hadn't been for one of his specials.

'Lovely, thanks,' said Fflur. She stood on the landing, nodding, dazed.

'I'll find you a towel. I'll just show you your room.' A roaring snore erupted from behind Paul's door and she jumped, eyes swimming again. 'It's downstairs, actually,' I said. 'At the front.'

'Oh, right. Lovely.'

We went back downstairs to the front bedroom. On the pillow was a tiny dead wasp. Fflur was polite enough not to mention it.

'Thank goodness you weren't full,' she said, beaming at the room as if it had a dressing table and complimentary bubble bath. I swallowed a splinter of cheese that had got stuck in my teeth and handed her a t-shirt to sleep in. She sniffed it and her hand flew to her mouth.

'I am so sorry! I really didn't mean to do that. Now I look like some middle-class snob who thinks homeless people stink.'

I grinned. 'I wash things,' I said, 'before I give them out.'

2

The words aren't coming. I look round the Learning Centre, which is essentially a classroom with some leaflets and antique computing equipment in it.

From the window, you can see the part of the grounds designated as garden. The sweeping curve of flower bed is still asleep under a thick frost, but the roses have been cut back and there's a butterfly bush and a magnolia in waiting. It's hard to be sure from here, but I think the network of dead twigs might be a dormant clematis.

'Sometimes it's easier not to start at the beginning,' says Carol, twiddling her necklace which is made of safety pins, beads and sequins. 'When you start at the beginning you can run out of steam before you reach the end. In fact you don't really know where the beginning is until you've written the end.' She winces, her thumb caught on a sharp bit of necklace; she's given herself the Writing Therapist's equivalent of a needlestick injury.

My head hurts. The pain feels as if it should be visible, should have a texture on the surface. I imagine circling with my pen the area on my scalp where the underside is rawest. My eyeballs are swollen hard and pushing up into my forehead. They taste of petrol. There are iron filings where my blood used to be. I dream of the day I'll be able to really go to town with the diazepam, and the inside of my head will pixelate. There's a Romanian woman here who trades in something that can't be too unlike Colin's palinka. That might be a good way to chase valium. Perhaps I'll give her the nod, in advance. In fact, as she also trades in fortune-telling, maybe she's already worked this out for herself. Maybe she's got supply and demand sussed. She complains, though, because she's used to reading tea leaves and you don't get a lot of those in here.

I let several minutes pass, kneading my left hand with my right; experiment with Carol's non-verbal skills and her nerve to see a silence through. She does active listening as if I am talking; she makes little blinks and nods in response to my nothings. When I shut my eyes, she says, 'The end is arbitrary *too, Shona. A writer chooses where to end her story – that's quite empowering, I think. Every story everywhere is linked to an infinite number of others; existence doesn't divide itself into measurable chunks. There are no fences to stop stories seeping into each other.' I scratch my crotch (I do try not to, but the regrowth of pubes is a bristly business. If I catch myself in time, I sit on my hands). 'Your job as a writer is to shine a torch onto a little piece of that eternal jigsaw. You might not even know what's there until you switch on your torch and start scribbling.' I open my eyes and stare at her boots, which are Victorian-petticoat leather lace-ups. 'Write something about yourself that you think might surprise me,' she says.*

There's nothing surprising about me. Except, I suppose, that I'm not a lesbian. I did have hair, but it was a very nondescript length and it got hacked rather than trimmed. (I tended to do this when I did my toenails, since I had the scissors out.) And of course I'm stocky, chunky, porky – Nain has used all those words and more – and I shove on jeans and really skanky trainers where some women (strange word, I usually think of myself as a girl. Not *girly*, but definitely a girl rather than a woman) faff about with skirts and tights. I do remember very distinctly the sensation of putting on tights – after PE at school, or in the swimming changing rooms. Horrible. It felt like trying to stretch dolls' clothes over the branches of a tree. I moved quickly on to the over-the-knee sock stage, which was hardly better, pulling scratchy ribbed grey elastic up onto sweaty thighs, and feeling them gradually slide down around my ankles so that I had to stop at every corner to pull them up. One day a friend of Nain's said, *Ooh, you were having trouble with those tights.* She'd been watching me, sitting in a traffic jam laughing at this itchy runny-nosed teenager lumbering along battling with her socks. And Nain said, *Oh yes, I have spies out,* and laughed, and I've never quite got over the idea that I'm being watched wherever I go.

Carol's tactic has worked (and she looks rather smug about it). She's got me writing again and I'm back to the Shelter, the following morning.

In the morning, Gloria rang from the office.
'Hi Gloria,' I said. 'How are you?'
Colin was scraping scrambled egg onto plates and Paul appeared,

breathing stale air into the room. He stuffed his hand inside his trousers and rearranged himself, squinting at the sunlight coming through the window.

'Bearing up,' said Gloria. 'I've had another visit from the Powers That Be.'

'Oh?' I said. Paul began to chew scrambled egg with his mouth open, as if that proved something.

'We need a face-to-face on this one, Shona.'

'We're full,' I lied. 'Are they really suggesting we kick people out? What purpose is that going to serve?' Despite Colin's humming, I sensed that Paul was listening to every word I said.

Gloria sighed. 'Shona,' she said. 'People are dying. You have to take this seriously. My chum in Environmental Health –'

'Must dash,' I said. 'Catch up later.'

'Don't get militant on me, Darling. I'm up to my eyeballs here. You are the only Shelter still open. I daren't ask if you're keeping up your prophylactics.'

'I am. Every day. I'm not stupid.'

'No. Just terribly stubborn.'

I put the phone down and Colin sniffed at length and said, 'Breakfast's up.'

Paul had finished his egg and was slurping down his tea. He was twenty-four and bald; he didn't even have eyebrows or eyelashes. He had come straight to us from prison this time without passing Go, dry and drug-free. Under normal circumstances, I'd have been pushing Gloria for a medium-term bed in a halfway house. But she'd locked the doors on it, so now there was just Colin and me, opening up each night and kicking through the hate mail in the hall.

'Good morning!' Fflur had washed and put make-up on. She looked at Paul. 'I'm Fflur,' she said. 'Did you sleep well?' When nobody spoke, Fflur looked at me for help.

'He thinks you're a social worker,' I said.

She laughed.

'I make jewellery,' she told him. 'Colin, you're a bit of a star in the kitchen. What can I do to help, Sweetie?'

'All in order,' said Colin, turning puce. 'All in order. Tuck in.' He put a plate on the table and Fflur settled herself opposite Paul.

'Goodness,' she said. 'That's more than my usual tablespoon of muesli.'

15

I swallowed a little snort. I'd had a Twix with my antibiotics.

When breakfast was over and people were leaving, I took Fflur aside.

'Look,' I said. 'I don't know what you're planning today but you should probably go to the doctor.' Fflur bit her lip. 'You've got enough to sort out at the moment without worrying about the great lurgy.'

'Do you take anything?' she said.

I nodded.

'Do you think they'll give them to me? I'll have to tell them I was here.'

I put my hand on her delicate little shoulder.

'Just to be on the safe side.'

There was a brisk knock on the front door. Colin said, 'So,' and coughed. Fflur smiled at me weakly. Suzy came trotting down the stairs, calling that she'd left her stuff in her room just today if that was alright with me and she was going to see some friends who might have a bit of work. She opened the front door and slipped out into the sunshine, passing Gloria who was waiting to come in.

Gloria was wearing a surgical mask, a shower cap and washing up gloves. Fflur's hand shot up to cover her mouth. Paul hung over the banisters and gawped. He specialised in delinquent facial expressions and liked to use his stark white baldness to frighten posh people.

'Gloria,' I said. 'Come in.'

She sat on the edge of the armchair and I clicked off the television and sat on the sofa. She kept her bag on her knee.

'I'm sorry,' she said, tucking her mask under her chin so that she could speak. 'You have to shut. As from now. There's no space left for debate.' She rubbed her hot pink cheeks and grimaced. 'Rosacea's worse than ever,' she said. 'Absolute pain.' She put up a gloved hand to stop me interrupting. 'The corpse in the shed. It was Alan Turner.'

'That figures,' I said, slouching back into the sofa.

'Shona, a man who stayed under this roof has died of this – this *plague* thing.'

(Alan Turner had one set of clothes, which he spring cleaned each Easter Sunday. He was always scratching; his fingernails housed thriving ecosystems. He claimed to have caught HIV from a mosquito on a cruise ship. Sitting in the kitchen under a poster we had which listed 'ways you can't get HIV', he'd say: 'They stab away, see. Don't care if you're not a homo or a blackie or whatnot – it's blood they're after. And they don't go rubbing alcohol gel into their feelers.' He loved telling people this; it made him laugh in a breathy, whistly way. 'What's the point in us fussing about with soap and that when they can just buzz up and stab you?' At this point, he'd jab a fingernail at whoever hadn't escaped. He generally got newcomers; anyone who knew what was coming would be out of jabbing distance well before he got this far. Paul said one breakfast time that if Alan so much as touched him, he'd have him for assault.

'I wouldn't touch you with a barge pole,' Alan told him.

'Barge pole!' Paul yelled. 'You flatter yourself, mate.' He slapped him on the back and then spat on his hands in mock panic and wiped them on Alan's shirt.

'You –' spluttered Alan.

'I'll have you both banned,' I muttered. 'Just to shut you up.'

Paul waggled his tongue at me and Alan put his knife and fork together on his baked-bean-smeared plate.

'Thank you, Colin,' he said. 'When you're ready with the coffee, garçon.'

Colin cleared his throat and poured a luke-warm cup of coffee. I wondered, as I often did, how Colin had been put in a position where he was responsible for keeping the peace amongst bullies like Paul and walking death-traps like Alan. If he'd rubbed either of them up the wrong way, they could have felled him with a little finger. Maybe that was it. Maybe it was his total vulnerability that kept him safe. Maybe it was myself I should have been worried about.)

'Alan Turner was a chain-smoking alcoholic with HIV,' I told Gloria. 'It's a surprise he lived as long as he did.'

'Nonetheless. We need to be on the safe side.' I raised my eyebrows. 'Shona, Darling, please.' She shut her eyes for a moment and sighed. 'There is no point in having this discussion. I wish things were different. I really do. And hopefully they'll get on top of this soon and it will turn out to be just another fizzled firework and we can all get back to normal.'

Footsteps crashed up the stairs. Colin came into the day room with his nose twitching.

'There's a policeman at the door,' he said.

'Does he want Paul?'

Colin laughed, scratching his neck.

Gloria jumped up and I followed her into the hall. Fflur was standing on the bottom step, clutching her handbag.

He wasn't a policeman I recognised. He looked at me kindly and unrolled a roll of red and white tape. Behind him, two men in luminous yellow work jackets were setting up barriers in front of the house. The students next door were hanging out of their upstairs window to watch.

'Can I help you?' I said.

Gloria made a little squeak.

'I'm not sure how to break this to you, love,' said the policeman. 'You're quarantined. Shouldn't be for long.'

'Nobody here has any symptoms,' I said. 'We check.' Fflur had her hand over her mouth. Gloria had her hands on her hips.

'Sorry, love,' said the policeman. 'I'm going to need a list from you of everyone in the building. And I'd ask you not to let anyone in or out. Just until, if you see what I mean.' He hooked the tape over the fence at one side.

'Until when?' My voice had gone up a notch. The policeman stopped unrolling the tape.

'Until the next directive,' he said. 'Environmental Health changes its mind on a daily bloody basis, 'scuse my French. So you'll probably be let out tomorrow. Then there'll be another set of instructions.'

'If you could just let me through,' said Gloria, indicating her shower cap. 'I've only been here ten minutes or so and I'm well protected as you can see.' She laughed encouragingly. The policeman looped his tape round the other fence and ducked underneath it to hand me an envelope.

'That explains the procedure for you,' he said, and took out a notebook. 'Could I have your names, please?'

We all stared at him and he looked sympathetically back at us, in the manner he used perhaps with victims of minor crime.

There was a crash from Paul's room and a series of swearwords.

'Paul?' I heaved myself upstairs, feeling sick and suddenly exhausted.

He was leaning out of his window with a cigarette in his hand.

'Rather rude,' he said.

'Who are you talking to?'

Paul sucked his cigarette and tapped ash out of the window. I stamped over to look out. A policewoman was brushing the ash from her jacket.

'This is your last warning!' she shrieked. 'Close the window now!'

'And if I don't?' shouted Paul and spat fruitily in her direction. I nudged him aside.

'Do we really need to keep the windows shut?' I said.

Three greasily pubescent boys came out of the house opposite. One of them pointed at us and they laughed.

'You do, Madam, yes.' I've always found the term 'Madam' faintly offensive. 'Please make sure all windows are secured now and instruct all occupants to –'

'We'll suffocate,' yelled Paul. 'Air is a human right!'

The boys in the street lit cigarettes and muttered to each other and Paul made an obscene gesture at them.

I eyeballed the policewoman, ignoring the elderly woman who had stopped right beside her to tut and the gym mother in the tank who was pulling up on the kerb.

'Could you give me some idea of how long this is likely to last?' I said. 'I don't have food for lunch.' Strictly speaking, we could have eaten tomorrow's breakfast, but still. And we'd need milk for tea.

'Supplies of food are on the way, Madam. You'll be kept informed. 'Please. Shut the window.' She turned to the gym mother in the tank, who seemed to be lost.

I pulled the window shut.

'Wankers,' said Paul.

I appear to be the only person who took up the offer of Life Writing Therapy. We had a 'taster session' at which we were invited to write a letter to a teacher we remembered from school. The word school *filled the room with attitude straight off. One woman wrote* Dear teachers, thanks for nothing, *and held it up. 'I was chucked out of six schools,' said the girl next to her, who was fatter than me and had horrible skin. This set off a cacophony about achievements in the area of expulsions, truancy, fighting and lesson disruption. I sat quietly with my guilty secret – I had a grammar school education, got good GCSE results, and was never kicked out of a lesson let alone a school. I got a report one year from a religious studies teacher whose register I was on by accident and who had in fact never taught me. It was indistinguishable from the reports of teachers who saw me twice a week.*

So as far as I know I am the only one who signed up, and at first I thought it would be weird with just me and Carol. I thought I'd feel conspicuous, that maybe she'd stare at me when I was writing and I'd be paralysed by the silence. But in fact it's fine, and it's nice to let my guard down a bit without the others around. They remind me of infant school when we had to choose partners in PE and no one wanted to go with the boy who had eczema on his palms. Now I'm the untouchable. Admittedly, to some of the women here, I'm more of an enigma. There was quite a trail of bodies, and the weapon was unique, after all, and seems to lend me a certain je ne sais quoi.

'Have you written much before?' asks Carol, leaning back in her chair and looking quietly interested.

'Not since school,' I say. 'Which was a very long time ago.'

She smiles. 'Not that long ago. Certainly not as long ago as me.' She chuckles. She's difficult to age. Her hair might be ash blonde, but it might just be ash; it depends on the light perhaps. There's a lot of it, and she's strewn with so many trinkets – necklaces, earrings, reading glasses on chains and sunglasses on her head – that you'd have to look right up close to see how deep her wrinkles are. I smile obediently; nonsense, Carol, you're not old by anyone's reckoning.

'Did you enjoy school?' she says.

I don't have a clear cut answer to this. There must have been lessons I enjoyed. I know I liked sitting on the carpet for story time when I was little, but that's not really what she's asking. I must have been relatively interested in science in secondary school, because there was vague talk of dentistry. But it would be an overstatement to say I enjoyed school. I was detached, on the fringes of it all, cynical before I knew the meaning of the word and really pretty friendless.

3

I sat on the bathroom floor with my head in my hands. Gloria was fuming. I had tried to apologise, and I was too tired to try again. She was right when she asked the policeman to let her out; she'd only just arrived, and people who'd stayed the night, several nights, had disappeared before we got taped up. Suzy was going about her business unaware that her things were in quarantine.

I'd wondered about escaping through the back door. You could have hidden in the jungle for a while surviving on crane flies. But the police guard had got there first, and as far as I could tell from an unauthorised peer through an upstairs window, had matted what looked like barbed wire into the undergrowth.

My packet of anti-tubercles was in a drawer in my bedroom at home; I'd only brought one dose with me. Maybe they'd bring some with the supplies we'd been promised. Or maybe the money that had been spent providing me with these magic capsules would now be wasted and I'd be left as open to the plague as anyone else. I'd rung Nain, assuring her that I had my medicine. I'd laughed a bit and told her to watch out for me on the news, waving from a window. She treated me to a few choked sobs and her brave voice, which was guaranteed to wind me up even when I wasn't sleep-deprived and locked in with the windows shut.

There was a knock at the front door. I scrambled to my feet and bolted down the stairs. Fflur and Gloria were there before me, and Gloria opened the door. She still wore the washing up gloves and the shower cap but she had abandoned the face mask. The summer had decided belatedly that it had a last spurt of energy to use up, and the sun was hot. It felt unreal, a mirage perhaps, the product of my fuggy, stale mind.

Two young men stood either side of a large plastic box on wheels. They lifted the lid, and inside was a slightly smaller box.

'Could you take it without touching the larger box, please, Madam,' said one.

Beyond the tape, a small camera crew were filming a reporter with her back to us. Gloria stepped forward and took out the smaller box with exaggerated care. The reporter turned and gestured to the door.

'How many of you are there?' she called.

Gloria stood holding the box, seeming to consider for a moment.

'Five,' she said loudly and clearly. 'And all completely well. We look forward to going home later.'

'Those of us who have homes, that is,' shouted Paul from upstairs.

Gloria turned purple. The delivery men wheeled away their uncontaminated box, ducking under the tape. One of them waved at the camera and the other one elbowed him.

Gloria carted the box into the kitchen and put it on the table. Paul came down and Colin stopped watching television and came over to look. We'd closed the curtains; they didn't quite meet but it meant the starers had to come up close to the window to see anything, and most people weren't prepared to risk that. We watched Gloria open the lid in silence. Fflur sneezed. Gloria glared at her and wafted her hands about.

There was a bottle of milk, two loaves of bread, butter, cheese, smiley face biscuits, crisps, and three little pill boxes.

'Good,' said Colin. 'That should do us.'

'Colin, you eat more than that by yourself.' I hated myself when I snapped at Colin.

'Shall I make some sandwiches?' said Fflur brightly.

I took out one of the pill boxes. It had Colin's name and date of birth on it and three bright blue capsules inside. I let Fflur take out the stuff for the sandwiches. She found the bread board, a knife and a cheese grater I didn't know we had. Colin opened a packet of crisps. I gave him his pill box and, without looking at anyone, I took out the other two. One for me and one for Gloria.

'Mm,' said Colin. 'So.'

'Does anyone not like cheese?' said Fflur.

'Oh, I get it.' Paul roared his best intimidating laugh. 'Those pills are to protect you from me.' He gave a little round of applause.

'Paul,' I said. 'Just leave it. Please. None of us asked to be stuck here.' Fflur had stopped buttering and was watching us, the knife sticking up from her hand. Gloria popped a capsule into her mouth and swigged from her tea.

'Is there – one for me?' she asked quietly. Paul looked at me, curious.

'Sorry,' I mumbled. 'It's only because we've already got them on prescription.' I crushed the box in my fist. Paul made a face at me and gave a huge fake cough. 'It's just policy,' I said weakly.

'Like locking us all in is policy,' he said. 'That's really going to stop the germs spreading.' I glanced at the closed window and sighed.

'Paul,' I said. 'I see your point. And I'm sure you wish you'd got out when everyone else did.'

'Nah, not really,' he said. Then suddenly he patted his pockets. 'Wank,' he muttered. Gloria shut her eyes and sighed. 'I've only got three cigs left.'

Colin tipped back his head and poured the crisp crumbs into his mouth. He smacked his lips and put the bag in the bin. Fflur had returned to her sandwiches.

In the delivery was a slip with a phone number on it for the Government Helpline for Quarantined Households and Institutions. After lunch, I spent an hour on the telephone listening to some eerie classical music and a voice which repeated every two minutes that I was in a queue. The phone was in the corner of the kitchen and it was possible to sit on the bench by stretching the cord straight. After ten minutes I had my head on the table. After twenty, I had eaten a packet of crisps and three smiley face biscuits. At about the half an hour mark, I had to call Gloria to take over while I went for a wee. Then she went back to leafing through her diary and sighing and I took the phone again and tried to do some yoga postures and ignore the music.

Eventually, the music stopped and there was a ringing tone. I rolled my shoulders and breathed out, nodding frantically at Gloria.

'Praise be,' she said, and came to stand beside me. The phone clicked and there was a dialling tone.

'Fucking bloody wank!' I shouted. Paul made a whooping noise and I wanted to kick his head in. Colin slunk from the room in long lolloping steps. I stamped out, ran up the stairs to Suzy's room and shunted her stuff out of the way so that I could throw myself onto her bed. It was always Suzy's room, Suzy's bed, despite regulations which required her to move out every week or so. She had two recycling bags, a Bag 4 Life and a silver make-up case. I buried my head in her pillow, which smelt of hairspray and something herbal.

After a while, Gloria tapped on the door. She crept across the room and stood over me with her hands on her hips.

'I think we're going to need something of a blitz mentality on this one,' she said. I bit down hard on the back of my left hand, leaving teeth marks. 'We might be let out tonight, but it seems increasingly likely that it could be tomorrow. Or ...'

'I just wish someone would bother to communicate with us.'

'I know, Darling.' She folded her arms and sighed. I pushed myself into a sitting position.

'Gloria, I'm sorry. I know this is my fault. I'm surprised you're still talking to me.'

'I'm furious,' she said. 'But I was actually quite impressed by the way you stood your ground. Most people would have put themselves first.' I looked at my trainers. 'And you may yet turn out to be right. Perhaps the disease did spread in Shelters. But it might spread even more quickly now they're shut.'

I shrugged. Downstairs, the phone rang. Gloria bustled from the room, tripping over Suzy's stuff, and I followed her, wanting to push past her on the stairs because she wasn't fast enough.

Fflur had answered the call. She stood very straight, smiling pleasantly into the receiver and nodding.

'Yes, absolutely. Here she is.' She handed me the phone and Gloria pursed her lips and cocked her ear to listen in.

'Hello. Shona Davies speaking.'

'Hello. I'm calling from the Quarantine Unit. This is a courtesy call to check that all is well.'

'A courtesy call?'

'Do you have sufficient supplies of food, drink, essential toiletries and any medication occupants usually take?'

'Um. Well, no. We haven't got much to eat.' I turned to Gloria. 'Do you take any medication? I mean, other than your prophylactics.' She swallowed and mouthed something at me. 'Hang on,' I said into the phone. 'I have to check about the medicines.'

'HRT,' hissed Gloria. 'And my rosacea stuff.' She patted her cheeks.

'HRT,' I repeated into the phone. 'Oh, OK. Gloria, do you have the name of the –'

'Oh, forget it,' she said. 'One day won't kill me.'

'It's fine,' I said. 'We can maybe leave that for now. Look, I tried ringing that helpline number and got nowhere. No one has told us anything.'

'I'm not sure that the helpline is up and running yet, Shona.' The way she said my name, I think I would have preferred *Madam*. 'Is there anything I can help you with?' I was stumped by this. I wanted to shout at her that I'd had very little sleep, that Colin and Paul smelt, that my grandmother would need post-trauma counselling and that locking up five healthy people was not going to help anyone.

'Do you know how long it will be before we can get out?' I said.

'I don't have an actual estimate, I'm afraid. We will do all we can and keep you informed of decisions.'

4

I think I am right in saying that what Carol is wearing is a kaftan. *She is also wearing a very long, complicated necklace. As she settles down, arranging her things, I wonder if I have ever worn a necklace. I must have. A daisy chain at the very least. I find myself stroking my neck, searching for the memory.*

'OK? Do you want some water?' says Carol.

'No, I'm fine. Right.' *I sit up straight: model student. Goody-goody.*

There's someone turning over the soil round the ground cover today, in the curved flower bed outside the Learning Centre window. I'm tired out from doing nothing and if the window was of the opening variety I'd jump out and go and help. There are some girls whose names are down for gardening, but they spend most of the time outside the office whining that they've got colds or periods and aren't up to it. If it didn't clash with Carol, I'd try and get my name down for it. But Carol has become the focus of my week; I think I'd be lost if I couldn't write. Words shuffle themselves about inside my head during the long hours alone. And when I'm in the canteen or the showers, remarks print themselves on an endless tic-a-tape behind my eyes. Cow from first floor has four yogurts on her tray and no one does anything about it. Key-jangler supreme joking with bitch from next door; bullying's a sociable pastime. *I hover above it all, watching the tic-a-tape.*

This place plays a mean trick with time. On the one hand it snatches whole chunks of your life, dangling the days from its jaws and drooling. On the other hand, it slows time down until it's no longer tangible. The rest of the world may still be turning on its axis, but it's left us behind. We're stuck outside the space-time continuum, with a high-pitched drone where the ticking of a clock should be.

If I came from a different background – rural East Africa, say, or the Gurnos Estate – I'd probably cope better with having so little to do. But I'm burdened by the compulsion to be constructive. I need lessons in how to be.

Just be, without having to do or say anything to prove or justify my existence. I've experimented with squatting on my haunches in the corridor and watching the world go by, but I always look at the clock in the end and not many minutes have ticked past.

'*When you write,' says Carol, 'you can be a time-traveller. You can go backwards, forwards, jog on the spot or turn in circles.'*

I was turning in circles on the landing with my eyes shut. It felt important at the time. And for want of any other way of improving the situation, arbitrary superstitious landing-spinning seemed worth a try. An old-fashioned *bring bring* startled me from behind Suzy's door. Wondering vaguely whether the helpfulness of answering someone else's phone outweighed the nosiness/privacy-intrusion factor, I banged straight in and rummaged through her stuff. The bottom of a recycling bag full of clothes and hair straighteners was flashing and vibrating and the quickest route was to tear a hole in the bag and get to the phone that way. The recycling bag was expendable: I had more than anyone could reasonably hope for in a lifetime because it was one of Colin's responsibilities and he took it pretty seriously. I managed to cut off the call before I'd worked out what to press and I dropped the phone on the rug and lay down beside it.

The Bag 4 Life was full of the sort of shoes that look completely different in a size 5. I was wearing the trainers I'd got from the boys' section of Peacocks. Luckily for me, the local lads had left a size 8 wide fit. I rolled onto my front, letting out an oomph worthy of Nain, and rummaged. Suzy had also been at the children's wear; she had a pair of white canvas buckle-ups coated in jellies. I stroked the jellies. I was aware that not licking them was a good sign. She had a scuffed denim shoe with a strap that had come off and, although I tipped out all the others and couldn't find its pair, I spent a while trying to thread the torn strap back through its loop. It was an effective meditation; when the drone of the television filtered back into my consciousness from downstairs, it felt like a small victory to have shut it out for a while. Then Suzy's phone jiggled on the carpet and said, 'How *you* doin'?' I was too bored to return to the nosiness/privacy dilemma, and I read the text without hesitation. *Had sooo much fun 2day thanx babe it ment alot x.*

I rolled onto my side and knelt up, fiddling about to see if I could mark it unread, revolted by my ferreting and envious of Suzy for getting called babe by someone to whom she *ment alot.*

I remember a girl at school saying, 'Shona, do you ever have fun?' and I said, 'What?' with a little sneer to show I thought it was a stupid question. She smiled sadly and said, 'It's just you don't strike me as a very fun sort of person. I'm interested to know what you do for fun.' She put her head on one side and I thought about spitting down at it; she was shorter than me.

'Maybe we just have different ways of having fun,' I said. 'Maybe you just pretend to have fun. Maybe fun doesn't even exist.'

The 'different ways of having fun' conversation was misquoted until I left school in the sixth form. It quickly became 'there's no such thing as fun.' When Mr Herbert confiscated a lipstick and it was whispered that he wanted to put some on, when we narrowed the aisles in the exam room by squashing the rows of desks together because Mrs Green was fat, and when someone hung a red-felt-tipped tampon in the religious studies display case, the class laughed conspicuously until someone said, 'Ssh! There's no such thing as fun,' and then they'd sit up straight and make faces as if they were forcibly constraining hysterics. We were kept in for a long time with the tampon hanging on display. Mr Herbert took his briefcase and left as the Deputy Head arrived. She wore her glasses at an angle that could reduce you to chalk dust. I burnt as red as the felt tip while the Deputy Head lectured us in scientific detail about the colour of blood. And when we were finally let out, some little cat gave me a look which seemed to suggest that the incident was somehow my fault. 'There's no such thing as fun' became a sinister little motto that could be used as a label or a threat.

The little cats I went to school with are running the country now. They're housing lawyers and breast surgeons, investment bankers and media studies teachers. As far as I know from Facebook-lurking, I'm the only convict with a background in greasy baps and homeless support work.

We had a second delivery in the evening. A selection of Indian takeaway dishes, individual butterscotch trifles, some milk and another two loaves of bread. Fflur shared out the poppadoms.

'Oh,' said Colin, frozen in the act of changing the channel on the television. He sounded desolate.

'Colin?' I glanced at the screen. A policeman wearing thick gloves was cramming a dog into a cage.

I patted Colin's arm.

'At least you didn't have to put your dog through that,' I said. Then I wished I hadn't said it. He cleared his throat. 'Sorry,' I said. 'I didn't mean. Sorry.' I had almost forgotten about Colin's dog. 'Colin, can I ask ... What did you do with your dog, when it, um ... passed away?'

'Nothing yet,' he said. Ah.

'So the dog is still at your flat?'

'Yes.' He shrugged. 'He'll be smelly now.' I patted his arm again and tried not to look at Gloria. Fflur was poised with a serving spoon over a foil dish of basmati rice. She was trembling a little. 'He is *covered*,' murmured Colin sadly, 'in those black boils.'

When the food was finished, I went upstairs and curled up in Suzy's bed with my clothes on to indulge in my favourite pastime, daydreaming about Dan. Dan came to stay for a week at the Shelter. We worked our way through an economy-sized packet of condoms and I spent more time in his bed than on guard in the day room. When Dan's stay was up, he wrapped his arms around me and kissed me goodbye, speaking urgently and firmly about The Future. He was holding my head in his hands, which were slap bang over my ears, so I didn't hear much of this at all. Then he shouldered his backpack and said, 'And I will get sorted. It just might take a while.'

I fell asleep mid-fantasy and dreamt instead that I was married to Manky Mark, the drug addict I lived with for a few weeks to consolidate my lack of self-esteem. In the dream, Dan turned up at my house and we were mesmerised by each other. I suggested I could show him round the garden; a chance for some illicit light petting. We tripped over the skeleton of the Christmas tree I dumped there years ago, and rolled on warty-headed clover, absorbed in hands and faces. Gloria dragged me away and hissed that I would ruin the children's lives, that they would end up in *a unit* if Mark and I split up. I introduced Mark to Dan and they shook hands but it was screaming with tension and mutual disgust. And all the time I was trying to tell Gloria that I didn't have any children and she'd got it all wrong.

I woke up slowly, sweating and stiff, thinking that I was married to Manky Mark in the waking world, cowed from Gloria's fury and unsure where I was. My mouth was foul and a spot had sprung up solid and painful on my chin. I dragged myself downstairs to get some water. No one had turned off the lights and the whole house stank of curry. Colin was watching television, picking at his feet. I didn't speak and he didn't show any sign he'd noticed me, so I glugged down some water and rubbed my face with wet hands. Maybe it was a good thing Dan hadn't been here to get locked in with us. In my daydreams I was sparkling with loveliness, not crusty-eyed and sweaty. I liked to think of him planting a soft kiss on my neck. His hair was scruffy and overgrown and his chin was scratchy with stubble.

I refilled the mug and took it back upstairs. Paul was snoring thunderously. I lay down, trying to shut out the sound and drown myself in sleep again.

Dan wasn't my only crush. There were others, but I admired them from afar and it was no doubt all unrequited. When I was newish at the Shelter and knew almost nothing, for example (this was in the days before my freckles became age spots and when I could walk straight away in the mornings), there was a young man called Tom who often stayed there. Tom had schizophrenia and halitosis. He was desperately embarrassed by the stench and mostly kept his mouth shut. He had the grin of an American sitcom actor, laughed like a child, and spoke with his hand masking the lower half of his face. He confided in me once that the effects of chewing gum lasted only seconds, and mints caused a saliva problem and gave him a weak little cough that smelt a lot worse than it sounded.

One night, when the Shelter was full – sleeping bags on the floor and couples sharing single beds (this was before Gloria's time) – Tom came to the door. I hated turning people away; I never got used to it.

'Not to worry, Shona,' he said. 'Thanks anyway.'

I made a *sorry* face and shrugged, which must have really helped. 'You could get yourself admitted to Whitchurch for a bit,' I said. 'Have a few weeks off?'

He was so surprised by the suggestion he let his mouth spring right open. 'If it snows, maybe.' He flapped the air around his face away from me down the path. 'Sorry.'

'Is it really that bad?'

He stopped flapping and looked straight at me. 'You can't go out,' he said. 'The fresh air rights are worse than prison.'

'Fuck.'

'Fuck indeed. It's a forward-thinking city, this. If the deterrent is strong enough, people might stop being schizophrenic. Perhaps they'll introduce the death penalty – get rid of us altogether one way or another.'

Where we lived, everyone claimed to have found Whitchurch patients lost in the street in their pyjamas. In fact the patients were mostly dressed in generic semi-homeless garb, and the staff were often indistinguishable.

Tom was moving sideways to the gate, balancing the courtesy of not turning his back with that of trying not to breathe at me.

'I'm sorry,' I said. 'I shouldn't have said it. I just thought, you know ...'

He clicked the gate into position behind him, rolled his shoulders back and stood up straight. 'Well now you know,' he grinned. 'The snow would have to be pretty thick.'

I was left wondering if he'd ever been kissed or if his sitcom actor lips and his gentlemanly ways had been wasted. I shut the door, wondering if I should train as a dentist after all and whether a hospital could really be so unpleasant it was worse than sleeping in a car park.

'You little cock-tease!' Oh God. Paul was whooping about something and Fflur and Gloria were rising to it. I had locked myself in the loo, resting my head on the wall and gazing at the soap dispenser, which had a sticker on it saying, *calming and relaxing, energising and invigorating.* This always struck me as something of an inflated claim, for a dribble of soap.

Paul shrieked, 'You've said it now! You can't take it back!' He played a drum roll on something metallic – the draining board or a saucepan, I supposed, and Gloria's voice rose above the noise. Her words were indistinct, a shrill, strident blur. I considered jumping out of a window. If it hadn't been for the barbed wire and the crane fly headquarters, I might have done. I looked at my face in the tiny mirror and rubbed my finger over the tight red spot on my chin. I dragged myself downstairs into the main room.

Colin was turning up the volume on a television cookery competition. Paul responded with a crescendo of his one-man kitchen band. Gloria was gesticulating with both hands, flushed with outrage, and Fflur was waving the washing up brush and shouting, 'Er – excuse me!'

'Glory Glory Hallelujah,' Paul sang this like a football fan goading the opposition. Gloria shrieked, 'You're only hearing what you want to hear!' and he did his roar-laugh.

'For heaven's sake,' said Fflur and she dropped the scrubbing brush into the water. She gazed into the sink as if she wanted to immerse herself. 'He'll stop quicker if you ignore him,' I said quietly.

'What's that?' shouted Paul. 'You'll throw me out? I wish.' He banged a saucepan against his forehead. 'They could use you inside, Glory-Ah. You could talk people into submission.'

I made a don't rise to it gesture at Gloria, grabbed a benefits leaflet from the side and took it out on a stray crane fly. Wiping it off the leaflet onto the side of the bin, I decided I'd done it a favour and put it out of its misery. It can't have had many friends, with the windows shut. Fflur looked so unhappy I wanted to apologise. I should never have let her in.

'The silver lining,' said Gloria, 'and let's face it we need to focus on the positive here, is that you and I have an opportunity for a proper chat.' She mirrored my body language carefully and I wasn't sure if I was in for some CBT or NLP or a dizzying mix of both. 'I know you weren't entirely happy with the appraisal Sandra wrote.' I've never been sure what hackles are, but I know they rise whenever I hear the word 'appraisal'. I swallowed and hoped someone would come in and interrupt – anyone, Paul even – but they were distributed about the Shelter as unobtrusively as if Gloria had paid them off for a while.

She'd made me a coffee, which was never a good sign. I drank it, looking neutral with a hint of don't-push-me. 'And since then there's been something of a stand-off really, hasn't there?' I finished my coffee and raised my eyebrows. 'You're a tough cookie, Shona.' God, appraisal and tough cookie in the same conversation. I could have done with one of Nain's diazzies. 'And that's a mix, perhaps, of Nature and Nurture, mm? But don't shut us all out, will you?' She smiled generously. I shook my head a fraction. 'Everyone needs people,' she said gently. 'Even if they're not essentially a people person.'

That was the phrase that had tipped me over the edge in the appraisal: *Shona isn't naturally a people person and might like to look at training opportunities which would help her to engage with clients and colleagues more effectively.* This from Sandra, who spends her day in a tiny office and says,

'What now?' whenever the phone rings. Who stropped out of a meeting when she didn't get her own way over a policy detail that would have had little bearing on anything. Who refused to talk to an admin temp until she was so upset she left. Six weeks after Sandra produced this vitriolic document, I found her dabbing at her eyes in the toilet at head office. 'I'm so angry,' she sniffed, her hands shaking as she took mascara from her handbag and fiddled with the lid. She smelt of perfume. (This is yet another sign of my complete failure as a woman, that all perfume smells the same and makes me sneeze.) 'Gloria's listed concerns on my appraisal, bloody woman. Concerns. I work my socks off for this twisted organisation and that's the thanks I get.' I turned on the tap and watched the water for a while, then I turned it off. I still hadn't been to the toilet, but I didn't feel like going with her there. 'Oh Sandra,' I murmured, 'I know how you feel,' and backed out.

So now Gloria was NLP and CBT-ing away in the kitchen at the Shelter and all that seemed like a previous incarnation.

'Have you heard from Mum recently?' For a second, I wasn't sure who she was talking about.

'Uh, no. Not for a while.'

'How's your grandmother?'

'Fine. Nain is fine. Thank you.'

Dad and I moved in with Nain before I could walk. She always said my Bloody Mother should have been dragged back kicking and screaming. I think she was jealous; she never had the chance to run away because my grandfather got there first. He was a sad old alkie by all accounts, though at Dad's funeral he looked quite dapper. And it's my own fault Nain's a hypochondriac because of the time I moved in with Manky Mark, mostly to punish her and rebel against something, though I wasn't sure what. And naturally Mark was a junk-filled waster and I was miserable and quite scared by all the shadowy lurking and dodgy characters in and out at all hours and the extent to which even rebellion was a cliché, and I seized the opportunity of Nain getting a slight cough to insist that I was worried about her and should come home to look after her. I think the doctor was puzzled by my theatricals, having seen me through abandonment and bereavement without a murmur, but she referred Nain for a chest x-ray to keep me quiet. Unfortunately, Nain enjoyed the appointment so much she took up medical investigations as a hobby and then as a full-time occupation.

'Is Nain ...' Gloria tweaked her hair a bit under the shower cap. 'Is she your only Significant Other? You had a partner for a while, didn't you? Is that ... over?' I made my neutral-with-a-hint-of expression, though I'm not convinced that's how it comes across.

'There was someone, yes.' I was defiant; it felt important to challenge my reputation as a sad lonely person. 'In fact we have something of an understanding. It's just not quite the right time for us yet.'

Gloria looked irritatingly sympathetic. 'Be careful though,' she said gently. 'That may not be entirely ... I just think that if a man really loves you, nothing will stop him beating a path to your door.'

'Maybe he's met Nain.'

'Am I right that there have been girlfriends as well as boyfriends?' She put her hands up in surrender. 'I'm not prying.'

'Gloria, I'm not a lesbian.'

'Bisexual?' She looked very surprised indeed. I stood up.

'I like to have sex with men,' I said. She coughed. 'From time to time,' I added.

And of course that was when Paul appeared in the doorway cackling and shifting globules of snot around his nasal system.

'Happy to oblige,' he shouted. 'Unless Colin's keeping you busy.' He bellowed up the stairs, 'Colin mate!' Gloria stood, tucked in her chair and stared at him until he moved enough for her to get through the door. 'Hey, Colin, you never told me you were screwing Shona, you dirty poofter!'

I pushed past him and went to lie across the mat by the front door and wish I was dead.

Staff numbers are low, and we're going downstairs for tea. The key-jangler supreme is charged with herding us. Her name is Huggins and she has a spiky self-possession about her that must be exhausting to sustain; multi-striped blonde melange hair and matte dulux on her face. Her eyebrows are fiercely groomed, too, but none of this quite distracts attention from her hooter of a nose.

Elena, the Romanian gypsy woman, is reading Huggins' palm while we wait on the landing. She's camping it up a bit, making trance-like faces and muttering. Huggins rolls her eyes.

'Just tell me what the lines mean,' she says. 'I haven't got time for the patter.'

Elena is waiting for surgery on both knees, and serving two years for arson. She has all the time in the world.

I wonder what makes someone choose to become a prison officer. Do careers advisers suggest it to people with a penchant for being unpleasant, to give them an acceptable outlet so they don't end up on the other side? Some of the Keepers of the Keys here are nasty little shrews; they'd have fitted in well in my class at school. Key-janglers. Safe-keepers. Custodians. Custody is a funny word, encompassing as it does both the ownership of children and the locking up of adults.

Admittedly, the therapeutic/punitive balance must be a challenge. It would be simpler, perhaps, if the day were divided. Bullying in the morning and sympathy after lunch. As it is, we get bellowed at on the way to the library and patted on the shoulder as we're banged up in our cells. It's difficult to know how to behave. A lot of the women here do ranting interspersed with sullen gloom. *I'm so fucking angry you have no fucking idea fuck fucking fucky fuck.* Their shouting gets in through the pores on my scalp.

In the tea queue, I fantasise about Colin's fry-ups. About takeaway pizza and chocolate bars for breakfast. About a crackly plastic bag in the newsagent, with sweets and a can of drink in it, and I'm counting out the change while the world's grumpiest shopkeeper huffs and puffs. Strawberry juice – it can't really be strawberry, can it? I'm guessing it's mostly grapes or apples, with the odd strawberry crushed in for colour – in a fridge I browse at leisure. Tea whenever I think about it, coffee sometimes. Biscuit dregs in the bottom of the office tin. Palinka, and a hangover to follow.

And when I finally get to the trolley, and take my tray and sit hunched over it, I coat the fishcake and the watery cauliflower and every one of the soggy chips with powdery, feather-light salt. I cut the fishcake into four and eat it piece by piece. I eat all the cauliflower and all the chips, all the while contemplating the sponge waiting in the bowl, and picturing Fflur's face as she slides a batch of cakes out of the oven.

When I came out of my trance on the doormat and wandered sulkily back into the day room, Gloria was scratching under the rim of her shower cap, scowling into the telephone.

'Alan Turner was a chain-smoking alcoholic with HIV,' she said. 'Are they surprised to find disease in his lungs?'

'Go Gloria!' shouted Paul. He made a drum roll on the table with his hands. I shushed him and leant closer to the phone.

'Just how long do these cultures take to grow?' snapped Gloria.

Fflur peered at the bottom of a sticky, near-empty jar of marmalade. 'Feb 2007,' she muttered and put it in the sink.

Gloria slammed the telephone down and hissed, 'Ye Gods.' I'd never seen her so scary. I wondered if it was worth mentioning the HRT thing, but I thought I'd hold fire for a while. 'Busybodies with more power than sense.'

'Mm,' I said. I looked accusingly at the telephone.

Colin cleared his throat.

'It's an interesting question, though,' he said, tapping the arm of the sofa and staring at the television. 'What happens to bodies when there's no funeral as such, and no one to claim them and so on.'

Gloria swallowed in the way she'd developed to demonstrate her valiant efforts not to scream at us all. Her cheeks throbbed a deep, hot pink.

'Yes,' continued Colin, 'indeed. I imagine the procedures are in place for disposal by cremation. Though there is the issue of paperwork. Hm. Uhuh.' He coughed and began to hum in time to his tapping.

'Fuck,' said Paul, 'I need a cig.'

I couldn't blame him; his need for cigs probably outdid my need for chocolate, and we all cope with these things according to type. Everyone can be fitted into one of three categories: the world is made up of Bullies, Victims and Rescuers. I developed this theory at the painful age of thirteen, from an analysis of the excruciating dynamics of girls' friendship groups. I saw myself even then as a Rescuer-Bully hybrid, which isn't quite the paradox it first seems. And I stand by this theory today. It works for most people: Nain is a clear cut case of Rescuer turned Victim. My Bloody Mother – Victim. Colin – Victim thinly disguised as Rescuer. Fflur – Victim/Rescuer hybrid. Bald Paul – Bully. Dan – Rescuer (King of). Dad was hard to categorise but in the end he was a Victim through and through.

My attention was caught by the television and the phrase 'barrier nursing'. An MP with particularly hairy nostrils was saying, 'and monitor the situation on an hour-by-hour basis.' The camera panned back to reveal an ambulance pulling up behind him and a hospital porter pushing an empty wheelchair. The programme cut to the studio and they moved on to a piece about a haulage company which had employed a driver without a license.

'That was the university hospital,' I said. 'Colin, what else did they say?'

'So, patients with poor immune systems are most likely to succumb,' he said, cracking his knuckles behind his neck. 'And I imagine smoking is a risk factor. The link between smoking and TB is pretty much established fact so far as ...' I tuned out. Gloria had left the room. Fflur was kneeling on the draining board, cleaning the inside of a cupboard. Paul was flicking a piece of grot with his fingers, making a goal out of the salt and the tomato ketchup. '... and there's been another death,' said Colin. 'Poor chap.'

I had developed an embarrassing little habit. Each time there was a homeless death on the news, I had to hold my breath for ten seconds so that it wouldn't be Dan. For all I knew, Dan was living in a semi with a garden and a water feature in the driveway, but it was hard to imagine. My throat constricted. I shook my head. Dan was tough – he'd travelled the world. His immune system had seen it all. He was rock solid.

I was on the verge of sleep in Suzy's bed when her voice drifted into my dream and I woke up. I staggered downstairs to find her tearing a strip off the police officer stationed outside.

'I need my stuff!' she shrieked. 'For God's sake.'

I opened the front door and the policeman grabbed his radio and held out a hand in traffic-stopping pose. It was cold where the sun had left a naked night sky, and the air smelt of garlic.

Suzy laughed. 'They won't let me in Sho',' she said. 'Can you get my stuff?'

The policeman shook his head. 'Sorry, ladies. This may sound a bit belt-and-braces but you're not permitted to pass anything out.'

'Belt and –?' said Suzy.

'What about the Russian doll boxes?' I asked. Suzy looked lost. The policeman shook his head.

'No can do.'

Suzy opened her bag to demonstrate the contents. 'Look. All I've got is mascara, twenty pee, two cigs –'

'And a collection of condiments in little sachets,' said the policeman. 'Do you take the cutlery too?'

Suzy clamped the bag shut and folded her arms. 'I don't even have any knickers!' she shouted. A wolf whistle came from the direction of next door's front room and she stuck up her middle finger. I sat on the doorstep. The policeman's eyes widened and I said, 'I'm behind the line,' and pointed at the tape. The Day Room door opened and I stood up sulkily. I wondered if I should let Paul make a break for it. Would the policeman tackle him or were we too radioactive? I imagined a Spiderman net-throw stopping Paul as he ran down the road. But it was Colin, and he tiptoed past without looking at us, up the stairs to the loo.

'Sorry.' The policeman was moved, I think, by the expression of resignation on my face.

'Please,' wailed Suzy. 'Look, I live here. All my stuff is here. My phone –.' She slapped her forehead. 'I need my phone. Sho', can you just go and read my texts and see if I've got any missed calls or anything?'

'Er – yeah.' I shrugged. 'Where is it?' I could feel my nose growing. Colin flushed the toilet.

'In my room,' said Suzy. 'Probably on the bed. Or in one of the bags.'

'Two minutes,' said the policeman. 'And close the door while you look.' He planted himself, arms folded, in front of the tape.

Gloria comes to visit. Her perfume precedes her into the room, along with the clanking of her Statement Jewellery and the fraying ends of a conversation she's been dominating in the waiting room. She is wearing her bright pink jacket with a coordinating sparkly scarf.

'Yes,' she's saying, 'this is exactly it.' She scans the room, spots me (it would be hard not to) and bustles across to stamp lipstick on my cheek. 'Darling!' she says. 'Hello!' She sits, hands folded on the table between us, and bestows a smile on me while she analyses my appearance. She's a knight in bright pink armour, and it must have taken her all morning to travel down. She's been to visit the Home; she assures me that Nain is being well looked after, though she's still trying to call the police when she can't find her toothbrush. Colin, she tells me, is 'bearing up' in Whitchurch hospital. Her smile is particularly firm as she tells me this. 'He's into billiards,' she says. 'There's a snooker table – or is it pool? Are they the same thing? Apparently he's a natural. Which is something. Passes the time for him.' She grinds to a halt there but not for long; she wipes her sunglasses and sticks them back on top of her head. 'I've not been to see him for a few days, which I must. I've been too busy to draw breath somehow.' Her rosacea gives her away, she's kicking herself for boasting about how busy she is, and her cheeks flare and spark as pink as her scarf. 'Sorry,' she says. 'Getting tactless in my old age.'

Last time I was locked up, we were on the same side of the door. Gloria's seen firsthand how well I deal with having nothing to do and nowhere to go.

'Now,' she says brightly, 'what else did I mean to tell you? Ooh, I know.' I smile. She is very, very well-meaning. And she's clearly delighted to have news for me. 'You will never guess what bald Paul is up to.' She pitter-patters her fingers on the table. He's joined the circus? Got his own chat show? 'He's enrolled on the peer mentoring project,' she says. 'He's very committed, could be the making of him. The other day he came in wearing a shirt.'

5

Gloria had just put down the phone on what appeared to be a satisfactory discussion with her dermatologist, when she suddenly went pale and shrieked, 'Oh!'

I don't think she had ever come across someone who lit his farts. Her face went stiff and the edges of her shower cap crackled. Her fingertips twitched a little, but otherwise there was no movement. Paul had dropped his trousers and hooked his pants out of the way with his thumb. His legs looked startlingly white and girly in their hairlessness. Twisting his top half round, he flicked his lighter twice and the flame popped up. Then he grit his teeth and pursed his lips and the flame turned blue.

'Haha!' He pinged his pants back into place, triumphant. 'Colin, mate, did you see that? Methane.'

Colin cleared his throat and said, 'Yes, um, yes. Bunsen burners and such – '

'Tea, Gloria?' said Paul, heaving his trousers up and letting them slide halfway down again.

'Not if you are making it,' said Gloria, blinking a lot.

'I'm on it,' said Fflur. 'Don't rise to the bait, it will only encourage him.'

Paul laughed his evil villain laugh and threw himself on the sofa beside Colin. Colin stiffened and made a series of bizarre coughing sounds.

'Come and drink your tea over here, Paul,' said Fflur. 'Give Colin some space.'

Paul's eyes stayed on the television but there was a dangerous shift in his expression. I steered Gloria to the table and we sat down and took our tea. Fflur left Paul's mug by the kettle and sat down with us.

'We need some more sugar,' she said.

'Er, yes,' said Colin from the sofa. 'Sugar's running low. We usually get granulated but last time it was demerara, which is fine in terms of dissolving in tea and coffee and in fact some people ...'

'This is completely irrational,' I said, my knuckles tightening on my mug. 'If we'd listened to them and shut the place, we'd all be free to walk the streets, but because we didn't we're locked up. It's effectively a punishment.' Gloria sighed. Fflur stared at her bracelet, rotating it slowly on her wrist. 'Fine,' I spat. 'Because *I* didn't listen. But if a homeless charity can't stick up for the homeless, then there's no hope, is there? And it can't really be safer to sleep rough. Do they have any idea of the numbers of people in these shelters they've closed? It's ridiculous.'

Gloria swallowed. 'Shona, Darling. You are a powerful advocate. But sometimes idealism gets in the way of pragmatism.' Gloria had a degree in Social Studies. Class of 1974. And she'd been, while it lasted, a card-carrying Social Democrat. I folded my arms and made a point of biting my tongue.

She flexed her fingers inside her rubber gloves. On the television, the news was being repeated word-for-word as it had been already several times that day. Colin was tapping his knees and humming. Paul was flicking his lighter and passing his finger absent-mindedly through the flame.

'Surely pragmatism must be informed by idealism?' said Fflur, rubbing her eyes. We looked at her. 'Actually, sorry, I read that somewhere and I can't follow it up.'

'Woohoo!' shouted Paul. He leapt off the sofa, smacking at the edge of his t-shirt where his lighter had caught it. Colin sprang up, arms flailing, and the sofa was instantly engulfed in flames.

I grabbed the fire blanket from the kitchen and fumbled with the strings. Gloria snatched up her diary and her handbag and rushed from the room, shrieking, 'Out! Everybody out!' I threw the blanket at the sofa, but already the little table beside it was up in flames. 'It's too late, Shona,' shouted Gloria from the hall, 'just get out!'

In the hall, we shuttled frantically about whilst the fire built up behind us and Gloria cursed because her rubber gloves made it hard to turn the key in the lock.

'Help!' screamed Fflur. 'Let us out! Gloria for God's sake let someone else do it!'

Gloria got the door open and we exploded into the street, knocking our police guard aside.

'Fire!' I bellowed at him. 'Ring 999!'

I imagine the police have 999 on speed dial so maybe this was a stupid

41

thing to say, but he got onto it while Gloria and Fflur clung to each other and Colin talked to himself and twitched his nose. Paul had disappeared by the time I'd thumped enough on next door's front door to establish that they weren't in.

We watched from the other side of the street as the fire reached the front room where Fflur had been sleeping and smoke and flames danced in the window. A fire engine screeched round the corner and the policeman flagged it down.

Paul had scarpered but there was uncertainty as to what should be done with the rest of us. We stayed obediently where we were while the street came out to watch. They stood by their gates, arms folded or hands in pockets, pointing things out to each other and sucking in their breath. A police car arrived with two more officers – a man and a woman – who guarded us at a safe distance.

'I take it we are free to go?' said Gloria bossily, removing her shower cap and fluffing out her perm.

'If you could bear with us, Madam,' said the policewoman, squaring her shoulders.

'Well, we can hardly go back into the Shelter,' said Gloria. 'As you can see.' She made her pleasant-but-firm face and stuffed the shower cap into her handbag. The policewoman's radio buzzed then, or at least she pretended it had, because she turned away from us and looked busy and important. The fire fighters were damping down the remains of the bottom floor of the Shelter, calling to each other about structural damage.

A car turned into the street and the policeman put up his hand to stop it. While he bent to talk to the driver, a woman jumped out of the other side with a camera and started snapping pictures of the Shelter, the onlookers and the fire fighters. She looked around, beady-eyed, spotted me and pressed the shutter. It was on machine-gun mode, clearly, because she held it in place while I scowled and turned away. Swinging the camera over her shoulder, she took out a dictaphone and strode towards us.

'I'd stay away, Madam,' said the irritating policewoman. 'These individuals have been under quarantine.' If the journalist hadn't been sure, she certainly knew now who the lepers were.

'However,' said Gloria. 'As charity officers and support workers, we are well-protected by prophylactic medication and pose no risk to public health.' They bristled at each other and the journalist snapped away.

'Do you suspect arson?' she said. 'There's been bad feeling toward the Shelter from the local community.'

'No,' said Fflur. 'It was an accident.'

'You set the Shelter on fire from the inside?'

I stepped on Fflur's kitten-heeled shoe.

'I'm going home,' I said. 'I've had enough of this farce.'

'I think Shona speaks for us all there,' said Gloria and trotted off down the street while the journalist wrote down my name. The policewoman fumed and hissed into her radio. Colin, Fflur and I followed Gloria, eyes down, full-steam ahead.

On the corner, we were stopped by a police car mounting the kerb inches from our feet. Before we could even think to retreat, we were surrounded by police officers in surgical masks.

'Vagrancy in city centres and residential areas is a crime,' explained a tall policeman with an unfortunate haircut. 'And you are all known to have been in direct contact with contagious disease.'

'Oh, for God's sake,' I said, giving him a withering look. Colin was trying to hide behind me. 'We're not vagrants. And this side of the seventeenth century, we use the term 'homeless'. We are support workers. On prophylactic medication.'

The police officers shuffled about a bit. The tall one got into the car and made a phone call. I could feel Gloria's rage sputtering in the air. When he came back, he said, 'Can you all give me home addresses?' and Fflur drew in a sharp little breath.

'Yes,' I said. 'Do you have a pen?'

He took down my address, where I said Fflur was a tenant, and then Colin's and Gloria's. Even after forty-eight hours in the Shelter, Fflur's appearance was so unquestionable, it wasn't her they looked at twice. They had Colin's flat confirmed and then they said it looked as if we were free to go. As we backed away, one of them said, 'Where's the fifth occupant? There were supposed to be five of you.'

I shrugged. 'There was a homeless man,' I said. 'I don't ask for details.'

Benny wants a visiting order; she wants to come and see me. It's quite a journey, but perhaps she's planning to apply for a travel grant and have an afternoon's shopping while she's at it.

This puts me in a position of some power, because in here, you can only be visited if you want to be. I could turn my back and say no. But I decide to get the form. In a twisted, screwed-up sense, it shows less interest than refusing. She might see refusal as a challenge, or as evidence of my emotional investment in the idea of her visiting me. But she'll get the form, and it will be up to her to apply to spend time with me. That feels right, somehow.

Carol tells me someone else might be joining us for Life Writing, and I nearly get up and walk out. Already I feel possessive of these sessions, of Carol's gentle, discreet probing. The experience of someone being interested in me, of being asked questions by someone who stays where she is to hear the answers, is a novelty I'm not keen to share.

We wait – waste – ten minutes for this usurper, and then Huggins rings through to say she's changed her mind. Carol looks disappointed. I'm not sure I constitute a Writing Group, and I guess it's possible the funding might be withdrawn if numbers don't improve. I'm relieved to have her to myself still, but the worry has seeded in my mind and I find it hard to concentrate at first.

'It sounds like it was a traumatic time,' she says, nodding. 'Being locked up like that.' I look out of the window at a roll of black canvas that's been plonked by the flowerbed. I think the intention is to cut holes in it to let plants through whilst suffocating weeds underneath. Carol gulps. 'Sorry,' she says. 'That was crass.'

'I'm fine,' I say, and smile at her clumsily. 'At least Paul isn't here. That's a bonus in itself. And some of the women in here are quite friendly.'

She rescues us both. 'So you took Fflur home with you?' she says. 'After the fire? Do you want to write about that?'

'I never thought I'd be in debt to Paul,' I said, keeping my head down and walking briskly.

'Do you think he did it on purpose?' said Fflur. She was trotting to keep up with me, adjusting the strap of her bag.

'I'm not sure. I don't think so. I just hope he finds something constructive to do with his time. Oh, shitting hell.' My language had suffered from incarceration.

'It's just that I – oh, I see. Is that your house?'

We'd turned into my street; a row of identical thirties semis, with hydrangeas outside and 'No junk mail or salesmen' stickers on the front doors. Except our front door stood out now, because someone had painted a Black Death style red cross on it. Fflur bit her lip and hung back.

'My grandmother will explode when she sees me,' I said. 'But there's nothing to be alarmed about.'

'Are you sure this is OK? For me to come? I could – '

'It's fine,' I said. 'Anyway, I owe you. You've kept me sane. If it wasn't for you, I'd have been stuck in there on my own with a bald hooligan, a twanging autistic and Gloria.'

We had gravel laid at the front after Dad died, because the grass turned into clover and I kept treading on bees. There was a rather battered cherub-gnome thing which went missing from time to time, but today it was placidly guarding the hydrangea.

'Who do you think painted the cross?' whispered Fflur. She took a lip balm out of her handbag and rubbed it on her lips.

'Oh, just kids,' I said.

I tried the door, but it was locked.

'Hello? Nain,' I called, wriggling my key in the lock. I got the door open, but the chain was on. 'Nain, it's me.' I made a face at Fflur, who smiled rather uncertainly. 'What you have to understand about Nain,' I said quickly, 'is that she is supremely bad-tempered. She can make you feel guilty by moving a mug from one place to another in the kitchen – Nain! It's me! Can you hurry up, I need the toilet – the sound it makes is different to the sound of anyone else moving a mug, do you see what I mean? – Hello? Nain? – she can nuance the opening and shutting of a cutlery drawer. And the way she leans on a sweeping brush ...'

Nain appeared, looking suspicious. As if someone with a voice exactly like mine might have stolen my key.

'Shona?' she said.

'Can you undo the chain? I need a wee.'

'Who's that?'

'This is Fflur, my friend.'

'Hiya,' said Fflur.

Nain began to cry.

'Nain, it's OK. I'm back now.' I shifted on my feet and squeezed my pelvic floor shut. There is nothing like standing at your own front door to make the need for a wee suddenly more urgent.

She unhooked the chain, looking from me to Fflur with teary eyes. Then she took a few steps backwards.

'Shut the door behind you,' she said quickly. 'Put the chain on.'

The hallway was cluttered with junk mail and folded plastic charity sacks. I made for the toilet but she shook her head.

'Leave your clothes in the hallway. I've got some alcohol gel, I'll get it now.'

I rolled my eyes at Fflur. 'We've had baths, Nain. And we are not about to strip in the hallway.' I edged past her and she shrank back to avoid touching me. I bumped into the broken mirror which had leant against the wall ever since I tried to put out for the bin men and it got rejected.

The bathroom was in a state. She must have spent a hundred pounds on antibacterial sprays, wipes and gels. They were oozing their contents over the shelf above the sink, round the bath and on the floor, though they were no match for the crusted flannels and dirty knickers.

Her tablets had been ransacked. She'd taken most of them, leaving empty blister packets and patient information leaflets everywhere. In the sink, her hairbrush was soaking in bleach. Despite all this, it was strangely comforting to sit on the toilet at home. I wondered if we'd always lived in such squalor. Had it grown worse in recent years or was it that I just wasn't aware of the rubble when I was younger? I was maybe wading oblivious through coffee cups and used tissues. Every now and then, when I looked up from the routine of my adult life enough to notice, I saw that if I continued to work for a homeless charity, I would never be able to escape my dreary house-share with Nain. My job was a temporary, studenty sort of pastime; it was going nowhere and neither was I. But routine has always been something I crave and dread in equal measure. So I stayed at home with Nain and watched the mess build up, too tired to do anything about it on work days and too lethargic when I had time off.

Leaning in close to the mirror, I squeezed the spot on my chin and the pus shot straight out, as satisfying as the pop of a spider when you squish it in a tissue.

When I emerged, Nain and Fflur hadn't moved. We stood in the hallway listening to the cistern hiss. The house was bottom-heavy; everything happened downstairs. We had the bathroom, kitchen, front room and my room downstairs, and upstairs it was just Nain's room and a very small room that used to be Dad's. It was rare for me to go upstairs, unless the fruit flies spilled over, in which case I'd go and remove anything in the process of decomposing.

We had an attic, too, and every now and then it occurred to me that I'd never been up there. There could have been something – or someone – living up there. It was probably more hygienic than the house.

'How are we off for food?' I said. 'Do we need to get anything?'

'I could go shopping,' said Fflur.

'Let's both go.'

Nain panicked. 'No,' she said. 'I've got some cold potatoes and ham.'

'Great,' I said. 'Come and eat, Fflur.'

We had a little table in the kitchen, with a wipe-clean table cloth and three very old chairs. I could see Fflur itching to get her hands on the work surfaces. There were used teabags and spilt sugar, scrunched up tissues and receipts strewn everywhere.

'I'm sure your kitchen isn't like this,' muttered Nain. 'But it's hard to keep on top of things when I'm not well.'

'Of course,' said Fflur, helping me to a slice of ham.

'And I'm on my own so much,' continued Nain.

I dipped a potato in salt and stuffed it in my mouth to stop myself from speaking.

'Would you like some more tea, Mrs Davies?' said Fflur, getting up.

'Oh, thank you. Yes. That would be nice. Goodness, I'm not used to ...' 'Shona?'

I shook my head. What I actually wanted was some of the strawberry juice I'd bought before my life was turned upside down, but the carton was empty in the fridge. I put it on a mental shopping list.

'It's been awful,' said Nain, 'you've got no idea. I can hardly pluck up the courage to go to the shops anymore.' She made it sound as if I'd left her stranded in a war zone for several weeks.

'Goodness,' said Fflur non-committally. I rummaged at the back of a cupboard and found some cooking chocolate.

'Shona,' said Nain. 'It's no wonder ...' It tasted like cardboard. 'And then, last night, I heard noises.' She covered her mouth with cupped hands and breathed in and out a few times. Fflur nodded sympathetically and I sucked the cardboard chocolate. 'I didn't know what to do. I mean, I'm used to being on my own at night, obviously.'

'Obviously,' said Fflur. She stacked the plates and ran the hot water tap.

'But it was so frightening. It sounded as if someone was trying to break in. I couldn't move, my heart was palpitating.' Fflur squirted washing up

47

liquid, murmuring noises of alarm and comfort. 'And then this morning, I found that awful cross.' Nain returned to her cupped-hand breathing and I sighed. I had been so relieved to be home, eating chocolate – albeit stale cooking chocolate – that I'd almost put it out of my mind.

'Oh, Nain, I'm so sorry. It isn't fair for you to get involved in all this.' I put my hand on her arm and looked contrite. 'But you can use your alcohol gel, that's really effective.' She sniffed and nodded.

'I'll see if I can get that graffiti off, shall I?' said Fflur. She'd put the plates in the rack to dry and was squeezing a dirty sponge. 'Should I throw this one away, do you think?'

'You're very good in the kitchen,' said Nain. 'Are you married?'

'Nain!'

'No,' said Fflur. She found the swing bin in the cupboard under the sink and threw away the sponge. Crouching down, she began to rifle through an assortment of cleaning products with fading labels. 'I was engaged for a while.'

I stopped mid-chew. I don't know why I was surprised.

'What happened?' said Nain. She looked completely recovered, eyes wide.

'He left me.'

'Bastard,' I muttered and stretched my arms high over my head, spreading my fingers wide.

'Awful,' said Nain. 'Was this recent?'

'Give the girl a break, Nain.' I lunged into a sideways balance posture.

'It's fine,' said Fflur. 'It's not a secret.' She selected a purple spray with an exclamation mark logo and stood, shutting the cupboard with her foot. 'We were going to go to Singapore,' she said. I swapped sides and put my weight on the other leg. 'He got a job there. Then about a fortnight before we were supposed to go, he texted me that he was going to go on his own. He said we needed time apart.'

'He *texted* you?' I'd been about to launch into my beginners' version of Salute to the Sun, but I was floored by this story. Fflur was far too nice to get dumped. Although she was probably well rid of him.

'He wasn't going on his own, of course. He was taking my ... my friend with him. My ex-friend.' Fflur shrugged and applied herself to the instructions on the cleaning spray.

'There are very few men of integrity left in your generation,' said Nain. I thought about asking her how many of these men she'd come across in her trips to local shops and monthly visits to the Luncheon Club. But I stopped myself; she'd had a hard time and it would take a day or two for her to get back on track. I'd have to get her another prescription too, if they'd let her have one.

Fflur nodded grimly. 'You are so right,' she said. 'He was one of those men who just doesn't understand that the whole point of presents is in the wrapping up.'

6

In the morning, I leant Fflur some clothes, and they looked quite cool, falling loosely round her shoulders and belted at the waist. She had a remarkable commitment to hair and make-up which completely disguised the fact that she'd escaped from a fire, scrubbed graffiti until her hands were sore and then slept on a rather lumpy sofa.

While she washed up the breakfast things, and Nain took her coffee back to bed because she'd had a bad night, I said, 'Should we contact your housemates?'

She blushed and wiped her face with the back of her wrist. 'I'm not sure the whole quarantine thing will help,' she said. 'But it's OK, I know I can't stay here. I'm so grateful to you. You've been a saviour.'

'You can stay here for a bit if you need to.' I doodled on the shopping list I was making. 'My grandmother likes you.' Little bubbles floated up from her hands as she pulled out the plug. 'How about family?' She dried her hands on the tea towel, sniffed it and bundled it up in her fist.

Our high street had three charity shops, a post office, a boutique with the Queen Mother's old dresses in the window, a butcher, a chain bakery and a greengrocer. On the roundabout at one end was a smaller version of one of the supermarkets which I never went into. I supported local shops on principle. I wouldn't have been seen dead in Tesco.

It was nose-scratchingly, drippily cold with a lazy wind that couldn't quite make up its mind. Nonetheless, it seemed the footwear equinox had been extended by the bonus sunshine we'd had, and half the population was still in flip-flops while the other half had progressed to boots or trainers.

'I'll pay you back,' said Fflur as we examined the bakery window. 'I really don't make a habit of sponging.' She adjusted her earrings. 'Although my ex housemates would tell you otherwise.'

I turned to her.

'Fflur,' I said, 'it's fine. Just now, you're a guest. And we can sit down later and talk things through. There'll be something we can do.'

She looked as if she were about to cry. Then she swallowed twice and set her glossy lips into a little smile.

'Thank you,' she mouthed.

We went into the bakery and bought a loaf of bread with seeds in it, which Fflur chose, and Welsh cakes spread with jam, which I chose. The assistant continued a conversation she was having with someone in the back room all the time she was serving us. She handed me my change, calling over her shoulder, 'I've said this time and again. It's no fun for me, and it's no fun for him. I wonder what the point is, now.'

We waited at the crossing for the slow line of traffic to stop for us. A truck had parked outside the boutique, and everything had to edge round it. The orange woman who ran the place was lecturing the driver, who was on his mobile and trying his best to ignore her. Fflur beamed at the car that stopped for us and we crossed.

'They'll have to let me have my clothes, though, won't they,' she said. 'I should definitely ask for my stuff.'

'Definitely,' I said with a mouthful of Welsh cake. 'I'll come with you if you want, in case these witches are even stupider than – '

We stopped in front of the butcher, staring first at a sign in the window and then at each other.

'They can't put that up!' said Fflur.

The butcher caught my eye through the glass and looked away quickly. I stormed inside the shop and tore the sign off the window.

'What do you think you're doing?' said the butcher. His apron was off-white and blood-spattered and he wore plastic gloves.

'I am taking down this sign,' I spat. 'Because it is offensive and bigoted and inflammatory and I –' He flipped open a drawbridge in the counter and marched over to take the sign from me: *No Dogs No Homeless.*

'This is my shop and I will put up whatever signs I like,' he said.

'You're asking for someone to smash your window in.'

'Is that a threat?'

A man with bushy white hair and rigidly upright posture came in, pushing a buggy with a scrawny, snotty little girl in it. He squinted at me suspiciously.

'What can I do you for?' said the butcher.

'You might want to boycott this shop,' I said loudly. 'The owner is a prejudiced idiot who won't serve anyone without a tenancy agreement or a mortgage.' The man tightened his grip on the buggy and peered at the display of skinned body parts. Fflur's hand was hovering near her mouth. 'Do you know what he put in the window?' I said. *No Dogs No Homeless.* I put the scrunched up sign on the counter.

The butcher stared hard at me.

'Too right,' muttered the old man. 'Don't want germs all over my chops.' He pointed at something revolting.

The butcher changed his gloves and prepared a sheet of greaseproof paper. I considered the pros and cons of smashing his window.

'I'm going to the Echo with this,' I said.

The old man took his package. 'That's where I've seen you,' he said. 'You shouldn't be free to walk the streets after where you've been.'

The butcher stopped halfway through ringing up the price. 'Tramp Flu started in that squat you ran. I'm not surprised they burnt it down.' His eyes flashed cold. I was feeling pretty violent myself, not least towards whoever it was who'd snapped me in the street when the fire broke out. 'Get out of my shop,' he said, quietly, dismissively. 'You are barred.'

'I'm vegetarian,' I said.

I stomped out of the shop and Fflur followed me, muttering, 'Outrageous,' in a ridiculously plummy voice. She stroked my shoulder and tutted, but I shrugged her off so then I felt guilty on top of it all.

'Sorry,' I said.

'Hey, you haven't got anything to be sorry about,' she soothed. 'That awful man should be – I don't know, arrested or something. He should try being homeless.'

I smiled firmly.

'Fflur, it's OK. You won't be homeless for long. We'll sort it.' She smiled back, her eyes watery; we must have looked like lovers making up after a tiff.

In the newsagent, I bought the Echo and the Daily Express. The man who worked there won prizes for grumpiness; he said as little as possible, and he huffed and puffed his way through each transaction as if it were the last straw. I'd been going there for years, and there had never been even a flicker of recognition. Until now, when he had hundreds of copies of a particularly unflattering full-length picture of me tied up in bundles on the front page of the Echo.

He chewed the cud a bit while he stared at me and then at my photograph. Fflur was reading the postcard adverts on the pinboard. He pushed my change across the counter and sank onto a stool, grunting something unintelligible.

'I could be a childminder,' said Fflur. 'I'd like that.'

I took the papers and hooked the plastic bag of chocolates and sweets over two fingers.

'Have I got something in my eye?' said Fflur, coming right up close and stretching her eyes wide. 'In the left one? It stings like there's a pin in it.'

I peered at her creamy-gold eye make-up.

'Nope. Probably an eyelash.'

The grumpy newsagent had humphed his way to the door and now he held it open, glaring at us.

'Oh, for pity's sake.' I was as surprised as he was when I exploded. The words just burst out of my mouth. 'You won't catch anything from me. People who work with the homeless take preventative medicine. I'm the safest customer you'll have all day. I could spit on you and you wouldn't catch anything.'

His jowls wobbled. He foamed a little at the mouth.

'Is that a threat?' he hissed. And Fflur got the giggles. She covered her mouth with her hands and scuttled out of the shop. I made a sound midway between a laugh and a sob and ran out after her, desperate to start on the sweets.

Our kitchen had never been so clean or smelt so wonderful. Nain stood in the doorway, nursing her tea and being nosey.

'Do you have brothers and sisters?'

'No, I'm an only child.' Fflur scraped the bowl with a wooden spoon, plopping cake mixture into little paper cases.

'And how about your parents? Are they local?'

'Nain.' I scooped a blob of mixture onto my finger and sucked it. 'Leave the poor girl alone.'

'It's fine,' said Fflur. 'Now, do you have a pinger?'

'Um, no,' I said. 'I could set the clock on my phone if you like.'

Nain frowned at me for licking the bowl. Halfway through the washing up, Fflur ground to a halt. She yawned and rubbed her eyes, leaning against the sink as if she needed its support. I felt suddenly embarrassed by the way I was hunched at the table, flicking through the paper.

'God, sorry. Let me do that.'

She let me nudge her aside and take the sponge from her.

'It's all catching up with me,' she said. 'Do you mind if we talk tomorrow. About – what I'm going to do.' She squeezed her lips together, trying not to cry. Her mascara was smudged. I realised something that had passed me by.

'Fflur,' I said. 'Can I ask you something?'

'Mm?' She sat down and put her head on the table.

'How old are you?'

'Nineteen,' she said, and fell asleep.

So now my guilt went through the roof. Not only had I got her quarantined, I'd been letting this child play Mum. And maybe these housemates of hers were just kids too. I abandoned the washing up and began absent-mindedly to fridge-browse. Not so young that anyone would be obliged to help her. But far too young to be familyless. I shut the fridge, uninspired, and stroked her hair.

'Fflur? You're having my bed tonight, and I'm on the sofa, OK? Come on.'

She woke up just enough to follow me wordlessly to my room and let me pull the duvet over her, shutting her eyes again as soon as she was horizontal. I went into the front room, where Nain was watching television with the subtitles on and the sound turned up. On the windowsill and the mantelpiece, we had a series of ornamental animals which Nain got free with a magazine she bought for the duration of the offer. They all stood on two legs and wore clothes, and whatever their eyes were made of hadn't stood the test of time very well, so they looked a bit diseased. Wedged between and underneath them were bills, letters, receipts, bits of packaging and torn out pages from television listings.

'You OK, Nain?' I said. She sighed. I imagined swiping my arm along the surfaces and sweeping everything, including the animals, into a bin bag. I'd been thinking about doing this for years.

I wandered back into the kitchen, took the cupcakes out of the oven and burnt my fingers and my tongue trying to eat one. I washed up a spoon, dropped it back into the water and dried my hands on my t-shirt. Then I went into the front room and sat on the edge of the sofa. I did some ankle-circling until they stopped clicking. I gazed at the television for a while. It was strange, not going to work. Gloria said the house insurance on the Shelter was complex. And not entirely fully comp. Or up to date. She was going to see if she could sort out 'alternative duties' now that I was a redundant Shelter support worker. Maybe they'd get a second night bus, now that we'd chucked everyone out onto the streets, and I could do a soup run. Or maybe it was time I looked for what Nain called 'real work' (not something she had first-hand experience of, but apparently it was my best bet considering I wasn't married, a failure she attributed mainly to my weight).

Fflur woke me up at half past five from a nightmare in which Dan, who was also Alan Turner, had become a dog and was prowling the streets in a pack. The taste of the dream was stuck in my mouth. My feet were cold.

'Shona? Are you awake?' Fflur's voice shook in a way that sparked the prickles of fear left by the dream, and I sat up, tensed all over. 'Can I turn the light on?' She switched on the light and I screwed up my face, blinking. 'Look at my eye.'

Her left eye bulged; the white was huge and shiny and seemed to be oozing over the pupil. Around it, her face was red and swollen. I swallowed.

'It's disgusting,' she said. A tear appeared in her other eye and she went to rub it.

'Don't touch it!' I said. 'Sorry, didn't mean to snap. Don't touch your face, OK?' She sat in the armchair and her lip trembled. 'Who's your doctor? Do you know the number?'

'It's in my phone,' she whispered. 'But they won't be open yet.'

'There'll be an out-of-hours service.' I stared at her eye. 'Maybe we should just go straight to casualty. Does it hurt?'

'Round the outside,' she said, prodding her cheek gently.

'Don't touch your face!'

She sat on her hands. 'Sorry.'

'I'll get us a drink. Stay there.'

She wasn't coughing. Or maybe she'd been coughing away all night and I'd slept through it. I'd have to call a taxi and take her to casualty. And we'd have to tell them where she'd been. We'd been shopping and made cakes when we could have been getting a prescription. She could have had two days of antibiotics by now, if we'd gone straight to the doctor when we got out of the Shelter. And I'd let Paul go tearing off to give everyone else his revolting germs.

I took two cups of tea through to the front room and we drank in silence. Pus seeped out of Fflur's left eye and she sat tight on the hand that wasn't holding her tea.

'Do you want anything to eat before we go?' She shook her head. 'I'm going to get a taxi,' I said. 'You should go to hospital.' She shook her head again, and it seemed to hurt her. She pressed the warmth of her mug against her cheek and sniffed. 'Fflur, they'll just make us wait for hours and then give you some antibiotics. It'll be fine.'

'Then I'll get some from my doctor, when they open.' She swiped at the pus with her knuckle.

'Let's be on the safe side. Considering you've been in the Shelter. I know you're not coughing or anything, but ...'

She put down her mug and sank back into the chair.

'They won't care if I'm coughing or not. They'll quarantine me again and this time I'll be on my own.'

She had a point. But she looked worse than when she'd first come in.

'I'm sorry, Fflur. I don't think we should wait. Come on.'

I stood up. She looked at me and didn't move.

'I'm not going to hospital. I'll ring the out-of-hours service, OK?' I folded my arms. 'I'll get my phone.'

She went to get her phone and I edged the net curtains aside and peeked out onto the street. An image as clear as a memory, of a moth-eaten dog that somehow embodied Dan and Alan Turner; I hiccupped a lump of vomit and swallowed it automatically. I scrambled for a tissue and spat into it but it was too late and my throat was burning from the acid.

Fflur came back silently, her phone to her right ear. She sat in the armchair again and let her right eye fall shut; her left eye wouldn't quite close.

'Oh, good morning,' she said, sitting up straighter. 'I'm sorry to bother you, but I've woken up with an eye infection.'

'Be honest,' I mouthed, pointing at her face.

'Yes,' she said. 'A little.' I held out my hand for the phone and she turned away from me. 'Yes, it is a bit ... around my cheek,' she said, 'and my forehead. But only on the left ... about two o'clock this morning.'

'Fflur!' I said. She ignored me.

'Fflur Huntington. Tenth of the seventh, nineteen-ninety.' *Nineteen-ninety?* That was last week. 'Ah. Well, it probably says Longacre Road, does it? But in fact I don't live there anymore.' I sighed. I'd started to feel sick again. 'I'm staying with a friend ... no, it's not that I don't have an address, obviously I'm calling from somewhere ...'

'Fflur, stop,' I mouthed, but she wasn't looking at me.

'My friend's house. That's – what? Two nights.' She sat on her free hand.

'Lie!' I hissed.

'In a Shelter,' she said quietly. 'The one that burnt down.'

That was it. They refused to send a doctor or to let her anywhere near the health centre or the hospital. They gave us directions to what they called an Emergency Barrier Clinic.

'I'm not going!' Fflur shouted, throwing her phone on the floor. 'Ouch. God, it hurts when I shout.'

'And you'll wake my grandmother up. That's two reasons not to shout. Let's sit down for a minute, OK?'

I sat on the sofa. Fflur blew her nose gingerly, winced in pain and said, 'No way am I going to some leper colony.'

I nodded.

'I imagine it's quite frightening,' I said, 'but it's the quickest way to get some antibiotics. And some pain relief.'

'You sound like you're quoting from a bloody text book,' she shrieked. 'Stop talking to me as if I'm one of your homeless people. Would you like it if the doctor refused to treat you?'

I shook my head and then nodded again.

'No one is refusing to treat you. You just have to go to this clinic they've set up.' I looked at the name of the road I'd scribbled on the newspaper. It rang a bell. There was a footstep on the stairs. Fflur grabbed a cushion and hid behind it.

'Shona?' Nain shuffled into the room, hunched in her dressing gown. She looked at the cushion in front of Fflur's face and frowned. 'What's going on?' she said.

I stood up, wondering if I could possibly construct some explanation, and decided it might be quickest to force Fflur's hand.

'Fflur's got a sore eye,' I said. 'Do you have the number of that taxi firm you used?'

Nain wrapped her arms around herself, glaring at me.

'You know I have a compromised immune system,' she whispered.

'Nain, your immune system is tougher than you give it credit for,' I said. 'Go back to bed and I'll bring you a cup of tea.' She touched her eyelids as if to check they were still there, and looked warily at the cushion.

'I've got some eye drops somewhere,' she said. 'And some antiseptic wipes.' Fflur let the cushion drop, sighing. 'No!' cried Nain. 'It's Tramp Flu! Oh, Shona, what have you done?'

We walked along the river, parallel to the railway track. The trees were dropping hard-shelled, dagger-spiked conkers.

'Look at the horse chestnuts,' said Fflur, sniffing.

'Yeah, I love conkers,' I said.

'I had a thing,' said Fflur, 'for painting them.'

Between the conker trees were chestnuts of the edible variety, with furrier, fluffier shells and delicate nuts waiting patiently for squirrels. The conkers were vicious little bombs – either they hit soft ground and the spikes got lodged, or they hit harder ground and split on impact. I picked up one that was only half out of its shell. I peeled away the case and stroked the smug shininess, the immaculate sphere with the gentlest of thumb prints on the top. I could have filled my pockets but we were pretty focussed on getting to the clinic (more fool us).

There hadn't been much rain for a while, and the river was low and slow-moving. A man in waders and a bulky anorak with pockets everywhere stood in the middle with a fishing rod. He didn't move at all as we passed; he was as much a part of the river as the tree roots that were alternately submerged or revealed according to the weather. A train rumbled past.

'Look, there's a river gnome,' I said. Fflur didn't look up. She trudged on, her face an alarming jigsaw of germ-infested red and panicky white. I was glad it was early. At least we were spared an audience.

We passed a mass of conkers that had fallen so hard and fast they'd shot out of their shells and smashed open, exposing squishy innards underneath the tough mahogany exterior. And beside these, there were embryonic conkers that had fallen too early, deformed, shineless little things spat out by their cases to rot.

The Emergency Barrier Clinic had been set up in the old post office depot. Clearly the taxi firm was well aware of its new purpose, because they'd told me to get real even when I suggested they drop us off a few streets away. The footpath divided, and we took the murkier of the two options, heading away from the river past a little swamp where bicycle frames went to die. The path was narrowed by brambles and vast Sleeping-Beauty weeds. The derelict industrial estate was just beyond the swamp.

'Nearly there. You OK?'

Fflur pressed her handbag to her side, and gave a little grunt of acknowledgement. A swarm of gnats flew up our noses and into our ears. Fflur coughed, supporting her cheek with her hand.

'Don't tell me not to touch,' she said tightly. 'Oh God, what's that smell?' She stopped, looking at me for the first time since we'd left the house. 'I'm not going any nearer this place. Forget it.'

I tried not to breathe. Pushing past a great wall of nettles, my sleeves hooked over my hands to protect my arms, I forced my way through to the road. I could see the back of the old post office warehouse and a little white van at the side, but that was it. No leper colony.

'It's OK,' I called. 'That smell is just the stagnant water. It's not so bad by the road.' I turned back and held the nettles out of the way for Fflur to pass. She picked her way through, covering her mouth and nose with her hand. And then she screamed. I followed her gaze and saw the source of the smell. The plundered body of a cat lay in the undergrowth. I grabbed her hand and tugged her past.

We stood in the empty road, looking at the back wall of the warehouse. It was a plastic-ridged construction that looked as if it hadn't been intended to stay up long enough to weather. Someone started the engine of the van and manoeuvred away.

'What do you think?' I said.

Fflur let go of my hand and adjusted the strap of her bag.

'I think I need some antibiotics,' she said.

I nodded and we marched towards the warehouse, the smell dissipating as we left the cat behind. I don't know what I'd expected, but there was no one there. It was an alarmingly blank, windowless place. I took the address out of my pocket and looked at the road sign. Fflur rummaged for her lip balm and slicked it over her lips. I looked around, but with the van gone the place was deserted. Then the prison-metal door opened and a fat Jamaican nurse in a surgical mask, shower cap, gloves and a plastic apron appeared. She seemed puzzled by us.

'Can I help you?' she called. She had a strong valleys accent. Fflur indicated her face. 'Have you rung your doctor?'

'They told me to come here,' said Fflur stoutly. 'I am of no fixed address.'

'OK,' said the fat nurse. 'Are you coughing too? Breathless?'

Fflur shook her head, her hand on her cheek.

'Try not to touch it, lovely.'

'We just need some antibiotics for her eye,' I said. 'It's very ... localised.'

The nurse opened the door and called to someone inside. Then she looked at me hard and said, 'Do you have any symptoms?'

'No,' I said. 'I've been taking prophylactic medication. I work in a Shelter.'

'Oh. The one that –'

'– burnt down. Yes.'

She disappeared inside and neither of us ran away. A second, very young nurse emerged, carrying a clipboard. As the door clanged shut behind her, I caught a glimpse of a blue screen and a schoolroom table.

'Hi,' she said. 'Can I take your name and date of birth?'

'Fflur Huntington. Double F-l-u-r. Tenth of the seventh, nineteen-ninety.' The nurse noted this down and smiled.

'That's lovely, Fflur. If you could follow me.' We made to follow her but she stopped and put her head on one side, smiling at me rather painfully. 'We're asking partners to stay outside, I'm afraid. We'll look after her.'

Fflur gasp-squeaked.

'But I – I take prophylactics,' I said. 'I'm a support worker.'

The nurse continued to smile.

'I see,' she said. 'And I'll have to ask you to wait outside, I'm afraid.'

I stepped back and they disappeared into the warehouse. I took my phone out of my pocket and clicked the button to see the time. It was twenty past seven. I was starving and the nearest shop was a petrol station about a mile away. There was no way I was going anywhere without Fflur. I felt as if I had fed her to the lions. I wished I'd never let her into the Shelter in the first place; I should have marched round to her house and insisted they let her in. Or forced her to tell me where her parents were. Instead I'd brought her to this bizarre clinic place that wouldn't even let me in. I looked at my phone again. Only six minutes had passed. I caught the rancid smell of the cat on the air. In my head, the image of the cat merged with visions of Alan Turner rotting in the shed.

There was a long drawn-in gasp behind me followed by violent coughing and retching. It was an Alan Turneresque character and he was shuffling towards me from the direction of the road, clutching his ribs. He had drool round his mouth, vomit-splattered clothes and crazy hair. He carried a plastic bag and, as I stared at him, he took out a bottle of whisky and sucked as if it was an inhaler. He scratched his armpit and his chin fiercely, contorting his face. There'd be Sun readers muttering about the benefits of Tramp Flu. I had to stop him going into the clinic until Fflur came out. I prayed to a God I'd never believed in that the tablets I took were a strong enough defence, and approached him. He smelt like the cat by the river.

'Do you want to sit down for a bit?' I said. 'We could sit against the wall and wait for the nurse to come back. She's got someone with her at the moment.' His piggy little eyes peered at me between the folds of skin that sagged around them. He let himself crumple to the ground. I held out an arm in moral support and crouched beside him. 'How long have you been feeling rough?'

He laughed and this made him cough more. He screwed up his face, thumping his fists on his chest. I glanced at the door in the hope that Fflur might be nearly done. My head had started to ache in a way that scrambled my thoughts. I didn't know how I'd persuade Nain to let us back in. She seemed to feel doubly betrayed because Fflur had been such a nice girl. As if she'd put on a disguise and underneath she was a rude, unwashed layabout just itching to spread her germs like spray paint on a wall. Keeping stink bombs and razor blades in her squidgy white handbag.

'You a volunteer?' said Alan Turner's twin brother. He spat to one side of him.

'I'm here with a friend. She's in there now.'

He nodded and dragged on his whisky.

'She bad?'

'No. No, she's fine. Just a –' I pointed to my eye. 'Just a bit of infection. Very localised. No coughing.' He wiped his mouth on his sleeve and sniffed. It made him cough.

A hundred yards down the road from the warehouse, a Mini Cooper pulled up and a man got out, talking to the driver as he fastened a buckle on a bulging satchel. He shut the door and smacked the window, and the car pulled away. I watched him survey the scene, already holding my breath but not yet believing myself. Then as he walked towards us, I realised it had to be him. He had the walk of someone who'd walked so many roads in so many far-flung places that he was relaxed wherever he was.

The homeless man coughing himself to death beside me seemed amused by the sudden dumb paralysis that overtook me. Dan kept coming, step by step, and I stuck out my chin and prepared myself for the worst. It was so like him to approach his doom so casually. To treat his symptoms like just another traveller's bug. An irritating side-effect of life on the road.

Swallow the tablets, wrap your feet in bandages inside your boots. He'd treated rough sleeping the same way; he'd slept under the stars in Africa, so why shouldn't he do the same here?

As he came nearer, I saw that he didn't look ill. His skin had the same weathered softness I remembered and he wasn't coughing. I staggered to my feet, looking right at him so I could see the exact moment when he realised it was me. He blinked theatrically and smiled with about sixty percent of his face. Trust Dan to let so little show.

I took a few steps towards him, away from my spluttering companion. Dan came just near enough to stroke my arm fleetingly.

'Shona,' he said. I bit my lip.

'Hi,' I said, and it came out cracked. He looked around.

'What are you doing here? Has the Shelter been shut?'

'Um, yes. Yes. And burnt down, actually.' He widened his eyes. 'Not on purpose.' He kept looking at me, but it felt ridiculous to be talking about anything if we couldn't first acknowledge what there had been between us. 'You must have heard on the news.'

'I've been away. What happened?'

'Paul. The bald one who goes to prison a lot? He started a fire. We were quarantined. Because that man who died in the shed turned out to be Alan Turner.'

'Quarantine. God.' He ran his fingers through his hair. It was shorter than it had been, and less dusty. 'But you're OK? You're not ill?' His hand reached out to stroke my arm again, like a little gift he didn't know he was giving.

'I'm fine. I'm here with a friend. Someone I was locked in with. And you...?' I held my breath.

Dan patted his satchel.

'Business,' he said.

I was relieved, furious, excited, humiliated. And I said, 'Oh. Right.'

He was overtaken by a huge yawn. He looked around, and jerked his head in the direction of the door where Fflur had disappeared.

'How long have you been here? Has there been much action?'

I stared at him.

'I'm working as a journalist,' he said, and yawned again. 'Jetlag,' he said. 'I only got back yesterday.'

'Oh. Right.' It was so like Dan to be just back from somewhere. Either that or about to go.

'Vietnam.' He said. 'It was good fun.' Fun? Dan did *fun* now? 'But no rest for the wicked, hey?' He nodded at the door again. 'They might not want me taking pictures in there. I'm wondering about a bit of cover.'

My destitute lover had become James Bond since he left the Shelter, and not thought to let me know. He wandered over to the man slumped by the wall, who was gazing at his empty whisky bottle. The poor bloke seemed to have given up breathing much, as if it was too much effort.

'You alright, mate?'

The man waggled his fingers a bit. Dan touched his shoulder. 'Shall I help you up? We'll get you into this clinic shall we?'

My own shoulders actually hurt where Dan wasn't holding them.

'Shona?' I folded my arms and looked at him. 'Could you get someone to come out to this gentleman?' I hated him for a second. For stating the obvious and for touching the dying man so gently.

'I'll see what's happening,' I croaked, and made my way to the door with creaking knees. I knocked hard, taking out some of my wrath on my knuckles. I needed to grab Fflur and go, then I could shut myself in the toilet or somewhere and steady my head. I thumped again, this time with the flat of my hand. The young nurse opened the door a little.

'Is Fflur ready to go?' I said. 'There's a man here who needs ...'

She looked past me and her face went stiff. Turning slowly, I saw Dan crouching beside the man's body, apparently deep in thought.

'Was he one of yours?' said the nurse. I frowned at her. 'From the Shelter? Where you work?'

'No. No, I don't think I've seen him before.' She nodded and let the door go. I held it open. 'Is Fflur OK?'

'Could you wait outside, please,' she said tightly.

'Look, some information would be good here,' I said. 'Fflur has been with you a long time. Long enough for your next patient to pass away in the car park, for God's sake.'

She sighed.

'I'm sorry,' she said. 'I also wish people wouldn't leave it so late before they come.' She was being called from inside. 'I need to ring the police. I'll be with you when I can.' She let the door clang shut and I clenched my fists. I stared at a cigarette butt and a woodlouse. Then the door opened again and the nurse came out with a sheet.

'I'll do it,' I said, and took it from her.

'Make sure you cover his head. Obviously.' She didn't stay long enough to notice that Dan was now taking photographs of the dead man.

I marched over to him and shook out the sheet.

'Your readers enjoy a corpse, then,' I said, and, holding two corners, I billowed the sheet high in the air and let it float down like a covering of snow over the man on the ground. It was my first dead body but I didn't feel drawn to stare. I was glad the eyes were shut and I arranged the sheet so that the contours of the face were lost in the folds. Dan took a shot of the covered body and tucked his camera back into his satchel. He scribbled in a tiny notebook and lit a cigarette.

'Poor sod,' he muttered. I turned away, checking the time for some reason on my phone and trying to ignore the pain in my head. 'Shona, are you OK?' I kicked a piece of grit and felt the gassy bubble in my stomach where my breakfast should have been. 'Hey, don't shut me out.'

I set my face hard and looked at him.

'I could use your help,' he said. He slipped the notebook into his jeans pocket. 'You must have your doubts about the ethics of these places.' I tried to get a balance between looking directly at him and looking away, but somehow nothing felt natural.

The clouds were dark enough for rain. The sheet would become more transparent with every drop.

'This set-up is just a way of trapping germs. Like a jam jar when you're trying to keep wasps off your picnic. I want to see if there are proper oxygen masks in there, and IV antibiotics.' His eyes narrowed and he dropped his cigarette and stamped on it. 'There could be other people in there covered in sheets. It's disgusting.' There was ice in his voice. I felt like a little girl who'd been fobbed off by the grown-ups.

'Fflur,' I said, gaping at him.

'I'm sorry. I know some of these people matter to you.' The scary edge to his voice receded. I had a dangerous urge to fling myself at him and talk and talk until I felt better. Suddenly, he doubled over, coughing and clasping his hands on his stomach.

'Dan?'

Not looking up, he muttered, 'There's someone coming. Work with me here.'

The Jamaican nurse strode up and took his elbow in her gloved hand.

'Come with me, lovely,' she said. She looked at me and murmured,

'There's an ambulance coming for the dead man.' Dan stumbled and groaned until I took his other arm and we made our way to the door.

The nurse held the door open. 'I'm sorry,' she said to me. 'Could you wait by there again please.'

Dan fell forwards, grabbing my hand.

'I'll help you get him inside,' I said. Dan gave my hand a little squeeze and let me pull him to his feet. The nurse gave in and led us inside, past the screen and the schoolroom table where clipboards and plastic masks lay scattered.

There were rows of patients. A skinny girl with blue hair was lying on the first trolley, retching into a kidney dish. I scanned the rows for Fflur. A man with a Father Christmas beard snored and grunted. The younger nurse had her back to us, intent on doing something with his feet.

'Hold onto him while I make up a bed,' the Jamaican nurse told me, and went to a stack of sheets and criss-cross blankets.

'Cover me,' hissed Dan. He fumbled surreptitiously in his satchel and I tried to look as if I was comforting him while I blocked him from view.

'This is mad,' I whispered. 'They won't let you out. And you'll catch it.'

'Are they looking?' I glanced up. Fflur was in the far corner, standing on tiptoes with her phone held up above her head.

'Quick,' I whispered. He sprang up, pointed the camera, took three shots and collapsed again. The Jamaican nurse came back and he looked at her beseechingly.

'I don't have to stay, do I?' he wheezed. 'Could I just have a prescription?'

'It's policy,' she said. 'You can talk to the doctor when he comes. This cough of yours. It comes and goes, does it?'

Dan straightened up.

'Er, yes. In fact I'm probably fine. I've always been a bit of a Drama Queen.'

'Are you a journalist?'

'Sort of. Freelance.'

'Well, you've got your photos. You'd better go before you catch this and become a public health hazard.'

I'd caught Fflur's good eye, and she rushed down the aisle between trolleys of spluttering people.

'Did you get any of my texts?' she said. 'There's no reception in here. And they won't let me out.' She shot a look at the nurse.

'Do you have a prescription?' I asked.

She rolled her eyes.

'The doctor will be here soon,' said the nurse.

'We'll get one from my doctor,' I said. 'Come on, Fflur. We'll go now.' I moved away towards the screen and the nurse made a barrier of herself in front of Fflur with her hands on her hips.

'Please,' she said. 'Be reasonable.' Her colleague came over to gang up on us.

Dan had taken the opportunity to wave his camera slowly around, taking film of the warehouse. Now, he held up his hands in surrender.

'They're experienced professionals, Fflur,' he said. 'They're not fooled by a bit of make-up. We'd better go.' The nurses looked at each other.

'You've taken quite a risk here,' said the younger one. Dan put his camera away. 'What are you going to put in your article?'

Fflur and I backed away and escaped.

'Oh, thank God –' she began and stopped short. A police car had arrived and the van had come back. Two men in spacesuits were loading the dead man into the back and a policeman was overseeing the procedure. Fflur put her hands over her mouth and stared. The spacemen shut the back doors of the van and spoke briefly to the policeman before climbing in and pulling away. Then the policeman turned and walked towards us. Fflur ducked back inside.

'Good morning,' I said.

'Hello,' said the policeman. 'Do you work here?'

'No,' I said. Fflur backed out of the door, wearing a surgical mask, holding her phone between her ear and her shoulder, and squinting at a clipboard. She managed to keep the left hand side of her face completely out of sight.

'My shift's over,' she said busily into the phone. 'Yup. See you in a mo'.'

'They're waiting for you inside,' I told the policeman. Dan emerged, also on the phone and carrying a shower cap, and I trotted after him.

We were rescued by the Mini Cooper. Fflur and I scrambled into the back and Dan got in beside the driver.

'Don't touch anything!' said the driver. 'There's alcohol gel in the glove box.' He looked at Fflur in his rear view mirror and nearly stalled the car.

'It's very localised,' she said. 'And I'm not coughing.'

7

The big window makes a sauna of the Learning Centre. Some snowdrops and crocuses have broken through. Purple and white, exuding a Fflur-like strength. I imagine outside it's probably still cold – there's a stiff breeze playing with the trees, and Carol has with her a technicolour dreamcoat made of knitted mohair squares. She's having some issues at home I think and the professional sheen is a bit diluted this morning. Her mind is on her mobile, which she turns over in her pocket every few minutes.

'Do you want to give me a miss today, Carol?' I say gently. 'I won't tell anyone if you slip off early.'

She laughs – sighs.

'You're very pretty,' she says, 'when you forget to scowl.'

I blush, burning hot all over my face. I don't remember ever in my whole life being told I'm pretty, or even trying to be pretty. Maybe I borrowed Nain's lipstick or dressed up in her nighty or something when I was little, but if I did I don't remember. In fact I'm not sure I remember Nain ever having any lipstick. In recent years, she's developed skin allergies but in the days when she was too busy for those, she might have had lipstick. Probably not very bright, muted perhaps.

'Perhaps you feel uncomfortable with the compliment.' Carol crosses her legs. I can't look at her. I'm waiting for my face to deflate. She waits and eventually my Rescuer tendencies kick in and I say, 'I've never had any lipstick. It's never even occurred to me to buy one.'

She blinks and smiles. 'Have you ever tried one on?'

'I don't think so.' She turns her mobile over in her pocket.

'Let's write about lipstick,' she says. I look up and she catches my eye skilfully. 'Make a list of colours for lipsticks.'

Pink, red, I write obediently. By mauve, I'm stretched. But I manage gold. Natural. And shimmer. I'm pleased with that one. I drag my pen across the paper with a flourish which is the code we've developed for 'I've finished.' She's *texting and she pretends not to notice. I flick the loose flap on the plaster on my thumb. My bladder is attention-seeking.*

I cross my legs and write: Blue. Green. Camouflage, khaki. Diagonal stripes. Clown-face-clown-chops, old lady spidering, shiny snowflakes, white like that shitty cow in the sixth form, ointment on crusty cold sores you can never take your mind off. And if you smile, or say a word with a long 'e' sound, *pop* it breaks along the fault line and it's bleeding again just when you thought it was beginning to heal. *Cold sores, herpes,* the shitty cow says *herpes, Shona has VD!* And in personal and social excruciation, they hand out leaflets about STDs and she mouths, 'Shona', without seeming to move or catch anyone's eye and the class of young women who will be lawyers, doctors, teachers and financial advisors in a few years' time are giggling prettily with the effortless cruelty that carries them through their school days. And I have thick yellow crusts in the armpits of my shirts which the washing machine just impacts. Cold sores under my armpits.

Carol has stopped texting and is engaged in a supportive silence so loud it breaks through my repugnant little foray into my past. I do one of my lines, but it's unconvincing and she can tell I'm on a roll.

We did what we should have done in the first place and got hold of a prescription using the name and address of Fflur's most obnoxious ex housemate. She was given strict instructions not to leave the house and sent home. Nain, however, was less tractable. She'd stuffed my bedding and the cushions from the front room into the wheelie bin.

'This is my house, too,' I called through the letter box. 'You can't do this, Nain.'

'I'll go,' said Fflur. 'She'll let you in on your own.'

I doubted it. I rattled the letterbox and rang the bell again and again, knowing I was being stared at. Nain poked the nozzle of a cleaning spray through the letter box and pulled the trigger, sending blobs of diluted bleach raining onto my jeans. I sat on the step beside Fflur.

'We could go back to the Shelter,' she said.

I shook my head. 'Not if we don't want ceilings falling on our heads.' I pinged the ring pull on my empty Fanta can. A small boy on a scooter veered into a lamppost, mesmerised by Fflur's disfigurement. Behind him, a girl pushing a double buggy and smoking quickened her pace. It was cold still, getting colder all the time.

'That man,' said Fflur. 'The journalist. You knew him.' I pinged the ring pull again and it snapped, ramming my fingernail. 'Sorry,' she said nosily, 'it's not my business.'

'He was homeless for a while,' I said. 'I vaguely remember him from the Shelter.'

'Oh, right,' she said. I leant back against the door. I felt lost, abandoned, and it had nothing to do with being locked out of my house. But Fflur was still there beside me. Foolishly imagining that sticking with me might be better than going it alone. And there was one person who wouldn't think twice about letting us in.

'We'll go to Colin's.'

We persuaded Nain to open the door wide enough to post us some clothes and a toothbrush, and we got the bus to the housing association flats where Colin lived. Panting after ten flights of steps, we knocked and he opened the door.

The right hand side of Fflur's face went pale.

'Shona,' she hissed. 'It smells like the cat by the river.'

'Oh God,' I mouthed, 'I forgot'. Colin batted away a drowsy fly and looked at us.

'Colin,' I said. 'Is your dog still here?'

'Yes,' he said. 'In a manner of speaking.' Fflur took a tissue from her bag and held it over her nose and mouth. Colin was staring at her. 'It was all the cleaning that did that,' he said. 'You were touching things a lot at the Shelter, and you're not used to the germs.'

'Colin, could we come in, do you think?' I said.

The flat was small and sparse and cold and damp; one room for kitchen and sitting room, a tiny bedroom, a toilet and a shower. The dog was in its bed in the main room.

'We have to bury it. Or burn it,' I said through gritted teeth, breathing as shallow as I could. Or put it in the green bin. (I didn't say that.)

Colin chewed his lip. Fflur took a bottle of water from her bag and swallowed a double dose of antibiotics.

'Burial,' he said, to the bleached spot on my jeans. 'Something to visit.'

I thought. I saw myself turning up at a veterinary surgery, asking them to cremate this decaying animal, Fflur beside me with a plague-ridden face.

'The old rec,' I said. 'After dark.'

'Would you like a cup of tea?' Colin swivelled his eyes at the ceiling and wrinkled his nose.

'That would be lovely,' said Fflur. 'Do you mind if I sit down? It's been quite a day.'

'I've got two different types of tea. Earl Grey in case my dad comes, which he probably never will but anyway. I think it's related to age. People pass fifty and suddenly they want Earl Grey.'

My heart ached for him. He was making a joke, and he'd been stuck here with his only friend dead and decomposing. I laughed.

He became industrious at the end of the room where there was a microwave, a one-ring hob, a sink, a very small fridge and a kettle. Fflur was on the chair at that end, and although there was an armchair and a deckchair at the other end, I would have to pass the dog's bed to get to them.

'I wonder if ... Colin, do you, um, have a sheet or a blanket or something? We could cover the dog up a bit.'

He looked surprised by the suggestion.

'Righto,' he said, and left the room.

'Fucking hell,' murmured Fflur.

I poured hot water into two mugs and a plastic tumbler and opened the fridge. It contained an open tin of baked beans. I looked at Fflur. She looked at the fridge.

'Here we are. Just the ticket,' said Colin, coming back with a striped fleece blanket.

'Is it one you mind about?' I said, shutting the fridge quickly. 'Only it might get a bit – '

'He liked this one,' he said, burying his face in the blanket. 'Here.' He pushed it at me, starting to hum.

I draped the blanket over the dog, holding my breath. I wasn't keen on my new role as undertaker, and the delinquent snarl on the dog's features brought my nightmare swimming back. I went to the sink, lathering a tiny soap remnant vigorously over my hands even though I'd managed not to actually touch the animal or its bed. I saw germs with legs and teeth crawling over the soap bubbles and shook away the vision in case I turned into my grandmother before my time.

We buried the dog after dark. It felt as if I was bereaving Colin all over again. I lifted the bed, which caved in to wrap itself around its contents, and the blanket slipped. I flinched and had to grit my teeth to keep myself from leaping backwards and dropping bed, blanket and dog. The disease-saturated foam padding was a poor shield against the alarming texture of the body; I didn't know rigor mortis gave way to an eerie floppiness, if you left it for a day or two.

'Colin, could you just –' I nodded at the blanket. He draped it more securely, clearing his throat as he did so, and we trooped out of the door. I let the weight of my load rest on the railing as Colin performed a little locking-up routine that involved standing on one leg and leaning on the door. He began to walk away, towards the steps, but as I steeled myself to follow him, he pivoted on his heel and started again. I gritted my teeth harder.

This happened twice more, and I had just decided to force the issue when Colin said, 'I've battened down the hatches,' and marched off. Clearly I was chief pall-bearer.

On the second landing, we heard hard, drunken voices. The stairwell was too narrow to pass if you were carrying very much, and I backed against the wall. Fflur pulled her hair in curtains across her face, so that just the tip of her nose peeked out. Colin hummed a drum roll, shuffling from one foot to the other, and I realised he knew exactly what was coming. Two boys appeared, skinny and spotty, one carrying a plastic bag of corner shop vodka and the other playing with a box of matches. They looked delighted to see us.

'Has your granny died?' one of them said, to Colin.

'I bet he killed her,' said the other. Colin sneezed, nodding and looking at a hole in the concrete wall.

Fflur said, 'Excuse me, boys,' and they cheered. She tossed back her hair.

'It's the elephant woman!' they roared, shoving us out of the way and running.

'Ignore them,' recited Colin, 'they'll get bored of it in the end.'

At the old rec, I dumped the dog on the ground and shook out my arms. Colin did a bizarre quickstep in the direction of the shed and twisted the numbers on the padlock.

'How do you know the combination?' whispered Fflur, though there was no one around to overhear.

'This is where I hide out,' said Colin, rotating his finger in his ear. 'Where I used to hide out – when I got chased after school. Or in the holidays. My dad said I needed fresh air and exercise, and I'd have to sit in here until they got bored of it. They always do, in the end. The same the world over. So. Now then.' He ducked his head and went in, unable to straighten up in the tiny lean-to.

Fflur mouthed, 'Bless,' and I sniffed and massaged the pins and needles out of my hands. I'd maybe have a deeper well of sympathy when I'd got the dog under the ground.

Colin emerged brandishing a shovel and twitching his nose. He gazed around, shielding his eyes to help him see in the dark.

'So now,' he said. I chewed my lip, prodding the ground outside the shed with my foot.

'Where we came in,' said Fflur gently, 'the ground was softer. By the tree.'

The sky lit up with the sound of machine guns and sparks rained down over the flats. Fflur gasped and Colin cleared his throat.

'Is it,' I said tightly, as if it were their fault, 'fireworks night?'

From the other side of Colin's apartment block, a small crowd cheered. An identical firework shot into the sky – same bangs, same white sparks. There'd be a limit to how many of those could be considered entertainment, even by local standards.

'Should we do this another time?' said Fflur. 'On a quieter night?'

Colin coughed in agreement. My jaw ached with gritting my teeth.

'I am *not* carting this fucking dog back up those steps.'

They were silent. A more impressive firework squealed upwards and sprayed blue stars for three or four seconds.

'Ooh,' said Fflur.

'Do you know,' said Colin, conversationally, 'I don't think I've ever been to a firework display. Though to be fair, I did construct a scarecrow one year.'

'A guy?' said Fflur.

'Er. Yes, oh, I see. Guy Fawkes. Remember remember and so on. Not just any old scarecrow. You are very right.'

'We used to go to the green near us,' said Fflur. 'It was a family tradition for a while.'

Colin thwacked the shovel into the ground.

'Best over and done with,' he said to the sky and began to hum. He thwacked the ground again but it was too hard and the shovel bounced. 'It could be a sign,' he muttered. 'Do you think? A sign that burial isn't right?' He clutched the shovel to him and shuffled backwards, shaking his head.

'Best over and done with,' I said and grabbed it from him. He wandered over to the slide, which was warped in the middle and graffitied all over.

'Actually,' said Fflur, 'I think fireworks night is on Wednesday, but they often go on for a week or so.' I looked at her and she helped me drag the dog back towards the tree. I placed the shovel experimentally and stood on the blade. The earth gave fairly easily, and I managed to gouge out a bit. I glanced back at Colin. He had the air of a mourner crazed enough to make off with the body, and I leaned hard on the shovel.

'How deep are we going to go?' said Fflur. The shovel met squishy softness, and the earth tumbled in on itself. 'Oh my God, someone's coming.' We froze, and a car alarm went off outside the flats. 'Perhaps we should just do it quickly, get it over with.'

I started digging again, hitting the edge of something very hard.

'Shit, there's a rock or a brick or something.' I experimented in each direction, but it seemed to grow bigger with every prod. 'Oh, for fuck's sake.' My back hurt. I wondered if the firework display had reached its finale with the blue stars.

'Shall I do a stint?' said Fflur. She sounded as if we were Girl Guides taking part in a sandcastle contest.

'I'm fine,' I said, ramming the shovel into the ground, 'and your shoes aren't exactly made for digging.' I flipped up a crisp packet and a wedge of glass.

After a while, when I'd dug a hole about half the size I'd imagined, and I was thinking that if we jumped on the dog a bit it might be enough, Fflur said, 'Shall we make a cross? Or something?' I looked at Colin, who was tapping his foot and talking to himself. Fflur stage-whispered in his direction, 'Do you want to – um – say goodbye or anything? Before we do it?' He shook his head, foot waggling to some frantic rhythm of his own.

We pulled the bed to the edge of the hole and tipped out the dog and its blanket, holding our breath, working quickly. A skeletal paw got caught on the side and I had to kick it down. Then, Fflur with the shovel and me with my feet, we shunted the mound of earth and rubbish over the top.

'There,' panted Fflur. I was swamped by the nausea I'd been holding back, and I swivelled out of the way just in time to avoid throwing up all over the grave. Fflur hovered and I batted her away, splattering myself with sick, feeling as if it would never stop coming.

When I stood straight again, gasping, Fflur and Colin were standing together in silence with their backs to me.

'ok,' I squeaked. 'I'm ok. Sorry about that. Colin, could you put the shovel back and we can go.'

Fflur smiled tightly at me. Colin rocked from side to side, humming.

'Are you religious, Colin?' said Fflur. 'Or spiritual, perhaps? Without, you know, any particular ... framework?'

'Please,' I whispered hoarsely. 'Let's just go.'

'Would you like to create something from the landscape here that might serve as a memorial?'

'Oh, for God's sake.' I wanted desperately to wash my face and brush my teeth. I felt like Alan Turner resurrected. But Fflur was nodding slowly, as if Colin was responding. 'Fflur, please.'

'Hmm,' said Colin. 'I don't think I'm wrong in saying that the very earliest religions – certainly festival-wise – are, were, the Ancient Greek Tragedies and Comedies. Frogs? Were there frogs involved? Funny what you remember from the chaotic mass we call schooling. I had a Classics teacher called ...'

My head hurt already, and Colin's voice was a migraine-inducing drone. I began to walk away, in search at least of some better air. Colin's monologue segued seamlessly from Ancient Greek Theatre through education to techniques for training horses.

'Do you have the key to your flat?' I said. 'I'm sorry. But I have to sleep. Wash. You could sit here for a bit if you like.' He poked about inside the neck of his t-shirt and produced a key on a string. He had to tug it free from a threadbare little dreadlock that had formed in his hair and got caught up.

'I could stay here with you,' offered Fflur. 'We could say a few words.' I wrapped the string around my wrist.

'It would be for our own comfort only,' said Colin, cracking his knuckles. 'The heap of bones, hair and rotting flesh you have kindly laid to rest is hardly in need of platitudes.'

The whites of Fflur's eyes shone in the darkness, the swollen one particularly luminous.

'Perhaps you're right,' she murmured. 'We may never know in this life.'

Colin locked the shovel in the shed and we made our way back to the gloomy tower where he lived.

'Do you have any gin at all, Colin?' said Fflur, as we started up the first set of steps. 'And tonic?' She paused, leaning on the wall. 'The shop might still be open. Those boys had a bag.'

Colin put his finger to his chin in an exaggerated posture.

'I have some palinka,' he said. 'It's Hungarian. Eastern Europe, as was. There was a man next door for a while, jolly chap, who used to come and visit me. Interesting history, the Hungarians.'

'Palinka?' said Fflur, looking at me.

'Absolutely,' continued Colin, taking the steps two at a time. 'Double-distilled fruit brandy. Apparently, all sorts of fruit are used; I think it's a case of what's available. Mulberries, for example. Whatever they are.' He seemed thoroughly energised by the idea. Fflur started laughing, and had to clutch her cheek as we followed him up the endless flights of steps. 'Intriguing. Dracula territory. In fact Dracula is claimed by various places. It's a marketing ploy, obviously. Kol showed me photographs. I had assumed he was Polish ...' He kept talking all the way up. His sentences became disjointed as he ran out of breath, and it was almost impossible to follow what he was saying. But Fflur was delighted, in a slightly hysterical way, at the prospect of the double-distilled fruit brandy.

I woke up foul-mouthed and aching. My back felt as if it would never straighten up. There was nothing odd about sleeping in an armchair next to Colin, though the smell was worse here, full of dog and death.

Two unlabelled bottles with the sticky dregs of best Hungarian home brew stood accusingly on the table. I staggered to the sink and drank straight from the tap. My stomach made a sound like Donald Duck. The water tasted wrong.

Fflur came in, groaning.

'I can't believe I was so stupid,' she said. 'You're not supposed to drink on antibiotics. I'm sorry if I was a girly mess.'

I washed my face and ran my hands through my hair, and then I looked at her.

'Fflur! Your face. It's going right down.'

Her hands flew to her cheeks and she prodded experimentally.

'It hurts less,' she said. 'Praise be, as Gloria would say.' She picked up the kettle and frowned at it. 'I'm surprised it's so skanky here,' she whispered. 'He was so domesticated in the Shelter.'

I nodded. 'Grief, I suppose.' I opened a bare cupboard. Other than the half-eaten tin of baked beans, there were no signs of shopping or cooking, not even an empty biscuit packet in the bin. I thought of all the pizza and crisps and the fry-ups he produced each morning. I watched Fflur fill the grimy kettle. It was quite possible that Colin only ate at the Shelter, that he wasn't in the habit of shopping or cooking for himself at all. And that now, without the Shelter to go to, he was more adrift than I'd realised.

At the other end of the room, he choked himself awake on a sudden, tumultuous snore and shook himself like a wet dog.

'So,' he said. 'Ahah,' and cleared his throat for a while.

'Black Earl Grey?' said Fflur. She had a Maid Marian look about her, of having dashed through a forest in mortal peril, branches tousling her hair – and bruising one side of her face, though not too hideously. The swelling had gone down and the eye was altogether less scary. Handing out mugs, she opened her mouth to speak and changed her mind. She sat down, and got up again, and stared out of the tiny window at the boy on the street who seemed to spend his time waiting for someone to show up – though when they did, they just did a bit more waiting together. She was getting on my nerves now, and Colin looked as if he might be revving up for a soliloquy. She turned to look at me and sighed.

'It's just – this.' She waved at her cheek.

'The antibiotics are working already,' I said. 'Put that 'elephant woman' remark out of your mind. It was rubbish, anyway. And they weren't exactly grade one gorgeous themselves.'

She was shaking her head, batting away my reassurance.

'If the antibiotics work this fast – and it was pretty bad – why is the infection killing people? What Dan and the other guy said, in the car, I think they're right. If people were being treated properly, they'd recover.' I sipped my black tea. I wondered if the water was coming out of a tank and not mains; there was a hint of dead pigeon to it. 'It's the kind of thing you'd expect in South America or somewhere. I don't know anything about South America. But do you see what I mean?'

'Mm,' I said. 'But then you weren't coughing. It's the TB that's getting people.' Fflur pursed her lips and folded her arms, deep in thought.

'Have you been in touch with ... anyone?' I tried to let the sentence hover but I had to say 'anyone' because she didn't help.

'I've decided not to go and collect my stuff,' she said. 'I'm having a fresh start.' I nodded as if this was an obvious move. 'Let them sell it all on eBay. They won't make much.'

There was very little battery left on my mobile, and patchy reception in the flat, but that didn't stop Gloria getting through.

'Shona? Gloria.'

'Hi. Look, if we get cut off it's because my battery is almost dead and I don't have a charger with me.'

'Where are you?'

'Colin's flat. Fflur's with us.'

'Good Lord. I imagine that's an eye opener for her. You get all sorts in those flats.' My phone beeped once, beginning its countdown.

'Do you want me to come into the office?' I said half-heartedly. 'While I'm spare? I could get onto some builders ... do some fundraising ...'

Gloria sighed. The phone beeped.

'Perhaps you could come and fend off these rags. I'm being pestered. There's one young hack who's insisting on speaking to you personally, but I'd rather you and I had a little conflab first.'

My insides turned a tight little somersault and my foot started jigging about.

'What's his name? The one who wants me?'

Fflur stared at me.

'Hang on a mo'.'

'Gloria, the battery's going to –'

The phone cut her off; with so little charge left, the connection was too much effort. But my inner battery had been kick-started. I swigged my tea, stuffed my phone in my pocket and grabbed the bag of stuff Nain had deigned to give me.

'I have to go to the office,' I said, scrambling for my toothbrush. 'There's an investigation thing about the fire and some journalists and things.'

I scrubbed my teeth, drawing blood, and spat into the kitchen sink.

'Journalists. And things,' said Fflur. 'Of course.'

'What are you grinning about?' I wiped my face on my t-shirt and caught a whiff of armpit. Fflur shook her head.

'Nothing,' she chirped. 'None of my business.'

The office was on an eclectic street: there was Bob's Ardware, stuffed so full of sharp, spiky metal things it would have been dangerous if anyone ever went in there, a Polish store you couldn't see into for special offer posters, a Private Shop, which for some reason boasted a display of sewing machines, and Tariq's Fabriqs, which had swathes of glittery sari material in the window. Dan was standing on the corner of the street, texting. I felt excitement swirl up inside me and despair at the same time, where the pessimist in me dwelt. What would I do if he didn't look up? Walk past and go up to the office? But he was waiting for me; it would be silly to miss each other. Perhaps he was pretending to be immersed in his text; maybe he'd seen me coming and grabbed his phone. So why was he there, then? Maybe I'd jumped to a conclusion I wanted too much.

I passed Yvonne's, the mildewy dress shop which had recently rebranded by sticking up a piece of paper that said 'Vintage'. There were mannequins in the window in a series of contorted stretches, and, according to a notice on the door, they also did hairdressing.

'Shona!' Dan sounded as if we were amicable acquaintances. As if we'd never spent the night wrapped in each other in the dark.

'Dan. Hi.'

'Hi.' He breathed in slowly as he looked at me and let out the air in a sigh. I wished I was someone who didn't have to fill a silence. Who could smile enigmatically and wait for someone else to speak first. But words came out of my mouth of their own accord. Apparently I was going along with pally but slightly detached.

'Did you file your copy, as they say?'

He did the slow breathing thing again and I wanted to thump him. A girl in a tiny skirt walked past, and he made a point of not noticing her.

'Are you going to speak?' I said. 'Or shall I go to work?'

He rifled in his battered leather messenger bag. 'I took these last night.' He thrust his camera into my hand. 'It's getting worse. There were at least two more deaths.'

The photographs were Armageddon. A close-up of an arm with maggots in the boils. A queue of people in varying states of decay. I looked at Dan's face, at his dirty stubble. (Not that I was in a position to judge, where personal grooming was concerned, that particular morning.)

'You should stay away,' I said, handing back the camera. 'You're putting yourself at risk. There's nothing new, by the way, about homeless people and maggots. There was a guy in the Shelter a few years back – '

'Where's your friend?'

'Fflur? Why?'

'She's in hospital, isn't she?'

'Hospital? No.'

He looked at me hard and put the camera back in his bag.

'She needs treatment, though. And she's not homeless, is she? She didn't look as if she'd ever slept rough.' He seemed unsettled. His assurance and confidence had got knocked somehow.

'She got some antibiotics from the GP. They're working already.'

His eyes flared and his mouth hovered between a grin and a scowl.

'She just walked in looking like that and they gave her pills. It's ...' He puffed out an indignant sigh.

'Fflur's bought into your conspiracy theory,' I said lightly.

He pounced. 'Would she speak out? Do an interview? We could set her up with a hidden dictaphone and –'

'It's complicated,' I said. His hands were adventurer's hands, strong and brown. I watched the knuckles bend and flex as he felt in his bag for something. I couldn't look at his face for long; it was all I could do not to reach out and touch it.

He waved a torn piece of front page at me, from a national that had bought his photograph of the dead man under the sheet. He insisted we had to get a story into the next day's paper, about Fflur getting the pills straightaway because she was posh.

'It's awkward,' I said. 'Fflur used someone else's name. She was chucked out by her housemates, so essentially, yes, she was homeless, but she hasn't got this plague thing. MRSA is actually fairly common in the community.'

'Who told you that?'

'The nurse at the health centre.'

'So Fflur didn't have Tramp Flu?'

'You can't call it that.'

'Everyone calls it that.' His smile was lopsided, his eyes sparkling at me as if just for a second there was only us. 'Even persons of no fixed abode, so no need for your diversity of discourses here.' He thought for a moment. 'Whose name did she use?'

'Her old housemate. Some little cat who pretended to be friends then kicked her out.'

'And the little cat's address? She gave a false address? As long as you have an address, they'll treat you. Shona, you're a darling.' My face must have flinched when my insides did, at the 'darling'; he did his slow breath in routine. I adopted the faraway expression of a schoolgirl who doesn't care that she's going to get told off. 'Shona, it's ... I really appreciate you saying you'll help.' He stroked my elbow. My *elbow*? We'd made each other come and now we were back to *elbow*-stroking?

'I'd like to see the Shelters open again as soon as possible,' I said, though I wasn't sure if this was true. 'Rough sleeping can't be good for vulnerable people, whatever anyone says.' I wished he'd touch my elbow again. A car screeched past, nearly mounting the kerb. We leapt to one side and Dan's arm shot round me. Whatever else I might have rambled disappeared with the sound of the engine and I stood gaping silently with Dan's arm round my shoulders.

'Shona!' Gloria was dashing towards us, handbag flying, perm bouncing. Dan gave me a minute squeeze before he let go, murmuring, 'Is that your grandmother?'

'Hello, Gloria,' I said. 'This is Dan. Dan, Gloria.' And then, back in fill-every-silence mode, I said, 'Gloria works at Head Office, which is a strangely grand title for the second floor of that building, above the ex-camera shop,' which was a mistake because I couldn't follow it up with, 'And Dan stayed at the Shelter about a year ago. We had sex a lot and he was supposed to come back when he'd *sorted himself out*, which presumably he has because he's now a cool journalist and I imagine he has somewhere to live, but clearly he doesn't want me after all.'

'I'm a journalist,' said Dan. When she sniffed, he said, 'Sorry,' and gave her a smile I was jealous of.

She tilted her head to one side, and said, 'You're the one that's been pestering me.' She threw her arms in the air. '*Endless* messages and calls.'

'Three,' said Dan.

'Well, you've found her,' said Gloria, looking suddenly suspicious. 'What are you after?' She was doing Joan Collins. Dan made an unreadable face and Gloria's rosacea flared up. She squinted at the sky and shrugged off her jacket. 'Hm,' she said. 'Shona, I'm dashing to a meeting with one of my government chums. Michael Blakelock MP.'

'Good to meet you,' said Dan, adjusting the strap on his shoulder.

'OK,' I said. 'Right.'

Gloria strode off and I looked at a lamppost.

'Michael Blakelock MP?' said Dan.

'Youngish. Hairy nostrils. She collects local MPs, eats them for breakfast.

Tell me you didn't really think she was my grandmother.'

Life Skills. They want to teach me to boil eggs and fill in forms and use washing machines and shop on a budget. It makes me want to crush their faces under the heel of my hand.

Benny comes for her visit. She quite enjoys the atmosphere; I think she'll come again. And she does conversation, and asking how I am. It's a bit surreal. I sulk at first but she tries so hard in the end I give in and we talk like normal people. She smiles when I tell her about Gloria's visit, and her eyes soften.

'The Life Skills might kill me,' I tell her, 'but I'm going to Life Writing, and I actually enjoy it. I've written loads.'

'Really?' She narrows her eyes. 'You know I've got nearly ten thousand words on a memory stick, don't you? I'm writing my autobiography.'

'Wow. That'll be something.' I roll my shoulders; I'm stiff from the flimsy mattress. I'd be better off sleeping in a chair.

'I've designed the cover, too,' she says.

She looks so grateful that I am talking back and not just staring blankly and letting the seconds tick past. She's clearly mellowing with age. Either that or she wants something.

8

So I trogged after Dan, flushing every time he touched my shoulder or something and trying to pretend I didn't go over and over memories of the nights we'd had a whole year ago. When we got to the clinic, the fat Jamaican nurse who'd admitted Fflur and then let us escape was just leaving, looking exhausted. She frowned at us, shaking her hair out of the shower cap and wiping her arm across her forehead.

'See for yourselves,' she muttered. 'They're getting antibiotics and TB drugs, they're just too late. People need to come earlier.'

'They're scared of this place,' said Dan.

'Aren't we all?'

'The work that needs doing is out in the community,' I said, 'actively seeking people out.'

'It's illegal to be homeless. And you have to register as homeless by coming here. These people are in an impossible position; no wonder they're hiding out God knows where. I have to go home. I haven't seen my little girl for two days.'

'Thanks.' Dan gave her that smile he dealt out so liberally.

A scream. An angry, frightened, absolutely-lost-it scream. We rounded the corner to look, Dan flicking the lens cap off his camera with one finger.

A thin, pale woman with a studded face was clinging to another woman, who she held tight in her arms so that all we could see was a tumble of red-golden locks and a rumpled sleeping bag.

'I'm coming with her!' she screeched. 'No one's taking her away!'

Two spacemen were opening the back of a van. This one was more of a truck, really. Nearly a lorry. One crouched to speak to the women, but got nowhere. He stood again, hands on hips, frowning.

Dan moved towards them and I opened my mouth and put out my hand to stop him, but found instead that I followed him. He crouched and looked into the screaming woman's face.

'Breathe out ... and in ...' he said, and she did, and all the time he held her gaze like he was hypnotising her. Her breath stirred the red-golden locks.

'I'm Dan,' he said. 'What's your name?'

'Alice.'

I looked into the back of the van and wished I hadn't. Five ex-people loaded up, shoes pointing at me.

I looked down at Dan, shaking. He stroked the red-golden curls.

'What's her name, Alice?' he said.

'Kylie.'

And then there was a policeman there, wearing a face mask and plastic gloves.

'Are you all registered?' he said. I flailed around a bit; I knew I wasn't looking my best and Dan was dusty at the best of times.

'We're support workers,' I said. 'Here to – support people.'

He frowned. 'Sorry,' he said. 'Sorry. You should wear masks, though. Even with the prophs.'

Dan was gently prising apart the two women, his eyes fixed on Alice. We all watched as he laid Kylie on the ground and her hair fell away from her face. She was beautiful. Porcelain-cheeked, princess-serene. And stone cold. Dan seemed to nod without moving his head and Alice went limp and allowed the spacemen to roll Kylie onto a stretcher and slot her into the shelf unit on the truck.

Dan stayed kneeling by Alice, who was silent now. The policeman looked a bit spare so I said kindly, 'We'll sit with her.' He looked relieved.

'Take her in when she's ready,' he said.

Alice was about to protest about that but Dan – who seemed to have a talent for telepathic communication – gave her another imperceptible nod and she kept quiet. The policeman left us to it.

I was hovering in a half-squat position I couldn't sustain, so I humphed down onto my bum and crossed my legs. Out of the corner of my eye, I saw our policeman reassure another that we were legit. Dan clicked something in his bag.

Alice rubbed her studded face with both palms.

'Was she ill for long?' murmured Dan.

'She didn't have any boils,' she said. 'Just a cough. And it wasn't even that serious. We were registered with a doctor, too, but the smug witch on reception knew Kylie had been in a hostel.' She pressed her temples where the memory threatened to explode from her head.

Dan had her hand loosely in his; he was circling his thumb over hers. We sat in silence while the death truck lumbered away.

'Was Kylie strong?' said Dan, still stroking, apparently meditative. Alice frowned a little, as if his voice was coming from a distance. 'Until the cough came,' he said. 'Was she healthy?' Alice nodded and sniffed, putting a finger under each eye and pressing hard. 'I'm sorry to ask this,' murmured Dan. 'Did Kylie ... was she HIV positive?'

Alice sat straight up and took her hand out of his.

'What are you trying to say?' she said, haughtily protective. She staggered to her feet, brushing grot and bits of tarmac off her combats. Dan shook his head and sighed gently. She folded her arms, glanced down at me. The spare part.

'I can tell you categorically,' she said. 'Kylie did not have HIV.'

Dan nodded, as if to say he'd known that all along but needed her to confirm it.

'And she wasn't using drugs or alcohol?' I said. If we were going to get anywhere, perhaps I'd better do bad cop. Alice sighed. I thought she might be about to spit on me but then she laughed.

'Kylie was a vegan,' she said. 'She did yoga and took flower remedies.'

Then there were three WPCs with shower caps under their hats and face masks across their mouths and noses.

'Have you come to register as homeless?' said one.

Dan stood, smiling. Alice backed away.

'Can I ask what you are all doing here? I need you either to show me some ID and give me an address or to get in there and register.' She jerked her thumb at the clinic.

I dug in my little backpack for my bank card. Alice fled towards the river. The police chased her, boots thundering.

Dan chewed his lip, his hand in his satchel clicking off the dictaphone. 'Wow,' he muttered.

I felt tired and stupid and scared. Kylie's tumbling curls and princess skin had imprinted themselves on my mind. The way her expressionless face had seemed to rise a mile above us.

'She was no Alan Turner, was she?' I said.

'I wish I'd got a photo.'

'Of Kylie?'

He scratched his head. 'Your friend Gloria was off to see that MP.

How much power does she wield?' An ugly little laugh snorted from one corner of my mouth. He was irritated. 'Does she know people in local government?'

'Yes. Yes she does.'

'Can you get hold of her? She needs to ask questions. They can't hide behind the compromised immunity thing now, not with beautiful young women on their death trucks.'

The 'beautiful' was a kick and the 'young' didn't help; Dan was six years younger than me, and when you're either side of thirty, that matters.

'Come to the office,' I said. 'You could play her that tape.'

He took out his phone and dialled, and there was a police car coming so we both began to move backwards, reaching for bank cards.

'Rory?' he said, into the phone. 'I've got an interview with a woman whose girlfriend's just been parcelled off to the morgue ... no; police everywhere – completely healthy, whole new story.'

I didn't like the way his eyes fired up. The way he was so animated by this death. He told me to go and see Gloria while he tried to find out where they were taking the bodies. Then he stopped and put his phone away.

'Shona,' he said. His face crinkled into that smile, and it had my name on it.

'Right, see you then,' I said, bristling.

'Shona,' he said again. 'You're fantastic. Thanks.'

I left quickly, my head aching suddenly as it remembered to be hungover.

At the office, Gloria was on the phone, stabbing her hair with a prong.

'Uhuh,' she said. 'Uhuh ... uhuh.' She raised her prong in greeting and I made some tea. I gazed out of the window for a while. In the street below, a group of foreign children took photos of each other gathered round a bollard with a sack over the top. I wondered how I knew they were foreign. What was it about their faces or their clothes? And how on earth had their parents let them come to the plague capital of Europe? I drank tea and reached into the biscuit tin for a digestive.

The office was small and musty. There was a big desk, where Gloria sat, and a filing cabinet by the window and a little sink. There were also piles of cardboard boxes everywhere, full of fliers and minutes, and some hooks on the wall with a coat that had been there forever.

When Gloria finally came off the phone, she yawned with her whole body.

'Good Lord,' she said. 'That young lady had a lot to say.' I finished my tea and scrabbled in the biscuit tin for the crumbs, waiting for her to go on. 'A health and safety report on the Shelter,' she said, looking at me meaningfully.

I waited. Was I supposed to go and write one? Look for an old one? Tut because it was a waste of time?

'I think my health and safety file went up in smoke,' I said, buying time with a voice that could go either way.

She glugged her tea. I could hear it swilling in her mouth.

'There are some forms we have to fill in,' she said.

'Naturally.'

'And a visit from Environmental Health.'

'Oh.'

She opened her desk diary and began flicking through pages.

'Gloria,' I said, leaning on the filing cabinet. 'You realise that homeless people aren't being admitted to hospital? There's a clinic set up on the industrial estate.'

'Yes.' She grabbed a pen and wrote rapid notes in huge handwriting. 'Barrier nursing in an isolation ward,' she muttered, as if she were an expert on such things.

'But it's not a ward. It's a warehouse. It's like –'

'Shona, Darling.' She looked up. Her reading glasses made her quite scary. 'Cardiff is the epicentre of an epidemic. It's sensible to separate people. There are lots of places doing the same thing now, anyway. Bristol and Swansea, for certain. Newport, I think.'

I drew a zigzagging line in the dust on the top of the filing cabinet, on the edge where it wasn't covered with stuff.

'Have you been to the clinic?' I said.

She looked in her top drawer.

'Yes, yes I have.'

'When?' It came out confrontational, so I added, 'recently?' to try and dilute it but it made it worse. She stopped pretending to be busy and leant back in her chair to look at me.

'I was on the consultation committee that set it up. As a representative of the charitable –'

'But it's horrible.' She did, admittedly, look slightly uncomfortable. No wonder she'd kept quiet about this particular committee. I felt a bit stupid. 'You're in a good position to use your influence then.'

'Oh? In what way?'

I retraced my zigzag. 'People are not being treated properly at the clinic. It's a wasp trap. A way of drawing them away so they can't spread the germs.' She was looking at me as if I were overstepping some mark or other. 'If people were given the right treatment, they'd get better. But they're dying, Gloria.'

'The Alan Turners of this world are dying. Even with medicine, you need some strength to fight disease. And –'

'I saw a young woman die there. A healthy, strong young woman.' It wasn't quite true, she may well have been dead before I arrived, but it made the point nicely. Gloria swallowed and examined a nail extension. 'You have to speak out. It's inhuman and unacceptable!' I thumped the filing cabinet. Gloria stood.

'I admire your principles. But you have wound yourself up about perceived injustice where there is none. Why would it be in anyone's interests not to treat people? Heavens, they're rounding people up to treat them even before there are any symptoms.' Her nail extensions were getting quite a battering. 'The injustice is in being homeless in the first place, Shona. But that clinic is the safest place to be. There's no under-treating going on. Far from it.'

She could make words her own by sheer force of repetition. I was on the verge of telling her about Fflur, but I was terrified she'd have her arrested and registered and banged up in the warehouse. And I couldn't be sure Fflur had had whatever killed Kylie. Fflur had no cough and Kylie had no boils. The warehouse was full of the unlucky sods who had both.

A selection of newspapers sat accusingly on Gloria's desk, and most of them had photos I was pretty sure were Dan's. I didn't know at the time, that he had been aching for a by-line. He'd cherished fantasies of a little photo and his name beside his words and pictures. And now, when he was right in the midst of the big story and could have got himself A Career, he chose to remain anonymous.

His apocalyptic photographs had been arranged in montages that left out any hint of nursing care. It looked as if people had been stacked on trolleys and locked in to die. The papers were divided into the scourge faction, who seemed to feel that stricter segregation was an ideal way to kill off the homeless population safely, and the less extreme faction, whose prejudice was born out of fear; they were keen on donations of money and blankets. *The Big Issue* took a sturdier stance, but no one read it anymore on account of not wanting to go too near the remaining sellers. It seemed only a minority took the view that the industrial estate clinics were unacceptable and that hospital was the correct place for the victims of what was now widely known as Tramp Flu.

Gloria was furious.

'The last thing anyone needs is ghastly photographs of homeless people. Not great PR.' She hooked her handbag over her shoulder and rammed her sunglasses onto her head.

'Where are you going?'

'Coffee morning.' She opened the door. 'Brand awareness.'

The next day I met Dan by the river and we wandered about a bit, not quite settling on a conversational style – work or play, flirty or matey. We watched a gaggle of children who should have been in school (but whose teachers were probably secretly glad they weren't) throwing something at each other in a plastic bag. The weather was drizzly and cloudy; it could have passed for any time of year.

After a while, we walked halfway across the ricketiest bridge, where the water isn't too deep or too fast despite the little weir, and leant against the rail. Dan watched the dogs swim and I tried not to. From time to time, a cyclist came across, ignoring the 'dismount' sign and wobbling all the boards.

'Do you know any doctors?' said Dan. He hitched his jeans up a bit.

'Lots,' I said. 'Nain is on a lot of lists.'

'Waiting lists?' He jumped experimentally and the bridge wobbled.

'And follow-up lists. And referral lists. And lists of patients they don't feel up to seeing while they're trying to give up smoking or get over their divorce.' I stopped, hoping I wasn't being too irritating.

'I mean a friend who's a doctor. Someone we could meet for a drink.' I focussed hard on the *we* to shut out the sense of being technically useful in the manner of a hinge or a ball and socket joint.

A trout, shiny, silvery, in a moment of weakness, its mind on something other than survival, got marooned on a little rock where the water was shallowest, and a blackbird dropped out of nowhere, stabbed it in the eye and began to eat it. A paddling dog shot towards them, tongue out, and its owner called merrily, 'No-o, Sidney, leave it,' as if the monstrous scene were rather cute.

'I don't have any friends, Dan. Useful or otherwise.'

Dan stroked my cheek with the crook of an index finger. I shook him off and turned away to leave the trout some end-of-life dignity.

'School friends?' said Dan, shaking out a cigarette.

'I'm thirty – over thirty. Mid-thirties, really ...'

'Don't you do Facebook?'

'God, no.' I stepped to one side to look at his face. 'Do you?'

He laughed on an out breath, scattering a puff of smoke and spit. 'I bet you have an account.' He was really laughing; he held his fag out of the way and grabbed hold of my wrist. 'You do!' he shouted, wrenching my arm into the air and spinning me so that his arm was round my waist. I shut my eyes and he breathed into my neck a couple of times. When he let go and started smoking again, I said, 'Two of the girls in my class became doctors and there's another one who probably did. But I haven't spoken to them for years. And the first two were dainty little thugs who used to flick ink at a man on the bus because they said he was weird.'

Dan flicked his fag butt into the water. 'And he talked to himself and had BO?'

'You met him too.' I snuck a look at the trout. There were other birds there now.

'What about the other one? Did she flick ink at weirdos?'

A bobbing pony-tailed blonde jogged past us, the boards quivering under her feet.

'No, Debbie was OK. A bit nondescript. I sat next to her in chemistry.'

Dan turned his back on the jogging angel. There was a guinea-pig-sized dog splashing around and a teenage boy shouting 'Molly' at it. Other than that, and the birds belching over their fish supper, we were alone now. Dan took out his fag packet and looked at it.

'Gloria probably has chums in medicine,' I said.

Dan smiled. 'I want to try out a few ideas on someone.' He put the fag packet back in his pocket.

'I'm sure Gloria's chums can be very discreet,' I said, and we grinned at each other and I had to scratch my nose and say, 'OK. I'll Facebook her.'

'Good girl,' said Dan. I made a don't-patronise-me face.

9

I decided I'd given Nain long enough to stew and that pretending there was nothing wrong might be the best approach. I wanted to go home. I wanted Dan to grab hold of me and declare his love. I wanted the Shelter back. And the steadiness of nights of rescuing people from the streets instead of watching them die and not knowing what to do about it. What was I going to do with Fflur? And at what point should I decide that Colin was in need of a mental health assessment? He'd probably come through better without any busybodying. Fflur's administrations and thorough spring cleaning might work better than a social worker or community nurse crippling him with embarrassment in his own home. Fflur was busy ignoring her homeless, jobless crisis. Her eye was recovering by the hour and she seemed quite chirpy. Was I secretly glad she'd had a grotesque disfigurement when she met Dan? Possibly. Right. Pull yourself together, Shona. Rap on the door. Rat-a-tat-tat.

'Hi, Nain.'

I fixed an uncomfortable grin on my face and hopped about in a cheerful manner. Nain flung open the door and burst into tears.

'Shona, I've been so worried about you. I haven't slept for God knows how long. Fireworks make me feel like I'm back in the war years. And I *cannot leave the house*. It's just me and the television, and that's awful, *no one* seems to know what to do. They had a *government expert* on this morning and he didn't know any more than anyone else. Tramp Flu is sweeping across the country – and we have definitely got it worst – and we're powerless to stop it. There are only so many precautions you can take.' I'd manoeuvred past the invitations to ring for takeaway or adopt a child in an unspecified part of Africa, and other handwritten, hand-delivered envelopes I suspected of containing letters about my audacity and general nastiness. There was a spindly spider knotting together the corners of the ceiling.

'Nain,' I said, 'do you need a diazzy?'

She smudged her glasses on her blouse. 'None left,' she sniffed. 'And I can hardly go to the doctor, under the circumstances.'

'Maybe she'll come out and see you, if you ring?'

The carpet was crawling.

'But what if she's a carrier?'

I sighed and she followed me into the kitchen. She'd been eating tins from the back of the cupboard. Chickpeas and sweetcorn, mainly.

'She's probably been nowhere near anyone contagious. They've all been shepherded into a warehouse on the industrial estate.'

'Oh, thank goodness,' she said. 'But can they be sure they've got them all?' I tore a piece of card from a packet of cornflakes and found a biro. I wrote, *bread, milk, eggs*. Nain hugged herself. 'It is such a relief to have you home.'

'Although, strictly speaking, it was you who wouldn't let me in.'

'I wasn't in my right mind. And that girl's face blew up like a balloon.'

'Fflur's fine. The antibiotics started working straight away.'

'Good,' she said, though she sounded a little disappointed. 'Good.'

I tweezered a scrunched up support stocking between finger and thumb and dropped it in the bin.

'I might've got the pair somewhere,' said Nain, but she didn't take it out again. The crackling sound in the air around her was a lament which sang of hardship and loss, of the life she could have lived and all the things she'd never have got round to even if her daughter-in-law hadn't been a bolter and her son hadn't indulged in alcoholic melancholy (or melancholic alcoholism, depending on your theory of these things) and premature death, leaving her with a granddaughter round her neck.

I plugged in my mobile, showered, washed my hair and swilled with mouthwash, changed my clothes, settled Nain in front of something about converting garages, and set off for the library and the shops.

Some people were wearing face masks in the street, random people – a suited gentleman, a woman pushing a wheelbarrow full of plants, a stick thin girl with the shiniest, straightest hair imaginable falling past her waist.

In the library, I bagged a computer and experimented with some neck exercises while it choked on error messages and terms and conditions. I remembered Debbie Wong, and I was pretty sure she'd remember me. She wrote down everything the chemistry teacher said, in handwriting that looked like typescript. She had Chinese hair and round eyes, she said she wasn't allowed boyfriends and she cried silently the day the maths teacher left.

Her father was a dentist. I was supposed to do work experience with him after my GCSEs, but I got tonsillitis and missed it. There were vague plans to set it up again, but they never came to anything. Her mother worked as a lab technician at another school. Debbie did the work experience with her; she came back saying she'd decided to study medicine.

Debbie's Facebook photo was available for general viewing, but the rest was under wraps. Her hair was shorter than at school and her glasses were now purple, but it was definitely her. She was pictured clutching a baby in a panda costume, against a backdrop of sofa and cushions. I stared at her, looking for something in her expression that might tell me how she'd receive a friend request. I put, 'Hi! Do you remember Miss London's chem lessons? Would be good to catch up. Shona Davies.' I added, 'Need to pick your brains about something!' but I deleted it. She might turn out to be a specialist in sexually transmitted disease.

I'd have happily stayed in the library, where no one looked at each other and you could hide behind shelves of how-to books on knitting and beekeeping. Outside in the street I wasn't welcome. I was a germ dealer, a leper-toucher. I was going to have to consider Tesco. Sitting on the free bus with the grannies, clutching my reusable bags. Maybe I'd go vegetarian after all to spite the butcher, who stood in front of his door when he saw me coming. The woman in Star Fruit grabbed a basket and insisted on picking out my stuff for me, and not because I was a local VIP.

I queued in the chemist for some herbal lozenges that said on the back 'may help to induce a feeling of calm and aid sleep.' Nain was probably beyond herbal lozenges but perhaps if I gave her enough. My mobile rang. It was a stout fanfare of a ringtone that I'd set absentmindedly waiting for Gloria to finish her endless phone call. A woman with a pushchair smiled at me. The pharmacist was a hobbity little man, a wizard who conjured up haemorrhoid gel and statins, cough syrup and highly addictive headache tablets. He had a sort of burrow where he ate his sandwiches and took customers for confidential conversations. I imagined him uttering the words 'The test was positive,' and rubbing his hands together in the way he did when he wasn't counting pills or weighing something interesting in the manner of an ancient alchemist.

The screen on my phone said 'Dan'. Dan and I had exchanged numbers – something he had avoided during our heady week of lovemaking, but clearly now our relationship was a practical one this was fine. I said 'Hi,' and looked at a display of shrink-wrapped, security-tagged make up.

Dan said, 'Shona, where's Colin's granny?' The woman at the front of the queue swung her leg up onto the counter and unwound a bandage from her knee. The hobbit peered at it, rubbing his hands. 'All we need to do is produce her.'

'Dan, what are you talking about? I've never met Colin's granny. I didn't know he had one. What's she done?'

He laughed. The woman with the knee took a tube of something and paid in coins from her pocket. The pushchair lady was next.

'Word on the street is you buried her. Illegally.'

'What?'

The man behind me groaned. I shrank into my little bit of space, not wanting to breathe his recycled air.

'I'm supposed to investigate rumours that you were seen smuggling her body out in the night.'

'What?' The groaner prodded my arm. 'Hang on, it's my turn.'

I handed over the Serenity lozenges and a five pound note. Behind the counter was a shelf of animal delousing products. I gagged. 'Oh fuck,' I mouthed, but it came out audible.

'What's going on?' said Dan.

I took my change and edged past the central display, trying not to knock anything off with my bulky carrier bags.

'It was his dog, not his granny.' The hobbit and the groaner stopped in mid-exchange. I let myself out, the glass door ding-donging. 'Colin's dog died the day – or possibly the day before – we were quarantined. This is revolting, I know.' The ghost of its smell wafted around me. 'You have to understand this creature was Colin's only friend. Apart from me, I suppose. Oh God.'

'Shona?'

'He's very dedicated to his job. So he came to work – presumably he'd have dealt with the dog the next morning if we hadn't been locked in. And then he was a bit traumatised.' I felt suddenly hungry, irritable. 'I don't know why I'm getting defensive here. Just because you're a journalist, people have to tell you everything, do they?'

He sighed. 'I wish. I need your help here. We have to get the nurses to talk. That fat Jamaican one knows more than she's letting on. What's Gloria said?'

'That she won't have anything to do with it.'

He cursed. He sounded as if he was smoking crossly. I wanted to tell him not to smoke so much. And didn't want to sound as if I had domestic aspirations towards him.

'OK,' he said. 'But you have to help me. People are dying.' Déjà vu. And always spoken as if it were somehow my fault. As if they'd stop dying if I only tried harder.

I dumped my bags by the front door, and a hydrangea twig tore a hole in the plastic. Scrabbling for my key, I treated Dan to a huffing silence as a demonstration of something.

'Can you get here?'

'I do have a job, you know.'

'Doing what?'

'We're ... collecting blankets. And jumpers and things.'

Nain was making a silent pantomime of relief at my return. I sat on a kitchen chair, shook out some sweets and read the leaflet that came with the lozenges. Dan was talking to someone else, just too quietly for me to hear. I thought about clicking the little red button but the bastard got there first.

Nain was quiet when I said I was going out again. She was pale, and she managed to shoot more powerfully from her tremoring hand on the TV remote and her brimming eyes than she could have with a rant.

As I approached the bus stop, I passed a woman smoking and saying into her phone, 'I know ... jump in front of the train like that woman did and hold everyone up ... Got the girls round tonight. Get lashed, yeah.'

On a seat under the shelter, a teenage boy, hood halfway, was playing loud thumping music on his phone. The music was such an effective social deterrent that two women and a man stood just outside the shelter, getting drizzled on rather than going too near. I passed the time with an experiment: I sat a couple of seats away from him, caught his eye and smiled. He started to sing along. When the next track began, it was migraine-inducing white noise, and I told him so pleasantly, by way of conversation. He switched the track.

94

'What are you into?' he asked politely. I panicked because it's one of my all-time most dreaded questions – I have no idea what I'm into and I never have had. I wanted to say 'Tudor Rock' or something but I just swallowed and mumbled a bit. He said, 'I do have an iPod, but the battery's gone.'

'Oh, right,' I said. I wanted to ask if he was addicted to music, why the idea of going anywhere without it was so unthinkable. But the bus came then, and I could hardly track him to his seat.

I kept my head down on the bus and didn't look the driver in the eye when I bought a ticket. I don't think he looked at me either, so I wasn't thrown off the bus but sat slumped at the back staring out of the window as the streets got skankier and the people pushing prams got smaller. We idled on the flyover while an angry little jam took its time to disperse, and I had a clear view down onto the landfill. Smoke wafted across the skips where sofas and televisions languished with their insides hanging out. It came from a crackling fire, with bony animal legs sticking out at awkward angles. From where I sat, you couldn't see the heads. The streets would be clear of lolling tongues and fleas. And it felt like my fault. I felt personally responsible for this mass cremation. I watched smoke swirl and the pyre shift and jerk as each body sank into itself and took up less space. As if they had waited for me to be watching before they lit it. I let my breath steam a barrier on the window to wipe out the sight. Did eyeballs pop or melt? Did fleas explode when the flame hit them? And whose idea was this, to burn cats and dogs because people were dying? Didn't history show that that just left the rats free to spread the plague?

I got off the bus and went into the corner shop to buy some food and loo roll to take to Colin's. There was a group of young people to navigate, across the door and on the street, and I went for complete blanking as the most direct route. Passing the rec, I wondered if the earth looked odd to anyone else, where it was disturbed at the edge. Or if people swigged their cut price vodka, smoked and snogged each other unaware that they were sitting on a skeleton.

I puffed up the steps, my calves burning. Next door to Colin lived a woman who wore her dressing gown all the time and entertained on a rota. She was leaning on the doorframe, squinting at a notebook.

'Hello,' I said.

She adjusted her dressing gown cord. 'It'll rain again,' she said, and she disappeared inside and shut the door.

Fflur let me in. She was on the phone. I gave her a little wave and went through to the kitchen.

'I'm *trying*,' she was saying. 'But if I take just any old job, I won't have time to really make a go of the jewellery business and all that will be wasted … I know … exactly. Something part-time …Yes … In fact I don't feel like justifying myself to you. Are you going to help me or not?'

I leant through the kitchen door to give her a double thumbs up, but her voice grew quieter and I realised I wasn't supposed to be listening. I pretended I was just doing a little hand jive to a tune in my head. She'd spent whole days in Colin's company so I think I got away with it. I pottered about, opening the loo roll and putting the shopping away, and Fflur ended her call rather curtly.

It turned out she had been wanting to ring me; she'd been looking out of the window a lot, chewing her lip and wishing I'd come back. But she said she didn't like to bother me and I'd done enough already, both of which felt more like accusations than anything else. Colin was talking a lot but had stopped communicating altogether. She said she'd tried making spider diagrams to see if she could find any connection between what she'd asked him and what he said, but she was stumped. 'Do you think he's losing it a bit?' she whispered, clutching the handle of a new digital-age mop. 'It's been a bit stressful. With the quarantine. And the fire. And of course the dog, and –'

'Yes. Yes, I know.'

She swallowed and trod carefully to the sink to squeeze a contraption on the mop, gritting her teeth. Her jeans looked new.

'Has your Nain forgiven you?' she said. 'For bringing the lurgy into her house?'

'Vagrants' syndrome? She's delighted; she copes better with something to panic about.'

'Vagrants' syndrome. Is that the proper name?'

'I was being facetious.'

'All five vowels in the correct order,' she said, hooking the mop onto a tack in the wall. 'My dad taught me that word. He loved word games.' She looked even more beautiful than usual; a chocolate box daddy's girl. And I wanted so much to know what had become of her daddy, or what had wedged itself between them so that she couldn't admit she needed to come home for a while.

The mop was too heavy for the tack and it fell to the floor, taking a chunk of plaster with it. Colin didn't flinch. I picked up the mop and threw the plaster and the tack in the bin. Fflur made a guilty face and I shrugged.

'I *think* some of what he says makes sense,' she said, wiping the rim of the fridge door with an earbud. 'If you listen carefully.'

I looked across at Colin. He'd grown a rather unflattering beard, and didn't seem to have changed his clothes.

'Does he eat and drink?'

'Only when he thinks I'm not looking. I've been leaving plates of food out. Like he's a hedgehog.'

She pulled the earbud out from the rubber bit and looked pleased with the grime she'd picked up. I had a sudden image of the earbud emerging from Colin's ear and had to blink fast. I watched her kneel by the fridge and mummify a knife with kitchen roll. She slid this underneath and swept it from side to side. 'I was thinking I could sell my jewellery through eBay. You don't have the same overheads and you can make it to order.'

'Supposing eighty percent of them do it for reasons of personal advancement,' said Colin. 'Power, money and so on and so forth.' He appeared to be addressing the deck chair. An air freshener puffed like a little dragon, sending a plume of sickly-sweet particles into the air.

'Has he washed? At all?'

Fflur looked at the air freshener and shook her head. 'I haven't even witnessed any toilet activity.' She blushed. 'I don't mean witnessed. Obviously I wouldn't actually follow him in. He must do it while I'm asleep or out.' She tapped the table with a finger. 'And I don't think that's a coincidence. Do you want some salad?'

'Er, yes, go on then. Can I get you a cuppa, Colin?' I said brightly. 'I'm brewing.' *I'm brewing?* I watched myself assemble three mugs of tea in a set of bright pink mugs that had appeared on a little stand with hooks.

10

Colin had some interesting neighbours. There was a young man with particularly long arms and a lot of hair who laughed all the time. He liked to perch on the edges of available surfaces – bus stop seats, walls, yellow grit bins. He'd sit for a while, entertaining himself by flicking through amusing thoughts in his head until he became a Neanderthal Humpty Dumpty, rocking so much he slipped off his perch.

Less innocuous were the Disaffected Youths (I'd say Juvenile Delinquents but then I'd start singing, which is best avoided.) They seemed uncomfortable alone or in pairs but came into their own once three or more were gathered together. I think this was to do with pavement barricading, which is easier with three of you to spread out. In fact there was an affiliate member who was so big he could block a pavement on his own, but he was well over forty so he didn't really come into the same category. He was like a giant toddler, and his tantrums were hurricanes. You secured anything in his path and then ran for cover. At the base of the flats was a Community Noticeboard with hinged flaps that looked as if they had originally had glass in them and were perhaps opened by a nominated member of a residents' committee and then locked when a notice had been posted. Now the system involved a local band sticking fliers all over it with wallpaper paste, the Disaffected Youths scribbling on them, and then the Giant Toddler tearing them down as part of a rampage. He shattered car windscreens too, tore seats from the bus shelter and liked to finale by vomiting on the steps.

The Disaffected Youths saw the Giant Toddler as something of a role model. Whiling away their time by persecuting a family of Burmese refugees and throwing rubbish at a Pakistani lady with limited English, they dreamt of the day when they'd be obese enough to block a pavement single-handed and have brains so pickled their speech would be effortlessly incomprehensible.

Fflur came into the kitchen and sat cross-legged on the floor with her back against the wall, tipping out beads, rolls of thread and medieval surgical implements onto a tray. She said, 'Good. I'm glad you're here,' and held up a twirly necklace that looked like an optical illusion or a puzzle of some sort. 'Who do you think of when you see this?' She twisted it to and fro to help me think. 'I'm going to do celebrity endorsement. In some form or other. Is that a good idea, do you think?'

'Mm, definitely.' I examined some mini cheeses in the fridge, wondering which one to start with and why I'd bought them instead of normal sized cheese.

'I'm so glad you said that,' said Fflur. She leant her head back against the wall and her eyes swam a bit. 'Shona, I know you'll say this is frilly, but I feel like you were sent to rescue me. I would have ... who knows where I'd be if ...' I picked the cellophane off a nice young camembert and put it in my mouth.

Fflur laughed and sniffed. 'Can I have one?' she said, dropping the necklace on the floor.

From the sitting room end, Colin said quite loudly, 'I wish fish dish.' He came across to us, tapping his forehead in time to his footsteps. Fflur sucked on her cheese, waiting for clarification. When it didn't come, she said, 'If I had one wish, I'd wish for a hundred more. We used to say that at school.'

'We did too,' I said, blowing my nose on some of the scratchiest loo roll I'd ever come across. 'I should have got tissues.'

'Tissues,' said Fflur, patting her pocket. 'I'll start a shopping list. Is there anything else we need, Colin?'

'Cremation,' he said, banging his head with his fist. 'I wish I had cre-mate-ed my dog.'

'Oh,' said Fflur. 'Mm.'

'Is it too late?' said Colin, managing some fleeting but desperate eye contact.

'Yes,' I said. 'It is. Too late.' I left no room at all for doubt here.

'Point taken,' he said. 'Point taken point taken,' and he wandered back to his deck chair to catch a bit of television.

I felt a bit perkier for seeing Fflur. It certainly beat sitting at home with Nain. Even with Colin smelling away and chuntering on to himself.

We ate our way through the cheeses, none of which was quite ripe, sitting on the floor arranging beads in different line-ups. Fflur had boxes with measurements and grooves where you lined up the beads before you threaded them. It was nice, trying out colour combinations.

'I've put down Cameron Diaz, Judi Dench and both Minogue sisters,' said Fflur, wiping cheese off her hands and kneeling up. 'And I want to try and get onto a reality television thing. Do you know anyone in programming?'

'Gloria's bound to have chums in programming,' I said, 'whatever it is.' Fflur exploded in a crying-laughing fit. 'I'm serious,' I told her. 'Gloria has chums everywhere.'

'Oh Shona,' she gasped. 'Oh, Shona.'

I put a blue bead beside a green one and plain wood either side.

'Some of the girls I went to school with had parents in television,' I said. 'But they existed on a different plane to me. They'd have been nice to you, though.' I stood up and tried to touch the ceiling.

'Why?'

I looked at her. 'What do you mean, why?'

Gloria had erected, with the help of some volunteers, a six foot by three foot banner saying *Help the Homeless!* The exclamation mark irritated me; Gloria had been to many a charity ball, and she never saw the irony. In the face of Tramp Flu, collecting jumpers was probably about as useful as saucepans for battle ships or hair from barber shop floors to bung an oil spill.

They'd arranged themselves outside head office, banner overhead and three boxes at their feet labelled in marker pen: *knitwear, undergarments* and *foodstuffs*. They stood and waited: Gloria, Sandra of shitty appraisal fame, and three students – two girls and a boy. I watched from the street corner, wondering what the minimum on duty might be. A car pulled up, hazards flashing, and a woman got out and opened the boot. She swung two hefty plastic sacks with the People's Dispensary for Sick Animals logo (their loss our gain) onto the pavement.

'Must dash,' flapped the woman, hopping back into the car and cutting up a taxi. The taxi hooted as the students fiddled with the knots on the plastic sacks and Sandra continued a long phone call. I took a deep breath and approached.

'Hi,' I said.

'Hi,' said the boy and one of the girls. The other glanced at me and found me wanting at some primitive level. Sandra smiled tightly and turned away with her phone to her ear and her hand on her hip.

'Hello Darling,' cried Gloria. 'Super. We've got a great team on this morning, look.' She gestured at the students. They were sorting the contents of the People's Dispensary for Sick Animals sacks, though they were struggling a bit category-wise. The silent one held up a twiddly plastic candlestick and the others shrugged. And there seemed not to be an obvious place for lift-the-flap picture books or the sequinned clutch bag either. 'Hmm,' said Gloria thoughtfully. 'OK. I think we'll relabel the underwear box and call it 'misc'. If anyone does bring undies, they can go in knitwear.'

'What do you want me to do?' I said. 'You seem pretty organised here.' A fire engine shot past, scattering traffic. I've always been alarmed by fire engines, even before the Shelter went up in flames – fire spreads quickly, quicker than a fire engine can go, anyway, and I start looking round for an exit and wondering how near it is.

'OK. Right,' said Gloria, plumping up her hair and squinting at the sky. 'Cross fingers the rain will hold off for a bit longer. Now then, what I see you doing, Shona, is *engaging* with donors.' I had an image of people handing over their internal organs.

'What do you want me to say to them?'

Sandra coughed, pocketed her phone and sighed. The students finished emptying the sacks and put them in the misc box.

'The central message,' said Gloria, 'is that fear of the homeless will make the situation worse. Proactive support is –'

'Proactive support,' I said quietly. The students' ears pricked up. 'And the warehouse clinics come under that heading, presumably.' Sandra looked puzzled and dangerous. Gloria's cheeks burned and she loosened the top button of her quilted jacket.

'That is a matter for the Assembly in negotiation with Downing Street,' she said. She always spoke of these places as if they were as familiar to her as her own front garden. 'Clearly the charitable sector can't steer policy making at that level, however much we would like to. What we're about is –'

I rubbed my face. Sandra looked quite pleased that I was squirming and that Gloria was unsettled. Fortunately a man with a small child on his shoulders arrived. He had a medium-sized dog on a lead and was carrying a tricycle and a pile of jumpers.

'Hello *you*,' said Gloria to the child, reaching up to tickle its foot. The child flinched and clung to its dad's head, obscuring his vision with its miniature arms and fists. It buried its face in its dad's hair and sang a secret little song. The medium-sized dog got restless and the dad said, 'Ta-ta then,' handed over the jumpers and trotted off the way he'd come.

Sandra was on the phone again. The more talkative of the two girls said, 'Oh, there's something very attractive about a guy who looks after children and animals.' The other one lit a fag and harumphed. The boy looked undecided and got involved in refolding a jumper to avoid taking sides.

Some very thin drizzle was teasing us now, but it didn't look committed enough to settle in and could probably be stared down, certainly by Gloria.

'The rain will hold off,' she told the sky. 'For an hour or so, whilst we do the filming.'

'Filming?' I slid my hood up over my head and pulled the cord tight around my chin.

'Right on cue,' sang Gloria. Michael Blakelock MP, complete with nostril hair and a touch of dandruff, climbed out of a car and exchanged mutterings with his driver, checking his watch and patting his top pocket. The car pulled smoothly away and Minister Mike surveyed our tableau.

Gloria put out both her hands to squeeze both of his, kissed his cheek and said, 'Mwa.'

Minister Mike cleared his throat and proceeded to greet us all individually and with a very firm handshake.

Debbie Wong had come home to Cardiff to be a consultant psychiatrist and she lived in one of the expensive apartments on the waterfront with very few neighbours because no one else could afford them. Dan and I got off the bus a stop too early and had to walk down the long, straight road in the rain, checking off numbers. The rain paused for breath and returned as a heavy shelling of hailstones. Dan put his arm round my shoulders in a brotherly gesture and steered me into a tiny shop on the bottom corner of an apartment block.

'Shit,' he said to the woman behind the counter. 'They're made of steel those things.' He let me go and brushed melting hailstones off his jacket. The woman said nothing. She had fluorescent yellow hair with a shimmer of tangerine and her face was shiny. I looked at the front covers of the magazines on offer: *Sex to make him fall in love with you. What YOU need to be HAPPY* and *One rape too many.* Dan was buying chewing gum and checking the screen on his mobile.

'Do you want anything?' he asked.

'No, I'm fine.'

'Magazine?' He had his private joke expression on his face – I was never sure if I was in on the joke or the butt of the joke, or both. I sneezed several times in a row and opened the door. Dan waved at the shop assistant. 'Bye. Thank you for your hospitality,' he said and I sniggered and then wished I hadn't.

Debbie opened her front door as soon as we knocked.

'Shona,' she said. 'Wow.'

I laughed a bit and wiggled my bum for some reason. Then she laughed and we shook hands. I said, 'Thanks for agreeing to meet up.' She laughed again. She flicked her eyes over Dan's face and flushed.

'This is Dan,' I said.

Dan gave her a full-on Dan grin, shook her pudgy little fist warmly and said, 'Fantastic flat. I have *got* to see your views.'

The flat was immaculate, and Debbie had put out biscuits on a plate and a jug of something unappetising.

'Ginger tea,' she said and poured us all some. I sat on the beige leather sofa, which sank lower than I'd thought it would and farted loudly. Debbie sat on the floor and insisted Dan sit beside me, the biscuits in front of him on a solid wood coffee table.

'Long time no see,' said Debbie. 'How are things? So are you guys married?' She giggled and slurped her ginger tea. Dan drank some of his, looking at me with interest. 'Not yet, huh?' said Debbie and made a gesture which seemed to say *we'll leave that one for now.*

'Dan's a journalist,' I said. Debbie's face turned suddenly cold and I could see how she might look when she had to section someone for distasteful behaviour. Dan put down his tea and held up his hands.

'Guilty,' he said. 'But I'm as ethical as they come.' Debbie's eyes were locked with his, but she was warming through at the sound of his voice already, the words were secondary. 'I'm not story-structure led or sensationalism-seeking –' (the alliteration had a hypnotic effect; Debbie began to hum) '– I'm very much focussed on perceptions of truth and moral certitude.' He spread his hands to indicate that the concept was too subtle for words and suggest shared understanding between highly intelligent people. Debbie copied the gesture, which I thought was clever because I tend to nod emphatically when people do this and it doesn't fool anyone.

'We're investigating Tramp Flu,' I said earnestly, wondering if the filling in the biscuits was chocolate or chocolate flavoured, which is very different. Debbie pushed the plate towards me.

'I hung up my stethoscope a while back,' she said. 'I'm not really the best person to ask.' She looked at Dan.

Dan sighed. 'We need someone who can be discreet. And Shona suggested you.' I bit down on my biscuit and scraped a few millimetres of cheek cells with it.

'Do you have questions? Or answers?' said Debbie, topping up our tea. Mine was still pretty full. Dan did coy *I'm just a layman* prevaricating, pretending to drink. 'I read on the net about the germ warfare theory.'

'It could be,' said Dan with just a hint of melodrama. 'In fact –' he glanced at me. 'This is something I've not yet voiced. I haven't entirely ruled out government conspiracy.'

Debbie's antennae pricked up. How dare he turn up in her flat on her day off? I allowed a pause. I'd not seen Dan squirm before.

Carol says I need to do more positive self-talk. She's right; the constant rattle of revulsion can't be a worthwhile use of time and energy. The noticing a hundred times a day what I've already established yesterday and all the days before that since I can remember (really – we're talking five or six years old here): that there is so much of me, that I stick further out into the world than I should, take up more than my share of the space available. As if by jutting, rolling, sticking out, I'm trespassing on other people's space. And the delicate thin people either stay quiet and meek in smug keeping with their neatness or else enjoy making the most of what they've got left over by filling it with living, breathing more fully instead of keeping it all in, afraid to breathe too much for fear of swelling even further. My posture is a continual apology for my bulk. Nain, incidentally, is about my size, though this has never been acknowledged. Benny's wiriness is, I think, down to more than just cigarettes and twitching; there could be something genetic involved

104

which she withheld from me out of spite. She's scraggy too, now she's knock-ing on a bit. Sagging where her skin's reached out for flesh it never found. I wonder if she looks at herself and sees the absence of flesh. Sees what isn't there instead of what is. It's an inverse form of self-hatred, but it might be just as violent as the one she cursed me with. Or maybe it's more wistful, the longing for, rather than the wishing away, which will always be more aggressive, more energy-sapping. Longing for, you can do with a puff of a cigarette or a sip of something glutinous – these would look greedy on someone who's wishing away. The wishing away of yourself is a more immediately destructive business. Actually visualising – no, more than visualising, it's a multi-sensory activity – imagining that you could slice, sculpt, melt, grate away at your edges. Of course when you actually start trying, then you've taken it a whole step further. It's quite difficult here, though there's usually a chance to hide a hair clip in your knickers and the edges of those can be good if you buff them on the side of the bed frame. I asked Benny to smuggle me in something sharp and discreet, but she was against the idea. Not so much because of the risk of being seen to be complicit with my self-harm (as if she could ever be vindicated) but more because of the attention it affords me. I get watched, and that's something she's never been. She looked quite snooty when I asked her; no Darling, it simply doesn't do to go sawing away at yourself. Rather gauche, don't you think? *And she has definitely indulged – you don't get herringbone lines on your arms from sunbathing with your watch on. She is of course far too old for self-harm now, and I imagine that irritates her. Fifty-somethings aren't a priority target market for concern groups, on the outside.*

Debbie rang when I was sitting at the kitchen table doing a crossword from the local paper. It was so easy it was almost difficult.

'Hi Shona? I've put out a few feelers. And I really think we can take this disease at face value. TB is latent in quite a proportion of the population and it's poverty and poor health that allow it to flare up.'

'But TB doesn't give you boils.' I sucked in my tummy and did some token marching on the spot.

'No. But the MRSA is riding the same wave; people are weakened by one and more likely to succumb to the other.' I drew an elephant's bottom on the edge of the crossword and made its tail really long, swirling it round the very short paragraphs in the paper. 'Imbalances in public health are there in most societies,' said Debbie. She made a little 'uh' sound that suggested I relax my tunnel vision.

'Yes,' I said firmly. 'You're probably right.' I started on a circular pig.

'Do you think your friend will keep looking for people to blame?' she said carefully. I joined the pig's squirly tail up to the elephant's.

'I think he's absolutely right there's someone to blame.' Clearly the instinct to defend Dan was urgent because I suddenly sounded like Gloria pre coffee time. 'Herding people into a warehouse is making things worse almost as quickly as –' my pen tore a hole in the paper, ruining the edge of the crossword. 'It's a pretty effective form of genocide in itself.'

'Hey,' said Debbie. 'I can tell this is something you feel strongly about. But believe me, doctors don't get to pick and choose – everyone gets treated in this country. I mean, you know, we resuscitate murderers, it's –'

'What? How are we talking about murderers, for God's sake?' My eyesight was fuzzy; I could see crossword squares wherever I looked. 'I'm sorry to dislodge your world view, but –'

'Uh-huh.' Debbie made *I-hear-what-you're-saying* and *absolutely-not* noises while I took hold of myself.

'Sorry. You weren't suggesting.' I blinked the crossword squares back into place.

'No. I used the wrong example there. It was inappropriate.'

'Yes.' I had some cheddar sticks and peanut butter in the fridge, but the reception was patchy on that side of the kitchen. 'OK,' I said. She talked for a bit about the long-term pattern of epidemics in society until I cut her off. 'Thanks, Debbie. Thanks for looking into it. I'll talk to Dan. We just ... well ...' I edged a bit nearer, wondering if I could hook the fridge door open if I stretched enough. 'Right.'

'OK.' Debbie laughed.

'Well, thanks –'

'Do you want to meet up for lunch? Coffee or something? Ginger tea?' she laughed again.

'Yeah,' I said. 'Great.' She drew the laugh out a bit and I struggled with the etiquette for fixing a date with someone you're both pretending you used to be proper friends with and you only got in touch with because you've become a sort of personal assistant to a man you're desperate for attention from. 'We could –' I started, but Debbie said, 'Not to worry. Cheers,' and put the phone down.

What use was a psychiatrist when you had boils and lung disease? The cheese sticks were a bit hard where I hadn't sealed the cling film tightly enough but I ate my way through them, scraping the edges of the peanut butter jar. Quite a bit of cheese broke off and it made an interesting paste.

Dan didn't answer his phone and then the next time I tried it went straight to voicemail. I imagined my name flashing on the screen and Dan clicking *busy*. I wondered what it was that he was busy doing. Never a healthy route to go down but I couldn't help it. Generally, it took the form of an anonymous other woman sitting across a table in a cosily cool cafe-bar, communicating with him through economical little gestures and amusing asides. From time to time the other woman became Fflur or Suzy (though oddly never Gloria), and I felt as venomous as if my imaginings were real. The venom turned rapidly to self-disgust, of course, because I was clearly a jealous covetous ferret of a woman incapable of loving or being loved. The downward spiral became so automatic it could take place subconsciously and within seconds, so very quickly the act of clicking on his name on my contacts list was enough to have me grinding my teeth and scowling.

I scuffed down the high street, wondering when charity shops had achieved such a monopoly – every other shop front was a hospice/animal-rescue/save the other side of the world establishment full of characterless clothes and vhs tapes (five for a pound). The two most recent attempts to open chic little deli-cafes had been more pitiful than usual, lasting only weeks. I held my phone in my hand so I could stare at it every few steps in case Dan rang back. I glared at the butcher through his blood-shot glass and he glanced up. Most people can tell when they're being stared at; it's something I discovered early on in my career as an icily detached anthropologist. If you're looking out of a bus window at someone approaching on the pavement and you try to catch their eye, they will look back at you. Even though the street and the bus are full of people, they sense you staring. Maybe it's just me. Maybe I have a particularly hard stare.

I decided I'd walk from the traffic lights to the roundabout and back, and then try again. I thought about stopping for a seasonally-iced biscuit in the bakery, but the queue was coming out of the door. When I reached the traffic lights, I leant against the churchyard wall and rang him. It was a risk; there was a limit to the number of missed calls I wanted with my name on them.

It rang five times while I made a tight fist of my left hand and stared at the sky until it hurt my eyes.

'Shona!' He sounded breathless and suspiciously jovial.

'Oh, hi.' He'd caught me off guard; it sounded as if *he'd* rung *me*.

'Where are you?'

'Why?'

He laughed. 'No reason. I just like to picture you when I'm talking to you.'

That did things to my insides. I giggled like the carefree schoolgirl I'd never been.

'Well,' I said. 'I'm leaning on the churchyard wall in the high street, if that helps.'

'Yes. Yes, it does. Thank you.' I surfed a three or four second silence, sensing his sideways smile. 'How can I be of help?'

'Um. I spoke to Debbie. She rang me.'

'OK.' There was a lot of pressure in that OK.

'Basically, she just said Tramp Flu is exactly what it seems. She said it was inevitable some people would talk about terrorists and germ warfare, or government conspiracy or whatever, because they always do when there's a panic. But it is what it is, and it's just that somehow the weather conditions or the movement of people this winter has triggered or magnified things.'

'She said it in those words?'

'I didn't record the call, but that was the gist of it. It was good of her to ask around.' Dan sighed. I was faintly amused, as well as irritated and desperate and all those other things, because I realised Dan was sulking. He was too cool to sulk, but I could almost feel him stamping his foot. I could hear him breathing. 'Shall we talk about something else?'

'What?' He was rather taken aback. I was pretty surprised myself.

'Um. Anything, really. I wasn't thinking of anything particular. I just thought ...' I had my eyes shut now, I couldn't quite believe my own audacity. 'I just thought it would be nice to talk about something else. For a change.'

'I know,' he said. 'I'm sorry, Sweetheart.' I took the Sweetheart in my hand and curled my fingers round it gently. 'I'm a bit single-minded.'

'A bit ...?'

'I need to get out more.' I heard a coy little giggle escape from my face and echo down the airwaves. I heard him smile. 'Maybe I should lighten up. Wear a red nose and get a squirty ring.'

'A squirty ring?' I realised I was beaming all over; a lady with an expensive coat and newly set hair smiled as she passed by in a slipstream of hairspray.

'You must have had those. Going-home bags at birthday parties always had squirty rings.'

'You went to parties?' I squeezed in against the wall to let a rhinoceros of a man steam past in a bulldozer for the disabled.

'Yes. Of course I did. Squirty rings 'til about six or seven, then football or swimming for a few years and then we graduated to throwing up in each other's gardens.'

The rhinoceros held up the traffic as he bulldozed his way across the road.

'Did *you* have parties?' I said. 'When it was your birthday?' The need to know felt intense – I wanted to magic myself into Dan's past, to know him, to see the little boy who became the man of my dreams.

Dan sniffed. 'One. My mum did pass the parcel and squirty rings when we were on the cusp, and I got teased a lot so I told her I wasn't bothered after that.'

I laughed. 'Say no more.' I was floating, it was lovely.

'I still got invited, though. I wasn't a total outcast.' Dan was laughing too. 'I wasn't some nerd who had to spend lunchtime in the library to avoid getting his head kicked in.' I thought of Colin hiding in the shed by the rec. 'How about you? Did you do parties and stuff?'

'Er, no.' I don't like birthdays, particularly my own, though other people's are bad enough, because of the pressure to make sure they have a Nice Day. I cleared my throat. 'Not really, no. But I wasn't a nerd. In retrospect that would have been better. It worked for Debbie. Nerding's an investment, it sets you up for life.' The sound of Dan's laugh was wonderful. 'I was just a misfit, but I never liked parties anyway.' I watched a Whitchurch hospital regular stagger past with a lot of luggage.

Dan was rustling, reaching for a cigarette. A girl in a mesmerising sari, bright sky blue and hot pink, walked past me without a glance. She was chirruping into her phone in an Indian language and she was quite clearly flirting. Successfully. I wanted to stop her and ask for some tips.

'I'd have invited you,' said Dan, sucking on his cigarette.

'Thanks.' I was flat now, tired. Flirting was exhausting, it seemed. Maybe your stamina improved with practice.

'Anyhow,' he sighed. 'Thanks for trying with Debbie. We couldn't have known she'd be a dead end.' This felt very much as if it was my fault. 'It's a shame we can't just sidle up to the Chief Medical Officer or the Minister for Health or Homelessness or whatever and say, *Right, listen to us you chinless wonders.*' He made a sound like the last suck on the cigarette. 'We'll have to rely on Gloria's chums.'

11

Passengers at airports were being scrutinised and anyone even slightly grubby was banned from flying. People were holding their breath at the check-in desk in case a stray cough or sneeze escaped, and trying hard to look affluent and perky. There was footage on the television of people outraged that they'd been deemed too scruffy to leave the country – or, more to the point, enter another one.

The Australians put a ban on British imports as well as British visitors, which was viewed as extremist at the time but perhaps they were simply ahead of us. They stopped even stopovers at Heathrow or Gatwick, and anyone too pale was viewed with suspicion. Rabies they had, scorpions, venomous snakes and skin cancer, but Tramp Flu they were holding out against. India was alarmingly relaxed and positively welcoming. Perhaps for the homeless population of Mumbai, Tramp Flu was a drop in the ocean. Other than India (and the Falkland Islands, who showed admirable solidarity – your disease is our disease), the rest of the world was quick to name and shame the UK as the home of Tramp Flu. There were people in far off lands who were talking about Wales as if they'd always known it existed.

Gloria's tame MP nabbed a slot on telly and explained that it was in fact a very good thing that Alan Turner had chosen to die in someone's shed, because if he hadn't, he might have done it somewhere secluded and rotted away quietly without becoming a warning beacon to us all. He spoke as if he had personally seen to the closure of the hostels, and kind of implied that the fire at the Shelter had been his radical solution. As if burning the source of the germs would help to get rid of them. And there seemed to be no doubt in his mind that the Shelter really had been some sort of foul epicentre, despite cases of Tramp Flu now being diagnosed across the UK. He did some enigmatic nodding and some hand gestures and face-scrunching to show that, though some things were to be regretted, he wouldn't be apportioning blame. And some bastard put a photo taken of me the night of the fire on the screen. I look guilty, like someone snapped on their way to court, perverting the course of justice perhaps. Fortunately, Nain was deeply involved in adjusting her wrist splints at the time, and I was able to position myself between her and the screen and engage her in conversation about the Velcro straps until the danger had passed.

Dan and I joined a crowd of people in front of the hospital jumping up and down in Minister Mike's face. I felt like a rather gormless football supporter, carried along with the tide, unsure exactly what I was supposed to be doing. Then a voice slashed through the chaos.

'Would the Minister like to comment on the barbaric and arbitrary culling of animals?' She repeated this, and various bits of it – 'Barbaric! Arbitrary culling! Minister!' (Puff puff, leap, leap) 'Minister, animals! Animals Minister!' And whilst there were maybe fifty people altogether jostling and shouting, plus aides, the odd police officer, a clinical manager woman in terrifying spikes and the people trying to catch it all on camera, her voice and her face crawled to the front of my awareness and began a slow throttle of my windpipe. She saw me, gasped, and made a snappy decision to keep leaping about for a while to buy time while she decided what to do about me. She looked as if she was skidding to a halt and ready to bite but the Minister chose the moment to address the matter of the cull. He spread his hands in the manner of a schoolteacher surrounded by children demanding to be picked first, and sighed so that his nose hair quivered and stilled. Turning to Benny, he cupped his hand around her bicep. Lower and it would have been aggressive, shoulder height and it would have been patronising; the bicep-cup was clearly a device he'd found to work. Benny snarled and pawed the ground, and he said, 'OK, I hear you want to talk about the animal issue.'

'Animals aren't issues,' she hissed. It was on the tip of her tongue to say, 'they're people.' I could see her form the words, but Minister Mike continued.

'It's a terrible price to pay and a painful priority to ... prioritise ... but the limitation, the damage limitation, has to be priority.' He sighed, deeply regretful, though largely at the collapse of his rhetoric.

'And animals aren't priority, huh?' Benny had her arms folded and was narrowing her eyes. He continued to look deeply regretful and allowed his silence to speak for him, and Benny shut up much faster than she would have if he had kept talking. He glanced at an aide, who snapped her fingers at the cameras and positioned herself in an upright starfish to let him through. As I backed away, Minister Mike took a moment to press Benny's hand, vicar-like, between his own sticky paws. She treated him to an *I haven't finished with you yet* glare, but her heart wasn't in it. She must have guessed I was planning to make a run for it just as soon as I could get control of my thoughts and my legs. A woman tried to tackle her about how she dared to say some mangy dog was more important than the welfare of children, but Benny scooted past her, dodging a tired-looking guy kicking a tripod stand that wouldn't fold in on itself.

'Look who it isn't,' she said loudly. Reluctantly, I looked at her. It made my teeth ache. The crowd began to disperse. An ambulance siren shot past outside the hospital grounds. I lost the stare-out and flicked my eyes to the tarmac. She let a delicate breath of false laughter escape, as if I'd tried to say something amusing and failed. *Right, I'm going*, I told myself. *I'm not sticking around to be treated like this.* She took a step towards me and I saw it before she got a check on it: she needed me to speak to her – no, she needed me to need to speak to her. So obviously I looked at my watch. Pathetic, but I didn't have a lot of thinking time. She produced a leaflet from the khaki camouflage-print bag slung across her body, and held it out like a challenge. I made a confused face – *you what?* And she had to stuff it back in the bag.

Dan appeared by my side, ignored her completely and hung something round my neck.

'Press pass,' he said. He took my arm and began to pull me in the direction of the disappearing posse.

'Shona love?' Benny sounded hurt, stoic and threatening all at once. She was pretty jealous of the press pass too. Dan stopped and turned to look at this bristly-headed guerrilla and then at me, irritated, fascinated.

I shook my head and sighed. I let Dan go to the press conference while I went with my mother to the pseudo-Italian cafe-bar over the road from the hospital.

Benny, like many victims of the smoking ban, was clearly unused to sitting at a table for longer than a few minutes at a time. But she'd decided to check me out and she wasn't going to risk losing sight of me until she'd scratched that particular itch. She wriggled her hand around in a button-down pocket on her combats to forage for change, and counted it out on the table. Having established that she had £1.67, she asked the stunning Chinese waitress for biscotti and a 'builder's tea'. I tried not to stare at the waitress. She had achieved a dreamy haze of colour above her eyes so that you couldn't tell where it started or finished or where the lavender became baby blue above her thick, soft lashes. I made a point of looking bored and the waitress smiled with slightly forced serenity as if I was a child or perhaps a pet of some sort.

'Coffee, please. Milk, one sugar. Thanks.' I could feel myself blushing as the waitress retreated. I rearranged some greasy sachets of mayonnaise and ketchup. Then Benny and I had a little battle as to who could look least interested and most immune to the pressure to start a conversation. This lasted, impressively, until the waitress returned. At the counter were some fudgy cake things behind a bullet-proof case. I told them silently that I wasn't in the mood, I was just there to fulfil some perverse kind of daughterly duty. Then I'd be off. Stuff to do. *Stuff.* I knew that Benny would be wildly jealous of my involvement with *stuff.* She loved that kind of thing, and it didn't fit with her mental filing system in which I slotted neatly into 'Conformist, mundane. Plain, bordering on invisible.'

A woman in a suit and a man carrying his jacket on one finger strode into the cafe and sat at the table in the middle.

'God, Viv will walk in on Monday and say we've hijacked her job,' said the woman, sniggering.

'Yup. That's the vision,' said the man, tugging his tie loose. They launched into lads-with-business-clout banter, breaking off for a moment to order a bottle of wine without looking at the menu.

'We've got an underground animal shelter going,' said Benny, leaning back in her chair, and falling on her sword in the *who'll-care-enough-to-start-a-conversation* battle. I conceded victory elegantly.

'Underground?' I said, making little scrabbling paw actions.

'You were always so *literal,*' she sighed. 'I mean the location is need-to-know. The owners hand them over after dark and they're taken to the centre anonymously.' I began on my coffee. 'There's a coded system of identity and care plans. It's taking off.' She snapped a biscotti, exploding crumbs and splinters which she picked up one by one on a licked finger.

The woman in the suit guffawed at something her colleague said about Viv's incompetence.

'So you don't think the animals are involved in disease spreading? I've seen some pretty gross animals. Boils and coughing up blood.' She looked long-suffering and generally superior.

'It is so rare,' she said, 'for an animal disease to be contagious to humans. Rocking horse shit.' She bit down hard on a biscotti (the plastic sheath said *almond snap*). I swallowed a mouthful of coffee and looked at her.

'Rocking horse shit,' I repeated.

'It's a medical term,' she said condescendingly, 'meaning extremely rare.'

I took a biscotti/almond snap. It was thin and managed to be both sticky and dry at once which isn't great in a biscuit. My jaw hurt as I forced it into swallowable globs.

'Did you finish that access course?' I asked. 'Are you qualified to use terms like rocking horse shit?'

She'd launched into the nursing access course with gusto: a year of literacy and numeracy, essays on social issues and time on the wards in a nurse's uniform, shovelling shit in the name of work experience (possibly rocking horse shit). Nain sniffed a lot, because Benny had never completed any section of the free education she'd been offered and the grant she was given to cover uniform costs, books and a laptop was incredible. I think she even tried for a childcare grant but someone found out I was in my thirties. She covered her tattoos in starched polycotton and found a way to pin a cap to her stubble. When I saw her in her uniform (she came round on a flimsy pretence of needing someone's number) I allowed myself a brief foray into a parallel universe.

Now, she sniffed at my question.

'Ridiculous,' she said. 'Lot of tossers.' Clearly, when she realised she had to wipe people's bums, she'd scarpered almost as quickly as she had when she saw how often mine needed doing as a baby. 'Busy at the Shelter?' she said, pierced eyebrows raised.

At home, I said, 'By the way, I bumped into my mother.'

Nain clasped her throat, gripped the back of a kitchen chair and sank down into it as if she were breathing her last. I spat my chewing gum into a tissue and did a couple of lunges while I waited.

'Where?' she croaked. 'Did she see you?'

I stood up, my knees clunk-wobbling into place. 'We went for a coffee.'

'You planned it!' she shrieked. 'Don't *by-the-way* me, Shona Davies.'

I yawned and gave up on my stretches. 'Why would I do that?' I said. 'I fancy a take away.'

She narrowed her eyes. 'Where from?'

'Chinese?'

She considered this. 'Do you think they're in the clear?'

'I don't think you can get Tramp Flu from chow mein, Nain,' I said, and rummaged in the overstuffed letter rack for a menu.

'All I'm saying is the delivery staff are a bit of a mix,' she said darkly.

I ordered chow mein, sweet and sour pork balls, fried rice and prawn crackers, and wandered into the front room to stare at the television.

Nain spent a while rearranging the mess in the kitchen and then she came to sit with me and wait impatiently for the take away.

I had a mouthful of pork ball when she said, 'So what did she have to say for herself, then?'

'She's working in an animal rescue centre,' I said, and then I had to repeat it when I'd swallowed the pork ball. 'She's hiding people's pets, to avoid the cull.'

'Typical,' said Nain. 'People are dying and all your bloody mother cares about is animals.' I ate the remnants of the chow mein straight from the foil tray. A chunk of garlic burst as I chewed and I knew it would stay with me through at least one teeth brush. 'She didn't finish the course then?' Nain dipped her finger in the polystyrene cup of sweet and sour sauce. I shook my head and shuffled back into the sofa, shutting my eyes. 'Typical,' she sniffed. Everything Benny ever did was 'typical', which is odd when you consider the extreme range and unpredictability of her behaviour.

'She invited me to visit her animal place,' I said, garlicky and sleepy. Nain made a sound of such epic ridicule that I said, 'I'm going, actually,' to see if she could top it.

She froze for a few seconds, and then set about trying to stack the slimy foil dishes, bowls and spoons. I kept my eyes shut, fantasising as I sometimes do about a switch you could flick on your shoulder or somewhere to send yourself to sleep. It's not as simple as it sounds, because someone else would have to switch you on again, unless you had a very reliable timer. Nain dropped the dishes on the floor and tried to recreate the force of her epically derisive snort. It didn't have the same impact, though, despite the things spilling everywhere. I opened my eyes but didn't move. She gaped at me, sauce-sticky hands staining her clothes.

'You'd watch a cripple sweep the floor before you'd lift a finger,' she said. 'Look at you.' I got up, picked up the stuff and took it into the kitchen. She followed me. I dumped it all in the sink and turned on the tap full blast, so that it splashed in all directions. 'What are you so cross about?' snapped Nain.

'I'm not cross,' I said. 'I'm tired.'

'You're always tired.'

I turned off the tap and dried my hands on my sweatshirt. 'Yes, I am,' I said. 'Maybe I have ME or something.' I grabbed a glass to take some water to bed.

'ME?' said Nain. 'Is this a sick joke?'

'Sorry. If anyone has ME around here, it's you.'

'And what exactly do you mean by that?' she said, glaring witchily at me. I held up my hands in surrender. I didn't know what I meant; everything and nothing. My mother's capacity to cause an argument is impressive. She doesn't even have to be anywhere near you; she'll be winding people up from beyond the grave. 'You do realise,' said Nain suddenly, 'that this house is in my name.'

'It's a council house, Nain.'

'With my name on the papers.' She traced a signature on her left palm with the index finger of her right hand. I hovered in the kitchen doorway. Nain scratched her head with both hands.

'Would you like me to move out?' I said. She blushed and blinked. 'I was going to wait until I was a grown up, but I could go now if you need the space.'

'All I'm saying,' she muttered, rocking a bit, 'is that whilst you live under this roof I would rather you didn't go meeting up with your bloody mother. It's adding insult to injury.'

I glugged my glass of water and went to fill it up again. Nain swallowed and coughed and swallowed again.

'That's settled then,' she said. 'If she comes round, or rings, or sends one of her awful little notes –' (it was *years* since she'd sent me a note. I'm not saying they weren't hypocritical and sentimental, just that there hadn't been one for a very long time and it seemed a bit much to drag them up) '– then we ignore. Ig. Nore.' She made a gesture of finality.

'I'm exhausted. I'm off to bed.'

I was tempted to leave it there but it wasn't long since she'd left me on the doorstep begging for a toothbrush, so I thought it might be best to clarify things.

'Nain,' I said. 'I know my mother is a complete nightmare, but she's got some contacts that could be useful for – well, for a friend of mine who's ... campaigning, I suppose you'd call it.' Nain looked ready to explode; with tears, shouting, indignation, hurt feelings, and acute and chronic non-specific distress. I made a pathetic attempt to squeeze her hand, and she flapped me away. 'I'm just going to visit this animal centre, and see if they can help me, and my – my friend.' I felt my throat constrict around the word. 'And then I'll probably ignore her for another decade or so.'

'Shona, what's got into you?' Nain's voice was wobbly with fury. 'You hate animals, you can't stand your bloody mother, and you're choosing *them* over *me*.'

'I'm not choosing anyone,' I said. 'But I do have a life, and friends. I have places to go and people to see. I can't be here all the time.' I was tired, and it was an effort to remain vertical. Nain, however, was fired up by the exchange of unpleasantries.

'This is an ultimatum,' she said. 'Either you tell your bloody mother you've changed your mind and you're not going to her little flea pit, or you go and live with those *friends* of yours.' Her nostrils flared. She was rocking quite violently now.

'Nain,' I said. 'We're both tired. Let's go to bed.' I reached out to pat her shoulder but she shrugged me off. Her eyes went watery.

'Shona,' she whispered. 'Say it. Tell me you won't go.'

I sighed. The sooner I let her kick me out, the sooner she'd be pleading with me to come back, and I didn't like to leave her on her own too long.

'I'll get my stuff,' I said. 'I'm taking a bag this time.' I stomped out of the kitchen. From the hallway, I called back, 'With *several* changes of clothes.'

It's easy enough to get diazepam here. I don't have to lift a finger, so to speak. There's a girl with the figure of a model and she likes people to watch her take off her clothes. We shut ourselves into the showers or she drops into my room during handover, and she strips and wriggles and purrs. I get maybe 10mg. How she gets hold of it is her business, I'm afraid. She speaks very infrequently and very quietly. It makes you want to fill in the gaps, because she often doesn't reply even when you address her directly. Pure Victim; you'd have to dig deep to find much else. I suspect her of exercising on the quiet. That pert little bottom can't be effortless, however picky you are about your food.

Outside the Learning Centre window, the daffodils are flowering. Trumpets fanfaring out of the ground after long months lying low pretending to be onions.

Gloria rang, and I wasn't sure why. I had the feeling she was waiting for me to say something – as if there was a question she wanted me to ask, or a secret she'd found out and she wanted to see if I knew but she was waiting for me to mention it first in case I didn't. That sort of thing. I admitted to being at Colin's, though I didn't go into the business with Benny or the fall out with Nain. After a while I began a game with myself to see how little I could say. I wondered what Gloria's average talk-to-listen ration was. Ten words to one? I tried making notches on the edge of the newspaper in batches of five and established that it wouldn't be too ambitious to go for fifty-to-one. 'Right,' I said. 'Uh-huh.' And, 'No?' She told me about a meeting she'd had with Michael (she often omitted 'Blakelock MP' now) and how her chums in the House of Lords were muttering about new legislation on homelessness.

'What sort of legislation?' I said, using up four of my allowance but I reckoned she'd come back with two hundred no problem.

'Legislation to protect the most vulnerable end of the socio-economic scale,' she began. 'In a rather revolutionary way. A collaborative private/ public sector initiative that might be rather powerful.' She chortled; it was a sound that seemed to involve all her teeth. 'We've got some power houses in the Lords these days, it's not the fuddy-duddy institution people take it for.'

'No?'

'Oh, Shona, you remind me of me.' (God, I hoped not.) 'When I was your age I didn't believe anyone the other side of fifty was capable of anything remotely revolutionary.' I looked out of the window, sighing. The gentleman who lived on the ground floor was striding out with the previous day's newspaper rolled up and held aloft like a weapon, in order to purchase today's paper. He always took the precaution of timing his excursion so as to be home and dry before the Disaffected Youths were awake and could start throwing things at him.

After a while, Gloria interrupted herself and said, 'Hmm,' as if she had confirmed a suspicion. 'How are you?' she said. 'On a scale of nought to ten? Wellbeing-wise?'

'Um ...' I scrabbled about for an answer. My first thought was five-ish, but it felt non-committal. Six seemed a bit heady, though, considering, and four might sound ungrateful for the roof over my head.

'Five?' I said. 'Ish.'

'OK ...' She wanted more.

'And you?'

'Ooh,' she said. 'A good seven. Now promise to let someone know if you drop below four.' I'd suspected there was something about four. No doubt she had a chum in therapy. I had to get her off the phone quickly then, because I could tell she wasn't far off giving me the number.

'Well, I'll let you get on,' I said.

'Yes. I must dash. Let me just check my Post-its.' *Oh, please, don't try and make me See Someone.* 'Ah, I know what I've been meaning to ask you. Have you considered internet dating?' I was impressed. She'd had me so busy dodging the therapist I hadn't seen it coming. 'It's more your sort of thing than that awful speed-dating concept.' She spoke as if this was something we'd already discussed and agreed. 'Like you say, the great thing about the internet is that it can all be asynchronous until you're ready.'

'What?'

'You get time to reflect. And to plan. But don't over-edit yourself or you won't make any headway at all. These things are a balance.'

'Of course.' I wondered if I could get her back onto therapy.

'Right. God bless.' She was gone. I made a delinquent expression, shook the phone and tried to breathe regularly.

I stopped off at the office to use the internet. It felt as if I was selling my soul but I signed up to Tesco and booked a delivery for Nain. Then I made my way to the animal centre to meet Benny, reflecting that all of this was so out of character I didn't recognise myself. Except that I'd only really taken Benny up on her offer to impress Dan, and that appeared to have become my raison d'être.

'Believe me,' said Benny, 'these people are seasoned campaigners.'

'Seasoned complainers?' I murmured. 'Right.'

She adjusted her iPod. 'They really care,' she said (in a tone that implied maybe I didn't). 'They've done it all. They grew up on Greenham Common.'

'And spent their adolescence in tree houses?'

'Probably did. Look, I'm trying to be helpful here. I can introduce you to some influential people.'

'Mum,' I said. 'I appreciate it.'

A young woman came past and glanced at us, thinking she'd heard wrong. Benny's eyes flared and I made a little *whoops* gesture. She set off through a tunnel of stinking stables and I had to follow her with my breath held and an eye out for anything I had to sidestep. Dribbling horse chops protruded from stalls, snorting at me. The phrase 'looking down their noses' got stuck in my mind and wouldn't shift. A man who looked like Tintin scuttled past us, doing ostentatiously inferior body language and ducking out of Benny's way. I gave him a little wave, which he started to return but then got embarrassed about and abandoned half way. This distracted me for a valuable moment and I was suddenly up against a horse being three-point turned into its stall by jodhpur Barbie; I had to polka sideways to avoid contact.

'Julie, is Chips around?' said Benny, still striding ahead, and jodhpur Barbie blushed and said, 'Think so.'

At the end of the corridor of doom was a field labelled 'Paddock' and a portakabin. Benny tugged her headphones out of her ears and wriggled them down inside her top, ducking under the rail of the portakabin. She put her ear to the door and knocked.

'S'only Benny,' she said. She pushed open the door and went in and I had to choose quickly between posting myself under the rail – and risking a display of extreme non-agility – or going the long way round on the ramp. I went for the rail, in case the door slammed shut, and compromised with an ungainly knee shuffle.

Inside, the portakabin was stuffy and cluttered. There was a desk, where Benny was now perched quite girlishly, stabbing at a laptop but not looking at the screen. She was looking instead at a six-foot-plus button-nosed boy in pyjama bottoms and a 'Where's Wally?' t-shirt. He was on the phone, saying, 'Things are a bit different now. We tend to outsource the minor campaigns. Hey, can I ring you back? I have a meet.' He clicked off his phone as the door wobbled shut behind me and held out his hand.

'Sky?' he said. 'I'm –'

I shook his hand. 'Shona,' I said. 'I'm Shona.'

'God, sorry,' he said. 'They told me your name was Sky.'

'She's not from Geronimo,' said Benny, adjusting the angle of the laptop screen. Where's Wally laughed and rubbed his button nose.

'Right,' he said. 'Do you want to come in again?' He stepped back into the handle bar of a bike leaning against the wall and had to grab hold of it to stop it knocking over a big plastic sledge. Benny stood up and wandered over to a trestle table covered in mobile phones. She picked one up and frowned at it.

'Shona's looking for an intro,' she said. 'She's my daughter, would you believe it. She's a cold fish. You wouldn't know we were related.'

'OK. Hah. Ahah. Right,' said Where's Wally. 'Well, good to have you on board. Take a pew.' He unfolded a folding chair for me and I sat down, plopping my rucksack on the floor. 'There are basically three arms to the org. Four if you count admin, I guess. Anyway. There's what we call the SWAT team, bringing the animals in at night. There's care for the animals once they're here. And there's protest-slash-awareness-raising, which is fairly subtly handled for obvious reasons.' He fished in his pyjama pocket for a packet of chewing gum, taking a piece and offering one to me, which I declined.

'It's really the protest-slash-awareness-raising I'm interested in,' I said. I felt silly on the chair when he and Benny were pottering about.

'She hates animals,' said Benny.

'Not all animals.' Something about Where's Wally's button nose made me defensive.

Benny laughed and said, 'Name me one animal you like. Or just don't hate.' A wave of nausea hit me, carrying with it an echo: *Shona love, pretend for a minute. Pretend you're a normal little girl who likes cuddly furry things and begs for a pet. It's a tough ask, I know.* She grinned at Where's Wally, but he was baffled now and back to knocking over bicycles. Colin would have liked him. In fact if I'd had any oomph in me at all I'd have dashed back to Colin's and dragged him humming and fiddling to the portakabin to get involved. I could have introduced him to Where's Wally and the gang and he'd have spent his days fixing computer problems and feeding animals, instead of staring terrified rigid at his television. Guilt is generous with its time; you can fill whole

122

nights with it, no problem.

I was at the foot of the steps to Colin's place, steeling myself for the climb, telling myself it was good for my heart etcetera, when the Wicked Witch of the West appeared beside me. She usually cackled loudly and this was a useful warning to duck out of the way of any spell she might be casting. She had done something to the top corridor once, which Colin couldn't bring himself to talk about. He'd mutter, 'Oh, the corridor incident ...' whenever the cackling drifted in through the window or up the stairwell. 'Legendary. Legendary. Not for Ladies' ears.' Then he'd shake his head and clear his throat to show the conversation was closed. Today, she'd managed to creep up on me; I must have been deep in thought, or possibly part of me had already gone to sleep, exhausted by my outing.

'Spawn of Satan,' she said, and attacked my chin with a dried flower.

'Hi,' I said, and shuffled forwards, wondering if I'd be faster up the stairs than her or if she'd catch me and tackle me to the ground to curse me. She was a big woman, but you couldn't tell how much of this was layers of clothing. She wore several skirts at once and periodically switched them round so that a different one was on top. It is very likely that she did the same thing with her knickers, and I don't think this routine involved much soap or water. Maybe she turned them inside out from time to time.

Colin's domestic prowess hadn't entirely gone up in smoke when the Shelter did. He woke me later from a miserable swamp of a sleep, by standing over me saying, 'Ahem. Hah. Calling Shona to the planet.' I unstuck my eyes and squinted at him. 'Ah, good,' he said, 'you're awake. Now then. Wash day. Hang out the washing on the Siegfried line.'

'Ng? Wo'?' I'd been having dreams that were simply a chaotic continuation of what happened when I was awake, and just then I was about fifty-fifty as to which state I was in.

'Don't worry,' he tittered. 'I can handle bras and knick-knacks. No blushes spared.'

My mouth was dry and my tongue wouldn't quite unstick. I tried to make a bit of saliva to swoosh about, but there wasn't much to be found.

'You're going to do some washing?' I croaked.

'Got it in one. No flies on you,' said Colin. 'Now, chop-chop, stuff your dirties in the binbag by the door.'

'That's really good of you Colin.' I managed to stand. 'Thank you. Is there a machine in the building or do you have to go to a launderette somewhere?'

'Hm, pros and cons,' he said, following me round as I got a drink and sat on the floor to sort my clothes. I gave him everything I'd worn to the animal centre. 'There *is* a washing machine in the bowels of this establishment, but the room is predominantly used for activity of a paracriminal nature. So to avoid becoming minced meat, I frequent a little place a few streets away.' He blushed. I had a vision of him with a Dot Cotton type, coy and giggly as they loaded the machine together.

12

I was on my way into the office with nothing but good intentions, when a couple wearing matching green jackets with little mountain symbols on the collars stopped me and shouted, 'You stupid, stupid, girl!' and 'You will never understand what we are going through!' The woman had pruned grey hair and the man was balding; they both had the drawn faces of people who can't forget their pain even for a minute. The woman grabbed hold of my sleeve and shook my arm, gnashing her teeth. The man looked at me as if to say, *You take it, I can't bear it any more. Let her take it out on you.* She pressed her nails down hard into my arms, shutting her eyes with the effort. I tried to throw her off but all her strength was going into her fingernails.

'Let go you mad woman!' I yelled – I'd not had time to consider, or I might not have put it like that – and I hooked my foot round her leg and tried to trip her up. 'Don't you kick my wife, you little –' hissed the man and began pummelling my shoulder like a crazed masseur.

'For God's sake,' I shouted, twisting away sharply where my waist would have been, with the wife attached to my forearms and the husband thumping my shoulder blades black and blue. I didn't shout, 'Help', because there was something acutely embarrassing about being beaten up by middle-aged ramblers. They were in a violent trance, spewing anger and hatred; they'd even stopped shouting now, they were just concentrating hard on damaging me. I tried to head-butt the woman. 'Let go of me! Leave me alone!' Flailing around was getting me nowhere so I froze suddenly, catching them off guard. They jumped out of their trances and stared at me, foaming a bit at the mouth, colour in their cheeks at last. And then of course Dan was there. I had a paranoid impression he'd been watching for a while. He waded in, holding up his hands for calm.

'Hey,' he said. 'Hey, do you want to tell me what's going on?'

I looked at him, my chest heaving and my nostrils flaring. The middle-aged ramblers hung their heads. The man put his hands over his face and gave a huge sigh. The woman burst into tears.

'Shona?' said Dan, looking from one to the other.

I shrugged. I had the uncomfortable sensation I was in the playground being blamed for something I hadn't started. 'Crazy,' I hissed. 'They just launched themselves at me.'

The man pulled himself together enough to straighten up. 'Who are you?' he asked Dan quietly.

'I'm Dan,' he said. As if that explained everything. But he said it so confidently, so gently, that the couple seemed reassured. 'Do you want to tell me what's going on?' he said again, quietly, softly, lowering his hands.

'My wife ...' said the man. His wife was trembling now, hugging herself. 'My wife and I ... our son ... is dead.' Then he was shaking, his teeth chattering and the zip pull on his jacket quivering.

'I'm so sorry,' murmured Dan. I rubbed my shoulder where it throbbed and stared at him.

'Tramp Flu,' sniffed the woman. 'Twenty-eight.' They stepped away from us and her husband took her in his arms and rocked her, his face in her hair. I started to speak but Dan shook his head and I swallowed, indignant.

'If you had closed that place when you were told to do so,' said the man into his wife's hair. 'After the first death.'

I put my hands on my hips. 'Look,' I said. 'Excuse me –'

Dan actually put his hand over my mouth. Gently, and pretty intimately, but I have never coped well with being told off.

'Your son stayed at the Shelter?' said Dan. I pursed my lips, felt my eyeballs bulging.

'We think so. One of his fr – someone told us he may have been there.'

'He *may* have been there?'

'Shona, ssh. Did he die at the clinic? On the industrial estate?'

I would have liked to have rounded on Dan and lashed out at him in the same way they'd been lashing out at me but we were starting to attract attention. The Peter Storm couple lost interest in us and became absorbed in each other. 'Glad to have been of assistance,' I said and Dan said, 'Ssh,' with one of his minute headshakes. He slipped a business card – Dan had business cards? – into the man's hand and steered me away. I felt like a dog trying to jump up and lick people's faces the way he handled me.

'Where are we going?' I said, when he didn't let go and I realised I didn't want him to. I was still fuming, you understand, fuming.

'My flat. Well, my room. Bedsit. It might make bedsit.' I kept walking, my shoulder flickering under his touch. 'Is that OK with you?'

'I didn't know I had a say in it,' I muttered.

He ruffled my hair. That was a step too far. I ducked out of his way and hunched my shoulders round my ears in the manner of a teenage boy who's pissed off with his parents. We walked further apart for a while, down the endless straight road that is almost entirely B and Bs and makes me wonder how one town could need that many faceless bedrooms. What's more, some of them said *No Vacancies*. Maybe Tramp Flu made us more interesting as a destination. I wondered if maybe Dan was staying in a B and B. He kept going, determined, a bit too fast for conversation. My inner thighs sweated a little and a trickle formed down the small of my back. He stuck out his hand without looking at me as if he expected me to take it, turning down a side street with a pub on the corner. I followed him, ignoring the hand, and he grinned privately to himself. Then he stopped suddenly, flinging out his arm so that I walked into it. The house was a huge semi-detached thing.

'I'll have to smuggle you up,' he said. 'They'll never stop asking questions if they see you.' He still didn't look at me. I thought seriously about walking off and asserting my autonomy but I got the impression he'd catch me like a fish. Or laugh and leave me to it and then what would I have achieved? I'd have demonstrated my willingness and my stroppiness all at once. He went up the stone steps, mushy with leaves and litter. I watched from the street as he unlocked the vast front door. He peered into a dark hallway. 'They're out,' he said. I rammed my hands into my pocket and did the teenage boy thing again, looking at my trainers and a fire hydrant cover. Paralysis was setting in, stopping my thoughts and words, preventing me from going in or stamping off. My teeth were pressed together and my cheeks were sucked in in a weird pout. He left the door open with the key still in it and came slowly back down the steps. He stood facing me, head down like mine, and after a second he nudged my trainer with his. I shut my eyes. We waited for me to unfreeze. When I opened my eyes, I was gazing at his vast lace-up boots. I tried to picture his feet underneath them. Had I ever looked at his feet? He didn't move. I saw my foot shift forward and press down on his toes.

'Ow,' he said. I rubbed my foot to and fro apologetically. It left a dirty mark.

'I've had this place for about three months.' Three months! He'd been back in Cardiff for three months and for all I'd known he was in Darkest Peru. Or Edinburgh or somewhere. I sighed. He swallowed. He smelt of shower gel and cigarettes. I shrugged and went past him up the steps. He leapt up them, sweeping me in through the door and plucking his keys from the lock in the same movement.

He didn't turn the light on. I followed him up a staircase.

On the first landing was a cardboard box that had exploded like a volcano, spilling socks and a marked essay, a paperback and some heart-shaped speakers. Dan pushed it aside with his foot and went up one step onto a longer landing with two closed, stripped wood doors. My calves were complaining as we set off up the next set of stairs, which were even darker than the first. I felt like a Tyrannosaurus Rex lumbering upwards, trying not to sniff or wheeze out loud. The stairs creaked under my feet more than Dan's, which was rude. And then suddenly he flicked on the light on the top landing and I was revealed in all my puffing, red-faced beauty. My hands covered my cheeks instinctively, in a Fflur-like gesture, and I tried to look casual with a hint of impenetrability.

'Welcome to my humble abode,' he said and he seemed really shy and anxious for me to like it. Which I didn't, obviously, as it was quite bleak and faintly mouldy.

'Do you often smuggle girls up to your room?' I said, in a grim parody of flirtation. *Girls*. Women. You're the other side of thirty, Shona.

'Er – no. Actually, you're my first visitor. Male or female.' It wasn't just his words, his voice had changed. He seemed younger, less like someone who'd slept rough on every continent I'd ever heard of.

'I'm honoured.' It really didn't suit me, flirting. We hadn't bothered with it, the first time. It was more a matey thing that segued seamlessly into a sweaty thing. He pushed open the door to his room. I followed him in and he switched on the bendy desk lamp beside his bed and a fluorescent bubbling stick with plastic fish bobbing up and down inside it in colour-changing jelly.

'The kids gave it to me,' he said, with a very lovely little smile, clearing away a crumby plate from the table. He looked at me. 'The kids that live here. In this house.' He surveyed the room. 'I had a birthday,' he said, as if this was slightly odd and a bit embarrassing. His room was two rooms with a wall knocked through and a rattly, ill-fitting sash window at each end. It was pretty arctic.

'You're cold. It is cold in here.' He wrestled with an electric heater until it began to hum and blush. 'All mod cons.'

All mod cons. What a ridiculous phrase. So un-Dan.

There was a swivel chair, straight out of an office set in a seventies repeat on afternoon telly, a desk to match, the table and an ornate, double-sized antique wardrobe. Most of the floor space was covered by a flying carpet of a rug that looked as if it told a thousand tales. I sat on the swivel chair and plopped my backpack at my feet. He took some stuff out of his bag and fiddled with his camera, wiping the screen and the lens as if he were stroking a baby guinea pig.

'I've been after a by-line for so long,' he said, smiling at the table, Colin-like. 'And now they've sold my photos to a national and I've said I don't want my name on them.' He grinned. 'Perhaps it's enough to know I could've had one.'

'It's very cool.'

He stood beside me and my head was on a level with his stomach. The fabric of his t-shirt was worn in the way some people pay good money for. Halfway between purple and brown. Not tucked in, not untucked. And the zip of his tan-coloured jeans – battered, very cool tan jeans – had started to breathe. My throat went tight and my girly bits went warm and fuzzy. He pulled my head in to rest on his stomach. Actually, I may have leant in first, before his hands were on my hair. He massaged my scalp a bit, his fingers weaving in and out of my hair. And I shut my eyes and opened them again and drowned in the night sky of his t-shirt. My arms slid round his waist and my thumb hooked itself in a belt loop. Was that a pass? Was that asking for it? If your chin is inches away from a man's cock (albeit with denim in between), is it any more of a come-on to hook your thumb through his belt loop? Anyway, it pressed some button because he put his hands under my armpits, pulled me to my feet and started French kissing me smokily. It made me want to yank his clothes off but I clamped my mouth shut and wrestled myself out of his grasp. *Three months.*

'Shona?' His eyes were glazed. I picked up my backpack and threw it onto my shoulder, feeling my face ice over. 'Shona, what is it? Lovely?'

I raised my eyebrows and made a move towards the door. He put his hands up in surrender.

'You're leaving,' he said, as my hand touched the door handle. There was half a Superman sticker on it.

'Um, yes. I've decided I don't really want to be an occasional masturbatory aid.'

'Shona!' He flung himself at me, turning me to face him, furious.

'What?' I looked into his scarily angry eyes with my frozen ones. He sighed and looked at the ceiling, still gripping my shoulders. 'It's getting dark,' I said. 'I should go.' My voice was as hard as my eyes, threatening, nonchalant.

'You're angry with me,' he said, looking at me again.

'OK.'

He gave me a little shake. I raised my eyebrows again, which seemed to have become my weapon of choice.

'You are what I think about when I go to bed and the first thing on my mind when I wake up,' he said tightly, as if he had stomach cramps. I didn't flinch. I looked sideways down my nose at his right hand on my right shoulder. He took it off and wiggled the fingers. I turned to his left hand, feeling ridiculous and miserable, and he let go. He folded his arms and I left, down the dark, dank stairs, past the exploding cardboard box and out of the enormous front door. The sky, which hadn't managed anything other than a dull throb all day, had given up trying and was sliding gloomily into night.

13

I had to check on Nain of course, though it was tempting to walk away. She may have been a Victim, but she wasn't a Bolter, and I'm indebted to her for that. I had to promise through the letter box that if she let me in I'd ignore my mother for the rest of my life.

'Where have you been?' she cried. Her hair was sticking up in spikes. I managed to get the door shut behind me and I stood amongst the junk mail getting my breath back.

'Have you been pulling your hair out?' I said. 'Literally?'

'Yes. Literally. I've been stuck here wondering where on earth you've got to, and the telly telling me the world's falling apart –'

I patted her shoulder. 'I'm sorry, Nain,' I murmured. 'I'll put the kettle on shall I?'

She trotted after me, wheezing slightly, and nearly bumped into me when I stopped suddenly at the kitchen door. There was nothing on the worktops or the table at all, just crumbs and fluff. I took some tentative steps into the room.

'What have you done with the kettle?' I said.

'It's in the cupboard,' she said. 'Make sure you put it back when you've finished with it.'

I opened the cupboard above the naked surface where the kettle should have been. It was stuffed with things; the kettle, some mugs, the bread board, bread, a rolled up nighty and some used tissues. I eased the kettle out, but the lead was tangled and it brought with it the nighty and – serendipitously – a box of teabags. I plugged in the kettle and put the nighty on the table. Nain grabbed hold of it and sat clutching it and watching me make tea.

'A tidy house is a hygienic house,' she muttered. We listened to the kettle make some distressed gurgling sounds. 'Shona!' she shrieked, 'you didn't put any water in it!' Her shriek made me jump and I gave myself hiccups.

I unplugged the kettle and took it to the sink, the hiccups sudden and painful. Nain's breath filled the air around us. I started again on the tea.

'Have you been eating too fast?' she peered at my tummy. I tried to make a derisive noise but it got hijacked by a hiccup. I focussed on separating the vertebrae in my neck. 'As usual,' she said.

Poor Nain, it was only a straw but it broke my back. I snapped, 'Shut up. For once in your life, just button it. It's my business what I eat and how fast I eat it and –' Her lips wobbled and she pursed them. I was overtaken by a monster hiccup.

The front room looked different; Nain had lined up the ornamental animals on top of the telly and swept the bits of paper into a plastic carrier bag which hung on the door handle. The horse had lost an ear in the fray.

I sank onto the sofa, my head full of scribble-thoughts. My year of dreamy girly fantasy had come skidding to a halt as I walked out on Dan, and there was a pretty bleak void left behind. I wanted some really strong cheese. The sort that teeters on the dividing line between exquisite and foul, that leaves your breath and your fingers smelling for hours. That hypnotises you into eating more and more even though you know you'll regret it.

As a child, I made a point of my inability to cry. There was a revolting little episode in which I bullied another girl into being nasty to me, to prove how hard I was. We both got spoken to, but it never came to anything because the teacher couldn't decide who was bullying whom.

Maybe there was nothing too odd about that; proving toughness to classmates is a time-honoured tradition. But I sometimes went to bed at night purposefully thinking about really tragic things to see if it made me cry. Which is pretty tragic in itself. And now catatonic on the sofa, observing my lethargy stooping to new lows, I thought how maybe I hadn't changed much. I wondered about taking a leaf out of the Disaffected Youths' book and nipping out for some Value gin.

Nain's eyes were threatening tears as she watched me heave myself up to standing. She flinched in the manner of an abuse victim at a raised arm. It made me want to slap her. *She was asking for it, your honour.* It was the perverse leave-me-alone performance, which as a method of attention-seeking is dangerous. I pretended I hadn't seen her and stumbled from the room, a swallow stuck in my throat because it was so dry.

She'd left a shoebox full of stuff by the loo. I weed loudly and angrily and blew out a great sigh of self-disgust. Then I couldn't be bothered to do anything except yank up my jeans, slide from the toilet seat onto the floor, and poke vacantly through the shoebox. I was in such a haze of gloom that it took me a while to realise what I would usually have seen straight away; Nain hadn't left a shoebox absent-mindedly in the bathroom because she'd been looking through it on the loo. She'd put it somewhere she knew for certain I'd go sooner or later. It was either there or the fridge. The box was stuffed with letters, bills and cheque stubs from the early 1980s. There was a letter from the council offering me a place at Endbury Rd County Primary for the academic year 81/82. A tear off slip had been torn off and presumably returned to accept the offer. I remembered the resource area, where we painted and stuck, and I thought about Lisa Lewis, who was known as Spaz and who graduated from callipers to a wheelchair largely as a result of the imitations people did of her attempts to walk. My swallow got stuck again. Fuck, I'd have liked to apologise. I thought about Facebooking her in the library but she'd probably Not Now my Friend Request and leave me there. I didn't remember much else specific other than the 'go on, I bet you can't make me cry' incident when I must have been about nine.

The cheque stubs had Dad's handwriting on them, which felt only slightly less unsettling than his voice would have done if it had come echoing out of the box. *11/12/82 – £3.50 – Shona school trip. 5/3/83 – Shona school photos. 10/4/83 – Shona party £29.* I was expensive. Could I remember that party? I had a vague recollection of a badly lit hall and a magician. Clearly I did friends and parties to start with. *9/6/83 – Hamilton Solicitors – £152.68.* Interesting. There were letters with the Hamilton Solicitors letterhead and invoices for what would have been large amounts of money in 1983. I started reading with the same sensation I had about the cheese – the knowing it was going to make me sick but not being able to stop. Apparently my mother had made a grab for custody. I hadn't known she had a custody phase. I guess I wasn't as adept as I later became at interpreting adult over-the-head speak. I remembered the miscarriage phase, and I can't have been very old then, but I examined the asides Nain muttered at Dad and worked out what the word meant. And I remembered my eighth birthday when she did a visit and told me she had suspected stomach cancer. She held my hand as she said it. We were sitting in a cafe window, like a shop display: Mother and Child with Bad News. I remember realising she thought I cared. She was breaking the news sensitively and being brave for me. But as I hadn't seen her for seven months it didn't feel too huge.

I flicked through the letters. Custody. That would have been different. But she'd have given me back; it would have been a short-lived thing. Maybe they should have let her have me for a while. It would have been cheaper than the courts, and I was a tough enough kid.

'Shona? Are you alive?'

Nain pattered her fingertips on the bathroom door. I sniffed and got up, flicking my hands under a drip from the tap. I pushed open the door and made a huge effort not to slump against the wall in a heap of indifference.

'Have you been sick?' Nain said. I shuffled into the kitchen. She followed me. I sat down and put my head on the table, which smelt stale and sour.

Nain rummaged in a cupboard for her box of supplements and selected some oversized capsules. She made a pile of them, counted them and prepared herself a glass of water. She kept glancing at me and making faces, which created a crazy little cascade of wrinkles when she let go again. I took a cheese triangle from the bottom of the vegetable compartment and sucked it through a hole in the corner.

Carol keeps fiddling with the strap of her shoe, just behind her ankle. She inserts a finger between strap and skin and makes a face.

'Are you OK?' I ask. It sounds far too solicitous, as if an itchy ankle is something to be pretty stalwart about – or perhaps it just sounds sarcastic, as if I'm taking the piss. I really can't tell. Increasingly, I think I should just keep my mouth shut.

'I'm fine, thank you,' says Carol. 'These weren't a good buy, these shoes.'

She seems concerned about the unrelenting gloom in my writing.

'You know Life Writing doesn't always have to be absolutely true down to the last detail,' she says. 'The life we lead inside our heads can be just as important as the one we play out in the real world. What matters is the story that you want to tell.'

I take her up on the challenge, and write about the wedding:

Gloria is there, of course, in a rather bizarre hat to which she's added a few touches of her own. And a bright orange silk jacket that billows sail-like when the wind catches her. Bunched-up netting pinned to her left tit.

Colin, giving me away, humming *Here comes the bride, all fat and wide* and clearing his throat at socially inappropriate moments. Fflur, the prettiest, smiliest, most attentive bridesmaid anyone ever had, glowing so brightly that no one gives the bride a second glance. (*Bride.* It's not a particularly elegant word. It's more adjective than noun: *Oh she's alright, but she's a bit bride.* Or a verb, *God, she just bride and bride. We couldn't shut her up.*) So Colin shuttles me up the aisle at top speed, Fflur gliding behind us, and I'm wearing a t-shirt-shaped dress of a nondescript colour that hangs just below my knees, and a pair of white baseball boots. I've experimented with various coloured laces and that sort of thing, but even that feels a bit squirmy. The t-shirt dress just appeared – I didn't have to design it or faff about with it in any way. Then Colin and I reach the end of this great long runway, where we've passed Gloria several times – with variations on the hat – and Nain watching television and Benny with her feet up on the pew in front. There are some non-specific Shelter users there, milling about a bit and nipping out for a smoke. And at the front, in addition to a generic vicar person, is Dan. Sometimes he has his messenger bag with him. He's stubbly and warm and he gives a little nod that I play over and over again, squeezing every drop from it. I've never got as far as vows and kisses; it's the nod that I slurp like a lolly, and the sense that it's me he's looking at when he turns round.

14

I can't write today. The words won't be tethered by my head or my hand. I sulk a bit and stare out of the window at the magnolia, which is hovering tantalisingly between budding and flowering. At school, when we wanted to get out into the sunshine, we told the teacher we wanted to draw the magnolia tree in the quad; she had a thing about it and seemed pleased that we shared it. This magnolia is a different pink. It looks almost rude; I can't help thinking it's labia pink.

Carol runs her finger around the back of her shoe. She hides her irritation; she was hoping for a smoother time today, clearly. After a while, she says, 'Forget the story. You don't have to write sequentially, remember. And tangents are fine. I like a nice tangent.'

'OK,' I say, an image of the school quad filling my head; the air and the feel of lying on the grass with the sketch books under our heads for pillows.

'We'll try an exercise.' She's having a hard time not touching her itchy ankle. 'List five smells you like.'

'Right.' I squiggle a line on the top of the page. Carol starts writing too, so as to avoid staring at me while I write. I put:

Pickled onion crisps
Chinese restaurants
Dan's armpits

I shut my eyes. I can't believe I wrote that. I need to scratch the inside of my cheeks with my teeth but if I start I won't be able to stop. I bite the tip of my tongue and sniff.

'OK?' says Carol. 'Do you want a different prompt? We could leave that one.' I shake my head, opening my eyes, and stare at the wall for a while. Then I write:

Matches
Lavender

I swivel the pad to show her I've finished and she contemplates my list as if it's a poem or a watercolour. After a while, she says, 'And five that you dislike,' and twangs her ankle strap again. I write quickly:

Dog shit
Chinese restaurants after you've finished
Lavender
My own armpits

And I can't for the life of me think of a fifth. Carol gives me thinking space, adjusts her posture and makes a that's fine, well done *sound. Do I like or dislike the smell of lavender? I'm not neutral on this one – halfway between like and dislike is not indifference, it's having to sniff it and go back and sniff it again, and not being able to decide itches as much as Carol's ankle seems to.*

I'm bothered that I can't think of a fifth. The list feels incomplete. Fox piss, *I write crossly, and it makes me feel worse.*

Colin and I were busy letting our lives dissolve in companionable silence (with intermittent humming), when Fflur came in looking shifty and started setting the table. I sprang up out of my slump and hovered about straightening the forks a bit. It reminded me of the weeks after Dad's stroke, when I kept a mug and a tea-towel behind the bread bin so I could look busy at short notice. It didn't do much to stop Nain's descent into Victimhood; in fact it was a self-defeating tactic because it reinforced the very mindset it was designed to head off. Somehow Fflur had brought it out in me again. I couldn't read her expression, which was unusual. Something was going on. I looked at Colin for clues. As if.

She was wearing a yellow woollen mini dress which I hadn't seen before, with a tartan ruffle round the bottom. Her tights were the same green as part of the pattern on the tartan. I may not be very observant when it comes to clothes, but even I could see that since Colin had dyed everything, Fflur had been shopping. I was fortunate in that most of my clothes were mud coloured to start with, but prior to Colin's outbreak of domesticity, Fflur's had been baby blue, soft pink or white.

I straightened the three forks and swept some crumbs into my hand, and Fflur shared cold pasta from a plastic box between three plates. Colin stood, picked at a scab on his elbow and broke wind rather inefficiently, saying, 'Whoops, whoops. Oof, oops.'

Fflur beamed at him and said, 'Din-dins?' She blushed. 'Sorry. That sounded like you're a cat.' She sagged down onto a chair and picked up a fork. 'Anyway,' she said. 'Pasta. If you want it.'

'Mm,' I said. 'Pesto. Smells good.' The food made me want to cry. Never crying isn't the same as never wanting to.

'It's called 'sunblushed tomato' –' began Fflur, but at the same time Colin had paused in his progress towards us and was wafting his hands about saying, 'Just disperse it. Sorry to mar the ... hah. Global warming over here.'

Fflur gripped her fork and fixed him with a direct look. 'I am sick and tired,' she said, 'of the tiptoeing. Just for once, sit down and eat without faffing about and wittering. You don't even have to make conversation, just eat, for heaven's sake.' Colin froze in the middle of the room and Fflur burst into tears. 'I sound like my mother!' she shouted. 'I can't believe I've let you do that.'

I ate sunblushed tomato pesto pasta salad, wiping the corners of my mouth with my knuckles where they stung.

'Trump trump trump,' sang Colin earnestly and sat down at last. 'Nelly the elephant. Now then.' He squinted into the food and sniffed curiously. Slipping a pasta twist into his mouth, he launched into the swelling crescendo of the 'wooh' that leads if you stick with it to the rest of the chorus. I suspected Colin didn't know the chorus, though, which left him floundering about on that first wavering note longer than was good for any of us.

'Shona,' said Fflur, looking deep into her pasta. 'I'm really sorry about this but Gloria rang and she's got a friend called Fenella.' She wiped up a bit of sunblush from the edge of her plate with her finger. 'With a son about your age.' She covered her face with her hands and kept very still. 'I tried to get you out of it, but ...'

'What's this, what's this?' said Colin, rubbing his hands up and down his thighs. I pushed my plate away and stood up. 'Don't mind if I do,' he said, and started on my leftovers.

Fflur went to the sink and rinsed her hands. 'It's a Sunday lunch do,' she murmured. 'I'm so sorry.'

I wondered how Fflur had kept going when her fiancé dumped her by text message. I was envious of her in a way, because she had been so consistently close to a man they'd actually got engaged. Admittedly it had all fallen horribly apart, but she'd had the experience, the relationship while it lasted; I guessed there was probably sex, and maybe casual linking of hands or sliding of arms round shoulders at random times of day and in a variety of settings. Perhaps it's like being in a film. Or maybe normal people feel like it's normal to behave like that, that they somehow deserve it. I was in the same category as Colin, I reflected, who would never get anywhere near marrying. Unless of course there was a Colinette out there who'd slot in and hum away. They might have babies who came out fiddling and tapping, and they'd live in a house with half finished sentences littering the carpet.

Gloria rang again, more focussed this time. The clink of ice cubes and the sound of swallowing preceded her down the phone line.

'Gloria,' I said. 'Hi. How are you? Please understand. It's kind of you to invite me to your lunch party. I appreciate the –'

'Evening do,' she said, and gulped from her drink. 'I've altered things a bit to fit Michael's schedule. Very relaxed, gardening slacks really, so don't start a what-to-wear panic.' The word 'slacks' has always seemed a bit dubious to me; I've never heard anyone say it convincingly. 'Fenella is a big chum of mine. She's a tough cookie, too, is Fenella. Her first husband was a horror, he got court martialled for putting his paws up ladies' dresses in the officers' mess. Tim is from that marriage but he's always stuck by his mum, and he's very close to her second husband Jimmy. Jimmy's non-military, he's something in architecture, but he's not an architect.'

'Yes,' I said, 'mm. But –'

'And Michael will be there, so –'

'Minister Mike?'

She laughed and said, 'Ngh' through a mouthful of what sounded like peanuts. She chewed busily, somehow conveying a strong sense that the floor was still very much hers. I squeezed my pelvic floor and curled my toes under, wondering if I could just say, *No thanks Gloria*, or whether I'd need to be more specific.

'Is he married, Minister Mike?' I said, abandoning my pelvic floor as a lost cause.

'Uh. No. No he isn't,' she said. 'To all intents and purposes, no. Are you still anti-prawns?'

'What?'

'There's a rather nice dinner party menu in my foodie mag this month. With an Indian courgette and prawn dish. It sounds odd but you sprinkle cheese on the top and apparently it really works. I thought I'd freeze a batch for when it's my turn to feed the Evensong lot. But I know you're not that keen on prawns? I could do stuffed peppers for you?'

'No, it's fine. I just went off them after this roll I had but –'

'Oh brill. Super.' The sound of her swallow had an air of finality; she'd finished her glass. I felt a niggle of cramp under the toes on my right foot where I'd been curling them too tightly. 'Cheers then Shona. Speak soon. Bye.'

She put the phone down and I scratched the ball of my foot so hard it hurt.

'Let's think about letters,' says Carol, mirroring my posture. It strikes me how funny it would be to set her up with Gloria; if they were both mirroring, how would you know whose body language came first? 'The poor old letter is a rare breed now, with emails and texts being so quick and easy. But there's something about the handwritten word on paper you can hold in your hand.' I nod. Good point; subject of many feature articles perhaps, but important nonetheless. 'I wonder if you remember any letters you've written or received?' She adopts an expression which indicates that, whilst she would be fascinated to hear about any, it really is fine if I can't recall.

'Um ...' I'm looking up and to the left, which is where I seem to keep memories I haven't taken off the shelf for a while. Carol blinks and breathes patiently. 'I got a letter once from my mother's brother,' I tell her.

She nods. 'Hm, OK.'

'On that really thin blue paper that folded in on itself to make an envelope.'

'Airmail. Goodness, yes. I remember those.'

'I was about twelve. He said he'd only just found out about me and if he hadn't just moved to New Zealand he'd have very much liked to meet me.' I laugh a lot. As I remember, I laughed when I got it. Stuffed it in the bin I think. Mainly so Dad and Nain wouldn't find it. I could tough most things

out but Dad starting on about my Bloody Mother and tipping back the whisky
challenged my cool like nothing else.

Carol smiles. 'OK,' she says. I'm struggling for any other examples.

'I suppose passing notes at school counts.'

'Yes, good one. I'd not thought of that.'

'Mostly I just passed other people's notes on. I was never exactly the centre of
the social whirl.' Carol smiles rather sadly. I do not have a personality disorder.
I have googled and considered this at length and on balance I've decided I don't.
I would rather Carol said, Do you have borderline personality disorder?
And then I could say, Well, I can see why you might say that, but in fact I
don't think I do, no. *When people think it but don't say it, a denial on my*
part would hardly help.

When I don't say anything for a while, Carol says, 'And letters that you
have written. Can you remember writing to anyone ...?' She reaches down
for her bottle of water and sips supportively. I shut my eyes and swallow. My
oesophagus shakes and my bladder feels suddenly full. Carol sips and strokes
the water bottle, breathing steadily.

'I wrote a letter to my dad and my grandmother. After Dad's stroke but
before he died.' My fingers are gripping the sides of the chair, squashing the
spread of my thighs.

'Uh huh,' murmurs Carol.

'I wrote: I don't know what to write but I can hardly write nothing.
Sorry. Thank you.' *I wrap my arms around myself and grit my teeth. Carol*
passes me a tissue that smells of menthol and stings my eyes.

'It sounds as if that was a very tough time,' she whispers. I take a deep
breath and sit up straight again.

'I had grandiose plans,' I tell her, 'to fill my pockets with stones and jump
into the river.' I sniff. Carol waits. 'But I couldn't get quite drunk enough.
And before I got round to trying again, Dad had another stroke which killed
him off. So.' I look at her brightly. Next question?

'Do you want to talk more about that time? Or write about it perhaps ...?'
She plays with her extra long necklace. I try to work out if it's symmetrical.
'Or we could leave it there for today. Hm?'

'No,' I say. 'I'm good. What's the plan?'

She lets go of her necklace and lifts her hair away from her neck for a
moment. 'I thought it might be good to write a letter,' she says. 'A letter which
you'll most likely never send. In fact some people choose to write to someone

141

who has passed away. Or someone they have lost touch with.' She smiles and scratches her ankle. 'Whatever seems fruitful.'

'I'll write to Benny.' I'm surprised to hear myself say this. 'But I'll probably tear it up.'

Dear Benny,

Carol's been nudging around the topic of family and childhood, trying to look as if she isn't dying for me to take the plunge. So here goes:

I'll call you Benny, so that perhaps you'll read this instead of stuffing it in your pocket and then leaving it on a table somewhere for someone else to pick up. You did that once; you turned up after months of nothing and we went to McDonald's. You were fiddling around in your pockets for money. You left some receipts and things on the table, and I picked up a note when you went to the loo. It was spelt badly, on a torn out piece of lined paper. It was signed *Spanner*, and he'd poured himself into this note poor guy, because he thought you were worth trying to change. He said *come off the shit, Ben, do as you're told for once, there's a life out there waiting to be lived and you're sitting around here letting days go past.* He said *I'll be there, I've given up on myself but it's not too late for you.* And he said *don't do anything stupid, you're a mother and that's big.* So you must have told him.

I'm sure you can pretend very convincingly that you don't have any children. Kicking about like an eternal teenager, sniffing and pulling your hood up, smoking as though smoking's a hard job but someone's gotta do it. Speaking in grunts where sentences might be too much like social interaction and you're too hard for that. Oh shit. Now I stop to think about it, I see the children thing up close and it hits me like a smack on the really vulnerable bit of your nose that makes you cry and feel sick; I'm not the only one. You have other children. It isn't just me feeling hard done by and screwed up and carrying my chip like it's something to be proud of. How many? If I had a fag in my hand, I'd chuck it on the ground and stamp on it here. For emphasis and because cigarette butts are a great way to displace emotions you're not prepared to admit to. You've populated the planet with benefit-leeching flat-faced children. Do you give them lessons, Mum? Is it nature or nurture, the leech thing? And the bolting. You're a Bolter. A forgetter, an intermittent-on-your-terms-rememberer. A leech, a drain, an embarrassment. Ironically, I suffered less from parental embarrassment than my friends, firstly because I had no claim to cool other than aloof, so it didn't matter anyway, and secondly because you bolted so early on most people didn't even know I had a mother.

Your own experience of childhood is shrouded in mystery; a shroud made from stories-within-stories, and hints of limited subtlety and maximum shock value. You went through a phase of reading Alice Walker spin-offs with little punctuation and quirky words for genitalia. *Mmm-hmm baby girl, your sweet honey syrup taste good.* It never sounded the same in a Valleys accent.

The single most cringingly dire thing you did was to go on a television freak show and explain that you were suicidally depressed because you were a man in a woman's body. You had shaved your hair off (including eyebrows, so there was more than a passing resemblance to Paul from the Shelter even before you sat with your legs splayed out, rearranging your crotch from time to time). You introduced yourself as Benny, which was the first I'd heard of your new name, did a lot of crying and said you'd considered everything ('and I mean *everything*. Don't go there') to raise the money for treatment. Nain stared at the screen, turning a deeper and deeper shade of purple, her eyes huge behind her glasses. It put her off chat shows for a while; she said they couldn't be trusted not to twist the facts. Dad said, 'I imagine she'll get legal aid to persuade the NHS to pay,' and raised his lager at the screen. 'My love,' he said, 'you have surpassed even yourself.'

I tear the letter out of my notepad and shred it. Carol seems delighted, even though she never got to read it.

Fenella's husband Jimmy was very freckly. His hands, face and neck were so thickly covered that I had to distract myself from wondering if he was that freckly *all over*. I'd arrived first and when Gloria flung open the door to let them in, I had to back into the hat stand and a vast urn full of pieces of grass. Jimmy followed Fenella into the house, leaning over to grab the hat stand before it fell, and Gloria showered them in words. Fenella matched her and raised the stakes. Jimmy had a long-suffering half-smile in place and made no attempt to answer anything Gloria said to him. The word scrum moved through the hallway towards the kitchen, where Gloria struck up a refrain about how little effort she'd put into the bœuf en croûte. I stayed behind in the living room with Jimmy and he said, 'So how do you know Gloria?'

'I ... we worked together.'

'Tim, my stepson, was otherwise engaged,' he said. My face went very hot. Then I had to show that I was relieved rather than disappointed, but of course I went overboard and it was less convincing than Gloria's claim that she'd thrown the dinner together in about twelve minutes.

Minister Mike was also otherwise engaged and this challenged the nonchalance of the bœuf a bit because the croûte was drying out fast. By the time he arrived, I'd eaten all the nibbles and wanted to pass away quietly when Jimmy made a gentle witticism about my appetite. Gloria announced his entrance into the living room, twitching with the urgency of moving us all through to the dining room. I was hoping fervently there wouldn't be a hatch. I can just about cope with the existence of a dining room, but a hatch tips me over the edge. Anyway, I was full of Vietnamese Rice Crackers and Kashmiri Mix, headachey from sherry and desperate for a can of Sprite and a lie-down. Minister Mike's nose hair was less intrusive than it had been. Perhaps he'd clipped it a bit using one of those tools from the Sunday supplements. He wore, rather unsettlingly, a cravat. I had real difficulty not staring at it because I couldn't remember ever seeing one in the flesh.

Gloria's dining room had no hatch. It was a Victorian museum. The tablecloth had been fiercely ironed and mats were aligned with the shadows of the folds. In the centre was a crystal bowl filled with water, coloured glass nuggets and rose petals (these had absorbed a lot of water during the delay and the effect wasn't quite what it might have been). Fenella raved appropriately while we hovered for instructions on seating arrangements and Gloria made hand gestures indicating her lack of any forethought on this and then told us where to sit. My role as gooseberry was highlighted now because although Gloria had clearly shifted things around when Tim failed to show, you could see he'd been supposed to sit between me and her. As it was, I was marooned in the centre at one side, facing Fenella and Jimmy, with Gloria and Minister Mike at the far ends. Minister Mike was positioned for optimum drink-pouring duty and Gloria stood at her end plunging murderous instruments into the bœuf and pursing her lips about the croûte shattering everywhere. It looked like flakes of dry skin scattered over the tablecloth and some claret-coloured meat juice got splashed about too so it was all a bit visceral. Fenella jumped up and found a stain remover spray in the kitchen. I gazed at the water feature in the middle, wondering how I would manage to swallow any bœuf or croûte with a bellyful of vegetable oil from the nibbles.

Gloria had an electric cupboard on wheels from which she produced: brussel sprouts with flecks of bacon and seeds; matchsticked carrots in butter and sugar; miniature peas with twigs; and the nicest, crispiest roast potatoes I had ever seen. Not a prawn in sight. Fenella raved about all of it, collectively and individually, talking so much she managed to deconstruct the contents of her plate without eating any of it.

When Gloria declared it was *time for pud* and refused to let anyone help her clear away, Fenella got distracted for a moment in the scuffle and Jimmy began on an anecdote, directed exclusively at Minister Mike. I had to admire the glass nuggets again and try not to burp.

'... I said fine: go through via our drive and up the lane. Take out anything on four legs, they'll give you a medal. It wasn't until half an hour later when we were happily gutting one in the back garden and a chopper starts hovering –'

Minister Mike looked briefly uncomfortable. 'Joking aside,' he said, 'the cull isn't a public sport.' He made a politically ambivalent hand gesture. 'Although rabbits I'll make an exception for. There's one who treats my garden like a salad bar – '

'What's all this I hear about choppers?' shrieked Gloria, sweeping in with an acre of tiramisu in her arms.

'Six armed police officers,' said Jimmy, and glugged his wine. Minister Mike shook his head and sat back in his chair.

'She'd rung 999,' said Fenella. 'This woman. She said –'

'We don't *know* that it was a woman,' said Jimmy. 'What they told us first was –'

'Well no, it *was* a woman.' Fenella moved things about on the table to make space for the industrial pudding. Jimmy sighed. 'No, no,' said Fenella. 'You tell it. It's your story.' She smiled at Gloria, and Jimmy circled the tip of his finger around the rim of his wine glass. Gloria handed me a horse's portion of pudding, laughed and said, 'What a hoot.'

'Someone had rung the fuzz, anyway,' said Fenella, receiving her pudding graciously.

'Right,' said Minister Mike. 'Fair play.' He gave Jimmy a man's smirk.

'They said there were reports of an angry-looking man coming down the lane wielding a gun!'

'Six armed officers, two cars and a chopper!' shrieked Fenella, folding her tiramisu in on itself.

'Good Lord!' said Gloria, and we all spooned pudding into our mouths in silent acknowledgement that this police response to reports of a gunman had been entirely unwarranted.

'Anyway,' said Jimmy, his voice thick with coffee cream, 'it all ended well, with Graham arranging to go shooting with one of the policemen next weekend.'

Minister Mike guffawed and Gloria tinkled. Fenella put one hand over her face and slapped the table with the other. For want of anything else to do, I shovelled tiramisu into my face and wondered when I could leave.

I arrived back at Colin's saturated in sherry and gravy, exhaling bœuf en croûte and furious with absolutely everyone including the taxi driver who made me pay up front when I gave him Colin's address. I turned the key slowly in the lock, willing Colin and Fflur to be asleep. Colin, however, was hovering just inside and as soon as I was over the threshold he launched himself into an attack on the front door, locking, unlocking, relocking and finally leaning his whole body against it and saying, 'hatches battened, hatches battened.' He squinted at the edge where the door met the frame, running his finger down the gap, not quite satisfied with the alignment.

I shut myself in the bathroom and tried to pass wind at the very least. I kneaded my stomach with my fists and glared at myself in the mirror. When I finally ventured out, Fflur was waiting in the kitchen, leafing through an underwear catalogue and jiggling her knee.

'Thanks,' she said, 'I'm desperate,' and leapt past me. I brushed my teeth in the sink. Colin did a sort of pirouette and had to put his hand on the wall to stop himself falling over.

'Ahem,' he said, and went to bed in his deckchair. Fflur reappeared.

'Shona, lovely, why don't you have the bed tonight? You look like you could do with it.' She put her head on one side and blinked.

'Um, no. It's fine. I'm used to armchairs. Thanks.'

She wrapped her arms around her chest. Her pyjamas were the colour of Golden Delicious apples. 'What was your date like?' she said timidly, glancing at me and then at the fridge. Colin, nesting in the deckchair, made a sound that might have been a snore.

'Didn't turn up, thank God.' I filled a mug with water.

'Oh. Oh, Shona, I'm sorry.' She sighed and looked at me a bit more. 'I mean just because his mother's friends with Gloria doesn't mean he's not –'

'Fflur, look me in the eye and tell me you had nothing to do with this.' She bit her little finger and pink roses flowered under her eyes. 'I can't believe you – you – that is *so* ...' My breathing was ragged. 'I do not need or want to have men lined up for me. You think I'm some middle-aged mess-head, some sort of ... just because you're so fucking *symmetrical.* I do not need to be set up with some mummy's boy!'

Fflur's eyes filled. She put her hands on her hips, shook her head violently several times and puffed out a sigh. 'He might not be a mummy's boy. We still haven't met him.' Her voice quivered delicately.

'And we never will.' I stalked across to the fridge. 'Unless you're in the market yourself?' Tugging open the fridge door, I turned my back on her and glared at the contents. Half a plastic pot of marinated olives, an opened jar of korma paste, two bites of brie and an apple.

'I was going to go shopping,' said Fflur quietly. 'But I fell asleep.'

I shut the fridge door and swivelled round to lean against it. 'It's not your responsibility to feed us, Fflur,' I whispered, looking at the floor. It was unrecognisable as the floor we'd first met.

'I know,' she whispered back. 'I just ... I like to. If that's OK. But I won't interfere with the boyfriend thing.'

'Thank you.'

She wiped her eyes. 'Ni' night,' she said.

'Night. You keep the bed.'

She paused in the doorway. 'Shona, what do you mean I'm symmetrical?'

I ran the tap to splash my face. She waited.

'It's a compliment, lovely,' I said, drying my face on a clean, ironed tea towel.

'Oh. Right. Thanks.'

Outside, far below, the Wicked Witch of the West screamed, 'Come back here and I'll kill you!' Fflur put her hands over her ears and shook her head and we shared a restorative, conciliatory laugh. She blew me a kiss, and went off to bed, saying, 'Night lovely. And anyway, Dan will come back. I'm sure he will.'

15

With the hostels shut and homeless people rounded up and locked in warehouses, Tramp Flu appeared to be spreading much more slowly. I knew this would be making things harder for Dan, because however unjust the system was, no one could say it wasn't working. I spent a lot of time imagining myself achieving some breakthrough for justice, and his eyes softening and somehow the grotty little scene in his room being put behind us. Benny was all set to snare Minister Mike at the animal centre; I just had to get him there.

Gloria was trying to apologise about the non-appearance of my blind date, and I was kicking myself for not having written her a thank you letter. Now that we were in the office and I was trying to get a favour out of her, it was too late and would seem a bit like an afterthought. Maybe I should even have bought her flowers – it was bœuf en croûte after all. However, I ploughed on.

'Gloria, I wonder if you could use your chummy status with Minister Mike to lean on him a bit.' I placed a mug of tea on her desk and smiled sweetly, stopping just short of ingratiating. Her rosacea pulsed; she looked gently flattered.

'What do you need Michael for?' She tweaked her hair and leant back in her chair.

'Um, right, OK.' I sat on the edge of the other desk, scraping my nail on a pencil sharpener. You have to be pretty determined to self harm with a pencil sharpener, unless you have a very small thin finger. 'What it is, there's an organisation that has been, well, basically *hiding* people's pets. To avoid the cull.' Gloria sipped her tea and sighed at me. 'And Minister Mike is against the cull, isn't he?' She made a noncommittal gesture and swallowed some more tea. 'So what might be good now is if he could visit the animal place. To reassure pet owners. Ow.' I'd managed an inadvertent pencil sharpener injury. 'It would make him look good. MPs like being photographed with animals.'

'Shona,' said Gloria. 'You hate animals.' I looked at her. My reputation as an animal-hater was well dug in. Most people probably assume I hate babies, too, which is unreasonable because I've never really spent any time with one. God forbid. 'So what's all this about?'

'I feel kind of responsible,' I muttered. 'For the cull. If I hadn't panicked about Colin's dog – '

Gloria hiccupped. 'Ye Gods,' she shrieked. 'Don't tell me there was truth behind the midnight burial rumour. I told anyone who asked point blank that it was nonsense.'

'Good.'

'Largely because the idea of you handling a dog, even – especially – a dead one, sounded very, very unlikely.'

I sucked my finger where the nail had caught the pencil sharpener blade; it wasn't bleeding much, it was more of a comfort thing.

'I thought we'd get locked up or something. I'd only just got Fflur out of the warehouse clinic and if we'd turned up at a vet with ...' My stomach splashed revulsion up through my windpipe. 'It was revolting, Gloria. We're talking boils, maggots, rotting fl–'

'Thank you.' She swished her hands in front of her face. I went to the window for some air. 'Now then,' she said, picking up her mug and then changing her mind. 'Heavens above, Shona.' The way she was looking at me, she seemed suddenly like the mother I never had. I shrank and looked at my feet.

'It was a really stupid thing to do. But at the time, under the circumstances, it felt like a reasonable decision.'

'I see. Well.' She rubbed her nose. 'So you want to atone for your sins.'

'I want to make sure the cull is officially stopped and get the message out that animals are safe. There's been some vigilante stuff in some areas.' I stood up straighter and looked at her. 'I do realise that normal people get very attached to dogs and cats. And hamsters. Probably even terrapins.'

Gloria adopted an *I'll-forgive-you-thousands-wouldn't* expression. 'It might well be something Michael would consider,' she said. 'I'll pick my moment.'

I'd have coped with that if she hadn't winked.

Fflur was good enough to circle her birthday in her diary and leave it on the table. Non-birthday people should keep quiet altogether, and birthday people should provide warning. A birthday person who keeps quiet until it's too late is an irredeemable Victim, and asking for it.

I bought her flowers and chocolates and it made me feel like a suitor. She was delighted. She grilled salmon fillets and made a green bean salad, and Colin came to the table and ate like a normal person. Colin and I didn't know when each other's birthdays were because neither of us is a birthday person by any stretch of the imagination.

After the salmon and beans, Fflur's eyes became very bright. The food was finished and there was a gaping hole in the atmosphere. If ever anyone was a birthday person, it was Fflur, and I hadn't even thought about getting a cake. She slid the cellophane off the chocolates with a reverential expression on her face, saying, 'Yum yum.' I put the plates in the sink, furious with myself. A cake would have been easy, probably overpriced, but Fflur would have been disproportionately pleased.

'I'm sorry I didn't –' I said, but Colin took a deep breath and sang over me.

'Ha – ppy bir – thday to you,' he boomed, and his voice was remarkably tenor, 'squashed tomatoes and stew – oo – oo.' He coughed. 'And so on and so on.' The performance didn't quite live up to its early promise, but I was speechless. He'd produced a fruit loaf on a plate, *with a candle in it.* Fflur beamed and we all looked at it for a breath or two.

'Do we have any matches?' I said, thinking how most people I knew carried lighters and could set things on fire at a moment's notice.

'Yes,' said Fflur. She took a large, new box of matches out of the cupboard and gave them to Colin.

'You do it,' she said coyly. Colin's hand shook and he didn't make it with the first match, but the candle took at the second attempt and we all let out an *aah.*

Colin said, 'Aha. So. Do we – what do you think? Do we sing?'

'Sing in Welsh,' said Fflur, clasping her hands together. 'It will remind me of when I was little.'

'Ha. Aha,' I said.

'Right,' said Colin. We looked desperately at each other.

'Pen-blwydd hapus i chi,' I sang, flat as only a tone deaf self-conscious non-birthday person can be. Colin began a little behind me, and it sounded a bit like a round but we staggered through and more or less finished together. Fflur was delighted all over again. She blew out the candle and we all clapped and Colin said, 'I'll do the honours, shall I?'

Benny insisted on the guard dog. A suit, a pointy-faced female aide and a teenage boy with a camera and a boom arrived ahead of Minister Mike, to prepare the scene. Their first hurdle was me clutching the lead of a sabre-toothed bull-faced dog-monster. ('Which is scarier?' said Benny. 'Close run thing.') What I'd said to Gloria, about empathy and so on, wasn't just hot air. I really can see how some of these creatures might appeal to some people. Contrary to popular belief (Nain's and Benny's, anyway), I can put myself in someone else's shoes. And in the same sense that people send each other cards with pictures of kittens or teddy bears embracing each other, I can appreciate the aesthetic appeal of some animals. A cat with three shades of creamy-brown framing its face and a habit of tilting its head to one side might get you (temporarily) overlooking the fluff balls and the stinky food. And the Labrador puppy thing I can go with. They just need culling within a year or so, before they start parking their backsides on everything. But this monster I'd been handcuffed to would have worn a hoody if it could and hung around street corners sneering at people. It had a snout and a fat lip it seemed proud of. I got locked into a staring contest with it, and then it slunk away a bit, stretching the rope between us, dropped its bum and squelched out the contents of its bowels. It won the staring match. And then I could hear it laughing.

'She's the one that buried that dog in the night,' said the pointy woman. She looked at me, delighted with the link, her headline-producers churning. 'Witch,' presumably, for the midnight burial, 'Canine Queen' maybe – about as ironic as you can get. She'd get the arson link pretty quickly, and the quarantine-flouting, germ-sharing selfishness. What she perhaps didn't realise is that the tight set of my face, the teeth-clenching and the twanging nerves, were nothing to do with her at all, but the slobbering werewolf on the other end of the rope. I just hoped it would eat me whole; I couldn't have stood being part eaten. In fact the camera boy had my number quite quickly.

'He's lovely,' he said, grinning at me. 'What's his name?'

I swallowed. 'They're sort of anonymous,' I said. 'Seeing as though they're in hiding.'

'With the full knowledge of the owners in each case?' said Pointy

Woman. 'Is there any substance in the claims that animals are taken without consent?' I experimented with a little flick of my rope in her direction and slobber-chops waggled his muzzle at her. For a second, I felt almost bonded, animal and woman, united against Little Miss Prissy. But I was under no illusions; he'd have had her for a starter and I'd have been the main. And possibly the pudding.

'I would be happy to show you around,' I said. 'If assurances can be given that our – residents –' (this was probably going a bit far) 'are protected.' I looked at the camera boy. 'Maybe you could blur their faces? Like they do with assault victims and celebrities' children.'

'Absolutely,' said the suit. 'The Minister gives his absolute assurance of impunity.'

'Will he be joining us?' I said.

'Absolutely,' said the suit again. Benny led the party to the portakabin, where we were welcomed by Where's Wally falling over bicycles and failing to shake hands properly. Benny took the monster from me and made a performance of play-fighting with it in a way that came so close to French kissing I had to swallow a little ball of sick. The camera boy smirked.

Eventually, Minister Mike arrived and was shunted through, settled on a camping stool and photographed.

'Could we get that dog back in?' said Pointy Woman. 'For a shoot?' She was perhaps unaware of the image I had in response to this word.

'After the interview,' I said, straightening up and folding my arms. 'That may be feasible.' Minister Mike seemed OK with this; he was cyber-wittering away, his attention on a miniature computer in his left hand. 'Can you tell me why seriously ill people are being refused admission to hospital?'

He started the pre-waffle before he realised what I'd said, wading through his bullshit-buffer for a while and then skidding to a halt and putting his witterer in his top pocket. He glanced at Pointy Woman, who was hissing like a swan.

'We're here to talk animal welfare,' she spat.

'Lock the portakabin,' I said and, amazingly, Benny did so.

'Are you attempting to imprison a Member of Parliament?' said Pointy Woman, as if this was out of my league as an offence. I felt a little shiver of delight.

'Good Lord I think I might be,' I hooted. 'What a scream.' Where's Wally made a boom-ditty-boom noise and did a little shuffle-hop-down dance step. 'I want to talk about the warehouse clinic,' I said.

Minister Mike glanced at the suit – I think he was checking whether the clinic existed, officially like.

'Not animals, then?' He scratched his chin.

'You can do what you like with the animals,' I said. 'Rounding up dogs is fine by me. But cramming seriously ill people into warehouses seems an odd way to make them better. Perhaps you'd like to spend the night in there, in the manner of the rough sleepers' initiative. You remember that, I imagine. Some MPs and other selected persons slept in padded cardboard boxes in thermal sleeping bags bought for the purpose.'

I was undercover reporter supreme, human rights champion and queen of the protestors. It was a high point, self-esteem-wise. I could see pointy cogs turning in the aide's head: they'd have to avoid Minister Duped into Defending Inhumane Clinics, by going with Minister Faces Questions Head On about Most Important Issues of the Day. Of course it wasn't the interview he'd been briefed for, so he must have got in huge trouble afterwards. Made assurances he wasn't supposed to make, talked himself into grubby little holes.

Cashing in on my high, I plucked up the courage to ring Dan with my coup. I tried hard to sound nonchalant and cool.

'I've got a tape you might be interested in.'

'A tape?' Dan sounded amused, in that way he had of seeming to enjoy a private joke too adult for me.

'Yes,' I said. 'I got Minister Mike to say that he will personally review the facilities at the clinic.'

'Wow.'

'On tape.'

'So you said.'

'I could sell it to someone else.'

He made a very irritating noise, of the sort heard in primary school playgrounds. Clearly he was still smarting from my deeply regrettable remark about masturbatory aids.

'I didn't realise this was strictly a business call,' he said. 'I thought you'd given up on the whole thing. I'll have to –'

A silent growl rumbled through my chest. 'Don't take the piss, Dan,' I said. 'I'm not in the mood.'

He sighed quietly and I could feel the face he was making.

'Shona, I'm grateful. And I'm impressed. Thank you.' That of course was too direct and I was left in a tangle of feelings I didn't know what to do with.

We met in a cafe – I wasn't sure how I felt about that, whether it was intimate or business-like – so I could hand over my swag. I had photos of Minister Mike with a variety of revolting animals, distinguishing marks to be blurred. There was patting going on, and even a little tussle with a lolloping grey-houndish thing. And a tape recording of the discussion in which he agreed indubitably to review the clinic and to be 'transparent' about the situation and its development. We debated the best course of action here: Dan was for an upfront publication of the transcript, but he was awestruck by my media-savvy argument in favour of keeping Minister Mike on side and biding our time. We agreed that the tape might be mentioned in conversation with the hairy-nostrilled victim and his entourage as required.

And then we looked at each other and I stopped trying so hard to pretend that his smell wasn't that day so exactly of him that I wanted to put my face in the curve where his shoulder met his neck and close my eyes. He, on the other hand, was cling-wrapped into acquaintance mode and our meeting was clearly at an end. It seemed I had well and truly annihilated any chance of my dreams ever coming true.

16

On the television, the Minister for Health was looking increasingly persecuted, grey and lined; you could almost hear his wife shouting in the background, 'And we never see you at all nowadays! You'll make yourself ill!' He was on television most of the day; some of it was live, and in between they re-ran and analysed the live interviews. He yawned at one point, probably exhausted or maybe he was bored with answering the same questions all the time, and of course this yawn was replayed until programmes were having entire discussion slots about it. Had his health been affected by the stress? Was he really up to the task, now that he was so old and infirm? (In fact he looked well under sixty and a yawn seemed like flimsy evidence with which to condemn him.) Body language experts gave opinions on his body language, mostly asserting that the yawn had been a reflex action he couldn't have avoided, but at least it gave them all something to talk about in between repeating the news that experts really didn't know what was causing Tramp Flu or even whether everyone diagnosed with Tramp Flu actually had the same thing.

I went home to check on Nain and to turn the place upside down in search of the bits of paper I needed to sign on (Gloria had told me sympathetically but firmly that she'd sent me my P45. Hardly news, considering my place of work was boarded up and no one would go in – partly because of the germs, and partly because the ceilings might fall down, I suppose.) It seemed that having put everything into cupboards, Nain had then had to pull everything out whenever she needed something, and she hadn't got round to putting any of it back.

I was shunting the sofa aside when a young doctor appeared on the television. He was being followed and interviewed live on his way to work, and he pointed out that although MRSA was now under control, the whole coughing thing was in fact getting worse. And it was the coughers who were dying. Many of them were also covered in boils, but boils with

155

no cough had a much better prognosis. TB, apparently, was also lurking everywhere (by this time Nain was palpating her ribcage and breathing very deliberately), and sat latent in the lungs of healthy individuals (presumably including Nain). And we were back to lowered immunity, because it can be triggered by malnutrition and HIV. There was footage in a long shot of doctors and nurses lining up to go through police barriers to the clinic, wearing face masks and being swabbed. Clearly no reporter in their right mind (which didn't include Dan) would go any nearer. Bullet proof vests and war zones were one thing, Tramp Flu was quite another.

I paddled my hand around in the mess that had regrown on the windowsill since Nain's uncharacteristic tidy up, wondering if we'd end up on television ourselves, in a documentary about socially incompetent hermits who can't get through their front doors because of the rubbish composting all over the place.

'Nain?' I called. 'Have you seen my P60 anywhere?'

She hunched herself around her hot water bottle.

'If I knew what one was ...' she muttered.

'Good point.'

'What? Don't mutter, Shona. You know my hearing isn't what it used to be.'

The mantelpiece pig which wore dungarees and a bow tie seemed more than usual to be glaring at me through its blurry eyes. I'd filled in other people's benefit forms with the efficiency of someone who had a job and a home to go to. Now I was staring at my own, I felt like a fraud. They'd see through me, they'd scour every smudge for evidence that I was in fact a waster with a wide-screen telly and an x-box.

Fflur's mum is over from Singapore and they come to visit together. She's very much in the 'here's one I made earlier' mode. If you rounded Fflur out, cut her hair and carved a few lines on her face, they'd be identical. Rather different to Benny and me, who you'd be hard put to spot in a deck of Happy Families. Though there is something about our noses, which look as if they've been broken even in the baby photos. Dad had a Greek God nose, though it got a bit red and bulbous towards the end.

Across the room, my diazepam supplier keeps adjusting her bra strap. She reaches across her body, using her right hand to fiddle with her left strap and vice versa. I want to tell her to try unhunching her shoulders. They're rounded

forward more tightly than usual, as if she's trying to pull her head into her shell.
Elena the fortune-teller is refusing to speak to her visitor. He looks pretty
dodgy, and he's so grimy he could be her husband or her son; it's impossible to tell.
Fflur has brought in her catalogue to show me; she is blushing with pride.
The style is apparently 'a sort of emo'd-out Cath Kidston,' which I can't quite
picture until she shows me. There's a 'black leather necklace with ditsy pendant'
for £19.99 and a crocheted knuckleduster that's selling particularly well. Colin's
going to set up a website for her. She talks for five minutes without breathing
and then she stutters to a halt and grabs my hand.
'Sorry,' she says. 'Do you want me to shut up?' And I start crying. It feels
odd, and public, and embarrassing. Fflur panics to start with, as if she thinks
she'll get thrown out for upsetting me. 'Visitors are supposed to cheer you up,'
she says. She looks as if she might start crying, too.
'Shona,' says her mum, and her voice is very like Fflur's. 'You know it's
going to be alright. You've got Gloria and Fflur, and me now, if you like. We
women have to stick together.' She smiles anxiously. Fflur swallows and rubs
my hands. We sit like this for a minute or so and I don't know how to move on.
When the invigilator calls time, I squeeze Fflur's hands, wipe my face on
my sleeve for want of a ditsy-print hankie, and ask if I can keep the catalogue.

Nain used to make proper Christmas dinners, until Dad died. After
that she declared that, as neither of us needed all that food, we'd stick
to something lighter. I've been known to smuggle in Quality Street, in
preparation for a secret Christmas guzzle. And I buy mulled wine on the
quiet, for the smell as much as the alcohol.

Colin used to organise a Christmas dinner of sorts at the Shelter, taking
bookings from the first week of December. Alan Turner was a regular. Suzy
would disappear for a while over Christmas and she let us think she was
staying with family, by not saying that she wasn't. Each year I thought
about bringing home a guest or two for a bit of Christmas tea, but Nain
would have fainted at the thought so the plan never materialised. About
half those who signed up for Colin's feast never turned up; memories of
Christmas past can drive you to drink, and we were strictly dry at the Shelter.

Whilst I was serving up potatoes and turkey roll at the Shelter, Nain
would have a nap or ring her sister in South Africa for their annual natter.
(By then, we'd be up to speed with the news from South Africa, having
received their Christmas Letter before November was out. They had

large cards made with a photograph of their house, varying the angle slightly each year, and inside there'd be a thick, sharply-folded sheet of paper. Nain's sister wrote the thing, but nonetheless referred to herself in the third person. It all became a bit regal: *Angela is kept busy on the golf club committee.* Carol would no doubt say that this painful great aunt of mine was to be applauded for taking ownership of her own narrative. Perhaps I should have reciprocated: *Shona continues to form dysfunctional relationships and is fattening up nicely. Season's Greetings to you and yours.*)

After dinner and tinsel at the Shelter, I'd go home for telly and whatever indulgences I could sneak past Nain. Like many people, I was generally relieved to get past Boxing Day and then it was just a quick teeth-grit and New Year was done and dusted. We never had a Christmas tree after Dad died, just the skeleton of the one that died when he did, which took years to disintegrate in the garden. And taking down decorations is such a depressing activity that it was easier not to put them up in the first place.

The Christmas after the Shelter burnt down there were still two places for me to be – remarkable for someone with negligible family and friends. There was Colin's flat, and there was the place I still referred to as 'home'.

Well in advance, Fflur was making snowmen from cardboard tubes from toilet rolls, and lining them up on every flat surface. There were three jolly but lopsided prototypes on the top of the television. She must have been hoarding empty toilet rolls for weeks. There was a lot of cotton wool involved, and raisins and shards of carrot. And – this was one step up on your average snowman – they had beaded crocheted scarves.

Colin patted them from time to time and said, 'Hello little fellas.' When there were no flat surfaces left, Fflur made paper chains from strips of magazines and strung them across the ceiling. Colin followed her around, saying, 'Job for a man, this one,' and climbing up on chairs to reach the corners. 'Rather festive,' he muttered, and made pom-ditty-pom noises. 'Brighten the place up, boom boom.'

What Fflur really pressed for, which the rest of us could see was just not going to happen, was a merger. She suggested we take Colin over to Nain's, partly for the bigger kitchen and partly for the therapeutic value of the outing ('He has to go out sooner or later, it would be cruel to be kind.'). I tried to picture it, the four of us round the table, wearing paper hats. Colin reading, rereading and then analysing cracker jokes. Nain staring at him and escaping upstairs with conspicuous discretion. Maybe we could knock Colin out with a litre or two of mulled wine then, and Fflur and I could kick back with the cheese and biscuits, a bit of Value trifle and some Quality Street. But neither Colin nor Nain supported the plan; in fact you could say they were outright opposed to it.

'That young man must be a seething mass of germs,' said Nain. 'And not just Tramp Flu. There are all sorts of things lurking about in that area of town.'

'You don't feel there's an element of prejudice there at all, Nain?' She pretended not to hear.

When we put the suggestion to Colin, he laughed in the manner of a pantomime villain with a sideline in paedophilia. He heaved in air through the gaps in his teeth for a while and said, 'Well now, Christmas again. Still going with the twenty-fifth, I see. No change there.' He sniffed and gurgled. 'I'll hold the fort here, I think. Watch a bit of nonsense on the box and so on.'

'Honestly, Colin,' I said. 'Nain would love to have us all for Christmas. We'd be doing her a favour.'

'A great kindness,' said Fflur softly, reaching out to pat his arm. He lurched backwards. I wondered if he experienced human touch as a burn or a sting.

So Fflur and I abandoned the blended family thing and agreed to do dinner at Colin's and tea at Nain's.

On The Day Itself, Fflur was up with the larks. She was dressed prettily, fully accessorised and wearing an apron with holly on it. On the back of one of the kitchen chairs was a pastel pink chunky cotton cardigan with the tag still attached.

'Can I help?' I said and she surveyed the kitchen, assessing the situation.

'Roasties are parboiling,' she said. 'I've done the carrots and the sprouts. How are you with devils on horseback?' She was peeling shallots, her bead-threading expression on her face.

'Um. Devils on horseback ...'

Fflur laughed. 'Prunes,' she said. 'Wrapped in bacon.' Obviously. 'They're yummy.'

'I've had little sausages wrapped in bacon. At a conference buffet thing. I ate most of them. They were incredible.'

'These are sweeter.' Fflur wiped shallot juice away from her eyes with her wrist. She consulted a page she'd torn out of a magazine. '9am. Preheat oven.' We both looked at the microwave. 'Never fear,' she said. 'The chicken can go in the microwave. Everything else will do on the hob.'

I quite enjoyed doing devils on horseback. My hands got slimy with fat and prune juice, and I wiped them on my clothes without thinking, so before long I felt like a prune myself, rolling in bacon fat.

We had Radio Two on Fflur's phone in the kitchen and Colin was channel-twitching and humming a Christmas medley at the other end of the room. We opened a bottle of fizzy wine and drank it from some new glasses Fflur had bought 'in a little antiques place round the corner.' I wouldn't find a shop like that in Bath or Brighton, let alone within a twenty mile radius of Colin's estate.

'Cheers!' said Fflur. 'Bottoms up. Colin, are you having one?'

Colin said, 'Fizz fizz pop. Fizzy fizzy pop pop.' It was hard to tell if he was accepting or declining but she poured him some anyway. He took a sip, made a face and said, 'Apropos of nothing much.' He smacked his lips and sniffed. 'When I *go*, as it were, I'd very much prefer the ashes to ashes thing. Dust to dust and so on. If I may.'

Fflur looked briefly alarmed, but then she said thoughtfully, 'I think on balance I'd rather be buried. With my hands folded across my chest. It seems more peaceful. Like an eternal and lovely sleep.'

'Moving on,' I said. Colin cleared his throat.

'Yes,' he said, 'move along now, nothing to see.'

On the radio, they were doing vintage Christmas pop songs. Jolly little numbers that took me right back to those school discos I avoided like the plague.

Later, we left Colin humming the national anthem in front of the Queen's speech and, though I was interested to hear what One had to say about Tramp Flu, warehouses and such, we set off for Nain's with a vague idea of hitch-hiking if there were no buses. The husband of the Pakistani lady whose existence was made miserable by the Disaffected Youths appeared to be sneaking out of the flat next door. Colin's neighbour was ticking something off in her little notebook.

'Now *that* –' I hissed.

'– is probably a good arrangement all round,' murmured Fflur, and as usual it felt as if she was the grown up. 'His wife may be quietly grateful.'

Full of lukewarm chicken, devils on horseback and microwaved Christmas pudding, we should have been too full to move. As it was, the cold air on our faces, and the warmth of the fizzy wine in our blood made us expansive, energetic almost. Fflur linked her arm through mine. I don't think anyone had ever done this before; it felt nice, but a bit precarious, as if I shouldn't breathe too much.

'Happy Christmas,' she sighed. She took a little tissue-paper bundle from her pocket and gave it to me. 'It's just something I made. It's your colours.'

It was a long time since I'd had a present. It was a bracelet made of silver stars and dark green twisty beads that reminded me of pasta. I wasn't sure I felt silver and dark green, but I slid it onto my wrist and smiled at her.

We passed some people coming the other way and Fflur said, 'A merry Christmas to you'. They said, 'And to you,' and it struck me that on any other day of the year we'd all have blanked each other.

Fflur squeezed my arm and rested her head on my shoulder for a moment as we walked.

'Are you thinking about your mum?' I said.

'I try not to.' She plucked a crushed cider can out of a hedge. 'Mum's lovely, it's her partner I can't stand.' We walked on a bit and Fflur dropped the can into a bin attached to a lamppost. 'He's very controlling. I hate the effect he has on her. He's made her into a twitchy old woman.'

I frowned. Fflur was twenty, so it was quite possible her mother wasn't much older than me.

'How old is she?'

'Forty-two.' I gulped. I didn't have long left as a girl-woman if twitchy old bag was on the horizon. 'I know it's not that old,' said Fflur. 'She just acts old.'

I steered her round a pile of fresh warm dog mess.

'When was the last time you saw her?'

'When they left for Singapore about eighteen months ago. It wasn't a very ... loving farewell.' She covered her mouth with her hand. My arm was getting stiff in hers but I could hardly pull away when she was about to cry. 'I refused to go the airport to see them off. By then I was completely ignoring the man she called my stepfather. And I was hiding from Mum most of the time, too.' She let go of my arm and plumped up her hair a bit. 'She said, *Darling, we can Skype*, and I didn't say anything.'

A rabbit (actually it was huge – I'm not sure if that makes it a hare) ran across the road and squashed itself impossibly flat to dash under a fence just inches from the ground.

'I thought rabbits hibernated,' I said. 'What's Skype?'

Fflur laughed and hugged me tightly. 'I love you,' she said. 'You live in the real world like no one I've ever met.'

Nain was crying when we finally arrived; I think we'd lost track of time because we'd somehow walked all the way without getting round to hitch-hiking.

'This is the first time in living memory that I have *ever* had Christmas dinner on my own,' she said.

I kissed her. It was an annual kiss. 'But Nain,' I said. 'You don't even like Christmas dinner. We never have it.'

'Typical of you to focus on the food. It doesn't matter what you eat. What matters is being together.' She patted her cheeks and sniffed. Fflur kissed her.

'Forgive me,' I muttered. 'I didn't realise you valued my company so much. Probably because you keep kicking me out.' I handed her the tissues.

'The scones were warm,' she said. 'They were perfect and now they'll be rock hard.'

'Oh Nain,' said Fflur, and it sounded quite natural. 'We can warm them through a bit and I'm sure they'll be yummy.' Nain made some brave noises and we all went into the kitchen. 'Oh, you've got squishy cream,' cooed Fflur. 'That's just what scones need.'

'And damson jam,' said Nain. 'From the Farmers' Market. I've had it for ages but I scraped the crust off and it's quite fresh underneath.'

17

I know I'm not the only person who hates that dead week between Christmas and New Year, but I do have a good excuse. I was seventeen when Dad dropped his can of Special Brew and fell back on the sofa slurring his words. It was during the post Christmas pre New Year swamp, and I hardly took my eyes off the telly. I got his duvet and threw it over him and sponged the carpet a bit with a tea towel, but it didn't occur to me until I woke up very suddenly at four in the morning that he'd had a stroke.

He lived for a few grotesque months, dribbling in a chair and needing his bum wiped, and before I managed to run away or kill myself, he had another stroke and died in his sleep. I was so relieved I had to smash my left hand to pieces with a hammer, which is why I've never had a driving license.

I left school, where it was now generally assumed I was a lesbian (this was unrelated to Benny's sex-change crisis appearance on TV and based entirely on my refusal to wear make-up, buy clothes, replace food with cigarettes or show interest in extended foreplay). I abandoned my vague plans to become a dentist and got a job in a horrible sandwich/burger place, breathing grease-filled air until I couldn't scrub it off and saying, 'Do you want ketchup with that?' until I was so brain-dead I was squirting ketchup on the counter and stuffing the change between two halves of a bap. Manky Mark worked there between dole-signings for a while, which is how I met him. And it was a friend of a friend of his (someone who knew one of the dubious lurker people, but was actually quite normal) who told me about a job at a day centre. And I found I liked spending the day with borderline-homeless alcoholics loafing around doing nonchalance when inside they were torn apart. I'd found my spiritual home. And got myself on the payroll of an organisation that looked good on a CV and would eventually lead to Senior Support Worker at the Shelter. I wore glasses to the interview in an attempt to look intelligent and so that I could twiddle them and have something to do with my hands. The lenses were clear but they gave me a headache anyway and the morning was clouded in a tight nausea. There weren't many applicants.

Anyway, last year, in the wake of Christmas, I was sitting in front of the telly with Colin, my mind full of white noise where feelings might have been. The loo roll snowmen were looking a bit shifty, as if they knew something I didn't. Fflur cleared up around us and brought us tea and some sticky bread roll things with hazelnuts and syrup in the middle. And suddenly the news was full of a six-year-old girl with Tramp Flu. Her school would not be reopening in January. A sweet-faced woman reading the news speculated on how the disease might have spread to the non-homeless community and then a young man live outside a locked school gate speculated with her, in a dialogue that added nothing new to the story. It was a local school. I clutched the splintery sides of the armchair, staring, and realised I had a tummy ache. Colin started to talk in a monotone without moving anything but his lips and his fingers, which tapped on the arms of the deckchair.

'That's quite a development. A *school*girl. If she's at school, she's got to have a home, ergo, she isn't homeless. Do you need an address to go to school? Bed and Breakfast at the very least. The teachers wouldn't let you go home to a car park, would they? Shona, you're the expert –'

The French had been sniffy for weeks about keeping the Channel tunnel open but this little girl clinched the decision for them and now it was apparently locked and guarded by gendarmes.

My phone rang. I had set it to a free download of a polyphonic but tinny rendition of 'Super Trouper,' which suddenly wasn't funny anymore.

'Nain?'

'Shona? Where are you?'

'Colin's flat. You know that.'

'Just checking. You need to come home, love.' She sounded particularly jittery. 'I've got a cough,' she said, in a stage whisper. 'And a rash.' She paused, her bomb dropped, and I could hear her listening for the explosion.

'You've been watching the news.'

'The news?'

'About Tramp Flu spreading.'

'Well,' she said, 'it was only a matter of time. I imagine I caught it from you. You must be a carrier, even though you take tablets to protect *yourself.*'

I was looking at the screen, where they were now showing footage of the University Hospital. An ambulance drove past at a leisurely pace. A man in a wheelchair smoked a cigarette. 'Is she in hospital?' I said to Colin. 'In the University Hospital?'

Colin bit the nail on one of his long, skinny fingers and tore off a grimy strip.

'Shona? Are you on your way, love?' said Nain. 'I'll sit tight.' Her voice was like a hamster, gnawing at my ear.

'Yes,' I said. 'Yes, I'll come.'

I heard her deflate and begin to breathe.

'Good girl. There's lovely. I'll put the kettle on.'

'Well, it'll take me longer than that, Nain. I'll need to get the bus.'

She'd gone. I danced my thumb over my phone, changing the ringtone to something less grating, and scraped the inside of my cheek with my teeth.

'OK, Shona?' said Fflur, hovering in the doorway. She had a thick needle stuck in her top and she was winding elastic thread round two fingers.

'Yeah. Fine. I'm going home for a bit. I'll see you later.' I rubbed my eyes, thinking I could tuck myself up for a while when I got home.

'Rightyho. You get off,' said Colin to the television.

'Fflur, will you be OK?' I made a sideways nod at Colin, raising my eyebrows. He hummed Super Trouper, banging his fist in time, with an ironic expression on his face.

'We'll be fine, won't we Colin?' she said, winking at me. 'Will you let me know if you'll be in for dinner or not?' I stared at her. 'Pancakes,' she said, little dimples appearing on her cheeks. 'With chocolate spread and bananas.'

I wondered what he was like, Fflur's ex-fiancé. Older? I felt this was likely. Suit? Scruffs? Arty? Serious? Dodgy? I started thinking maybe Fflur was so nice she'd be one of those Rescuer girlfriends, taking on boyfriends who needed shaping up a bit – woolly edges, left school early, possibly dyslexic or with a mild speech impediment. She'd sort out that type with her eyes closed and one hand tied behind her back. But then what if she'd done the bad-boy junkie thing? Going round to his pit and briskly sweeping butts into bins and empties into the recycling. Opening windows and making beds. How tragic if she'd been doing all that only to be abandoned. Not tragic in that she'd be rid of him, obviously; the bastard would probably have let her clear up his shit for years, promising intermittently to try to kick the hard stuff. I couldn't imagine her being led astray, though, unless she was smitten beyond reason.

Nain opened the door in her dressing gown and slippers, carrying a thermometer and a tape measure. She ushered me in silently, glancing into the street and then bolting the door. She gestured me into the kitchen, gave me alcohol gel and sat down carefully. I rubbed gel obediently into my hands and checked the fridge.

'Aloe Vera juice? Fifty percent off? What the –?'

Nain looked as stubborn as a toddler. 'I sent off for it. From the TV Times. It's been used for centuries. For all sorts of things.'

I tasted it. It was foul. She passed me a mint from her pocket. 'I drink the whole dose in one and then crunch one of these,' she said, a fanatical gleam in her eyes. 'It takes the taste away.'

'Right. Fair enough.'

'You look tired, Shona. Flabby.'

I felt pretty tired and flabby. I sniffed. 'Yes,' I said. 'I might sleep for a bit.'

She choked on a sob and I tensed. Suddenly, I was bellowing.

'What do you want? You won't go to the doctor and you won't let the doctor in. You rang and I came home straight away and here I am.' She dissolved. I made some tea and put it on the table and waited for the juddering to blow itself out. We sat for half an hour sipping tea, making more, taking it in turns to sigh. I wondered if I was still being punished for getting Christmas wrong.

Eventually, she said, 'What are you up to all the time? With the Shelter gone?'

'Nothing much,' I shrugged. 'This and that.' We sounded as if we'd arrived at a party too early. 'I've been helping out some friends.'

'Friends? Who?'

'Um, Fflur. And Colin, who works at the Shelter, and –' I couldn't say his name. 'And Gloria,' I said.

'You don't like Gloria,' said Nain. 'You complain about her all the time.'

'Once. Or twice at the most. Don't paint me as some sort of people-hater.'

'You're not a people-hater, love. You're just not what's known as a *people-person*. You were never invited to parties and things when you were little, and you didn't care. You said there was no need for everyone to like you any more than for you to like them back.'

I wanted to drown the woman in Aloe Vera juice. I wrestled with the rusty back door key and stomped into the garden. It was parched and soggy all at once. Like the twigs couldn't be bothered to drink any of the rain so it just made them droopy. Our lidless black bin was half-full of rain water housing growths that blurred the animal-vegetable-mineral boundaries.

It wasn't that Dad was a gardener, but more that we stopped gardening after he died and then Nain even stopped opening the back door. If I opened it when she was in draught distance, she'd flinch and huddle. I planted bulbs from time to time, in the autumn, though I found it hard to get that clump effect. Rows of tulips or daffodils look faintly silly, especially if they're more than a few inches apart. Squirrels generally dug up about half what I planted anyway, to smash on the ground and leave for dead.

I considered lying down amongst the weeds and waiting for the ground elder to strangle me. I flicked some twiggy stubs with my foot and they came out of the ground – just last summer, they'd been a perky little bush of chrysanthemums in amongst the undergrowth. Dad's last Christmas but one, he bought a tree in a pot with roots, and we planted it in January just outside the front door. At the beginning of the following December, he gave me a pitch fork and told me to loosen the earth where I could, but when he came back with the shovel, I'd pulled the tree out in my hands. It had no roots to speak of; it had stood there all year without growing or dying. He looked at me, the shovel in his fists, and I thought he might make a joke about my strength. But he just said, 'You pulled it out.'

I looked at the tree. 'Yes,' I said.

To make it stand upright, we wedged it into a pot with rubble from a skip round the corner. It was quite slanted to start with and by Christmas day the star on the top was resting against the window.

I started on the hideous task of dismantling Christmas particularly early that year. I dragged the tree into the back garden and kicked it to one side. They're spiky, unwieldy things, Christmas trees, but if you ignore them long enough they crumple and shrink out of the way.

I stood now in the garden, surrounded by twigs and rotting weeds, and thinking that I might as well go back to the industrial estate and volunteer. Because someone had to. And because the idea of rotting quietly away in the corner was quite appealing.

Nain was in the kitchen, pretending to read a newspaper but looking out every few minutes to see what I was doing. In the end I stomped back inside and slammed the door.

'I'm going to watch telly,' I said, in the manner of a grumpy twelve-year-old. I was regressing fast; preteenage now.

'Yes, of course,' she muttered. 'Must catch the headlines.'

I slumped on the sofa and chewed my nails. The mantelpiece goat, which had always looked a bit dodgy as a result of the slant of its eyebrows, now seemed to be sneering at me. I wondered how I'd never noticed before that the sheep had its arms folded. The sense I got was of a ganging-up; the ornaments were planning an Orwellian revenge on me.

It was impossible to imagine Dan with Tramp Flu; he was always so impenetrable. But at the same time, it was an image that flung itself into my mind at regular intervals. He behaved like some sort of stupid martyr. As if his crusade was so world fucking important that it was inevitable he had to keep swarming round the virus until he caught it. Russian Roulette with Tramp Flu. Martyr. Idiot. 'Masturbatory aid?' Where had that come from? Was *masturbatory* even a word? It's not a word I'd want to have invented, really. It's pretty icky. I can take or leave sex altogether, in fact. Although when Dan was at the Shelter I was admittedly pretty keen. Gorging, really. Addicted.

I remember closing the curtains at two o'clock one afternoon and he said, 'You want to do it now?' and I felt like a sex fiend. God, it was lovely. He was a laugh, and it was matey and unromantic, but once he got down to it he was a very serious love-maker. He shut his eyes; he never spoke when we were properly at it. And when he was about to come his face would kind of snarl, like he was building up to a fight. I laughed once, when his top lip curled and his teeth were bared, and he made a growling, wolf-noise to cap it all. But I understood, too, because I always liked the sex more than the coming. However much I thought I wanted to come, because that's where it all leads, biologically-speaking, and you're wired that way, there would always be that moment when I'd suddenly gone too far and I couldn't have gone back. And I hated that. That few seconds when anything could have happened and I would have just grabbed his hand and shoved it back where I wanted it, to get where I was trying to go. It was something that had to be endured, got over with, a price to pay for the rest of it. It made me grit my teeth and shake my head and I felt angry with Dan and furious with myself. And then I'd want to get my knickers on, quick, which made me feel guilty and I'd lie wound together with him knowing that I should be properly appreciating the moment because this was what I craved and thought about all the time, but all I could think about now was not getting slime on the sheet or on him and whether it was OK to move yet.

Nain was gripped by the spiralling discussion on the television.

'Poor mite,' she said, tutting and sniffing simultaneously. (The sound was not unlike a truffle pig they had on Masterchef once.) 'That young girl is dying because her mother put the tramps before her.' I focussed my eyes. The screen extreme close-upped on a photo of a blonde tumble-locked little princess in a school uniform.

'She's not dying, Nain. And don't say 'tramp'. Tramps are characters in children's stories. These people are –'

'I know, I know. Don't nag me, Shona. I'm not up to it.'

A spokesperson stood beside the girl's mother. Spokesperson? Since when did I use that word without cringing and where do you find such things when you suddenly need one? But then the camera lingered on the mother and I sat up.

'I've met her,' I said.

The mother of the very white little girl with Tramp Flu was apparently the very black Jamaican nurse who'd admitted Fflur to the clinic. They were asking her what she thought about allegations that she'd given her daughter Tramp Flu through her own carelessness; had she taken all the barrier nursing precautions? Had she had regular testing? Missed a dose of antibiotics?

'Shona, stop ignoring me. Who have you met? When? How?' Nain looked ready to pounce. As if we might catch it from the TV.

'The mother,' I said. 'She works at the industrial estate clinic where I took Fflur against my better judgement.' I tweaked at a flap of something on my thumb, too hard to be skin and too soft to be nail. A blob of blood emerged, hovering. I sucked it.

'Right,' said Nain. 'We'd better get me to hospital.'

I lay down and put my thumb in my mouth and a cushion over my face.

'They might agree to put you down.' This was unintelligible perhaps through the thumb and the cushion. I pressed the cushion harder over my face, making sparkly dots dance and fizz. She did some more truffle-pigging and some muttering and then fell silent in front of a truly bizarre game show.

I woke up with the cushion still on my face. My arms exploded with pins and needles when I moved.

'You've been snoring,' said Nain. 'I made some soup but it's gone cold.'

169

I heaved myself up, dabbing at a streak of blood I'd left on the sofa.

She hadn't so much made soup as poured a tin into a bowl and micro-waved it. She had been known to make soup, but it had a gaggingly-thick skin and I'd generally discouraged it since.

'Thank you,' I croaked. 'I'll put the kettle on.'

By the time I'd made the tea and found some deep fried desiccated carrot peelings I'd bought as a possible crisp-substitute, the Minister for Homelessness had resigned. It seemed an odd response to developments, but it was reported in tones that implied it had been the only decent thing to do in the circumstances. He hadn't kept the public safe. Our very own Michael Blakelock MP of hairy nostril fame had already been invited to take his place, and he seemed delighted.

'There is in fact no need for anyone to sleep rough. Everyone, including the most vulnerable people, has shelter and treatment no-questions-asked.' He sounded as if he had already solved the problem.

Presenters and journalists led public horror that a ringletted schoolgirl hadn't been adequately protected from the homeless and the squalor for which it seemed they were responsible. I lay on the sofa eating desiccated carrot peelings while they interviewed the little girl's friend's aunt about how irresponsible everybody had been – MPs, nurses, the child (*she's only six. Her mother shouldn't have put her in a position where people stopped inviting her to tea and of course no one would hold hands when there were partners*).

Nain announced that she was putting her affairs in order. I sucked sticky orange dust from my fingers and she went off in a huff because I hadn't even looked at her.

On TV, a clean-shaven doctor with electric blue eyes was warning view-ers that emails offering Tramp Flu vaccinations were not from bona fide drug companies and that the truth was that, as we still weren't sure what Tramp Flu really was, there was no approved vaccine. At best, these internet scams would be sugar or vitamins. They might of course be dangerous. He made a 'keep calm' face. I wiped my hand on the sofa. Maybe Dan was right. Maybe there was a conspiracy to kill off the homeless, only it had got out of control. Or perhaps it was terrorists or Nazi-style state research. Or terrorists pretending it was Nazi-style research. Or Nazi-style research using the cloak of homelessness. Or something.

18

Outside the Learning Centre window, the rose bushes are growing. It's early yet and too far to see the really small buds, but they're on the way. When roses are wide open, when they're really fat, I can't take my eyes off them. They're too lovely to be real. I planted a rose in the back garden the summer of my GCSEs and it isn't exactly prolific but it does flower. When a butterfly lands on it, I feel like it's giving me a compliment. The tiny hard-shelled beetle things that breed in their thousands all over the stems are another matter. I've been known to squirt the bastards with so much pest-killer they drown in the stuff before they can overdose on it. This violence is driven by love, because if I didn't love roses so much, then I wouldn't hate the bugs. I probably wouldn't even notice them, actually; you have to bend down and focus, but once you've seen one or two, you realise they're everywhere. The rose chokes underneath them. Drenching them with pest-killer is the only way of rescuing the rose, and even then there's a Darwinian system of comeback, and you can almost hear the new improved armour-plated scuttlers laughing. Then this winter, during the frost, a miniature rose opened out on the end of a dead twig, and it felt like it was working on a new strain of its own.

I abandoned my New Year's Resolution to contract a particularly virulent strain of Tramp Flu and roll over to die when Dan turned up at Colin's saying if it was the sex that was the problem, we should do without it but please could we do the mates thing. He still wanted a Maid Marian, that was the trouble, so it was hard to tell if it was my company he wanted or my contacts. Which makes me sound like a high-flying networker, but in fact it was my inside knowledge of the grotty, gormless underworld he was after. And of course I was disappointed about the sex thing because my self-esteem had plummeted to an all time low and masturbatory aid seemed like a reasonable career choice. But as I hadn't washed my hair since I flounced out on him, I wasn't best placed to throw myself at him and caddying was the next best thing. So I found myself settling him at Colin's table with a bright pink mug of tea while we waited for Fflur to come back in and stop pretending she was making the bed.

'The point is,' he said, 'this child with Tramp Flu symptoms is in *hospital*. Not a warehouse.'

I swilled out my mug and upturned it on the draining board. I thought I saw some sort of skank-monitor on his face register the fact that I hadn't done much with the rim, so then I overdid it and ran half a sinkful of water with some vicious cleaning fluid Fflur had bought. I made efficient squeaking noises soaping the mug and listening to Dan's outrage.

'We need to find out what exactly is wrong with this kid. I'm pretty sure she's got respiratory symptoms rather than dermatological.'

I rinsed the mug, splashing my sweatshirt.

'You've been reading up, professor.'

'Don't pretend to be thick, Shona. You're an intelligent woman.'

I don't think I'd been called that before, and I was surprised how small it made me feel. He got up and prowled, picking up a tired loo roll snowman.

'What the –?'

'Fflur made them. For Christmas.'

'Of course.' He looked up at the paper chains and sighed. 'It'll be interesting to see how quickly the school mates start coming down with it.'

That annoyed me; I slammed the mug upside down on the draining board and a bright pink chip flew into the water.

'I'm sure dying schoolgirls make a great story,' I said (witheringly), 'but try not to look so smug about it.'

'She's not dying. She's got the full resources of the University Hospital on her case. There'll be IV antibiotics and oxygen and topical steroids if –'

I dried my hands on my sweatshirt. 'What are we hoping to achieve here? You want the homeless patients moved to the University Hospital?'

'And an apology. For letting things get out of hand because it was *only* homeless people affected. An acknowledgement by our mock-socialist government of their underlying fascist ambitions.'

'Right.' I didn't laugh; his face looked like an ultimatum. *Laugh and I'm outta here.*

The only spanner in the works was Nain, who rang to say she was having severe breathing difficulties. She certainly sounded as if she was being strangled, but she was good at that. I had Dan standing in the doorway,

172

jiggling his keys as if we were about to race off in a Dan-mobile instead of standing under a vandalised shelter waiting for a bus. And Colin was doing an especially loud and monotonous hum, so it didn't take much effort to be short with her.

'There's heavy snow on the way, too,' she said. 'It's dangerously cold.'

'Nain,' I said. 'I have things to do. Shall I ring an ambulance for you?'

'No. I don't like to put anyone out.'

'Except me.'

Wounded silence.

'Shona, you're family.'

'Worst luck.'

Fflur touched my shoulder and I realised I had my head pressed against the wall.

'I'll go, lovely,' she whispered. 'Tell your Nain I'll come over and get her some lunch.' She glanced at Colin. 'I'll leave some food out here.'

We persuaded Nain that, as a recovered victim, Fflur was the safest person to have in your home. And we abandoned Colin, with a little trail of delicacies which Fflur assured us he'd be more likely to eat if we were out. She said it was actually kinder to leave him alone from time to time because our presence was paralysing him. She got her things together to go and see Nain – 'We'll make cakes. She'll be fine'.

There was snow in the air ready to strike. The skin on my hands and face shrivelled on impact and I aged ten years in a second. I'd just been for a wee but suddenly I needed another.

At the bus stop was a young man in denim combat shorts and sandals with wide leather straps. I perched on a broken plastic seat.

'Won't they call security if we're caught poking around the hospital?' I said.

'Chicken,' said Dan, making little flapping movements with his elbows and grinning. It wasn't the dazzle smile he did to make you see things his way; it was a glimpse of the boy he was before he became ultra-cool-travel-the-world-and-lay-his-head-wherever-his-hat-fell. It was pretty special. I took the grin and tucked it in some internal pocket to fiddle with and gaze at when I was alone, or waiting for a bus without the real thing.

'Are you going for some journalists' award or something?' I muttered, pretending to text someone and feeling obvious. 'Undercover reportage?' I sniffed quickly before my snot turned to ice.

He sighed and raised his hand to hail the bus as if it were a cab in

Mayfair. I stuffed my phone in my pocket and trotted onto the bus behind him, huffing because he paid for me without asking.

Where the bus should have turned up the street towards the hospital, it swung all the way round a miniscule roundabout and doubled back. We stood and made our way down the aisle, Dan steady and me catching people's bag straps and coat hems and apologising.

'It's only ambulances up there,' said the driver, making a masturbatory gesture at a motorcyclist considering suicide.

'Can you let us off here?' I said.

The driver ignored me completely and we ended up walking about a mile back on ourselves. It was scarily cold, and I had to concentrate on not wetting myself and keeping sniffs to under three or four a minute.

In front of the hospital, two film crews were drinking coffee from a campervan that had maybe disguised itself as an ambulance to get through. Police officers were wrapping them up with Police Incident tape, going round in circles to herd them into a pen.

'Can I help you?' A huge policeman appeared in front of us, dwarfing Dan which put him in his place for a minute. He was a bit prop-forward, and there were jet black curls popping out from under his hat.

'We were hoping to visit ... someone from work,' said Dan.

'Which ward?' said the giant policeman, and blew on his paws.

'Dickens,' I said. Dan swallowed.

'Care of the elderly,' said the policeman.

I tutted. 'I know. She's outraged. She turned sixty and all of a sudden she's told she's geriatric.'

Suddenly, Dan put his fingers in his mouth and whistled loudly. 'Paul mate!' he called.

Paul the fart-burner was dressed in scrubs and manoeuvring a trolley with a rumpled blanket on it across the main entrance.

'We're visiting Gloria,' called Dan. 'She's on Dickens.'

Paul smirked and nodded at the policeman.

'I'll take them up,' he said, and – bizarrely – the policeman left us to it. We scurried over to Paul and the irony wasn't lost on any of us.

'What are you up to, Dan mate?' He made a gross leery face and wiggled his skinny hips.

'Actually, Paul mate, I might need a bit of a favour.' Dan sounded like an understudy for The Bill, it was a bit grim. Paul waggled his tongue and Dan didn't flinch.

So we got into the hospital under cover. Paul enjoyed that joke for several minutes; I was under the blanket, lying on my side (I was a bit concerned that there might be a pregnant silhouette if I lay on my back – I'd been going to check in a mirror but then I forgot about it when there was no hope of doing anything involving lying down in sight of Dan, and now it was too late). It was a relief to warm through. I flexed my fingers experimentally to see if they still worked. I curled up and Paul tucked me in (again, quite bizarre, but then the whole thing was a bit beyond) and I pulled up the holey blanket to hide my face. Dan put his hand on the hump of my thigh (with the blanket in between, but it was still rather nice) and Paul marched us along the corridors, flapping through great heaving rubber doors and past chamber of horrors sound effects. From one ward came the sound of a drunken, deep-voiced man yelling what sounded like, 'Olé!' I had visions of castanets but as we got closer I realised he was probably shouting, 'Ali!' and that Ali might be long gone. Paul pressed a lift call and picked his nose while we waited.

'Dossers' Disease has really taken off,' he said, in the safety of the lift. 'They're lining them up in the corridor.'

Dan made one of those faces you forgive people when you fancy them, but if you were married to them you'd hate. I heaved myself up onto my elbows.

'How the fuck did you get a job as a hospital porter, if you don't mind me asking?' I said. The strip light and the distorted mirror effect of the steel walls were not kind to any of us. Paul's head looked like the surface of the moon on a cheesy day. He laughed gratingly.

'Not too many applicants?' murmured Dan. Paul clicked his fingers and belched.

'Did you do that in the interview?' I said. 'Or did you go with the lighting the fart thing?'

Dan slapped me gently on the thigh. I tucked this into the same pocket as the grin.

'I was doing the pick-ups from the warehouse,' he said. 'As in –' he drew his finger across his throat, '– pick-ups. But now I specialise in hospital morgue runs.'

The blanket suddenly seemed a bit too close to my face.

'Honestly,' he continued. 'I'm fearless. I'll touch boils with my bare hands. I've done it all. I've stuffed my hands up –'

The lift pinged, thank God, but the remnants of the idea were left with me. As Paul trundled me out, two schoolboys in white coats stood back politely. Trolleys were lined up in the corridor with people who looked like they'd been there since the dawn of time. The relatives had kicked the patients off so they could have a turn lying down.

The ward was like the warehouse but with linoleum flooring. We were approached by a nurse in full nuclear protection and I sat bolt upright, which wasn't part of the plan, and cried out 'I'm fine now!'

Paul, the bastard, said, 'Let us be the judge of that.' The nurse folded her arms and looked at him as if I was his fault.

'Where am I supposed to put her?' she said. 'Just park her.' She glanced down the ward. 'In fact, check bay three. She's stopped coughing.'

'There we are,' said Paul cheerily. 'Problem solved.'

I was about to swing myself off the trolley but Dan's hand clamped down on my shoulder. The nurse left to catch some vomit in a cardboard dish that didn't look up to the job and I looked around and then up at Dan. He gave a slow nod as if to say *give it time*.

'Paul, where's the kid?' he whispered. 'The schoolgirl?'

Paul gestured with his head, and Dan checked no one was looking and helped me off the trolley (irritating? Gentlemanly? Couldn't decide). I dived into a cubicle that said 'Toilet for Patient's Only'. If they got me, I'd divert attention to the apostrophe. After a wee that seemed to go on forever and wouldn't be rushed, I emerged a new woman. I could hear Dan's voice, and I ducked past the Marie Celeste nurses' station and into a side room.

Sitting in an armchair, apparently asleep, was the fat Jamaican nurse from the industrial estate. And in the bed (playing with a modern day version of the little Snoopy tennis game I got from my mum out of the blue once in the post), was the schoolgirl Tramp Flu victim, as seen on TV. I looked at Dan. I felt horrible, like someone who stares when they go past a funeral, but Dan was buzzing. Paul had disappeared. The girl looked up from her game and Dan gave her his smile. She blushed and twinkled and glanced at her mother. Dan put his finger to his lips and winked.

'How're you feeling?' I whispered, as if it was any of my business. She shrugged, and pointed to her chest. Dan edged forward to rest his hands on the foot of her bed. He began to flick through the file of notes hanging on a bulldog clip.

'What've they done to you so far?' he said, with a conspiratorial eye roll. He ran his finger down the notes and looked as if he was about to nick a page as evidence, but the mum woke up. They looked at each other for a moment, and then she stood and her eyes bulged.

'What – who – oh God, I don't believe it.' She put a shaking hand on her daughter's shoulder. 'Have you taken photos? Of Lucy? Have you?' She was moving forward, about to strike.

Dan put his hands up.

'No, no.' He spoke quietly, calmly. 'I come in peace.'

She sank down, deflated, and rubbed her eyes until they were bruised. 'What are you doing?' she mumbled, after a while. 'You got your girlfriend to fake a bit of staph so you could get into the clinic, and now –'

'She's not his girlfriend,' I said. Somewhat unnecessarily, perhaps. Dan suppressed a grin. Mum seemed to like that.

'I'm Dan,' he said. 'I need to talk to you.'

Lucy tried to speak and it sent her into a choking-coughing cycle that involved her mother attaching an oxygen mask to her face and propping her up on some pillows. Eventually she sank back with her eyes shut and stuffed some earphones into her ears. Mum puffed out her feathers.

'What's your name?' said Dan, so kindly that she shrank again and told him.

'Natasha.' She swiped at her face with her palms.

'Lucy will be fine,' said Dan gently and convincingly. Then a bit more hesitantly, he murmured, 'Underlying health issues ...?'

Natasha shook her head. I fiddled with the hook where the notes hung, jamming a little screw between my nail and my fingertip. Somehow Dan managed to get round by the side of the bed and start browsing get well cards on the locker.

'I'm making a statement later,' said Natasha, settling sideways into the armchair so she could keep her eyes on Lucy. 'But we're not doing a tear-jerker special, I'm afraid. So you'll have to get the story with everyone else.' She examined her own nails. 'Although I do have some respect for you.' She sounded pretty grudging. 'There weren't many journalists who braved the industrial estate. You're a bit of a war correspondent, aren't you?'

Clutching a piece of pink notepaper covered with felt tip messages and smiley faces, Dan turned to face her across the bed.

'This statement you're making,' he said. 'I think you have a duty here.' Natasha snarled and rested her eyes for longer than a blink. 'Lucy will recover because she is being cared for in this hospital,' he continued. 'And she had a head start anyway because she's a well-nourished privileged little kid who gets wrapped up warm every night.' Natasha swallowed but kept her eyes closed. 'How many deaths did you see in that warehouse?'

She opened her eyes to look at Lucy and then scowled at Dan.

'Would you go away before you say anything else quite so tactless?' she said, and glanced at me as if I could do something about him.

Dan put down the notepaper and rammed his hands into his pockets.

'Please, Natasha,' he said, though he wasn't pleading, he was staring her down. 'You have to speak out. People will listen to you at the moment, you're today's news. And what you have to tell them is –'

'I don't have to tell them anything at all, boyo –'

Dan did his smile. 'Thanks very much.'

She glared at him and he did incorrigible but irresistible until she stopped foaming at the mouth. He sat on the corner of Lucy's bed then, as if he was a visiting teacher or something. I noticed she had some squeezy yogurts tucked in amongst the grapes on her locker.

'I could use my moment in the spotlight to talk about that bloody clinic,' said Natasha after a while and Dan nodded encouragingly. 'I could talk about the deal I make with myself: if Lucy gets better, I'll give up work and be a proper mother. I think a lot about why I was ever at that place.' She made fists with her hands and knocked her knuckles together. 'I went back to work because it was more interesting than staying at home cooking tea and washing PE kits. And perhaps there was something exotic about the clinic. It was a tempting antidote to PTA meetings and school runs. And now of course I wish I'd never even heard of –' I winced as she finished her sentence with her knuckles.

Dan did look a bit unsettled. He hadn't thought of this. That a nurse might in fact be a nurse less because she wanted to be than because she was bored with the PTA. We sat in silence for a bit and the beat from Lucy's iPod filled the space between us. We heard the nuclear-clad nurse on the telephone and Natasha looked suddenly puzzled.

'How did you get in here?' she said. 'It's barrier nursing and quarantined.'

'Friends in high places,' I muttered. It occurred to me that we might not be allowed out; the gate might be a bit one way.

'Maybe you could get your friends in high places to talk to the new Minister for Homelessness.' Natasha massaged her scalp in the manner of the seriously stressed. 'He's coming to nod at me tomorrow. Through a thick plastic barrier probably.'

'Ah, Minister Mike,' said Dan, smiling. 'He's a particular friend of Shona's.'

Natasha's phone beeped and she slipped it from her pocket, scowling. She clicked and glanced then pressed down hard to turn the phone off.

'OK?' I said. 'Can I – we – do anything?' She looked so miserable. So friendless. She gave a short little snuffle of a laugh.

'PTA,' she said, waving the phone. 'Oddly enough, we had a meeting once about kids who were organising barrages of nasty text messages. It felt worse than a thumping in a way, more devious. And now ...' She snuffle-laughed and had to rummage in her sleeves for a tissue. 'I'm getting shitty little texts.'

'The PTA?' I was outraged.

'They're scared,' she said, easing herself out of her chair to look through the window. 'Some of Lucy's friends are showing symptoms. It's snowing. A bit.' And then she started crying and bit her fist and turned away in case Lucy opened her eyes or heard a sob through a break in the playlist. 'I couldn't live with myself if – but if I had to *choose*, I'd choose Lucy. You know, if it came to one of those deals ...' Dan was up and right by her, holding her shoulders and looking intensely into her face.

'But of course it doesn't work like that,' he said. 'There's no choice here, no either/or. These kids will be fine. All of them.' He shook her a little bit. 'Really fine.' Natasha succumbed to the Dan treatment and pulled herself together under his gaze. Quietly, he added, 'It's the other kids who won't be. The ones we left out in the cold a bit too long. And then when they came out in boils we could hardly let them in.'

Snow was falling in satisfying round blobs that splattered gently on impact. I paused outside my front door, watching the street turn white and the dog mess and litter disappearing. The smell of bread enveloped me as I pushed open the door.

Fflur was in the hallway on her mobile, wearing an apron. She waved at me and made a blah-blah-blah sign at the phone. I shut the door quietly, shaking at the sudden change in temperature, and stamped my trainers on the mat. I crept past Fflur to the kitchen, following my nose. The hallway looked bigger. The broken mirror had gone, and there was no junk mail on the floor.

Nain didn't look directly at me. She was very busy checking something in the oven. The radio had been brought down from her bedroom and given a good wipe, and they were listening to Radio Wales.

'I hope you've taken your shoes off,' she said. 'Can you pass me that spatula?' She squinted into the oven and held out a hand. I found a plastic scraper thing on the side by the sink and gave it to her. She didn't do anything with it, just closed the oven door and put it down again. On the radio, the newsreader said that there were reports of two cases of extremely sick homeless people just north of Paris. Apparently the French were up in arms about the Channel tunnel having been shut too late.

'I'm gasping for a cup of tea,' announced Nain.

'Right,' I said. 'Yes, me too.' I filled the kettle, which looked somehow different in the way that men do when they've shaved off their beard and you can't quite put your finger on it. I curved my fingers round it while it boiled.

'I'll have camomile and rosehip,' said Nain. *Camomile and rosehip?* She looked at me still in my grubby jacket. 'Are you not stopping?'

I opened the cupboard but Fflur came in saying, 'They're on the side. In the pink tin.' She was suspiciously casual, pocketing her mobile and blinking brightly. She gave me a small pink tin, smiling. I prised off the lid and picked out a little pink teabag.

'Do you want one of these?' I asked Fflur.

'Er – yeah. Yes I will. Thanks.' Her mind was still on her mobile. The news gave way to the weather forecast. The cold snap was predicted to last at least a fortnight. It was winter, spring was miles away, and as headlines go I felt this one might reasonably have been bumped by something more newsworthy. I liked the onomatopoeia, though. Essentially, what we were experiencing was more a *cold splat*, or a *cold squish*. A *cold snap* was a nice spin, I thought. She sat down at the table and sighed sweetly. 'How are things?'

Nain shuffled from foot to foot a bit, as if it wasn't her place to sit down without being asked.

'Not great,' I said. 'Lucy Johnson – the kid in hospital? She's pretty ill.' I pulled out a chair and sat down. 'Is this bread for anything special? Can I –'

'Mm, yes, do,' said Fflur, and got up to make the tea I'd abandoned. I tried to tear the edge neatly off the warm loaf but a huge chunk came with it. Nain tutted so discreetly it was more a ripple in the air than a sound. I hate tutting. All my life I have been tutted at. I stuffed a piece in my mouth. It was delicious.

'Mm, bloody lovely.' Fflur handed Nain a cup of tea – not a mug, a cup. A delicately patterned china teacup with matching saucer. Nain put it on the table and sat down. 'Is that one of ours?' I said. A wodge of bread got stuck to the roof of my mouth. 'I've never seen it before.'

'We went to a car boot,' said Fflur. 'We got a whole set for ten pounds, with just a little chip in the teapot. So what's happening? Where's Dan?' She blinked at me, wide-eyed. I dislodged the last of the sticky bread with my fingertip and sucked it.

'Firing off letters and articles. For all the good it will do.' I ground my teeth a bit. The radio presenter suggested that people could text or email him their pictures of the cold snap (snow sculptures, for instance, or the four hundred lorries on the hard shoulder of the M25). Perhaps he was planning to describe them in vivid language for the listeners to imagine.

A small plastic chick on top of the fridge started leaping up and down making a noise like a vintage fire engine and Fflur got up and looked in the oven.

'It needs a bit longer,' said Nain, sipping her tea. 'I had a look.' She was experimenting with ways of holding the teacup. Fflur glanced at the clock.

'Tell you what I'll do,' she said. 'I'll switch it off but leave it in for a few minutes.' She turned the knob to zero and humphed down in the chair. 'Maybe it's a good thing Tramp Flu has crossed over to non-homeless people. Well, obviously not good. But it will shake things up. They'll have to let everyone into hospital now.' I shrugged and gouged another hole in the bread. 'They can hardly send Mr and Mrs General Public, and certainly not children, to the warehouse place.' She made a face. 'And you can't have one rule for some and another for everyone else.'

Nain was nodding sagely. 'Don't eat all the bread, Shona,' she muttered.

19

*B*ehind the roses, the clematis is growing too, winding its way around whatever it can find. It's as sinister as a triffid, really, in the way it sends out little shoots to grab the stems of other plants and the bits of broken chairs piled up against the wall. But somehow you can understand its neediness, its selfish clinginess; clematis only flower for a fortnight. Fifty weeks of growing and waiting, and then a two week exhibition when suddenly everybody notices them.

The magic of shifting shape, colour and texture only lasted a day or so, and then the snow turned to mush. It emerged that Strasbourg had discreetly disposed of the body of a Polish man found in a car park, and this turned out to have been not long after Alan Turner died. The television and newspapers were able to take a break from finding and interviewing anyone who'd ever met Lucy's family and to turn their attention to being rude about the French. *French Lied About Tramp Flu! The Big French Cover-Up: Did WE Get it From THEM?* The tunnel stayed firmly shut.

Germany grudgingly admitted a few suspected cases, but one or two of them just looked like they thought it would be fun to get on the news. The French government, however, was rolling out the warehouse clinic system conspicuously and with gusto. No one could accuse them of failing to protect the public. They boasted a capacity of a thousand beds for each large town or city, and several times that for Paris. There was a *Les Misérables* feel to it all.

Dan rang to tell me he was coming to Colin's.

'I need your help,' he said, and his voice made my breath shallow.

An hour later, he came staggering through Colin's front door with the remains of a girl draped across him, coughing into his chest. They were both sleet-splattered. Dan had a black binbag over his shoulder like a Value Father Christmas. He looked at me and jerked his head in the direction of the bedroom. I opened the door and he backed in, nodding at the duvet. The duvet cover was the pattern of First Great Western upholstery and Fflur had actually ironed it. It looked starched too, as if she'd sharpened the corners by sticking a pencil into them like Mrs five-eighths-of-an-inch taught us at school. Beneath the First Great Western surplus, a sheet had been hospital-cornered. Pinned against the wall as Dan lowered the girl onto the bed, I realised it was Suzy. Streetwise, carefree, spring-in-her-step Suzy, last seen casually entrusting me with all her worldly goods.

Her eyes were shut. Dan leant against the wall and panted.

'We need to change her clothes,' he said. 'She needs dry stuff.'

He started pulling off her clothes, murmuring to her softly. He looked pretty drenched himself. I scuttled obediently into the sitting room and grabbed a sweatshirt and some socks. On Suzy, of course, the sweatshirt was like a dress.

'Bucket. Or washing up bowl.' There was an edge to Dan's voice that made me feel as if something were my fault; there being so many steps, Suzy being so heavy, but so skinny and so revoltingly unwell.

Fflur had furnished the place with a washing up bowl but it was too nice to let people puke into it, so I rummaged in the cupboard under the sink and found a little stack of dog bowls at the back. These things were pristine under the external coating of moist dust that still clung to anything Fflur hadn't got her hands on. There was a pink one labelled 'hors d'œuvres', a green one labelled 'entrée' and a brown one labelled 'désert'. Each had a line drawing of a doggy face licking its chops staring out from the base, which was enough encouragement to put them right in the firing line. I selected the green one, largely because of that irritating little voice that pipes up with arbitrary instructions such as *if you use the pink one she'll die and if you use the brown one you'll wet yourself in public*. At times like these, the race is on to move fast and take action before you find out what the remaining option will set in motion. You can be left in limbo, hovering indefinitely between contracting HIV from a bleeding Shelter resident and losing your Significant Other (Nain, recently replaced by Dan).

Dan was stroking Suzy's hair, picking a wet strand from across her face where it was anchored in a crack on her lip.

'Where did you find her?' I said, putting the dog bowl on the floor beside the bed. Dan sighed and rubbed his eyes so hard the lids turned inside out.

'She was hiding,' he said. His eyes reshaped themselves, red and raw from the attack. 'She knew the clinic would kill her.'

'Where?' In the sitting room, Colin turned up the sound on the telly. 'Where was she hiding? They've been arresting everyone.'

Dan stood up and walked me out into the hallway. He spoke through his teeth.

'That clinic is a dual-purpose amenity.'

I followed him into the kitchen, where he hovered about, fiddling with the loo roll snowmen and flicking the switch on the kettle on and off as if he'd never made a cup of tea in his life. Colin glanced at us, half rose from the deck chair, preparing his hand to shake Dan's, and then started humming and adjusted his trousers instead.

'Hi Colin,' said Dan. 'I'm afraid I've brought you another guest. Three little women you've got yourself now.' I plonked a cup of tea in front of him, letting it splash his sleeves. He looked at the tea, raised his hand in the manner of a courteous motorist and took a sip.

'Where's Fflur?' he said.

I shrugged. 'I don't think she signed out.'

He sighed. 'Don't get stroppy, Shona. It's important to keep tabs on each other. I don't want any of you wandering off without making sure someone knows where you're going and when you'll be back.'

'She's at mine,' I said. 'I think she's adopted Nain. Or Nain's adopted her. One or the other.'

Dan nodded as if this was part of his plan. 'But you'll stay here with Suzy for me, right? There's stuff I have to do, and I need to know you're both OK.'

I pursed my lips and took a punnet of tomatoes out of the fridge. I washed them and twisted the stalks off in efficient, precise little movements whilst I tried to form a retort. *Who the hell do you think you are? Just because you've travelled the world and thrown your hat in all the best saloons and there's presumably a girl in every port damn the bitches.*

'I've seen a bit of life too, you know,' I said. 'I once took a sock off an old guy who turned up at the Shelter and –'

'I know. His toes came off with the sock. Urban myth.'

'Yes. Well. I've lived the urban myth.'

Dan drank his tea. 'We have to get antibiotics. For Suzy.'

'You didn't smuggle any out of the hospital, then?'

He tapped his fingers on the table while he thought. Then he looked at me. 'No,' I said. 'And not Fflur either. You do it.'

He shook his head and stifled a hiccup. 'I don't think we should go faking symptoms. We don't know how far you can go now without being admitted.' I bit a tomato and it splashed seeds and juice onto my top. 'Could we get in touch with Debbie again? Ask her to get hold of something a bit – um – discreetly?'

'Dan.' I squished a bit of tomato between finger and thumb. 'No. Just no.'

He hiccupped again and it made him frown. 'You could Facebook someone else.'

'Shona has sent you a friend request. And asks if you could prescribe the following on the quiet like.' I turned away and stared out of the window.

'What about Manky Mark? Do you see him around at all?'

Dan's voice sounded horrible. He was tired and stressed and knowing what was in store for him must have made him cynical. As if there was nothing to be done but stare into the barrel of the gun. He was cannon-fodder. And proud of it. I wonder sometimes if he felt the only alternative for someone like him, once he'd finished being a cool young traveller, was to be an embarrassingly gristly middle-age peddler of travellers' tales. He'd become Conrad's Marlow, mumbling about the *horror*. And sending thousands of sixth form students to sleep.

He examined the ceiling for a while, where the magazine chains were sagging under the weight of a few weeks' dust.

'I'll go to the hospital,' he said at last.

'And?'

'I'll find out what Lucy's on and we'll get hold of some. Steal it if we have to.' He looked desperate enough to try.

'I'll come with you.' He opened his mouth to object and I shook my head. 'Suzy can sleep. And Colin's here. I'm coming. Someone's got to keep an eye on you.'

When I was at school, the art teacher told us one morning that she'd seen a painting with nothing on it at all except the colour blue. The artist, she said, had been so taken with a particular blue that he filled a whole canvas with it. I choked on my own laughter, and for months afterwards if I thought about it I'd snort.

And now I'm so ancient – older, probably, than the art teacher was when she said it, and I'm gazing at the lithodora in the flower bed, hypnotised by its colour. It's a mass of incredible, mesmerising blue, so intense it appears to move, hologram-like. Carol understands that I want to sit by the window. She seems to understand my need to stare at the lithodora without blinking. The blue is so fierce I want to eat it. The petals could do their wilting in my colon where decomposition is all the rage. Watching them sag where they are will be too drawn out as a death. I imagine spraying them with weedkiller to get it over with. Daffodils do it to me, too, when they're really going for it; it's the transience that makes me violent. So yellow, so chunky.

Carol tells me it can be best to avoid abstract nouns like Love, Hate *or* Pain. *You don't give weight to your experience by capitalising it, she says. Try shrinking it. Put them under a microscope and write what you see. The weight is in the mundane. The soggy toast and the metallic margarine. And then she suggests we do just that. Make a list of abstract nouns, global words that have lost their impact through overuse. And write about some of them – put them under the microscope.*

'Love,' she says, 'for example,' and I try out a few possibles in my head and then put: Dan refusing to leave his mother and his mother refusing to let him refuse.

'Wow,' says Carol. I'm not sure what she expected.

'Pain?' she says gently. 'If you want to try that. It's always your choice what to write and what not to write.' Her voice is soothing, cocooning. She's good at her job; she deserves to have people queuing down the corridor to get into her classes, and instead she just has me. Without hesitation, I put: Fflur, seventeen and so convincing she forgets for hours at a time she's making the whole thing up.

Then 'Jealousy': Visions in my head of Dan with Suzy. Knowing I'm the joke, the puppy that did as it was told and followed him round. And Suzy was the real person, who knew what it was like to sleep rough and wash in public toilets. And she was beautiful too, in an edgy, real-world way. Thin, hard, plucky. Her face was more defined than mine. Her eyes had outlines. She plucked her eyebrows until there was nothing left and drew them on with whatever she could find – I saw her use a felt-tip once – and it didn't look silly, just cool. And the reason Dan was so upset was because they'd been seeing each other for weeks. Weeks? They'd probably been together on and off for as long as I'd known them. I was lying in bed with my own hand up my nighty, and they were huddled up for warmth somewhere, wrapped in each other. Is that *jealousy, Carol? Is that the margarine that tastes like metal? And can you be jealous of someone who's dead?*

The slush piles froze; the pavements were one long slide and the roads were death traps. The up side was that Dan could exercise chivalry without it having to mean anything; it was quite natural to take each other's arms from time to time as we navigated a particularly treacherous patch. He was fine, on account of his seven-league boots which must have taken half an hour to do up in the morning. Maybe they even had studs on the bottom, because it's girly to slip. My trainers, on the other hand, had a mesh at the front that let in water so my toes were always cold. My feet squelched with every step.

He was telling me about his mother and her disastrous relationship history, which made his eyes go hard and his shoulders tense. Apparently she had a way of finding spongers; she was one of those incredible women who go out to work all day and then come back and wash up breakfast – swearing a bit at the oaf on the sofa but doing it anyway. Dan was nine, he told me, when he decided that when he grew up he would be very different from any of these men. He remembered his mother coming home from work – she was a care assistant in a hospice – and the resident man lazily raising a hand to high-five her without taking his eyes off the telly. This was repeated daily for ages, but on one specific evening, his mother was briefly in the way of the telly. Dan remembered her stooping down to pick up a plate from the carpet beside the sofa. And this man poked her shoulder with his toe and asked her what was for tea.

'I was nine,' said Dan. 'And don't get me wrong, I already hated him. But that toe was so ... double-jointed, so hairy and so ...' And this revolting *passenger* of a man (that was one of many names Dan had for him) stuck out a foot and used it to push her aside so he could see the television better. The foot was bare and filthy and the nails were jagged. A skinny, jumpy nine-year-old Dan glared at the foot and all it represented and knew that he could never, ever let a woman work to keep him in food and television. He would have clean feet with trimmed nails inside shoes he'd paid for himself. He would look after his mother, and any wife who came along (the wife he imagined was apparently a lot like a girl called Nicola from the top juniors, who was half Venezuelan and pretty mesmerising), and he would never, ever touch them with his feet.

With men like this for role models, Dan might easily have slipped into passive-aggressive uselessness. Or abandoned his childhood to become Man of the House and salvage something of his mother's time on the planet. As it was, he hovered guiltily between the two throughout secondary school and then ran away with a rucksack.

'God, how horrible,' I said. Dan made a shunting gesture with his hand as if to say, *enough*. He went silent, which I've never been able to handle in anyone when I've just said something, even if it wasn't tactless. I need a reassuring grunt at the very least or I assume I've just caused irreparable offence. As we got nearer the hospital, we could hear some sort of disturbance taking place. I tried to speed up, but I fell thwack on my bum and pain shot up my spine. Dan crouched down and hugged me briefly before putting me back on my feet again. I was ready to fall over every other step after that, it was so lovely.

We turned the corner near the pseudo-Italian cafe-bar. The front of the hospital was swarming with people who seemed prepared to trample on other people's children in order to get where they wanted to be. They were sliding on the ice, grabbing onto each other, falling and wailing. Most people seemed to want to get inside, but there was a significant number trying to get out, too, which made for a sticky front line scrum a few yards from the entrance.

In the street where we were about to cross, a car screeched to a halt and the car behind it hit the bumper and the one behind that dominoed into that one. Horns started up. The driver of the first car leapt out screaming, 'Help! She's stopped breathing!' She flung open the back door and yanked an unconscious teenage girl out of the car by the armpits.

SuperDan was right there, telling me to ring an ambulance and kneeling down with his ear to the girl's face. Two other people – a tall Japanese boy in full retro punk gear and a storybook grandmother with a spherical baby bundled up asleep in a buggy – were also ringing ambulances, but I punched in 999 anyway, my fingers shaking. Dan threw his jacket over the girl. A man in a tracksuit was squaring up to help. I think we all felt the painful ridiculousness of being so close to the hospital that it would be quicker to pick her up and run, but Dan launched into mouth-to-mouth. The grandmother got through first and I abandoned my phone call. She passed her phone to the mother kneeling on the pavement, who clutched it, nodding, her face stretched tight. The man in the tracksuit and the retro punk eased other people away. 'Give them some space, she'll be OK.' The spherical baby woke up and blinked fatly. 'Da,' it said. 'Da-doh.' Its grandmother bit her lip and took the brake off the buggy. She looked at me, uncertain. Standing around seemed almost worse than walking away, but they'd got her phone.

'Do you think she ...?' she said. 'We're so *near* to the hospital ... but.' She rocked the buggy so hard the baby's cheeks wobbled.

I crouched on the pavement, murmuring to Dan with his sets of five compressions and his deep shared breaths. 'Keep going. It won't be long now.' Willing him on. I felt my own breathing start to fall in with his rhythm. The mother was holding her breath as if she could let her daughter have her share. But with Dan doing that for her, it was her job just to nod at whatever the 999 operator was saying. The girl had black hair, so black I decided she probably helped it along, and beautiful eyelashes. Her face was pale, but it was still pink. Dan was keeping it from going blue. As he moved away for a set of compressions, I thought I saw a flutter in her eyelashes.

Dan kept the girl pale pink until a doctor was accosted, and just as the doctor was detaching a protective mouth guard from his keyring, an ambulance drew up and produced oxygen and tubes and things.

'You did good,' said the Japanese punk and rubbed Dan's shoulder.

The mother dropped the mobile phone and climbed into the ambulance, shuddering. People lingered a bit; we'd shared in something profound and we weren't sure how to move on from it. The doctor shook Dan's hand and said, 'Well done. Are you medical?'

'First aid,' said Dan. 'Years ago.' He looked deflated, as if he really had given away his breath. 'But I just followed my instincts there.' He shut his eyes and scruffled up his hair. The rest of the cast drifted away, with the odd backward glance and sigh.

'Look,' said Dan to the doctor. 'I need a very big favour.'

The scream of an ambulance siren a few streets away drowned out the doctor's answer. Dan took his elbow and drew him aside, muttering intensely, gesturing from time to time at me. The ambulance swept up into the hospital grounds, but the crowd wouldn't part and it got stuck in the siege.

I could hear only snippets of Dan's conversation, stranded like a lemon and unsure if I was supposed to be part of it. 'Lungs,' said the doctor.

189

'Sofa surfing,' said Dan, and 'gas chamber.' The doctor looked shifty, wary, glancing at the hospital as if someone might hear them. 'It's not somewhere you'd send your least favourite great aunt,' said Dan, and that seemed to clinch something. 'If this was your loved one we were talking about, you wouldn't even consider it.'

Love? Where did that one slip through?

'... resistant strains ...' the doctor was shrugging.

I changed the wallpaper on my phone with intense concentration. The doctor left, not really looking when he crossed the road, and Dan's face took on a manic expression.

'Shona, go back and be with Suzy. She needs you, and it's better if I do this alone. Better that you don't get involved.'

'What exactly are you planning?' I said, cocky, bolshy.

'As I say,' he murmured, 'better to stay out of it.' He brushed his hand over the back of my neck. 'See you later.'

He crossed the road then, but unlike the doctor he did so with exaggerated care, as if he was demonstrating the procedure to a small child.

'Wait,' I called. 'Dan!' I scuttled and slid after him towards the battleground, where the people desperate to get in were preventing the people who were desperate to get out from getting out, and vice versa. The police seemed uncertain as to whether they should try to form queues or go for riot-style dispersal.

'I appeal for calm,' said the steel-voiced manager woman, standing on a bench with a megaphone. She had on a deceptively pastel suit. 'All the children at the affected schools are to be screened in the safety of their own homes. This will take time and I ask you for your patience whilst the programme of tests is rolled out.' She handed the megaphone to a police woman and stepped unflappably down from the bench.

'And what about the rest of us?' bellowed a man carrying an adult-sized boy on his back. 'What about the other schools? Or are you still pretending those are safe?'

A lot of people were wearing homemade mouth and nose masks. A man in navy overalls and builders' boots shunted his way through, a girl in a fireman's lift over his shoulder.

'If you don't move, I'll get her to cough on you,' he growled, and barged through.

Paul appeared and threw a luminous yellow waistcoat at me.

'Alright, you ol' lezzy,' he yelled and thwacked me on the back. I kept my head down and clamped my hands on the trolley of equipment he was trundling. 'Dan's nosing,' he said, and his whole body smirked. We used the trolley to shunt a pathway through the crowd and into the hospital.

'Oh God, that sounds dangerous.'

'You want to go and see Lucy again, right? Oh shit, quick, hide in this store.'

He indicated a cupboard door and we squeezed in with our trolley, squashed up against piles of blankets and sheets. I never liked sardines as a child, it was worse than hide-and-seek and forty-forty put together. Paul laughed quietly. He sniffed, swallowed the product and told me, 'Stinky Tom died. He was – get this – found in the lavs at Central Station. There's style for you.' Stinky Tom? 'Schizo. You know Stinky Tom. Breath that knocked you sideways. Or was he before your time? He's been in a rehab place on and off. Probably a specialist centre for stinkers. Jesus, can you imagine?'

Tom. Gentle, kind, humble and now dead, presumably from Tramp Flu or one of its sidekicks. I felt responsible for his death, for some reason, more than any other. Was it an acceptable excuse, that I was so new when he was around, that I didn't know how to go about looking for help for him? Perhaps whatever I had done, he'd still have been front line fodder for Tramp Flu. But I'd always had that sense about him, that if it weren't for his extreme bad breath (and the schizophrenia wasn't exactly an asset either), he could have been an actor. Or a model, or at least a shop assistant in one of those horrendous shops that only employ people who look like models. I went into one by accident once. It was dimly lit, but you could make out the terrifying price tags if you tried, and the surly faces of the assistants. The effect was a bit like the Chamber of Horrors at Madame Tussaud's. Benny took me there once, when I was far too young. I think it was my birthday, possibly my seventh. She shoved me in front of her and shouted, 'Nobody's holding nobody's hand!' I registered the double negative even then, but I was unable to speak and was forever scarred by an installation of a waxwork man strapped into an electric chair. There was a voiceover which said something like, 'We're going to pass electricity through you until you are dead,' and then they did something with the lights so that the waxwork man's head appeared to jerk about and spontaneously combust. It made Benny laugh, gave me nightmares for months, and led to a stand-off about access rights.

Paul had fallen uncharacteristically silent. He'd even stopped chewing gum and closed his mouth.

'Sho'?' he said. 'You're not in shock about Stinky Tom are you?'

I swallowed. 'I'm sad to hear about Tom. He was a nice guy and he had a hard life.'

'Aah,' said Paul. 'Would you say the same about me?' He leant in close and tried to tweak my cheek. I ducked out of his way, knocking my head on a shelf.

'No Paul, probably not,' I said. 'But then you'll outlast us all so it's irrelevant. You're disturbingly indestructible.'

Lucy was thinner.

'It's hitting her chest hard,' Natasha sobbed. 'And she was never a wheezer. Obviously I'm glad she's been spared the boils and ... and so on. God, maybe she doesn't even have Tramp Flu and we're barking up the wrong tree. It could be something else. Lung cancer. In which case it would be a secondary. It would –'

Dan took her hands and breathed slowly, looking into her eyes until her breath slowed.

'We both know,' he said, 'that Tramp Flu is probably a mix. People are lumping it all together in a big panicky jumble but there's no test yet, no real diagnosis.' He was still holding her hands.

'I know,' she sniffed. 'I know.'

'TB hangs around most of the time. There's been a mass triggering –'

'I am A Nurse. With a degree in such things,' said Natasha, pulling her hands away from Dan's. He gave her his milkshake-grin.

'So she has TB. Probably. And she'll respond to treatment pretty quickly, hm?'

Natasha tucked some of her hair behind her ears. 'What are you after this time?' she said.

Paul stuck his head through the door and jerked it. Dan took Natasha's hand, squeezed it meaningfully and went to follow him. I was about to trail after them, but Paul said, 'Go home little lady, this is men's work,' and I nearly hit him.

I headed back to Colin's. Dandruffy flakes of snow wafted about undecided, flapping in my face and tickling my nose so that I developed a Colin-like tic trying not to touch it. My insides were scrambled. I didn't know whether to hope Dan had got hold of something for Suzy or whether he'd failed and we'd have to tell someone about her. I hung over the balcony, watching the Giant Toddler make hand grenades from frozen slush, stones and broken glass. He hurled them at people's backs, and it kept him out of trouble for a while.

As I loitered on the doorstep, some of the Disaffected Youths arrived next door. It seemed they'd had a whip-round for one of their group, and presented him perhaps with a birthday voucher.

After that the Giant Toddler mooched up, but the lady of the house sent him packing, saying, 'Come back when you can behave nicely.' He left placidly enough, spitting half-heartedly in my direction and sloping off down the steps.

When Dan finally turned up, he stank like a pub.

'You're drunk,' I said – in neutral tones, a statement of fact rather than an accusation.

'How is she?' He had a puppy dog expression on his face and a slur in his voice. I took him inside and shut the door, hiding my face whilst I pulled myself together; somehow I couldn't cope with Dan doing pathetic.

'The same,' I said. 'Sit down. I'll make coffee.' I kept my back to him whilst I made the coffee, hands shaking, lips pursed. He slammed himself into a chair and launched into a speech.

'It's funny, what matters to people. The creed and the colour and the skin don't matter so much as the class. The middle classes will find each other anywhere on earth.' I gave him some coffee, put mine on the table opposite him but didn't sit. His eyes flicked back through what he was saying, searching for a thread he'd lost. 'What I'm saying is. I've been around this world a bit you know.' He was shooting further down the rapids with every burp, further and further from the waterfall of cool. His face looked clowny, eye-googlingly nerd-gets-drunk-and-thinks-he's-amusing/entertaining/informative/possibly alluring. And I was furious. And unsettled because I spent most of my time and energy fantasising about him and it turned out he wasn't quite as cool as he seemed to be. My mind wandered as he rambled, to address the wider implications of this depressing insight. If the at-a-distance-in-your-dreams Dan was so hugely inflated – falsified even – then what was the reality of, say,

David Tennant on a down day? I had a vision of David engaged in fart-lighting at a boys' get-together round Paul's. Dan was rubbing his face in a manner that exaggerated its drunken slobberiness, and I had to look away.

20

Carol is late and I'm cross about it. Doesn't she know that even five minutes in here can be endless, exhausting? I run my biro down the spiral binding of my notebook; the sound it makes says something about the irritation I'm feeling, and the raggedy line turns the page instantly scruffy. I've experimented over the weeks, at Carol's suggestion, first with a neat, pretty notebook that Fflur gave me (with sweets on the cover and nice thick pages) and then with a corners-curling spiral-bound thing. It's this one I've settled on. My story is too grubby to have sweets on the front cover. Doughnuts, maybe, or slightly sweaty cheese, but perhaps the scruffy anonymity of my wide-ruled spiral pad is what settled it. And Carol's hypocritical, really, because at the start of a session she always says, 'tell yourself as you write that you can tear it out and throw it away, because that will free you up and stop the what would people think inhibitions.' But then afterwards, she says, 'resist the urge to get rid of it. Value the narrative you are constructing for yourself.' This advice has worked well, but leaves me stuffing notebooks under the mattress and putting out the pastel sweets one on display, in which I inscribe the odd platitude from time to time. Oh, Carol. The clock must be slow; I've been sitting here much longer than it's admitting. Oh, Carol, I am but a fool. Now I can't get the song out of my head. Nain liked it in the days when she used to put music on sometimes instead of the telly, but I thought it sounded like one long whinge.

It occurs to me that there is no reason I shouldn't begin writing on my own, while I'm waiting. It can't be that hard to come up with an idea. Why should I need the validation of a steadily-breathing poet with eclectic dress sense before I can write? It would be good to write – or draw, sing or dance or something, just because I want to, rather than because I'm told to. This thought, which should stop me chewing my lip and have me sitting up straight, in fact sends me into a spiral of existentialist doubt. If I can only write (I never draw, sing or dance, even if I'm told to) when someone else is watching, and *then when no one is watching I just sniff, fart and sprawl around stuffing my face, what does that say about me? Do other people only function when they're being watched?*

I roll my shoulders back and unslump in my chair, despite being alone in the room. And at last, there is someone coming. The knots in my face loosen. But the footsteps are wrong, and there are keys. It's Huggins and she tells me, without even entering the room, that Carol has cancelled. I hate Huggins and she hates me. I know instantly that Carol can't stand me, either. That the gentle warmth is an act, and that she judges me. I'm ugly, overweight, and my breath smells. I want to spit at her, to shake her until the elaborate expression of concern comes away and all you can see is the sneer behind it.

'I need to lock this door,' says Huggins. She waggles her keys at me and looks busy.

I wonder whether I'd feel better if I had a bunch of keys. Possibly each key is a notch of self-esteem and a really big bunch makes you positively arrogant. In my real life I had a Shelter key, a house key, a back-door key, a wafer-thin key to a little jewellery box I was given by a woman who used the Shelter (I never had any jewellery to put in it but the key sat there hopefully in the lock for years) and a bent key that had once fitted a bicycle padlock (I had a vision of myself at one time as a cyclist; 'Oh, I cycle everywhere, can't stand buses,' but the chain malfunctioned more than it didn't and the vision never really got established). The Authority Figures here have whole necklaces made of keys; great clanking chains they bestow ceremoniously on each other when they Hand Over.

In the corridor, I pass Elena. She tilts her head on one side and rubs her hands together.

'Fortune?' she whispers. 'I tell your fortune?'

I shrink away from her. I go back to my cell, hurl myself onto my bed, stretch my toes right down and arch my back. It's an instinctive stretch; my spine feels briefly as if it's part of me, and my knees get a rest from carting me around all day. I let the stretch go and sulk on the bed for a while, until my fingers itch and I find I'm opening my notebook.

Dan went off in a drunken huff because I said I didn't want to talk to him until he'd sobered up. *Who are you, my mother? No, not your mother, Dan, your nobody. I'm your nobody.* He texted me half an hour later, *U R not nobody.*

Then Fflur arrived with a clinical mask, a packet of disposable plastic gloves and some cut-price fondant fancies. She had on a thick white furry coat and a blue hat. She leant against the sink and listened to Suzy cough and retch in the bedroom.

'She sounds awful,' she said brightly. 'Can I do anything?' I scraped my teeth against a mouth ulcer. 'We could do the false address thing again.' She prodded a pink fancy. 'With my second bitchiest housemate.'

Colin clapped his hands and said, 'Ahah, back again.'

'Hello,' said Fflur. 'Tea?' But he'd slid the battery cover off the remote control and was busy rearranging its insides. The sun appeared suddenly and caught a warp in the window, landing a streak of rainbow on top of the microwave.

'She's not strong enough to go anywhere,' I said.

Fflur filled the kettle. 'You could ring – no, they'd … right.' She took a hair slide out of her hair and sucked it.

For a moment, my whole body shook and my teeth chattered.

'When we went to get stuff for her,' I said, 'another kid … she stopped breathing about two minutes away from the hospital car park.'

'Oh God,' said Fflur, squeezing her eyes shut and breathing into her hands. She pulled herself together then and said, in confidential tones, 'Suzy must have family somewhere. She's quite young, isn't she?' I fiddled with the elastic on the face mask.

'Dunno,' I said. 'Twenty-five? Ish.' We listened to a coughing cycle from chesty to throaty and back again. Fflur stabbed her hair slide back in and began some aggressive teabag-squishing with the vegetable peeler, which was the nearest implement to hand. I realised my backside was wedged against what had become the cutlery drawer. I passed her a teaspoon and she threw down the peeler.

'It's so unreasonable!' she cried, with such force that she had to stop making tea and steady herself against the sink. Her cheeks were flushed.

'She does have parents. She won't give us their number.'

'Well find out from someone else, for heaven's sake! What's her surname?'

I folded my arms and looked at the rainbow on the microwave.

'She uses Prince,' I muttered. 'But that's not her maiden name.'

'She's married?'

'I think she sort of was, for a while. He died of a drug overdose I think. But she uses his name.'

Fflur bit a yellow fondant fancy and scowled. 'How can you be 'sort of' married? God these are horrible.' At the other end of the room, Colin had begun to chant with a hushed intensity, 'Ashes to ashes, dust to dust,' like an underground vicar.

I tried a blue fondant fancy.

'They might be alright warm,' I said. 'With ice-cream.'

Fflur swallowed her bite and put the remainder in the crammed bin.

'I was just going to sort that,' I said, 'when you got here.' She made a tight face and pressed her lips together. She was trying not to cry. I nearly made a ridiculous remark about her passion for emptying bins, but unusually I stopped myself before the silence-filling began.

After a while, she said, 'Use the gloves. Please.'

She had to go, because she was running a jewellery workshop at Nain's luncheon club. So it was just me, Colin and Suzy. And I couldn't ring Dan and say things like, *How can I be in two places at once?* Or *I can't just drop everything to look after your girlfriend*, because I had nothing to drop. I was jobless and pointless. I was free to put food out for Colin as if he was a hedgehog and to encourage Suzy to sip Dailyvit with her tablets. She was so tired she learnt to cough in her sleep and I'd be curled up in the armchair with cotton wool stuffed in my ears, feeling like a used dishcloth.

Colin didn't seem to mind not sleeping. In fact he muttered and twitched when he was asleep and he didn't interact much when he was awake, so there wasn't a great deal of difference anyway.

Gloria comes again, to sit opposite me and smile firmly.

'Gloria,' I say, when I can get a word in, 'I've been wanting to say I'm sorry if I ruined things for you with Minister Mike.'

She twists a big transparent bangle she's wearing. The inside is filled with crumpled newspaper. I try to make out some of the words.

'I think he and I had finished our particular dance,' she says. 'He was irritatingly codependent, for a politician.' She gives a little chuckle.

'Mm,' I say. 'Fair play, then.' I never say fair play*, so it sounds odd, and I wonder if it will be one of those phrases that, having used once, I'll now use in every other sentence.*

'Incidentally,' says Gloria. 'Fenella and Jimmy have separated.'

Fenella and Jimmy. Fenella and – *'Oh, yes, of course, them. Sorry. I'm sorry to hear that.' I've turned into someone who says* I'm sorry to hear that. *Gloria sighs with her whole body.*

'They've tried. They went to marriage mediation and so on, but it seems they've come to an end now, as a twosome.'

'Fair play.' Inevitable: self-fulfilling prophesy. A particle of Gloria's perfume catches in my throat and I can't clear it without some attention-drawing growly noises. The conversations around us falter while I'm looked at and the invigilator moves towards me. 'I'm fine,' I say, still coughing. 'Sorry. Thank you.' Most of the conversations get going again; they hit the ground running now, with visiting time nearly over. At a few tables, where talk is more stilted or punctuated by gentle crying, people are still glancing at me. Too late now, to start a new conversation, relaxed, urgent or otherwise. They're dreading the bell so much they're willing it to ring.

Gloria, who looks so wrong here, so self-possessed, so dauntless, is running though a checklist in her head of things she's been meaning to tell me.

'Sandra has a new job,' she says, 'at the Arts Council. Oh, and Colin.' She slaps the table. 'Have you had an update? We've got a medical assessment that says he definitely does have Asperger's, and that the stress he was under was sufficient to render him unaccountable for his actions.'

I swallow, to stop myself coughing again. 'That's great news. Well done. So what happens now?'

The bell rings and the chairs scrape. A little light suffering is endured. Gloria makes a significant face as she stands.

'Shona Darling, it's good news up to a point. But Darling –'

'If you could say your goodbyes now, ladies,' says the invigilator, signalling the door.

'Indeed.' Gloria looks at him the way she looks at shop assistants who don't instantly have what she's after. 'Shona, if Colin can't be held to account for what happened, it does rather mean someone else might be.'

Suzy seemed to need to get things off her chest; I didn't have to say anything until the end, when she said, 'I did nothing wrong,' and I had to offer absolution in a series of sympathetic headshakes.

She was pregnant at twelve. *Twelve*. By a skinny runt (her words) who'd left school early to smoke full-time outside the Spar. Her main memory of the sex was hayfever. They were in the park in late May and the pollen was getting into its stride. Both of them were sniffing. Her lips itched and the corners of her eyes were sore. When he put his willy inside her, she thought at first it was his fingers. When she felt both hands squeezing her shoulders, she said, 'What are you doing?' but he was too far gone and that was that. (I did interrupt here. I said, 'Suzy, do you mind if I ask? Had you been drinking?' And she said, 'Yes. But I mostly blame the hayfever.') She never spoke to him again. A few days later she was with her dad and couldn't come up with a reason not to go past the Spar. And this runt poked his finger through his zip and waggled it, spluttering on a can of coke with a fellow lurker. Suzy's dad noticed but didn't get the personal significance of the gesture. He muttered about national service and they went into the post office.

'I did nothing wrong. I was just a kid.'

'You were really unlucky, Suzy,' I said. And I shook my head hard.

It was Colin's dressing-gowned next door neighbour who told me the news that made me sag deep inside. The end of the world was coming, after all, and not with a bang but a shrug. I felt more guilt than shock, a guilt impacted by my inability to cry like a normal person.

I was letting myself out of the front door, having invented a need for milk in order to escape the humming and coughing. If Colin had had a different channel on, I'd have heard it from the telly. The neighbour was leaning in her doorframe smoking and dabbing her eyes with a tissue.

'Hi,' I said, quietly and gruffly. She took her fag out of her mouth and watched some ash fall off it.

'That little girl,' she said. She didn't look at me; perhaps she could sense the grip she'd achieved on my attention. I knew straightaway she meant Lucy. 'The nurse's daughter. Who got Tramp Flu.' She blew her nose and dashed a tear from her cheek. 'She's dead, bless her.'

I had to hold onto the wall. She looked at me then.

'Did you know her?' she said.

I shook my head. In that moment, every cynical thought I'd ever had felt confirmed; negativity was no longer a lifestyle choice but a certainty and an eternity. The neighbour in the dressing gown carried on crying, and I noticed how slack my face felt, how expressionless.

'It is to be hoped,' she said, stubbing out her fag on the side of the balcony, 'that she was isolated quickly enough. From the other children. Or –'

I turned and fumbled with the door, needing to be inside again, to escape the image she'd just left hanging in the air. I found myself back in the hallway battening down the hatches and grinding my teeth.

Whilst I worked at being the world's most incompetent nurse, Fflur was working her sweet-toothed magic on both Nain and the house. I could just see them, sitting at the kitchen table threading beads, Fflur listening to Nain's reminiscences on a loop. The table had acquired a gingham cloth and a bowl of fruit.

'Shona's father was conceived on our honeymoon. On the Isle of Wight.' Fflur squeezed the pliers down hard on a crimping bead. She had no particular difficulty with an eighty-year-old discussing conception, it was just that the details tended to go up a notch with each repetition.

'There's lovely,' she murmured. 'I had a cousin who emigrated to the Isle of Wight.'

'We were so lucky with the weather,' said Nain, fondling a satsuma. 'Sunshine in the day, and we walked up hills and along beaches holding hands.' She rolled the satsuma around between her palm and the tablecloth. 'Then at teatime, we'd go back to the hotel and watch the rain set in as it got dark.'

'Would you like me to peel that for you?' Fflur put down her beads and reached across for the satsuma.

'Thank you, angel girl,' said Nain and handed it over. She played with the edge of the tablecloth and drew swirls with her finger. Fflur took a plate from the cupboard and segmented the satsuma, removing the pith onto a piece of kitchen roll. 'And there was no television in the hotel of course. This was not so long after the war – '

'Did you meet your husband during the war?' Fflur served up the satsuma.

'VE day.' Nain smiled softly. 'His call-up papers came through the letterbox when there were still streamers in his hair from the street party.' She sucked on a segment.

'It's seedless,' said Fflur.

Nain swallowed. 'He'd lost a brother, and his father was never the same. But his mother welcomed me with open arms. She'd say *the war took a son from me but victory gave me a daughter.*'

'She sounds a lovely lady.'

'Oh she was. She'd have loved you. She squeezed my hand as we left for our honeymoon and she whispered in my ear, *Bring me back a grandson. There's a good girl.*' Nain giggled, spraying satsuma juice and stroking her

201

left breast. 'Hand on heart, I can honestly say I did my best. And Shona's father arrived nine months later. Bless his soul.' She gave a huge sigh. Fflur sucked the end of some thread and concentrated on poking it through the eye of a very thin needle.

'He was an only child?' she said, job done.

'Yes,' said Nain firmly. 'We put all our eggs in the one basket.' Her shoulders quivered, her face folded in on itself and she began to cry. Fflur put the kettle on and found the tissues.

Suzy seemed to be getting better. I sat with my back against the open door; it was as far away as I could get and still be in the room. Her breath was a problem. The trouble was, the stench wasn't coming from her mouth; it was deep down inside her and I couldn't really get the mouthwash swilling round her lungs. Maybe I should have tried.

So I sat on the floor and listened as she talked between coughing fits. Three terminations. Assaulted in the street. I didn't actively invite her to confide the flashpoints of her life, but the situation seemed to draw it out of her. A job that turned out not to be; reporting the employers to the job centre and having her dole money cut off. Parents who pretended to believe that she worked as a beauty therapist and lived with girlfriends in a flat share.

'Dan and I were never going anywhere, you know,' she said, tugging a bunch of hair round to examine her split ends. 'You don't need to hate me.' She let go of the hair. 'I don't mean hate. You could never hate anyone.' *I don't know. I might rustle up some Hate, if I really put my mind to it.* I didn't know then, where these abstract monstrosities would take me. She allowed herself a tentative throat-clear – any more and it would set her off. I avoided her eyes and drew a circle in the carpet grime. Things were going downhill fast without Fflur to keep standards up. For some reason, I said, 'I'm sorry about your things, by the way. Getting burnt. Was there anything valuable?' *Only everything she owned, Shona.*

'Nah,' she said generously. 'I don't do *things*.' Relationships with people are difficult enough without getting involved with inanimate objects.' That put me in my place, then. She hurled and spat a globule of something into her dog bowl. 'Oh, sorry. That's better.' She massaged herself mid-rib-cage and flopped further onto her pillows. With her eyes closed, she said, 'How about you? Anything valuable?'

'No. No, I grabbed my bag on the way out.' Suzy sighed with pleasure; the expulsion of that particular globule had clearly been pivotal.

'You're a good woman, Shona. You deserve more.'

'Thank you.' *Damning with faint praise* was Nain's stock response to my school reports.

The sound of Colin humming a repetitive but jovial little ditty drifted through. We listened to a few bars and I thought Suzy was falling asleep but in fact she was crying with her eyes shut.

'Suze?' I'd never called her that before; it just came out.

She shook her head and stretched her fingers out like agonised starfish.

'I feel like shit,' she snapped. 'And I taste horrible.'

I pushed myself up off the floor, pins-and-needling in all four limbs.

'Do you want something to eat?' I said. 'That would help. Or a fizzy drink or a mint or –'

'Shut up.'

I felt my face twitch. Steel-plated, petrol-spined, I stamped the feeling back into my right calf and left the room.

I emptied out my bag to find my Sleeperz and a bit of cocodamol for good measure. The Sleeperz were double strength to begin with but I shoved four into my mouth as if this somehow made a point. I ate some crumbling white cheese dipped in salt to take the taste away and brushed my teeth hard. Colin was now fast asleep in the deckchair, twitching and rumbling away. Wondering what Suzy would say if I just walked in and took the blow heater, I curled up as compactly as I could in the armchair, ignoring the concertina-ing that this involved underneath my breasts, and settled down to wait for sleep.

After several minutes of trying to shut out the sound of snoring, coughing and television, I forced myself up and took the remote control from the floor. I turned the volume down bit by bit, keeping an eye on Colin's face and an ear out for any change to his rhythm. But it didn't help; I spent a good half an hour curled up again with nothing happening. Then, grumpily foggy, but still revved up by Suzy's vehement dismissal, I shuffled to the fridge and got the half bottle of white wine Fflur had left there. Stomping back to the armchair, my breathing heavy and my mouth set in a bulldog down-pull, I unscrewed the top and drank from the bottle. Elegance indeed. It tasted sharp against the toothpaste but I swigged most of it and then let my head drop back and my eyes sink deep.

I spent the night in a black hole off the coast of sleep and woke to a sour silence. For a while I hovered statue-like between the risk that movement would wake Colin and Suzy and flick the switch on their humming-coughing duet, and the urgency of checking on Suzy in the absence of any sound. It was possible that she had coughed just before I'd woken sufficiently to hear it and this was in fact only a brief pause and not even her longest; there must have been other times when she'd stopped for longer but the empty minutes had been broken up by the sound of the television or Colin's background chunterings. After a time, though, I couldn't pretend there was nothing odd in the silence and my paralysis began to look like lethargy. Not long after that I knew it was terror. Because if she had actually stopped breathing, then Suzy's last words had been 'Shut up.'

21

It turned out that another death in the flat was just what Colin needed to spur him into action. The day Suzy died, he turned off the television and folded up the deckchair. He jumped and tugged at the paper-chains, grunting like a tennis champion. He pulled down as much as he could and crushed it against his chest, then leapt at the corner of the ceiling above the telly, where there was a lot of sticky tape still attached to one end.

'So,' he said. It was more of a gargle than a word. 'Best to get rid of the evidence. That's Christmas out of the way.' This was the longest sentence he'd spoken in a while and his voice was slow and glutinous. He stuffed the paper chains into the bin, using his fists to compact them.

He appeared to be waiting to be picked up after that; he was patting his pockets, and striding to look out of the window from time to time. I rang Dan, leaning on the draining board and staring down at the street below.

'Shona?'

'Dan.'

He waited; maybe he was waiting to be forgiven. It was always hard to tell with Dan whether he felt he was wronged or in the wrong; he did impenetrable either way. But what I'd rung for was beyond wrong. I had to tell him that Suzy was dead. That her legs had swollen up like an elephant's. And that she was starting to go stiff now and I'd thrown up until my throat was bleeding. I made a keening sound and Dan shouted, 'No!' and I heard him start to run. 'I thought you said she was getting better!' There was traffic now in the background.

'I didn't say anything. We haven't spoken since –'

'Fflur,' he puffed. 'Hang on, I'm going to get cut off ...'

My muscles were seizing up; my throat was suffocating itself.

'How long will you be?' I squeaked. Of course he hadn't just abandoned us. He'd had updates from Fflur, kept tabs on us from a distance. There was a tremble below the surface of my face and a pus-filled scowl erupted, because I'd let Suzy die, and because Fflur and Dan had been talking behind my back.

Colin turned his attention to the loo roll snowmen.

'What about you fellas, eh?' he said. He picked one up and plucked some of its cotton wool fur experimentally. He seemed to be on the verge of telling me something, but he couldn't quite spit it out and he ended up making do with a little clicking sound. I couldn't bring myself to touch Suzy again. I stood in the doorway and stared at her, and I leant against the wall in the corridor becoming so conscious of my own breathing I thought if I stopped concentrating I'd pass out. But I didn't drape a sheet over her or even straighten the duvet, which was clamped between her legs.

Colin couldn't bring himself to throw away the snowmen, and he kept picking them up only to put them down somewhere else. In the end he marshalled them in formation on the floor, on the shadowy patch of damp where the dog basket had been.

'Colin, stop tutting,' I barked. I'd had no idea I was about to speak, let alone shout, and the explosion stayed up there above our heads and wouldn't dissipate.

It was too quiet. The snow was very grey. Where was the Wicked Witch of the West when I needed her? Or the laughing Humpty Dumpty man?

'Plan A,' said Colin, looking at the fridge. I waited, easing the muscles in my cheeks out of their spasm and aware that a faint intermittent whine was escaping from my face. 'Plan A,' said Colin again. 'Nothing to lose.'

'Oh?' I looked at Colin's elbow. He cleared his throat.

'I'll. Um. Get this one,' he said. I pressed my eyelids with the pads of my thumbs. 'Suzy was a nice girl.' Each syllable had to unstick itself from the roof of his mouth.

'Yes.'

'I'll get this,' he said again, like it was his round in the pub. 'I'll get this.'

I'd taken up the mantel of dazed weird person and was leaning in doorways biting the inside of my bottom lip and willing Dan to arrive. As if when he did he'd know instantly what to do and do it quickly with no mess. I bit my thumb to give my lip a rest and looked at Colin.

'You get on,' he said. 'Not to worry.' He tried to shoo me out with flapping gestures and loose nods in the direction of the front door. And I actually considered taking him up on this, that's what you have to understand about me. In my mind, I flicked through some possibilities:

go home and pretend none of it ever happened; get on bus/train without looking where it's going, find anonymous place to stay, take packet of something highly sedative in large quantities. But what then, what about the next day? All directions began with walking out of Colin's front door, and not all of them involved using the steps.

After half an hour or so, Colin stopped trying to get rid of me and went to measure Suzy. He muttered the length of her legs until he'd done her shoulders and then he wrote both measurements on the back of his hand. I whispered phlegmily, 'What the fuck?' and he tapped the metal end of the measuring tape on his front teeth and said, 'dimensions.'

'Ye Gods,' I breathed, turning away, needing to stare at the letter box.

'That's Gloria's line,' said Colin, and he sounded like someone you could chat to in a post office queue.

I steadied myself on the strange raised line that ran along the wall in the hallway halfway between the ceiling and the floor. I leant in close and nestled my head so that it was cradled by the two arms of a sickle shaped crack. The paper smelt dry; it was odd, I was thinking, that it didn't just smell of the flat. It should have absorbed the smell of the dog, Colin's sweat, Suzy, and the tea we were constantly making. Then I remembered how paper smelt when it was warm and purple-inked from the bander machine at school, before schools had photocopiers and printers were compact little boxes on people's desks. I shut my eyes and let my fingers trail over the bumps in the wall, wondering if that was what Braille felt like and how anyone ever kept living if they couldn't see anymore, and trying to remember what year I'd first used a printer and whether there were any of these halfway lines on our walls at home. Colin pocketed his tape measure, cleared his throat and went to the front window to watch for Dan.

I got up and went into the kitchen to sit huddled on the draining board staring out of the little kitchen window, watching the gentleman set out on his daily newspaper-fetching mission. He had on a battered military cap and he seemed to be wearing all his clothes.

When I saw Dan come round the corner into the street below, it was clear even from ten floors up what he'd been hiding from me. In a week, he'd lost more weight than I'd ever managed in a month of angry lettuce-cramming. He looked cold; his shoulders were curled inwards and his walk was different. He had on the grey knitted hat he'd been wearing when he first turned up at the Shelter, before I knew how incredible he'd look when he took it off and shook his dusty hair free. Now it was pulled right down over his ears. I pressed my back against the wall, fists tight, windpipe knotted. My teeth set themselves in a painful clamp which I had to use my hands to release. Colin turned a circle in the middle of the room and stood to attention behind the armchair. I pictured Dan trailing up the stairs, telling myself I might have got it wrong, that it hadn't been Dan at all I had seen. Maybe it was just someone who looked like him but was much thinner.

He knocked flatly on the door. *Bring out your dead*, I thought. Colin coughed and said, 'Right. Well. Bring out your dead. As they say.' He wiped his hands on his trousers and looked at me. I clambered off the draining board, which gave an accusatory clunk as it reshaped itself, and counted my steps to the front door. At ten and two thirds, I opened the various bolts and twists and pulled it open, looking at my feet.

Dan ran gloved hands through the greasy mat of my hair and held my head tightly. He was shivering.

'She was dying when I brought her here,' he said.

'Then why – we could have – *you* could have –' I crumpled in a snotty mess against him, gulped, wrestled my way out and still couldn't look him in the face. I ushered him rudely, sulkily, in and shut the door. Then I leant against the wall and shut my eyes. Dan's fingers reached softly round my neck, stroking little circles. He pulled me towards him so that our heads were resting on each other's shoulders.

'You looked after Suzy like no one else would have done.'

I thumped him. 'You dumped your sick girlfriend on me and left me to it!' He pinned me to the wall, rubbing wads of my flesh like Fflur rubbed butter and flour for scones. 'And Lucy? Did you know she was going to die, too?'

'Shona, love, I'm sorry. I'm so sorry.' He pressed his face into my filthy hair. 'I didn't know what to do.' He smelt odd. Acidic. Antiseptic. I wriggled sideways and left him propped face first against the wall in a frozen press-up. From somewhere I gathered some strength.

'Dan,' I said, loudly, in an experimental voice. 'The gloves and the mask.' He ground his face into the wall and made self-flagellatory noises. 'Suzy was HIV positive, wasn't she?'

'Yes,' he breathed, and brought himself to face me.

'Right,' I said, hands on hips, brisk. 'And you? Were you aware of this when you slept with her?'

From the kitchen, Colin set sail on a complicated aria. Dan grabbed my wrists and eyeballed me sweatily.

'I tested negative.' He shook my wrists and my arm fat flapped. 'Suzy had no chance against Tramp Flu.' He rolled up his sleeves. 'Is she in the bed?'

I had a fleeting hope that he might lift her in his arms and stagger out with her the same way he'd brought her in. Then Fflur could bustle in with a hoover and a damp cloth and we'd be straight again.

Colin appeared and patted Dan's shoulder, but I didn't have much space in my head to consider the incongruity of Colin touching someone voluntarily, because I was so winded by the sight of Dan. I'd slid down the wall and was sitting on my backside looking up at him. This skewed my perspective so that he looked malformed, with a swollen head and a shrivelled body. If he'd been a plant, you'd have sat him in a pot of water to drench his roots. And sprayed him with pesticide – which wouldn't have been such a bad idea, though by then he'd have had to inhale it to do any good.

Colin spread his hands, did slow nodding, drew in long breaths and kept saying, 'Well now, look.' He had the manner of a politician in an awkward spot.

'Dan,' I said. He coughed for a while, one hand over his ribs and the other shielding his mouth. I watched myself paw the wall and rock a bit.

Colin said, 'Déjà vu. Except last time it was the dog,' and took a few steps towards the bedroom-turned-morgue. 'Probably best if you two skidaddle.'

Dan finished coughing and panted until he could speak.

'I need to see her,' he said and stepped past us. Colin looked at his watch and tapped it. I shut my eyes and tried to work out how I could give Dan some of my blood, transfer a bit of my flesh.

He came out crying. I wanted to tell him not to; he couldn't spare the water. He avoided my eyes.

'All done?' said Colin, and cleared his throat. 'I'll do the necessary.'

Dan steadied himself against the wall. 'Do you have scissors?' he wheezed. Colin drummed his fingers against his head and said, 'Scissors.'

'Kitchen drawer,' I said. 'Fflur bought them for her beads.' Outside, it started raining very suddenly and very hard.

'Right-ho. Scissors.' Colin hopped into the kitchen and I pulled myself into a standing position. Dan was struggling not to cough. Clearly it would be difficult to stop once he'd started, so he swallowed and tried to keep breathing. Colin emerged waving a pair of scissors and stopped to turn them round and offer them to Dan by the handles.

Dan went back into the bedroom and Colin actually looked at me, directly, with eye contact.

'God knows,' I said. He made a googly face and blew a raspberry.

Dan came back and returned the scissors, a lock of Suzy's hair in his gloved fist. His eyes were still moist.

A firework exploded inside my head. I stormed into the sitting room, rammed my hands into my jacket sleeves, grabbed my dirty washing from the floor and stuffed it into my bag on top of everything else. I couldn't do up the clasp so I swept the bag up in my arms like a misshapen baby, stamped back into the hallway and hurt my fingers trying to undo the front door with my hands full.

'Allow me,' murmured Colin. 'Ashes to ashes, dust to dustiness.'

'No,' said Dan. 'What are you doing? Where are you going?'

'Home,' I spat. 'Thanks, Colin.'

I stormed out into a Siberian-league storm. My nose stung and my hair stuck to me like skin.

'Wait! Shona!' Dan came out after me, clutching his ribs. I shook him off and started down the endless steps to the street. Behind us, Colin slammed the door and scraped the bolts across.

22

When I wake up sometimes, I hover for a few seconds on the edge of sleep, peaceful. Then I remember that Dan is dead, that his son is very much alive. I remember where I am, and the internal trembling starts up. I feel constantly on edge, as if I am waiting for significant news of some sort. It's exam results, a biopsy, a jury's verdict, silence for the starting gun on sports day, all rolled into one. It's itching all over and sweating in every nook and cranny. Head pulsating and mouth dry, heart shaking, muscles paralysed. And of course, because there is really no news to be waited for, there's nowhere for all this edginess to go and all it can do is spiral in on itself until I can't think or move.

Every day, I remember everything that's happened, all over again. But, whilst Dan's death hits me like a hammer still, with each morning his presence fades. The sense that he is everywhere seems to lose its urgency and then its integrity, until it feels like a fantasy I invented for my own comfort.

I shouldn't, of course, have left Colin to deal with Suzy's body – especially after he'd left his dog festering for so long. But the sight of Dan with a lock of Suzy's hair in his hand and grief in his eyes was unbearable. And Dan didn't look so far away from wherever Alan Turner and Suzy and everyone in between had gone. I was running away from humiliation, jealousy and death. I scuttled down the steps and out into the street, past Humpty Dumpty who thought it was so funny he laughed himself off the car bonnet he was perched on, past a selection of the Disaffected Youths roaring at the rain and on towards the bus stop. The wind slowed me down and, even in his very weakened state, Dan wasn't far behind me. I never understood, at school, how to make my legs go faster. It didn't matter if we were running a hundred metres or eight hundred, I went at the same pace. However hard I tried, I couldn't send messages from brain to legs to speed up.

The torrential rain was gathering in great pools along the streets. The drains were badly bunged with the remnants of the Giant Toddler's snow bombs, and rivers of diluted slush ran down the gutters. The rain rubbed out the last of the snow, finishing off a really stubborn snowman the Disaffected Youths had missed.

There was a bus not too far away. I could have taken advantage of the severe coughing fit which stopped Dan in his tracks and shaken him off. But the sound he made sent me right back to the warehouse clinic and I knew that if I didn't stop then, I might never see him again.

When he got sufficient breath back, he held out the lock of Suzy's hair and said, 'We need to get these bastards under a microscope.'

Carol is off on long-term sick. Huggins tells me in passing when she's doing checks. Oh, by the way, the only interesting thing you ever get to do is cancelled for the foreseeable future. Her eyelashes are significantly denser today on one side than the other. I'm stuck in a whole-body expression of gormlessness, gaping at a map of fire escape routes. I want to say, Couldn't she at least ring in with the work? Or send an email? Fax through the exercises and any introductory spiel? *Carol's absence makes me want to tear up my notebooks or scribble all over the pages.*

Elena wanders past.

'Fortune, Shona? Fortune?' *she says, with a sideways smile, and I think,* Not fortune, Elena. Palinka. *She whines in a blended gypsy language that's just out of reach.*

I shut my eyes tightly. I want to scribble on my face, too, to press the point of the pen into my skin and zigzag hard. I bite down on my bottom lip; I'm breathing fire, my nostrils feel huge.

'You OK, Shona?' *says some randomer passing by. I grunt. And then, just under the surface of the mound around my middle, a doll-sized foot – or possibly fist, though I sense it's a foot – wriggles and thrusts. I put my hand over my t-shirt and nearly wet myself:* the baby is moving. It's a real one.

Back in my cell, I lie on my side, prodding my bulge experimentally to see if I get a reply. My knees and my back ache; I'm asking a lot of them at the moment. My notebook and pen are on the floor where I chucked them. For long minutes I do dribbly staring into space. The paralysis, the sensation that I'll never move or speak again, takes me back to Christmas, when I thought I'd lost Dan for good. The sensation of having been steamrollered flat is similar.

212

His death, when it came, had the opposite effect on me. I took his death between my jaws, shook my head from side to side and roared. I tore it to pieces and gnashed my teeth at anyone in my way.

We went miserably to Dan's bedsit, trailing up the stairs, glad no one was in. I yelled, 'You fucking martyr! You don't have to martyr yourself! No one's going to say, *he doesn't really care, look he's still alive!* And I stamped my foot and cried every single snotty tear I'd kept under lock and key for three decades. It was something of a torrent. I saw the life we would never have together flash before my eyes and all the sex we'd never had because I'd been such a stubborn little madam. 'Masturbatory aid' is the kind of accusation that sounds a bit ridiculous when the end is nigh. Why shouldn't we have indulged in a bit of mutual warming up? What exactly did I want from him before I'd take off my clothes again? I was hardly a staunch committer; I was a bolter in the making. I stared hard at the bubbling fish stick, which had gone dark and needed its bulb changing. Dan rubbed the snot from my face with a wad of loo roll, clamped my arms to my sides and glared at me until I looked up at him, feeling like a silly little girl.

'Shona,' he said, and his eyes were wobbling, 'you need to shave your hair off.'

I needed my hands to wipe my nose which was still going strong, but he kept pressing my arms and staring me out. I didn't ask why, because the next thing he said was, 'If we shave off all our hair, we can have sex.' He took off his hat, and his head underneath was completely bald. There were a few scabs scattered around on his scalp, and scratches and flaky bits, but he had a nicely shaped head and he didn't look too odd.

I scuffed straight back through the wind and rain to the nearest chemist in a lust and grief-filled daze, pushed the door open, my palm flat against the notice that said, *Stop! If you have any of the following symptoms*, etc, and grabbed a packet of disposable razors. The young woman behind the counter was faffing about with some leaflets and a hook they were supposed to be hanging on that was coming away from the wall, so I put a two pound coin on top of the till and left. She made a few shrill malfunction noises as the door shut behind me.

I hadn't understood in every clinical detail by then; I'm not sure I have now. But there was a connection forming in my mind – a memory of Paul with his jeans round his ankles and a very naked half-mast cock. Stark white skin everywhere – head, chest, legs, and no hair at all, not even eyebrows. And in beautiful, heart-rending contrast, Lucy's goldilocks curls on the hospital pillow.

It was colder in the room when I got back. The storage heater had gone clunk and was letting out refrigerated air. I shut the curtains on the rattly sash windows. A bus went past and the windows shuddered. We were covered in goose pimples.

Dan sighed, pulled me to him and kissed the top of my head. He ran his fingers through my hair and they caught on a tangle. I know most women would be anxious, hesitant if not actually reluctant, about shaving their heads, but I was more focussed on the part that was coming next. I'd have cut off my ears if he'd asked me to. I pushed away and he handed me some scissors. Scooping my hair into a bunch with one hand, I snipped away, crunching the scissors around too much at once and hacking until there were just a few electric wisps amongst the gorse. Dan foamed some shower gel in his hands and massaged my head with his eyes closed, breathing as deeply as his chest would let him. Then we both got hold of razors and went at it in a disorganised fashion, getting more impatient. We had to keep swapping razors because they clogged up so fast.

'Do you want to look in the mirror?' he said.

'Not really.' I took the little round mirror from him and found myself staring back from the magnified side. I swung it round in a panic and peered at my scalp. It was very red. I wasn't sure if my head was as nice a shape as Dan's, either, but I didn't want to hold things up so I put the mirror down and tried to smile.

'I'm sorry, beauty,' he said, and it turned out I did have a few tears left after all. I sniffed and shook my head. 'I've only just got there, I promise. I'd never have left Suzy with you if I'd known. Have you had any symptoms?'

'If you'd known about the hair? No.' He held the mirror up to his own face and shaved off his eyebrows.

'Eyebrows?'

'Everything.' I stared at him and he angled the mirror so that he could look up his nose.

'I've never needed one of those nose hair trimmers,' he said. And then he laughed and bent over, wincing. 'What's worse in a man?' he wheezed. 'Nose hair or ear hair?'

'Both pretty special in a woman,' I said. 'I've been looking forward to growing some when I get old.'

He took hold of my face very gently, kissed me softly and slid my eyebrows off in a few strokes.

He pulled his t-shirt and sweater over his head, shivering, and took out his chest hair with tweezers; it would have been rude to count but I think there were seven. He fussed around double-wrapping the hair and the razors in plastic bags.

'This is to do with Paul, isn't it?' I said. Dan paused. His belt was unbuckled and his jeans looked huge around his waist. 'God you're thin.'

'I'm about eighty percent sure.' He shook his head. 'No. Ninety percent.' I waited. I was keen to get on, you understand. 'Tramp Flu,' he said, clutching his waistband to stop his jeans falling down, 'started with the homeless because it's carried by lice.' Instantly, I was itching all over. I clamped my hands under my arms. 'What's happening now is scary because the lice have spread. They're not just feasting on grimy dosser skin, they're everywhere.'

I had a horrible image of something I saw in a school leaflet, a picture of a headlouse magnified a squillion times. It dampened my ardour a bit.

'They've developed armour. They eat soap for breakfast. They're clinging on to every last hair they can find.' He sank onto the bed and got his breath back.

'So the only cure is to shave off all your hair?' He made a so-so gesture with his hand, trying to breathe as steadily as he could. 'Well why the fuck didn't you do this before then?' I cried, choking on fury. 'What are you trying to prove? Have you told anyone any of this – Natasha, for example?'

He put his hands over his eyes; he looked as if I'd punched him in the stomach.

I tried to start again: 'I don't know what you think –'

'Ssh, ssh ...' he pulled me towards him, burying his face in my ample bosom. After a while I let myself stroke his head, circling my fingers round his ears and spreading out my hands over his scalp. He mumbled into my chest and sniffed. Then he had to sit up again to breathe properly. 'It's only in the last day or so I've really got there,' he said. 'And now of course it seems obvious.'

I nodded. 'Paul,' I said. 'The hairless wonder.'

'Yes.' I sat beside him, not quite touching. An invisible elastic thread vibrated between us; I swear you could have touched it. 'You know it's too late though, for me?' I felt my bottom lip jut out. 'Whatever it is the lice are carrying gets into the lungs. Maybe it's the first bite, maybe it's dose-related. I don't know. But the bastards are poisonous.'

We sat there with our bald heads bowed like a couple of monks, listening to the rattle in his chest and taking it in turns to sniff. Downstairs the front door opened and shut; there was a shout from the street and someone running on the stairs. The door opened again and was banged shut, making the whole house shake.

Dan twisted towards me, took hold of my face and snogged me until visions of monster-nits receded and all I could think about was getting my knickers off. He insisted on shaving each other's pubic hair as a prelude. Never in all my hours of fantasy had I imagined lying back on his bed stretching my under-carriage taut so he could get to the stragglers. We shaved our arms and legs; the razor caught on a raised mole on his shoulder and a perfect little circle of blood sprang up. He wrapped the razors and the hairs in toilet roll and stuffed it all in the plastic bags. Then we faced each other like a hairless Adam and Eve, shivering still and not knowing how to start. Then we both looked down at the exact same moment at his penis, and as we looked it struggled to its feet and rose to the task. We laughed – Dan carefully so as not to cough too much – and then we got under the duvet together and rubbed our hands all over each other until we warmed up. I crushed my face into his chest so I couldn't see or breathe and concentrated hard on getting in the mood. I was thinking how ridiculous it was that I'd just made a special visit to a chemist without even thinking about condoms. Protection had taken on a whole new meaning. But breathing in his sweat I was prepared to risk anything to sleep with him; Tramp Flu, HIV, nothing felt so important as the need to have sex with him there and then. As if sex would keep him alive. As if by risking my own health I could give him his back. Maybe I wanted to share whatever he had. Maybe I'd already decided I didn't want to live without him. It didn't strike me as horribly unfair; I'd never really believed I would do the relationship thing properly. The partner thing always seemed a bit grown up, a bit beyond my reach. I felt pretty honoured at the prospect of an hour or two wriggling around under a duvet together. I was never ambitious.

Sex exhausted him. He slept and coughed in turn, and I lay uncomfortably at his side taking up as little room as I could and massaging the pain in my hand.

A bile-choked dream. I'm carting Suzy down endless stairs, wrapped in a stinking blanket that makes me itch between the shoulder blades. Colin's dog digs a hole in the dirt by the bins and pants at me for praise. I look around; Suzy is piggy-backing now, her feet locked together round my middle and her breath alcoholic in my ear. Behind me, Colin and Fflur are searching rock-pools. My lips are fat and liquid, they won't shape the sounds I make. The dog's turned into my religious studies teacher in the body of my father and he's bellowing at me, Now! Do it now! *But when I go to drop Suzy into the hole, she's gone and I'm shaking shredded tissues from my back, static-sticky flakes that won't come off my fingers.*

Ambivalence. Indifference. Nonchalance. Take it or leave it, life or death, either way. There is no After. There is only now. I know this because I'm the girl who never cried, the girl who never remembers what her star sign is. The girl who wished her mother was dead, but killed her father by accident when the wish veered off course. And the doctor comes and wants to know if I have made any plans *for suicide. I think of Tom, who must have known his parents loved him. He took the opportunity to slip away with Tramp Flu to hide behind, because disease is easier to cope with than suicide, and he was so forgiving.*

'Have you written any letters?' asks the doctor, rather too routinely I think. Yes, but I've torn them up. Have I put my affairs in order? The house was never mine to sell; the council will reallocate it once it's been fumigated.

He writes in my notes and ruffles his hair. He's attractive, for a psychiatrist, but his eyes glaze over as if he's forgotten I'm there sometimes.

In my cell, I lie on my back and watch a long trailing string of cobweb dangling from the light. I discover by accident that I can send it dancing one way or another with my breath, even though it is far above me. The dance is slow-motion drug-hazy, as if the cobweb has soaked up all the stuff people have been fed lying underneath it and now it's drunk with sedatives. The walls, the wardrobe and the floor have all been shaken with a snow-shaker, and gossamer-thin plastic sheeting which crumples and reforms so thin, so almost not there, that where it should crackle, it merges into the silence. I imagine breathing it all in, and passing out in a cobwebby haze.

I spend perhaps an hour in my cobweb trance, bereft when it breaks off, covering my face in dust. I have to try and catch it in my mouth; it seems the only way to make the best of the situation.

Gloria wasn't in her office and she wasn't answering her phone. I decided it wasn't out of the question that she was nestled in with Minister Mike somewhere, and for want of any other ideas, I tracked her down in her Ideal Homes cottage.

I rang the bell and waited, surreptitiously sniffing my armpits. I felt a bit whiffy – I couldn't use the bathroom at Dan's until we were certain the family were all out – and I couldn't remember when I'd last put any deodorant on. I couldn't hear anyone, but the house didn't feel empty. I had that sense that I was being watched, so I stopped examining my armpits and stood up straight. I rang the bell again and followed it with a firm drum roll of a knock, clearing my throat. My head was freezing, even under Dan's hat.

There was movement upstairs. I thought about running, but I'd have looked pretty suspicious if they'd spotted me, and anyway I'd spent good money on the taxi. I glanced up at the top floor windows. Gloria opened one and looked down at me. She was wearing a peach-coloured silky dressing gown and she grimaced and blushed like a schoolgirl.

'Not a good time,' she mouthed, and made shooing gestures. 'Sorry.'

I slid off the hat and held it in my fist.

'Ye Gods, Shona,' she whispered. 'What have you done to your hair?'

'That's what I need to talk to you about.' I put my hands on my head and moved my scalp back and forth, which was a strange little tic I'd developed since I went bald. It wasn't smooth; already there were tiny pinpricks poking through my scalp and longer ones on my legs, which seemed to sprout shoots within minutes of shaving.

'Can't it wait?'

'No.' Her face puckered and she swallowed. She kept staring at my head. 'You know that little girl died? Lucy?'

Gloria nodded and screwed up her mouth. *Yes*, she seemed to say, *yes, it's as bad as it gets but we can't all grind to a halt.* I could read her expression as if she really was my mother.

'I need to speak to you urgently,' I said, and stared hard. She looked agonised, but she nodded, shut the window and came down to let me in.

She pulled me into the kitchen.

'What have you done?' she whispered. 'Are you OK? It's not breast cancer is it?'

My flesh breathed out in the warmth, and the skin on my scalp, my hands and my cheeks stung.

'No. Not cancer. I've shaved all over to protect myself against Tramp Flu.' I showed her my smooth arms and spiky legs. 'Maybe you should do the same.' (That was cheeky, but I couldn't help it.)

'What?' she frowned at me, a frown that spoke a thousand words. I sat down and this made her frown harder. 'Shona, I'm concerned by what you've done and I think we need to talk about it.' She tightened the slinky sash round her middle but it slipped again straight away. 'But I'm not *alone*,' she whispered, indicating the ceiling. 'This is not a great moment.'

'Gloria, I need you to pull some strings.' She tapped her foot and sighed. 'I need you to talk to Minister Mike.' She blushed and scratched her décolletage. I stared her out. *The one with the nose hair, I think you know him?* 'He'll listen to you.' I put my head on one side and looked knowing and a little flirtatious, when all I wanted to do was run back to the big draughty house, get under the duvet with Dan and cry until I stopped breathing. And the family of play people who lived underneath him could find us both when they came to investigate the silence. 'I have to tell him – I have to tell him –'

'Shona, what's the matter? What's happened?' Gloria had never seen me anywhere near tears before; like most people I don't think she thought I was capable. She pulled me into her perfumed bosom and rocked me about really quite violently, patting and shushing. 'Is it Dan? Is he very poorly?' It was more incantation than question, Gloria being one of those women with that global-scale maternal instinct that knows what's wrong with you before you do. I let her rock me for a minute, breathing in the fat droplets of her expensive aura. Then I placed my hands firmly on her breasts and stepped back.

'Is he here? Minister Mike?'

She pursed her lips and sighed, folding her arms. 'Yes,' she said quietly. 'Yes he is. And we would be grateful for your discretion. When one is in the public eye, it's –'

'Could you ask him to come down please? I need to speak to him. Now.'

She covered her face with her hands. 'Shona,' she sighed.

'I could go up and get him if you like.'

'For heaven's sake!' She stood between me and the door, shaking her head, desperation creeping over her face. Imminent bereavement and the gradual sediment of the winter made me stubborn, unembarrassable. I was ready to accost him in his birthday suit if I had to. 'Shona, for heaven's sake. Look, I'm prepared to put this to him if you like and arrange a meeting. Although after you twisted the animal business round, you're not his favourite person.' She gave me a headmistressy look. 'And one has to be allowed some sort of work-life balance. It's not always possible to mix business and – '

'Pleasure?' I said, and she went scarlet. 'No. But this isn't just his business, it's everyone's.'

She rubbed her face and looked crossly at her fingers which came away with mascara smudges on them. She licked her thumbs and drew them across the fragile skin under her eyes. 'Damn,' she whispered. 'Look, give me some sort of summary and I'll do my very best to pin him down.' We both sniggered then, but my snigger turned a bit snotty.

'Dan's worked it out,' I said soggily, proudly. 'We know what Tramp Flu is and it can be stopped.' Gloria folded her arms and rocked herself, sighing through her nose.

Down the stairs came the firm tread of a man preparing a flimsy excuse. I folded my arms and blinked at Gloria.

'Oh God,' she muttered, pulling uselessly at her slippery sash.

Minister Mike tapped on the kitchen door and coughed lightly.

'Hullo,' he said, in a very deep voice. He opened the door and looked at me as if I was the one caught indulging in a spot of lunch break adultery. '*You* again?'

'Minister,' I said, sticking out my hand. 'Shona Davies. We've met on one or two occasions.' He tried looking busy by checking his phone and shuffling about.

'Yes,' he said. 'Indeed.'

'I told her she should really make an appointment,' murmured Gloria.

'Er, yes. Absolutely. I offer regular surgeries. I believe the next one is –'

'Listen.' I stood beside a set of carving knives stuck to a magnetic plaque on the wall above the dishwasher. As non-verbal cues go, it was a few steps beyond passive aggressive. 'Dan has worked it out. We think – we *know* what's causing Tramp Flu.' Minister Mike rolled his eyes a little and Gloria looked long-suffering back at him. 'It's nits.'

They shook their heads and looked pityingly at mine. I could see them making fists though; they weren't immune to the itch reflex of the word. 'First it was body lice. Hence the epidemic amongst the homeless population. But then the lice ...' The word in my mind was 'evolved' but that felt a bit overstated, too reminiscent of dinosaurs and billions of years. I settled for, 'The lice *changed*. And now they can live on scalps. Which is why hygiene and a roof are no longer protection. To any of us.' *Mutated* – the word was *mutated*.

Minister Mike looked floored and I thought I'd reached the limits of his understanding. But then he said, 'I think that sort of mutation would be quite a leap,' damn him. 'It's an interesting hypothesis though and something that our research is no doubt looking into thoroughly.' He made the busy gestures again, and I leant back against the dishwasher with the knives behind me. 'I imagine boils can be a result of lice,' he said, turning a little green. Gloria sighed and put the kettle on.

'The boils may be a red herring,' I said. 'MRSA taking advantage. That's not rocket science.' I cleared my throat. 'I have in my possession a tape of an interview –'

'Oh God. You're not taping me again are you?' He looked around the kitchen. 'I have nothing to hide. Our policies are transparent and I think you'll find my actions stand up to close inspection.'

Gloria held up a packet of herbal in one hand and a packet of Tetley's in the other. Minister Mike shook his head and consulted his watch.

'Young lady,' he said (which was kind of him), 'are you medically trained? No? I just wonder what makes you suggest that a fatal lung disease might be caused by nits – by lice. Lice live on your *skin*.' And he strode out, without so much as blowing a kiss at Gloria.

'We're talking about kids here!' I bellowed, so loudly it hurt.

Gloria made tea in the ensuing silence, not bothering to offer me herbal but doing Tetley's for both of us. After a while, she said, 'Are you planning to use the tape at all?'

I shrugged. 'I don't know,' I sighed. 'What purpose would it serve, really?'

Gloria swallowed. She gave me a sad, irritating little smile. I gripped my mug.

'Shona,' she said. 'The great scientific minds of the day are getting there. I think we should probably leave them to it.'

'We don't need great scientific minds,' I said. 'What we need is a dermatologist. That woman you went to about your cheeks.'

'Rosacea,' said Gloria, reddening. 'And she was about twelve.'

'Ring her,' I said, 'and I'll lose the tape.' Gloria's lips puckered and she looked at me as if I'd just hung a tampon in a display cabinet.

23

I'm writing. On my own. Not because anyone is watching me or telling me to, but because I was lying on my bed feeling horrible and one thought led to another and I picked up my pen.

I wonder sometimes what would happen if someone got hold of my writing. Are my notebooks a booby trap of libel suits? What exactly is a libel suit? Some of the cast have got their real names: Gloria, Nain (though admittedly that's a bit generic. She's actually called Francesca and as a child they dropped the 'r' and called her Fanny, which presumably had to be stopped at some point). Suzy's name is in fact Sal (which I've told you now, but I owe it to her to make at least a nod to anonymity). There was no point in disguising Minister Mike of the hairy nostrils, since footage of the attack was apparently shown (repeatedly) on television and internet sites. Benny, of course, changed her own name long ago and it might just pander to her ego to start fiddling with it again. I might change it back and use her old one, come to think of it. That would get her going; Margaret isn't a name she ever really bonded with.

I've made Fflur promise not to tell me what she calls the baby, and I've promised not to ask.

'Ah, yes. Hello. I wonder could I perhaps have a word with Doctor Sharma?' Gloria fluffed her hair a bit, pressed her lips together and nodded. 'Yah.' *Yah?* Maybe dermatology secretaries inspired these turns of phrase. 'Gloria Myatt ... well, a while back – it was – no. Yah. It's probably nothing.' She looked at me. 'But it's quite urgent. Very urgent.' She made a strange face and jabbed a finger at me. I folded my arms and refused to look embarrassed. Gloria clicked off her phone and said, 'She's in clinic.' I flopped back into the chair and rubbed my eyes.

''Til when?' I snapped. 'Look, where does she work? We could just go there.' Gloria poured a cold cup of tea down the sink and polished the taps with a J Cloth. 'Doesn't she have a crash bleep or something we could set off?'

'I'm not sure dermatologists have crash bleeps.'

'Tell me how I get this across to you,' I said. Her face glazed over a bit. She fluffed her hair but it didn't do what she was hoping for and a thick wad of grey root got exposed where it parted.

'We can put your concerns on the agenda for the next SMT meeting,' she said, 'which is Thursday.' She opened a drawer and shuffled things about in it. My hands formed themselves into claws. I left the house with a strong feeling that I was performing in a film and that any sense of self had shrivelled away and passed into the shitty air.

I hunted down Doctor Sharma at the hospital and demanded to see her. She was curious, I think, or perhaps it really was the power of invoking Gloria's name, but she left her patients stranded while she saw me.

'Doctor Sharma,' I said. 'Would it be possible for nits to get into your lungs?' I was a smelly snorting lump but she seemed prepared to overlook that. She made a waiting face. So tidy, so neatly drawn, with hair like black velvet and skin like suede. 'Tramp Flu is …' I wanted to repeat exactly Dan's words but they felt silly in my mouth and just when I needed to sound rational and intelligent, I was overwhelmed by anger. It took all my effort not to smash my fist into the desk and scream. Ground-breaking medical theory was somewhat beyond me. Doctor Sharma was better at attentive silence than anyone I'd ever met. She supported me non-verbally through the eye of the storm and when I was breathing again she said, 'Tramp Flu is a blanket term. MRSA and TB are always hanging about. And they've got a hold and provided a breeding ground for whatever it is these poor people have got.' Her phone bing-bonged and she stroked her thumb over the screen without looking at it. 'Are you a mum at the school?' she said gently.

'No.' I coughed and a flicker of alarm crossed her face. 'But my – someone has Tramp Flu. And he's worked it out.' She made her waiting face but she didn't look too excited.

'I'm sorry to hear your someone is unwell,' she murmured.

'He is completely convinced,' I said. 'And so am I.'

'Is your someone homeless?'

'Intermittently. But not at the moment. Doctor Sharma –'

'Preeti.'

'Preeti. Dan believes that Tramp Flu is carried by nits. Nits that can burrow into your skin and get into your lungs.'

Her eyes widened; she looked really sad for me. 'Lice,' she said. 'Nits are the little white eggs. Lice are the black things that look terrifying under a microscope.' She adjusted the band in her velvet hair. 'And they don't burrow. They just nibble.'

'Scabies,' I said. 'Body lice. Crabs in your pubes. Are they all the same? Or are there lots of ... species?'

'Um, right. Body lice are different from head lice. Certainly body lice are a problem amongst the homeless community. We do see scabies in the general population. We get outbreaks in old people's homes.'

'And what if some kind of super-nit – super-lice, louse – mutated? A mutation.' I couldn't get the words in the right order now, I just had to get them out, and hope Dan's ideas would form themselves into something that made sense to this kind, patient, sceptical woman. 'Lice that could get into your lungs.'

She looked at me and then at her phone. 'This is very odd. But I've got a line from *Grease* in my head.'

'*Grease*,' I said. 'As in Lightning?'

'*They're fleas on rats. They're amoebas on fleas on rats.* Men.' She stood up. The package in my jacket pocket held its breath.

'What if?' she said, and it was kind of her to speak to me as some sort of an equal. 'What if there was a parasite on the lice? If the lice were carrying a parasite – or the parasite had a parasite – that somehow got inside you?'

'Yes?'

'However,' she said pessi-optimistically, 'middle class schoolgirls don't get body lice.'

'But Tramp Flu began with the homeless and some of them might have had body lice.' I stood up too; we were breathing fast.

'It would be quite a leap for a body louse parasite to adapt itself to living on a head louse.'

'But possible?'

'Possible. But it would be something of a first. Practically unheard of.'

'Rocking horse shit,' I said firmly. 'I know. But not impossible. There's a guy with no hair. Anywhere. Bald all over. He works as a hospital porter.

He was carting bodies out of the warehouse clinic when Tramp Flu was still a homeless problem. Natasha, the mother of the first schoolgirl, was a nurse there.' Preeti Sharma was listening to me now.

'That nurse is Jamaican,' she said, very much to herself.

'Well, yes,' I said. 'I suppose Lucy was adopted unless there's some genetic –'

'And this bald man is fine.'

'Fine. Drinks and smokes and doesn't wash. But no Tramp Flu.'

'You've shaved your head,' she said.

'And the rest.'

She swallowed. I handed her the package containing Suzy's hair and its residents, and she gave me a prescription for scabies lotion. She gave herself a good coating too, I'm sure, but she stopped short of cutting off her hair which is so lovely it looks photoshopped. Airbrushed. She gave me lotion for Dan as well, but she was honest enough to say that this would do nothing about anything that had got as far as his lungs.

'Yes,' I said. 'Yes, I thought that might be the case.' My insides were squeezed so hard I'd experienced the novelty of being unable to swallow food. Impressive. Dan was 'going home', as my dad would have said.

I shuffled out of Preeti's office, ignoring the waiting room full of people who hated me, and into the corridor, where bilingual signs listed everything that could go wrong with you: Dermatology, Orthopaedics and Trauma, Neurology, Antenatal (God forbid), Matters of the Heart ... I fell through a portal into a parallel existence, where the signs read: Grim Childhood, Unfit and Overweight, Love-Starved, Fear of the Future. I was in a dither as to which department I should visit first.

From the other dimension, through the rapidly-closing portal, my phone tooted and buzzed. I fumbled in the wrong pocket, and managed to answer it just before it gave up on me. It was Fflur, in tears. She sounded like a child.

'Would you come home?' she said. 'To your house. Just for a bit? I could really do with a chat.'

'Yes,' I said. 'Yes, of course. I'll come now shall I?' I had to go, I owed Fflur that at least, but every minute that I wasn't with Dan was a minute I'd never be able to make up.

'It's ... the man I told you about ... remember when I said he ...' She was overcome with sobbing.

Outside, it was biting cold. I buttoned up my cardigan from top to bottom, thinking of my maths teacher who was known for doing up all her buttons as if this was a ridiculous habit. My head felt raw.

Now that Preeti had added the amoebas onto the fleas, I began to understand more clearly. A parasitic life cycle. And if they got you when they were in lung mode you were done for pretty quickly. The amoebas-on-fleas that were suffocating the poor kid in her mother's car were at the height of their powers and when Dan pressed his face onto hers the bastards must have had a lovely time head-hopping. Marching straight off to his lungs and that was him written off. The memory of Dan's hair mingling with hers churned in my mind until I threw it up in a wire mesh bin inadequate for the purpose.

I arrived home and stood on the doorstep, feeling impotent without my key, which I'd left either at Colin's or at Dan's, I wasn't sure which. My nose was dripping and I didn't have a tissue.

Nain opened the door, tugged me inside and spoke in a stage whisper. 'Shona,' she said, 'we've had a few items go missing.' She humphed darkly and waited, her face camel-like, relishing the sour taste of the words.

'What have you lost?' I yawned pointedly.

'A five pound note has gone walkabout,' she said, her eyes flaring. 'And the shortbread tin by my bed.' She folded her arms. 'That could be dangerous. My blood sugar's going very low in the night.'

'I'll have a look. It can't have gone far. Where's Fflur?' I shuffled past her to the kitchen.

'Things have begun to *grow legs*,' said Nain, following me so close I could smell the chutney on her breath.

Fflur was sitting at the table in the kitchen. Her tears were delicate, diamanté-studded little things. Nain hovered and wrung her hands.

'Fflur?' I said. She sat up straight and looked a bit beseeching. I took a probiotic drinking yogurt from the fridge and waited, wondering whether to touch her or not. Lay a finger on me when I'm in a state and I'm likely to bite it off, but then Fflur has a much softer, smoother outline than me and a fresh cottony texture. I tugged off my hat without thinking. 'He's definitely not worth much crying,' I muttered. 'You're far too good for some indecisive little –'

Nain put her hand on her heart and sat down quickly as if she might faint. 'Oh Shona,' she whispered. 'Don't turn into your mother.'

'Ignore the hair thing,' I told Fflur. 'It's fine.'

Fflur opened her eyes very wide and then shut them for a second. 'My mum rang,' she said. 'Christian walked out on her.'

'I'm sorry to hear that.' The crust flaked off the words in my mouth. Nain began to rock in her chair, chanting something under her breath.

'He's changed his phone number and everything,' said Fflur. I squashed the empty drinking yogurt bottle in my fist. (I say 'bottle', but those yogurts are more like the mouthwash cap you swill from. There's a medicinal, dose-related feel to the whole event.) 'So,' she said. 'But I'm OK really. Probably she's better off without him.'

'At least you can make up with your mum now,' I said, thinking, *Excellent, Shona. Outstanding.* She squeezed her whole face up tight around her nose and a sob exploded, followed by a loud, indulgent crying spree. I tried to gesture to Nain that it might be best if she left the room. She pursed her lips and began to cry along. I sat with my hands clamped under my thighs. My left hand throbbed. I imagined myself back in Dan's room, the electric fire on and the duvet around us. My head on his chest, every wheeze loud in my ears.

Whether it was the quality of Fflur's crying or the way her fists were balled in self-hatred, I began to understand before she set sail on the story. 'Ah,' I said quietly. 'I see.'

She stared at me desperately. 'Is it that obvious?' She sniffed and swallowed, not taking her eyes off my face.

'No,' I said. 'Nothing's obvious. I just wondered.'

Nain jumped up and caught my eye. She put her hand to her cheek ready for an aside.

'I found the tin but not the biscuits,' she said, and began to rearrange the spice cupboard. Fflur made what my dad used to call an old-fashioned expression. She rocked backwards on her chair.

'You probably ate them in your sleep,' I said. I rummaged in my pockets, sniffing. 'Do you have a tissue?'

'I'm prepared to bet you're contagious,' said Nain. She covered her nose and mouth with her hand, panic in her eyes. And accusation. For bringing germs into the house and for not taking her dramas seriously. These specific charges overlaid the ongoing, more existential issues in the long-term black book. Incredible, what a fleeting cloud across the eyes can communicate when there are genes and history behind it.

Fflur said, 'I was in love with him. He was going to take me to Singapore; we were waiting for the right time to tell Mum.' Her face was hungry with the relief of talking about him. I wanted to kill him.

'Did you ever tell her?'

She folded her arms and stretched her face to halt the tears.

'Uh, no. No, we didn't. And then he changed his mind and took her anyway, which is what he'd always told her he would do.' Nain held her breath, clutching a fossilised jar of turmeric. Fflur laughed a tiny little laugh. 'So all the volcanoes and earthquakes that were supposed to rock Mum's world hit me instead. Served me right.' She sob-laughed. 'What sort of daughter would go off with – try and go off with – her mum's boyfriend?'

I was a bit stumped here; I was keen to express support and sympathy but the question didn't seem entirely rhetorical. I thought hard.

'A confused one,' I said. 'One whose head had been messed with. How old is this arsehole?'

A shocked little grin shot across Fflur's face. Then she realised she was going to have to tell me. In a hard, defensive voice, she said, 'He was forty-five last month.'

'And how old were you when he – when they went off to Singapore without a backward glance?'

Nain was brushing salt and mixed herbs from the inside of the cupboard.

'Seventeen,' whispered Fflur. 'Old enough to know better.'

It left a chemical shudder in me that took a while to shift. I stood up and put the kettle on. An oil-slick current was pulsing in my temples. I made the tea; I hadn't put quite enough water in the kettle, and I had to tip it so far the scum from the bottom splashed out into one of the mugs. I considered the pros and cons of changing the subject. Nain made one of her more irritating sounds: it was only an 'mm' really, but in a very specific tone. There was a finality to the rhythm that meant something had ended, a television programme, or a visit – the sound might be made a moment after the front door has shut – and the inference was very much one of ambiguity of response. It said, *I gave that time but enough's enough. Interestingish, but I can't be standing here all day.* On this occasion, the expression of superiority was accompanied by the firm shutting of the spice cupboard door. I gave Fflur the tea without the scum and she said, 'I pretended I was pregnant, obviously.'

My eyebrows raised themselves and I talked them down.

24

*H*uggins *pokes her statement nose in on checks and I write the same word over and over again until she stops trying to get a response from me:* Parasite. Parasite. Parasite. *When she's gone she seems to take the words with her and I give up trying to squeeze them out and drop my pen on the floor.*

I notice spots on my arm; is it usual, to have spots — of the zit variety — appear on your arm? My brain stalls. It's thinking, but sludgily, grudgingly, needing frequent rests. It offers me clear enough methods of escape, presenting them over and over, enticing, persuasive. My face itches. My breasts and my middle are vastly inflated, stretching as if to burst. Stretch marks are interesting. They start off hazily luminous and then they bed down in permanent purple to become part of the geography of my mountainous body. My hair is miserable, dishcloth texture; it didn't grow back thick or curly or blonde or anything as some people told me it might.

The doctor says all is in order. My blood pressure, she means, and the lack of sugar in my wee. As for the rest — arm zits, violent images on repeat in my mind's eye, and a general deterioration in spirits and wellbeing — that's unremarkable, apparently.

Lying in each other's arms, snatching moments between coughing fits, Dan and I squeezed in a bit of talking. He told me about a second stepfather figure, marginally less disgusting than the oaf who prodded people with his feet.

This man, he said, regularly turned off the television to do something constructive. He made matchstick models on a table he erected in the corner of the sitting room for the purpose and had tantrums if the table got jogged by a passer-by or a hoover lead. Dan was fairly certain that this man also cooked meals from time to time; he had a memory of eating chilli con carne so hot it made his eyes and nose stream, and knowing that he had to finish it.

During a table-jogging tantrum, this man kicked a hole in the kitchen door. A week or so later, in a mellower mood, he decided to fill in the hole and repaint the door while he was at it. Dan said he thought it was probably the school holidays, because his mum was out and he remembered sitting on the floor to watch. They had the radio on, and the stepfather swore amiably at things the presenters said, and tried to fill in the hole by painting over it more and more thickly. The paint wouldn't stay put, and the puddle on the floor grew quicker than the stepfather could shovel it back into the hole.

'Bloody useless,' he said. He looked at the puddle, plunged his hand in and splatted a handprint higher up the door. This made him laugh and Dan said, 'Can I do one?' They sploshed handprints all over the door and onto their cheeks and clothes. The stepfather grabbed a marker pen from the rubble in one of the drawers, shaking with laughter, and drew a big round face on the door. The two of them giggled and spluttered, adding lots of curly hair, a moustache and some zits. And then the radio told them it was four thirty, which meant Dan's mum would be home and the stepfather said, 'Better paint over it. She might have a sense of humour failure.'

Of course they piled paint on thicker and thicker but the face still grinned through at them. And with every layer, Dan's stepfather's temper got worse. Dan wondered if he would kick the door again and get his shoe covered in paint.

'We lived in that house for years,' Dan told me. 'With the ghost of the face leering at me whenever I sat down to eat my tea. The door was a mess but it stayed that way. Mum never said anything; maybe you could only see the face if you knew it was there. Or maybe my mum was just good at picking her battles.'

When things get really out of hand, Rescuers tend to self-destruct. We cope impressively with other people's disasters, but our own we don't know what to do with, which is why we develop grubby little Sleeperz habits, drink ourselves stupid or pick at our fingers with sharp objects. Bullies, on the other hand, go in the opposite direction when the going gets tough; they self-indulge. They drink, like Rescuers, but more expensively and without the noxious intensity. Victims manage to walk an intriguing line between self-destruction and self-indulgence; there tends to be a degree of both in their disaster-response procedures. Fflur is a well-brought up Victim-Rescuer hybrid and she's fortunate in that the Victim in her leans more towards self-indulgence than self-destruction. She took herself off to a bar and sat with some fizzy pink in a dangerously-stemmed glass. She didn't really mind going on her own; oddly, she doesn't have friends any more than I do. You'd have thought she'd be surrounded by people she referred to as 'the girls' and constantly texting, Facebooking and meeting up in wine bars. If she had any Bully in her, to temper the Victim or the Rescuer, she'd be sorted. But a Victim-Rescuer mix can make for a lonely time. Fflur is convincing to look at, but a lot of it's tissue paper and ribbon.

It turned out this sexual and social pervert had been grooming Fflur almost as long as he'd been involved with her mother. At fifteen, Fflur had turned down a boy at school, saying she preferred older men because they knew what they were doing. He generously responded by telling everyone she was a 'Grampy-fucker' and inscribing this on her locker in case people tried to move on. How did her white-bobbed mother not see what her daughter got for her sixteenth birthday? How could Fflur sleep on one side of a wall when on the other side the man she was sleeping with was sleeping with her mother? He must have had to work at wiping the grin off his face in the morning. It seems entirely prudent, on Fflur's part, to have introduced a pregnancy – especially as she made sure it wasn't for real. How was she to know this would be exactly the push he needed to make up his grotty little mind?

I'm invited on pain of death to Assertion. Some unidentified funding has been secured for a hideous trio of sessions: Assertion, Anger Management and Anxiety Management. Maybe we'll progress through the alphabet: Bullying, Boredom and Babbling Nonsense. Caution, Courage and Crochet. And so on until Zooming, Zoology and Zebra Keeping – and if you pass that you're up for parole.

We sit in a circle in the Learning Centre, on the plastic school chairs (mine has 'cock-sucker' tippexed on it), and an anorexic granny with dyed red hair comes in carrying a lot of brightly coloured but very slippery A4 plastic wallets which fall onto the floor. Her skin is burnt sienna and as fragile as airmail paper.

'Welcome,' she says. 'Hello, hello.' She tries to restack the plastic wallets. 'So I need to make a list of your names.' She gives up on the wallets and waves a register at us. The wall of rain is so thick you can't see out of the window.

Assertion, she tells us, is asking for what you want, politely but firmly. It's not Aggression, or even Passive Aggression, and it's certainly not Passivity. There are several women who have glazed over now; the vocabulary is beyond them and the chairs are too hard. The rain hurls itself at the window. Anorexic Gran uses an example: Your partner is unfaithful. *I sigh; this is a futile exercise as far as I'm concerned, because the likelihood of me ever having another relationship is negligible. I imagine a* Would Like To Meet *column:* Shona, 35, likes writing, sleeping and eating cheese. Dislikes birthdays, Christmas and animals of any sort. *I did one night allow myself a little fantasy that Dan had a brother just like him, who turned up to claim me. It was nice, but it felt a bit disloyal so I cut it short and thought about garlic bread until I fell asleep.*

Anorexic Gran lists the options for handling the hypothetical unfaithful partner. Do you (a) sew prawns into the hems of his trousers, (b) cry a lot and have sex on demand, or (c) shout, stamp and throw punches. The prawns, we decide, but it's the wrong answer. It turns out to be a trick question, which is hardly fair. Apparently they're all wrong. The correct answer is (d) state firmly, using prepared phrases, that you will not tolerate a repeat of such behaviour and that you need some time to consider the future. Assertion is Asking for What You Want. *The rest of us glaze over now, because she's clearly misinformed. The prawns or the stamping are definitely the way forward.*

Asking for What You Want. Preeti tries to get a pig-headed misogynist microbiologist to listen:

[The expression on the face of the microbiologist Preeti sort of knows is stubbornly arrogant. A jumped up dermatologist – a female one at that – thinks her opinion might be helpful to the Chief Medical Officer's team of doctors, scientists and pathologists who have spent months slicing up Tramp Flu victims.]

Preeti: You're looking on the inside of the body. What if this disease starts on the outside? On the skin? [She tugs her ponytail] Or in the hair?

Microbiologist [Sighs and makes room for her at the microscope]: That is a common or garden head louse, Doctor Sharma. They are all over schools, let alone hostels. I'm sorry but this is a herring of the red variety.

Preeti: Just listen for a minute. What if –

Microbiologist [Puts hand up in manner of traffic policeman]: Stop right there. I don't play 'what ifs'. You can't put 'what ifs' under a microscope.

Preeti: That's ridiculous. Your job is to explore 'what ifs'. Without 'what ifs' there'd be no questions to find answers for.

Microbiologist [Yawns. It's tough-going being a government-appointed expert]: *Hypotheses*, love, not 'what ifs'. There is a difference. We cannot pander to every empirical little whim [Facial expression takes on a new level of condescension]. Your interest is to be encouraged, however. Consultants should be as prepared to learn as junior doctors. There is always more to be learnt [Though this perhaps does not apply to himself].

Preeti [Becoming a little fiery]: Here's my hypothesis then. What if Tramp Flu is not airborne? Something that looks like TB but behaves like malaria? What if body lice developed a parasite of some sort that mutated into something which can now live on a head louse? [Microbiologist rubs his face. It's quite rubbery.] It would explain why the disease suddenly crossed over to the general public.

Microbiologist [Shuffling through papers – he's a busy man]: Doctor Sharma. Many, many disease-ridden corpses have been examined and at no point has there been a suggestion of a disproportionate incidence of head lice.

Preeti [More firm than polite now]: The TB/MRSA *hypothesis* isn't enough anymore. Why have TB and MRSA got out of control this winter, rather than any other?

Microbiologist [Looking at watch]: We're looking in depth into mutations of TB. It's a cycle that needs breaking. But you do not get TB from head lice.

Preeti [Shaking microscope as if it's his throat]: I think this head louse carried a parasite which entered this woman's bloodstream through her scalp. And the parasite was at a stage in its life cycle where it headed straight for the lungs.

Microbiologist: With all due respect, this victim was homeless ...

Preeti: Vulnerably housed. Irrelevant. She was unlucky to get nits when the parasites – which have a life cycle all bound up with the host – were targeting the lungs.

Microbiologist [Squaring his papers]: It's an intriguing 'what if'. And a dermatological view on Tramp Flu is perhaps something we should be seeking more actively, separately from the MRSA issue. I give you that.

Preeti: Could you just do one thing? Get someone – much more junior than yourself, obviously – to crunch the numbers. Find out if Afro-Caribbean people are succumbing to Tramp Flu.

Microbiologist [Stops for a second – this might be interesting – but shakes his head]: I see what you're getting at, and it's interesting.

Preeti [Following him out of the lab and down the corridor]: Generous of you. Look, what would you expect to see, in an autopsy, if my hypothesis is right?

Microbiologist [Opens a door with a digital key]: Rocking horse shit. But thank you for your interest.

We now have a shop on the wing. In a room the size of a large cupboard. Items are priced by tiny stickers – blue for 50p, red for 75p and green for £1. There are rails of depressing second hand clothes, and chemist rejects such as oddly shaped earbuds and deodorants without lids. The nail varnishes and lipsticks are tumbled up in a little basket, and some of them look as if they've never been used.

'Go on, I dare you,' says Huggins. My face burns up and I ignore her.

There are three of us and we're ready to be shepherded out. There's a woman who's bought a man's jacket for 75p, a young girl who's got more make-up in her pocket than she's paid for, and then there's me, reflecting on the fact that my life has shrunk to the size of a cupboard-shop. This is the highlight of my week, without Carol to look forward to.

Huggins ushers us out, all squashed up in the doorway, and locks up behind us with the briefest of glances at her key stash. Her fingers seem to find the key by themselves. We're shunted back down the corridor to the rest of our day, and Huggins pushes a lipstick into my hand.

'On me,' she says quietly. 'It's your birthday coming up. Push the boat out.'

Later, I find it in my pocket and take off the lid. The colour is nondescript. It is in fact lip colour. Push the boat out Shona. No one will notice.

Preeti begins phone calls by saying, 'Here is Preeti,' which makes, 'It's Shona,' sound rather plodding and apologetic.

'I think the parasite is *inside* the louse,' she said. 'That's why it's hard to prove.'

'Can't you just use a bigger microscope?' I was tired and foggy, but it surely wasn't impossible. These things could not be so tiny that they were submicroscopic. I wanted to pound my head on the wall. Dan's breathing sounded even more precarious in sleep.

'Yes, of course. I'm hoping that once a parasite is found inside the louse, the focus will be on finding it in the lungs or the blood, maybe in slices of scalp.' She was thinking aloud. It didn't help. 'I'm worried that the parasite might not leave enough of a trace inside the louse, once it's found its way inside the body. And we don't know what form they take as they go through their life cycle.' Dan coughed in his sleep and hauled in a wheezy breath. 'We just don't know what it is we're asking them to look for.'

I was lying on the floor, picking at grot on the carpet. It was a while since I'd bothered with telephone exercises. Or bus stop clenches. Or anything that involved any more effort than was strictly necessary to function. The fish lamp had blown a fuse or something, because the fish had stopped bobbing about and were all on the bottom.

'You still think we're right, don't you?' I rolled onto my back. The ceiling had jagged cracks across it. 'It's the most likely explanation?'

'I don't know about *most likely*,' said Preeti gently. I squeezed the phone.

'It's a possibility. It's still a bit of a 'what if'. Look, I've got a clinic now, I have to go.'

'OK.' There were tears behind my eyes, really viscous ones that were too thick to shed and would bung up the tear ducts if I tried. Even Dan had got this one wrong. Suzy didn't even have Tramp Flu; it was no wonder they couldn't find anything in her hair.

'I'm going to contact someone who taught me at med school years ago. I think he's retired now but he'll be about somewhere. He's a professor of infectious disease. And I'm going to see what I can do via the BAD.' (The British Association of Dermatology, she explained, settled for BAD, possibly because the dyslexics and the dentists nabbed BDA.) She was talking very fast; I could hear her computer clicking and pinging.

'Preeti,' I said, digging my nails into the carpet. 'Maybe Suzy died of TB. She had AIDS.'

'AIDS?'

I screwed up my pudgy face and hiccupped.

'HIV. Maybe she didn't have nits. Maybe just ... just TB.'

At Preeti's end, a door opened and someone spoke.

'I'll get some of Dan's hair. He's definitely got fucking Tramp Flu.'

Preeti was distracted now. 'You're doing daily lotion, yes? Take care. Gotta go.' I was coating myself in lotion. I was plucking out my eyelashes and washing the inside of my nose with bleach. And scraping the electrocuting comb in zigzags across my scalp, my crotch, my arms and my legs, pressing down hard.

It turns out there's another 'A' besides Assertion, Anger and Anxiety, and this 'A' is the scariest of them all. Animal Therapy. We are herded into a grass enclosure and encouraged to pat a horse, cwtch up to a couple of 'labradoodles' and take turns sitting on a bench combing the hair of a guinea-pig that looks like Dougal from The Magic Roundabout.

I cling to the diagonal wires of the fence, stunned by the inter-species love-in. The women rub noses with the little curly dogs and roll over on the grass playfighting. They pick Dougal up and hold him under their chins and say, 'Aw'. And they go right up to the horse. They purposely touch its sides and before I can catch my breath there's a vicious gang-leader of a woman with her face buried in its neck.

I plead allergies. Psychosomatic they may be, but they're severe. I've turned into a clematis; my fingers won't disentangle themselves from the fence and I'm dragged suffragette-like to the guinea pig bench. They manoeuvre until I'm forced to touch it. And pick it up. The scrabbling claws and the way it squishes in on itself leave a physical imprint on my memory and I already know the feeling will stay with me, thrusting itself into my mind at inappropriate times for the rest of my life.

The others think it's funny that I'm so scared. They grab the dogs and whoosh them into my face, growling (that's the women, the dogs are quietly stoic).

'I'm allergic,' I mutter, twisting my head to avoid breathing in fur.

'To people!' they shout. 'Shona's allergic to people!' and I'm back at school in a classroom with a blackboard and broken vertical blinds.

Dan looked beautiful. His armour had been peeled away and left just his baby skin, newborn-wrinkled and blotchy. I cocooned him in his duvet with just his face showing and knelt on the floor beside the bed, gazing at him and wondering what it felt like. I tipped out the contents of his bag, scattering scraps of paper and chewing gum wrappers, biros and tissues all over his duvet shroud. A brown marker pen without a lid rolled towards me and I grabbed it before it hit the floor. The ink was almost dried up; the cap had been off too long, but by going over it a few times, I wrote my name quite clearly on his stiffening forehead.

25

Benny comes again. *She is wearing a dress. It's nice; it has blue and purple swirls and the edge is fraying slightly where it swishes round her ankles. If her head wasn't sticking out at the top, you'd think it was lovely.*

'Hello,' she says awkwardly, and she's looking everywhere but at me, so it looks as if she's greeting the whole room.

I'm so fat now that I have to sit right back from the table. I rub my tummy.

'Hi,' I say. 'What a pretty dress.'

'Fuck off,' she mutters and sits down opposite me.

I'm anxious because I don't know where to get diazepam now; the girl with the stripping fetish is being released into the wild. She seems ambivalent about this. I asked her if the rumours were true, and she pulled in her head, tortoise-like, and gave a fake flicker of a laugh. It's true, though. Her things are in a bin bag by her bed.

I study the twiddly straps of Benny's dress, notice the crinkly freckled skin between them. Do fat people get creased? Or will I just expand until that bit of me is hidden by my chins anyway?

'Shona pet, there's something I want to say.'

Pet? Pet? Coming from Benny, it's as bad as Madam. At another table, a faded Gloria type is massaging her daughter's hand and telling a gently amusing anecdote.

'It's OK if you want me to look after the baby,' says Benny. 'For as long as you like.' *She adjusts a twiddly strap on her shoulder. The points of her nipples are showing through the crepe-paper fabric of the dress.*

'Um. No.'

Her face twitches. I can see her thinking but I'm wearing a dress. I bought it specially. 'I think I'm readier now,' she says, 'than I was. To be a mother. In a very real sense.' *She is sitting unnaturally straight. She looks like she's trying to stop her head falling off.* 'And you're going to have to give it to someone.'

Dan's view was that Benny had something formally diagnosable. Maybe there's borderline personality disorder in the genes after all. I look at the guard by the door, who invigilates with the same beady-eyed boredom the teachers did in school exams. He catches my eye and I glance at the clock. I could kick her under the table, maybe, and she'd swear and look difficult and get thrown out early.

'So ...?' she whispers.

'Benny,' I say. 'Mum. You're not having this baby. I'm giving it to Fflur. It's all arranged. With my solicitor.' Benny's mouth shrinks and her eyes narrow. I laugh. 'Mum, for goodness sake. You must be in your fifties now. Go on a cruise or something.'

She looks murderous. She very nearly explodes.

The snow came back the day Dan died. I put his jacket and boots on; it felt like I was wearing his skin. After I'd written my name on his forehead, sucked his earlobes and held his hands, plaiting my fingers with his, I went to get Preeti.

Entry and exit to the hospital were heavily policed now, with barriers and estimated waiting times. But there were more police than patients; maybe the snow was keeping people away, or possibly the parasites couldn't handle the temperature and were already on the run.

I stormed the entrance in my seven-league boots, huffing and stamping, and just when it looked like I was going to be asked my business, I snarled, 'Preeti Sharma, Dermatology,' and it worked.

I sat in her waiting room, sunk into Dan's jacket and wondering whether I should just stop bothering to breathe. I felt her hand on my shoulder and looked up. She steered me into her office and sat me in a chair, squatting beside me.

'Shona,' she said. 'What's happened?'

'Dan is dead.' I looked down at the plastic tiles. Something on Preeti's belt beeped and she tapped it briskly.

'I'm so sorry,' she murmured.

'I've got his hair in this bag.'

'Right. OK.'

'Head hair and body hair. I thought we'd need both. It's been off him a while, though.'

'Yes. Absolutely.' Preeti stood. Her voice changed. She sounded less like a dermatologist and more like a transplant surgeon on the way to theatre with a lung on ice. 'Can you get hold of Gloria's Minister?' I nodded. My heart thudded. You could have taken my pulse through my eyelids. She helped me to get up. 'Ring me,' she said. 'As soon as you know where we can collar him.' I squeezed her arm but I couldn't look at her; I'd have leant my head on her shoulder and cried.

It wasn't surprising my eyes switched off and my brain went on strike. I hadn't eaten for hours and that wasn't something my vital organs had prior experience of. The next thing I remember is crouching against a wall in the hospital corridor. I was clutching the plastic bag of hair and shuddering. Someone told me to sit tight. I moved and someone told me to hold my horses. Four or five people had attached themselves to me. It would have been easier if they could have agreed on a party line, but even through the haze I could sense discord. The central sticking point seemed to be whether I needed a nurse or a psychiatrist (I think I'd been muttering, possibly there'd been dribbling). Then, just when a couple of them had given up and wandered off, who should appear but Debbie Wong, looking for all the world like she was in charge. The Victim role she'd been cast in at school had left no outward mark; no one would have thought she was anything but a card-carrying Rescuer. She dispatched the loiterers and crouched in front of me.

'Shona? It's OK, I know her.' Her hand felt warm on mine. 'Shona, can you hear me? Are you OK?' I tried to shake her off and get up. 'Shona? What's been happening?' Her fingers found the inside of my wrist and she counted silently for a moment.

'All good,' I said. 'All good.' She stopped taking my pulse and looked at her watch. It was a serious, androgynous watch, for people to whom time is significant. I managed to stand, pretty shakily. She did the same, rubbing her back and considering me.

'You're a better colour,' she said. 'But you still look a bit dazed.'

'Yeah, I think I'll go and find a Coke machine or a couple of dozen Mars bars or something.'

She didn't speak. Clearly, she was still mid-assessment. I tried a rather grim little smile in the hope of stopping in their tracks any thoughts along the lines that I might be even vaguely dangerous to myself or others.

'Come and have a sit down,' said Debbie. 'I could get someone to make you a cup of sugary tea.' The way she took my elbow, I felt about ninety.

Or maybe it had nothing to do with age. Maybe it was her dealing-with-unhinged-persons elbow squeeze.

''s fine Deb, 's okay. I've gotta go, there's someone waiting to ...'

She wouldn't go away. 'Shona, you don't seem well. Are you here with anyone?' A growl escaped from my beast within, and I let it. 'Shona,' said Debbie, 'do you know where you are?'

'Yes,' I snapped. 'Of course I do.' It was taking all my effort not to throw up, let alone fend off unwanted psychiatric assessments.

'Do you know what day it is?'

'Yes I fucking do!'

'Right. Uh-huh.'

I staggered off, flapping my hands and repeating, ''s okay, 's okay, sorry, sorry,' in time to my steps, which probably didn't help.

I don't need to tell you how much I wanted to go back to Dan's room and be Romeo and Juliet. I'd lost momentum and I could easily have rolled myself up with him in the duvet. It wasn't strength of purpose or character or anything that stopped me, so much as the thought of having to get past whoever answered the door, and look normal and so on.

I sat on a bench in the hospital grounds beside the semi-frozen pond and watched ducks skate. A woman in a stripy dressing gown and reindeer slippers stomped past me every few minutes, doing circuits of the pond. Two very important senior doctors strode past, being very important and senior.

I rang Gloria.

'Gloria.' My voice came out like a bark.

'Shona?' She sounded terrified.

'I need you to get hold of Minister Mike. Urgently.' I scraped my knuckles to and fro on the freezing bench. 'Please. Now.'

Gloria sighed. 'I don't know that he ... I'm not sure of his whereabouts at the moment.'

'Ring his mobile. Give me his number. Gloria, I need your help. This is –'

'Shona, Michael and I are busy; we don't live in each other's pockets, and ... well.'

My hands were sore. My head hurt a lot. 'Shit, you've split up with him. Ring him anyway. I have to see him.' She coughed delicately. 'Preeti's sure we're right about this.'

'Doctor Sharma?'

'Dan did work out what's causing Tramp Flu – practically, anyway, and then Preeti made sense of it. We have to make people listen. I need to speak to Minister Mike. Today.'

'Shona, are you OK Darling? You sound awfully –'

'Dan's dead.'

She gasped. 'Oh, Darling.'

'He knew he was too late to save himself. But he was determined he'd be one of the last. People have to start listening to us. To me.' I had what I could only describe as central crushing chest pain – and I knew this wasn't a good sign. Could be indigestion, could be a heart attack. I had some monster version of PMT, too. My middle felt cramped and full, dragging and tight.

'Oh my poor girl,' murmured Gloria. 'If there's anything I can do – '

I interrupted the reflex bereavement-speak: 'There is. That's what I'm telling you. Could you get Mike round to your house? What's his weakness, what will clinch it? No, actually, don't tell me. I'd rather not know. Just get him there. *Please*.'

It was unheard of for there to be a pause in a telephone call with Gloria. She breathed heavily and thoughtfully for several seconds.

'Right,' she said. 'Look, I'll ring him. What I'll do is get him over to Fenella's.' Her voice went up a notch. 'She's apparently more of a pull than I am, in recent weeks.'

The week before my birthday, which I am trying not to think about, I am invited to attend Anger Management. Declining is not an option. I plod along sheep-like with the rest of them – which creates a stash of anger in readiness for managing, because it's the Learning Centre again, and I would much, much rather be going to see Carol.

I make sure I'm near the window. It feels like my room, not theirs, and my window and my flowerbed.

Anorexic Gran is in towering shoes and a dress that shows off the area where her cleavage used to be. She has a flip chart and she asks us to give her other words for Anger. We ignore her and there's an itchy silence while we pick at our nails and stare at our shoes. The baby is Alice-in-Wonderland huge now. It's found the Drink Me bottle and its giant limbs are outgrowing the walls and ceiling. I picture its head tucked to one side and a grimace on its face. Soon it will cry the tears and the animals will be swimming in the flood. Meanwhile, we're all picking noses or toes, rearranging hair and looking either superior or intimidated according to type. (The Bullies, Rescuers and Victims classification system really comes into its own here.)

In the end, twitching, Anorexic Gran teeters to her feet and writes 'annoyed', 'furious' and 'cross'. Her shoes really are Abba-tribute.

'Maybe you'll think of some more as we go,' she says, and opens her eyes very wide. She asks us to think of an occasion on which we felt angry. To consider our thoughts and feelings at the time, our behaviours, physical symptoms and the consequences of our actions.

Fenella and Jimmy's lane, scene of gun-toting rabbit slayers, was not as long or winding as I'd imagined. It was more than a driveway, but lane was maybe going a bit too far. Clutching my evidence, I crunched up the snow and gravel, separated from next door's lane/driveway by a thick bay hedge proudly boasting bright green leaves under its snowy coat. A gap further up led not to next door but to the cul-de-sac behind it. The cul-de-sac had a patch of grass in the centre with a weeping willow that looked like a spider's web covered in icing sugar. Beneath the willow was a monument to community spirit in the form of an igloo. It was so big you could have squeezed a family of Inuits inside, providing they conformed to type and were short and compact. The grass around the igloo had an after-the-party look; it was a refrozen swamp of dirty snow, sticks, stray gravel and sweet wrappers. It seemed a strange place to hunt rabbits, sur-rounded by detached houses with trampolines and inflatable football goals.

'Shona, hello.' Fenella spotted me snooping from the front door. She crunched over, arms outstretched. 'I am so sorry to hear about your friend. Was it peaceful at the end?' I pawed at the gravel, clearing a muddy patch. 'Goodness,' she said, 'Jimmy will have your guts for garters.' She swept the gravel back into place with her black patent boots. 'He's just had the holes filled in. His gravel's only just below his lawn in the pecking order.'

I had a vision of my guts strung out to hold up the trousers or stockings of some giant golfer, pecked by pigeons, and I struggled for a response.

'Is this where your friend shoots rabbits?' I indicated the cul-de-sac.

Fenella roared with laughter. 'Goodness no. Oh, you are sweet. I can see why Gloria's so attached to you. No, you see the cut-through between those two houses? That takes you through to the woods.'

'Oh, yes. Of course.'

'Come in and catch your breath.'

Gloria had risen admirably to the occasion. She had rung me back to tell me breathlessly that she'd told Minister Mike she had something to say which he might prefer to hear before she made it public. 'I've got him *scurrying* about,' she said. 'The poor man is in a blind spin.'

Dan's editor, who'd SWAT-teamed us out of the warehouse clinic the day Dan came back into my life, put together a media crew within minutes. It was an odd phone call, because I rang from Dan's mobile.

'Dan,' he said. 'You had us worried.'

'It's Shona. We've met before. You gave me and my friend a lift when we got stuck at the industrial estate.'

'Oh. Hi, Shona.'

'Sorry about this.' I set my face in preparation before I said it. 'Dan's actually dead, I'm afraid. But listen, I need your help.'

He rallied quickly. His story antennae were so finely tuned they trumped bereavement.

As Fenella showed me in, I glanced down the drive. I was interested to see whether Minister Mike would arrive in an anonymous car. Large sunglasses and a false moustache, perhaps.

'Jimmy's in town,' said Fenella, though she didn't say which one. She took me through to the lounge, where Gloria was in position on a plump white sofa, her hair mountainous and her lips scarlet. She was wearing really quite a short red dress under a bright pink jacket and her necklace was the same shade of brass as her shoes. She leaked perfume from every pore.

I sat on the piano stool beside a grand piano with a rug over it and a framed cross-stitch sign on top saying *please do not put things on top of the piano*. The plastic bag – Exhibit A – was on my lap. I imagined the microscopic murderers scuttling about inside, tying Dan's hair in knots as they scrambled over each other in search of skin.

'Gloria will be in situ here,' said Fenella. 'Apparently alone. I'll answer the front door fairly neutrally, and then be busy in the kitchen.' She was an impressive project manager. I'd use her again, if I needed to organise an assault-by-hair-clippings.

Outside, there was the sound of crunching footsteps. We froze. Fenella looked at the miniature grandfather clock on the mantelpiece.

'That's the crew,' she said, and dashed off to let them in.

Gloria's hand shook as she applied a fresh coat of lipstick. I watched her put the lipstick back and click her bag shut, and I saw clearly what I should have seen all along: that if it weren't for Gloria, I'd have succumbed to Victimhood long ago. She had been rescuing me for years, endlessly forgiving, endlessly warm. She sat up straight and shook out her hair, and I rested my hand on her shoulder for a moment because I'd have squashed her if I'd sat on her lap.

It was fortuitous that Fenella's dresser with integral drinks cabinet was so wide. Not a lot of people can hide three men, a boom and a largish video camera in their living room. I hid in the kitchen with Fenella, a plate of triangular crustless sandwiches and a tray of smoked salmon vol-au-vents. I wondered if the nibbles were part of the honey trap or for a celebration afterwards. I took a sandwich when Fenella wasn't looking and it got stuck to the roof of my mouth. I was scraping it off with a finger when the doorbell rang.

'At your stations, men,' she whispered and strode off to answer the door. I paced a bit, twanging, wishing I hadn't mistaken fish paste for pâté, wondering if anyone actually liked it. Fenella had been arranging flowers. On the draining board were some crisply chopped stalks and a small, sharp pair of scissors with orange handles. Nain's voice from somewhere inside me said, *Your grandfather used to give me flowers when we were courting.* I wondered if Jimmy had bought the flowers through duty, habit or a residue of romance. Possibly, Fenella had bought them herself.

I listened to her chirruping about the possibility of hailstones later in the week. As far as I could hear, Minister Mike said nothing. I picked up the scissors and cut my thumbnail too close to the skin. Fenella was coming back and I felt a bit weird getting blood on the scissors, so I slipped them up my sleeve.

She came in, held up both hands with fingers crossed and looked at the ceiling. We stood either side of the half-closed door, trying not to cough or breathe too loudly. The plastic bag trembled in my hands. The sandwich hovered somewhere in my throat.

When Gloria's voice grew audible ('I simply feel that you and I have some loose ends, Michael, and it seemed best to have this conversation somewhere neutral'), we knew she was blocking his exit and crept a few steps out of the kitchen towards the living room.

'Neutral? This is your best friend's home.'

'Hm. You seemed quite happy to oblige when I said –'

'Gloria, I'm sorry for putting an end to anything we might have had together. But I'm not sorry to have known you. You make me feel like no one else can.'

'Not at all. I quite understand, Michael. Far be it from me to stand in the way of progress.'

'It's not –'

'I don't wish to know any details, thank you. Could we change the subject?'

'Change the subject?' He sounded baffled, but then he let forth a low growl. 'What are you after?'

'Shona, sweetie, Michael will see you now.'

'Oh God no, spare me Shona!'

I made my entrance, brandishing my weapon.

'He's all yours.' Gloria waved me in and then stood across the doorway, her arms folded. Fenella squeezed in beside her, hands on hips. Minister Mike glared at me. He had as much hair growing out of his ears now as his nose.

'Minister, I need you to listen to me.' He was reddening, his eyes bulging.

'Young lady,' he snapped, 'I run regular open access surgeries where –'

The film crew sprang from behind the dresser and pounced, surrounding him. I thrust the bag forward.

'I need you to listen now,' I snarled. 'Tramp Flu is a parasite. Which lived originally on body lice –'

'Research suggests,' he began, so I shook the bag right in his face. 'This is assault!' he announced, as if anyone was on his side.

'Fuck the research. They're refusing to listen to common sense. The parasites have found a way ...' I was shaking; I had to steady myself. 'They have mutated. Adapted. Evolved. And now they can live on head lice.'

'Which is why Tramp Flu has crossed the great social divide and we are now all of us as much at risk as the next person,' said Fenella. She sounded like a BBC news reader. In the distance, a police siren started up.

Minister Mike was trapped between a plastic bag and a rolling camera, grappling for his phone and trying to shield his face.

'Well, look,' he said, 'if you could just give me some space ...'

'Tramp Flu is everyone's problem now,' I said. I think he could tell I was a woman on the edge.

'The theory is certainly one which will have been discussed,' he said, 'at the highest level.' He scratched the hair inside his right ear. 'Will you please take that plastic bag out of my face? Are you trying to suffocate me?'

'Suffocation might be quicker,' I hissed. The police siren grew louder, then deafening as we waited in furious stalemate and a car swept into the drive, spraying gravel.

'Lives could be saved so easily if you just –' My voice grew tight and I couldn't quite finish the sentence. 'Just. Listen.'

There was urgent banging and dingdonging on the front door, and Fenella dashed to let in the police before they damaged it.

'You've got some interesting ideas there,' said Minister Mike, rallied by what he perceived as imminent rescue. I bared my teeth and snorted.

Debbie and Preeti entered the room with two police officers, one man and one woman.

'Preeti!' I said. 'Please tell this idiot –'

Preeti made a speedy assessment of the situation. 'Minister,' she said. 'The parasite mutation hypothesis is something to look at urgently. I think Shona is right. I think people are being killed by parasites on the head lice in their hair.'

The police officers hovered, uncertain as to whom they were arresting.

'Nits?' said Minister Mike scathingly. 'You're telling me Tramp Flu is common or garden nits?'

'I thought nits were the white bits,' said the cameraman. 'The eggs.'

'Who are you?' Minister Mike asked, ignoring the cameraman.

'Doctor Sharma. Consultant Dermatologist.'

I thumped my fist on my head. 'Look! Do you think I shaved my head for fun?' I shouted. 'Believe it or not I'm a woman under here, and women don't tend to –'

Debbie put on her psychiatric voice. 'Shona,' she said. 'I need you to stop this crazy behaviour or we'll have to treat you like a crazy person. Do you understand?'

The police woman stepped nearer to me. Minister Mike's face registered such smug relief that it pushed me over the edge. I delved into the bag and grabbed a fistful of hair.

'Tell me you're not scared of this!' I shrieked. 'If we're wrong, there's nothing to be scared of, is there?'

'Madam,' said the police woman, taking hold of my arms. I shook her off, snorting fire, bunched the hairball in my fist and scrubbed Minister

248

Mike's face with it. His nose felt huge and bony under my hand. In my mind, the parasites were lobster-sized things crunching up his nostrils straight into his brain, bunging up his windpipe with their claws. Spikes stuck up his nose and tufts got into his eyes. I shoved it into his mouth as he tried to call out. He spluttered and spat, lashing out at his face, at me, at his hair. The police woman was saying, 'I'm arresting you for assault,' and grabbing my arms again. The scissors slid down my sleeve and into my hand, and in my last free millisecond I swung them up in one great sweeping arc in the direction of Minister Mike's face.

Then both police officers were on me, clamping handcuffs round my wrists, and the bloody scissors dropped to the floor.

26

O
n my birthday, which I intend to sleep through as far as possible,
I receive four cards.

One is from Benny and has a poem about *A Mother's Love* printed
in swirly gold lettering. Maybe it's ironic? Maybe it's a last ditch attempt to
break me. It's grisly, whatever the intention, and she's signed it *from your
mam*. I drop it in the bin and open the second one, which I know is from
Fflur by the handwriting and the flowery envelope. The picture on the front
is of two fat teddy bears having a cuddle, and inside she's written Dearest
Shona, Happy Birthday!!! Hang in there loads of love Fflur xxx. *The third
card is from Gloria, and has pictures of women from all around the world in
a collage. She's written inside,* When they let you out, you can come and
live with me. Please. Love Gloria x *I stroke it for a bit.*

The fourth card has been hand delivered. It just says Shona Davies E5A. *Who
can it be from? Lines from a children's book flicker through my consciousness:* It
can't be the milkman, because he came this morning ... It can't be Daddy,
because he's got his key. *It can't be Nain, because she's lost track of the date,
and it probably isn't Colin because he's in a Unit. I remember the title of
the book:* The Tiger Who Came to Tea. *It comes to me with the image on
the last page, of a tiger playing a trumpet. And:* Just then, Sophie's Daddy
came home. Framed in the doorway and flourishing his bowler like a star
in an old-fashioned variety show. *The tiger never showed up again, despite
the stocks of tiger food Sophie's mousey mother got in. At five years old, sitting
on the carpet in the infants, I thought this was rude of the tiger, but I also
suspected the timid expression on Sophie's mother's face of being a front. She
was maybe planning to bolt. Possibly with the tiger.*

*The card is from Carol. I'm excited – maybe she's coming back – and
angry – how can she have dropped off a card without coming to see me?* Happy
Birthday Shona. Writing's a blessing and a curse but I think you've got
the bug now. Keep scribbling. Love Carol. *Not* I'll be back soon *or* sorry I

abandoned you. *No reason, no excuse. And what a choice of phrase:* I think you've got the bug now.

If I hadn't been fiddling in the kitchen, I wouldn't have had scissors up my sleeve. If I'd gone out to lunch with Debbie when she suggested it, maybe she and I would have become friends and she'd have been less inclined to decide I was a danger to myself and others. Maybe she'd have checked things out with me first, given me a chance to explain. But I suppose the scene she found in Dan's room was a bit ITV murder mystery; it was only a matter of time before reasonable people felt I should be locked up.

The footage shows the police officers dragging me backwards by the elbows, and I'm shouting, 'My boyfriend worked it out! And if someone had listened maybe he'd still be alive!' It felt liberating to kick out, to ram my elbows into their sides. I used my bulk for once as an asset; even my bum was a weapon. It was better than swimming in the sea.

Preeti is there, hurrying after us, calling, 'Shona, it's OK. It's going to be OK,' and Debbie's on the phone looking detached and professional.

As I'm bundled into the police car, screaming, 'And stop calling me *Madam!*' Preeti's shaking her head. *The hair was supposed to go under a microscope, Shona, not up his nose.* And if you look closely, when the camera swings back to where Minister Mike is covering his face with a tea towel, you can see something of a Mona Lisa smile on Gloria's face.

I'm sitting on the floor staring at my cards and thinking how odd it is to celebrate birthdays – surreal, arbitrary, almost as bad as Christmas – when Carol knocks gently on the door. She's wearing a purple turban and has no eyebrows or eyelashes. She gasps at the size of me – I've gone from vast to gigantic during her absence – and I try not to gasp at her very naked face.

'It isn't Tramp Flu?' I ask, and she shakes her head.

'No, no,' she says lightly, 'but the prognosis is about the same. Hah.'

She'd be better off with Tramp Flu. There are hardly any deaths now. It was as simple as nit lotion, as obvious as insect repellent. And if it hadn't been for Dan, there might have been many more deaths while the experts searched for something more complicated.

'I can't stay,' says Carol. 'But they said I could come and give you this.' She takes a present from her bag, wrapped in artfully grainy yellow paper and a

251

straw ribbon. She tries briefly to hug me but my size and my lack of people skills get in the way.

When she's gone, I sit on the floor and unwrap a plain hardback notebook. I scrunch the wrapping paper in my hands and chuck it at the bin. I flick through the empty pages, but they're not quite empty; on the top of every third page, Carol has put a title. Gardens. *She's doodled a flower and a tree.* Friends and enemies. *She's underlined this with a wavy line.* My life story in a hundred words of one syllable. A letter I will never send. *No doodles on these. I grip the book and cover my face with it. Then I remember Fflur saying that the point of a present is in the wrapping, and I retrieve the paper from the bin.*

Dear Dan,

The days here are endless. By the afternoon I'm craving sleep. Doing things in tiny chunks and trying hard not to look at the clock. Because if I do look, depressingly few minutes have gone by despite my filling them with whatever bizarre little ritual I've improvised. I have to find things that take five minutes, because that looks like progress on a clock face. I swing my arms across my chest a hundred times. At thirty-seven I'm sure I've been doing it forever but I force myself to keep swinging, keep stamping on the spot. I get to ninety-nine and do a final big swing for a hundred. The hands on the clock of course have never quite reached the full five minutes. I have worked my way through so many sets of five minutes my brain feels diluted. Odd how the bigger I get, the skinnier my brain feels.

I don't dare start calculating how many sets of five minutes make a day. Or how many days I need to string together. Contractions, I'm told, become relevant and interesting when they are five minutes apart. I imagine my five minute units punctuated by earth-shattering tummy cramps. I try imagining Benny having contractions when I was on the way. Maybe she timed them with cigarettes. *Have you timed your contractions? How many cigs apart are they?* Flinging a half-smoked cig to the ground when they got closer together, furious that they wouldn't go away, then mad with the relentlessness of it all. She couldn't just pull her hood round her face, kick a bit of loose rubble about and ignore me until I went away. Not until after I was born anyway. Even so, I've started to feel a mote of respect for her efforts at that very early stage; my guess is she was no better at being pregnant than I am, just as repulsed, and startled by it all over again every morning. And as the parasite swells, the double standards set in. *Come on then, hurry up and grow. What are we waiting for here? Fully developed lungs?* And at the same time, the holding back, the denial that all this could lead to anything that lasts longer than five minutes.

You were a spring baby, Dan, and you died a few weeks before your thirtieth birthday. Somehow these two facts are linked in my mind. It's my lithodora complex. The unbearability of something so intensely beautiful. But you could have outlived the spring, however perfect you are. Were. Are. You could have turned thirty, forty, fifty, and found a way to be. You were the blue painting my art teacher loved, you were lithodora in bloom. But I would have lived with the autumn, Dan, if you had given me a chance.

Your son will be born in the autumn, and Fflur will mother him like no one else in the world. I have a Madonna and child image in my head when I think of them, which I try to avoid. He'll be weaned on fairy cakes. They're going to Singapore to live with her mother, so he'll have a proper grandmother too. Probably be spoilt by maids, but I've made Fflur promise never to let him touch anyone with his foot.

When we made love that day, bald as babies, I saw your face when you wriggled yourself inside me. You were complicit, silently wishing on a few zillion sperm. It's a primitive urge, I imagine, the sowing of seed whilst you can. As unforgivably irresponsible, perhaps, as hoping for a child you know you won't keep. An autumn baby.

The magnolia tree outside is opening out into rude pink blooms. The last few daffodils wink at me, daring me to look without flinching at their transience. And the clematis is doing a bit of yawning and stretching in readiness for its tantalising weeks of not-quite-there and its fortnight of narcissism. Spring is trying hard, going overboard on sun and rain, sometimes both at once, to make up for sleeping in so long.

I've got so much hair now, everywhere, and it feels like a betrayal. The baldness and the prickliness felt right; they were the punishment I deserved, the finale I'd earned. I'm told that when the baby's born, some of my hair might fall out again, which is fine by me. Job done. I'll have given you your son and I'll be able to sleep as deeply as a daffodil.

~

About the Author

ROMY WOOD is a recovering secondary school teacher, where as Head of Drama she staged various productions from 'Macbeth' to 'Les Mis'. She has an MA in The Teaching and Practice of Creative Writing from Cardiff University and lectures in Creative Writing for the Open University. She writes novels because they are easier to write than short stories and poems. She drinks too much Coca-cola, likes to win at Scrabble and walks the tightrope that is Bipolar Disorder.

'Word on the Street' is her second novel following her acclaimed 'Bamboo Grove' (Alcemi 2010). Romy lives in Cardiff with her husband and three children. She is a Member of The Welsh Academy.

www.romywood.co.uk

Lightning Source UK Ltd.
Milton Keynes UK
UKOW040859050613

211794UK00001B/11/P